B. F. Peterson

THE ELLYRIAN CODE

ANGRY
ROBOT

ANGRY ROBOT
An imprint of Watkins Media Ltd

Unit 11, Shepperton House
89-93 Shepperton Road
London N1 3DF
UK

angryrobotbooks.com
Here be dragons

An Angry Robot paperback original, 2025

Copyright © B.F. Peterson 2025

Edited by Eleanor Teasdale, Desola Coker and Steve O'Gorman
Cover by Alice Claire Coleman
Set in Meridien

All rights reserved. B.F. Peterson asserts the moral right to be identified as the author of this work. A catalogue record for this book is available from the British Library.

This novel is entirely a work of fiction. Names, characters, places, and incidents are the products of the author's imagination or are used fictitiously. Any resemblance to actual events, locales, organizations or persons, living or dead, is entirely coincidental.

Sales of this book without a front cover may be unauthorized. If this book is coverless, it may have been reported to the publisher as "unsold and destroyed" and neither the author nor the publisher may have received payment for it.

Angry Robot and the Angry Robot icon are registered trademarks of Watkins Media Ltd.

ISBN 978 1 91599 862 0
Ebook ISBN 978 1 91599 863 7

Printed and bound in the United Kingdom by CPI Group (UK) Ltd, Croydon CR0 4YY

The manufacturer's authorised representative in the EU for product safety is eucomply OÜ - Pärnu mnt 139b-14, 11317 Tallinn, Estonia, hello@eucompliancepartner.com; www.eucompliancepartner.com

9 8 7 6 5 4 3 2 1

For my sister Christina,
Without whose boundless enthusiasm for my stories
I might never have finished any.

PROLOGUE

Hazzar stood on the crest of a hill, watching the camp of four sleeping Edrei. They had come thousands of miles in response to the Dophkan Uprisings, seeking to uphold the ideals of their Order abroad. They had come to challenge the oppressor, to defend the weak, to sustain the impoverished, and to teach the way of peace. They had come to serve.

With them had come Hazzar.

He stole down the hillside by the light of the stars, approaching the dragon that lay at the edge of the camp. There was no moon tonight, and no one was awake to discern the stains on his cloak in the darkness.

"Lach," he whispered, and the dragon raised its head. Its neck undulated like a snake as huge reptilian eyes rose and turned to meet Hazzar's own.

Hazzar restrained himself from taking a step back. Lach's flaring snout and spike-rimmed face were formidable, and tonight Hazzar had reason to fear the dragon. He just had to hope his efforts to win its trust over the course of their journey had not been in vain.

Working quickly, he sketched a mental image of the city of Tarsh, back home in Ellyrian. Then he Projected the picture into the dragon's mind. *"Far brywethavèn i khyra?"*

he whispered, speaking the language his Order used to command the creatures. The words translated: *Will you take me there?*

The dragon studied him, its yellow eyes unblinking. It was hard to tell how much the creature understood. It could smell the blood on him, Hazzar knew, and he suspected it felt his urgency and trepidation. It had to sense that something had changed within him.

But whether it knew that flying him to Tarsh would be aiding and abetting treason, Hazzar did not know. As a Projector, he was unable to perceive the creature's thoughts, as another kind of Imager might. Projectors did not often interact with dragons.

The creature bobbed its head once, down and up.

"*Norim?*" Hazzar asked: *Tonight?*

Lach nodded again, and Hazzar took a deep breath and released it.

He began Projecting again, bending himself into an image of how the landscape would look without him in it. It was a complex enterprise that required total focus, and he stilled his mind to all but the task at hand as he crossed the camp to the general's tent and slipped inside.

He emerged moments later, an extra weight in his pocket. He kept himself invisible as he hurried back to the dragon's side.

"To arms!"

The shout startled Hazzar into dropping his Projection. The general had awakened and rushed out of his tent, and the two of them locked eyes as Hazzar became suddenly visible. Hazzar grabbed the lowest spike on Lach's neck as the other Edrei surged to their feet, reaching for weapons.

"*Livarräeast,*" he told the dragon: *Fly.*

"Hazzar?" Realization dawned on the general as Hazzar pulled himself over Lach's neck, straddling the creature at the gap in its spikes near the wingline. "Stop him!"

"*Krishest!*" the team's Intuiter yelled to the dragon: *Stop!*

Lach cocked its head at the woman, confused. Whatever message passed from dragon to handler, Hazzar could not perceive, but the animal continued to spread its wings, nearly quadrupling in diameter as the other Edrei rushed toward them.

Hazzar's mouth tightened in a smile as Lach turned west toward Ellyrian and beat its wings against the air.

"Hazzar!" the general bellowed, and Hazzar looked over his shoulder as they rose.

Pain seared through his face as the general's dagger sliced across his cheek, just missing his left eye. Hazzar lost his grip and might have tumbled from his seat, but the dragon shifted under him to bear his weight.

Hazzar clapped a hand to his face to staunch the bleeding, wondering how he would stay ahead of the other Edrei after the dragon left him in Tarsh. The Edrei were respected and trusted the world over, and he had become a traitor.

He touched the shard of black crystal concealed in his pocket, feeling the power that radiated from it.

His torn face was only the beginning of the price he would pay for it. When word of his actions reached Ellyrian, his House and his friends would disown him. The Council would strip him of rank and reputation – even his very name. He would be sentenced to death, and the Order would chase him to the ends of the earth to mete out justice.

I have become Hezred, he realized, remembering the man

from Jeshimoth who could not pronounce "Hazzar." The syllables he had used instead meant *without a name*. Now that error would be Hazzar's truest designation.

The irony settled over him like a cold mantle over the shoulders, a grave counterpoint to the green of the Edrei cloak he wore there. *Nameless.*

But Friada was dead, and the shard was already in his pocket. There could be no turning back now.

FOUR YEARS LATER

CHAPTER 1

Hatreth Justice

Power is seized by great men when weak men give way to fear
and the feeble qualms of excessive conscience.

– Hatreth proverb

There were few things in life Jadon truly hated.

He did not hate riding at the head of forty Hatreth cavalry
and signaling commands to them, though he felt redundant.
His father, the High Prince Hatreth, rode next to him and made
all the decisions, which Jadon merely translated. Nor did he
hate the hot summer sun on his dark clothing, though he was
starting to drip sweat after riding all day. It helped to know
he cut a dashing figure in the uniform of the Hatreth guard:
black lined in red, with a fieroq – the little creature of fire and
dark that was the symbol of their House – emblazoned across
the chest. Jadon did not even hate spending two weeks on
the road with his father, his father's right-hand man, Zar, and
two orange-robed priests of Aurantiacus. The priests were
ceremonial and boring, Zar was habitually silent, and the
high prince refused to discuss why the priests were there or
any other subject Jadon might have found interesting.

Jadon hated how pointless it was, and that he had been
given no choice in the matter.

Classes at Eshtem University, where initiates trained to join the Order of the Edrei, began in two days. All the other members of Jadon's class were gathering in Lystra. Most of them would ride out with the Eshtem caravan at noon the following day. The Hatreth column had passed through Lystra earlier in the morning, and Jadon had entertained the fleeting hope that his father might dismiss him from this absurd errand so he could join them.

Instead, the high prince had sent word to the Drei Masters that Jadon would miss the orientation ceremony.

Jadon was not surprised that his father, as Senator-Liaison to Eshtem, expected special treatment for his son. He just did not understand why his father would use it for such a trivial purpose. They had set out for Shenn when their soldiers captured three leaders of a rebel group that called themselves "Elteressi." The high prince had intended to try the rebels in person, but Jadon did not see why his own presence was necessary. Moreover, a messenger had met them on the road with news that the rebels had escaped, so the excursion had become even more pointless. All that was left was to hear the city's petitioners, and that could be done anytime.

As they approached the city, Jadon's attention was caught by a blackened field. Not a lightning storm, for the charring continued right up to the boundary stone, where all signs of a fire stopped. The neighboring crops stood tall, ready for harvest.

Past ready for harvest, Jadon realized, frowning. All these fields should have been full of workers, but several stood idle.

The people they passed as they rode into the city had mixed reactions. Some took one look at the Hatreth column and hurried off in other directions. Others stopped what they were doing and rushed closer when they saw Jadon's father. Shouts of "It's Lord Juaqen!" and "The high prince is come at last!" were raised, and a few began babbling about food shortages and the Elteressi. Most of them looked unnaturally thin.

Jadon had not known they were so hard-pressed, but it did not surprise him. He pitied them for thinking his father was here to help.

By the time they summoned the local Hatreth company and walked into the city hall, over half the city had gathered. The crowd had difficulty parting for the Hatreth princes as they made their way to the platform at the front of the room.

They were met by Captain Gregol and the city mayor at the steps.

"Your Highness," said the mayor, straining to be heard, "you have been long in coming. The people here respect your rule and have been waiting for justice for too long. They are hungry and ill-used. Did you not receive my messages?"

The captain scoffed. "The townspeople have not been supportive of our campaign here. Elteressi sympathies run high, and though we have been proceeding according to the law and our mandate, there have been complaints. Nevertheless, we have the matter in hand – or we did, until Lieutenant Firhelm surrendered my prisoners," the man amended, fondling his sword hilt. "All the same, we are honored to have you here. I thought you might want to deal with the lieutenant in place of the rebels, so I left him in prison pending your arrival. Shall I quiet the people and have him brought out now?"

"No," said the high prince. "We will deal with him later." With a cold look for the city mayor, he added, "We receive many messages from our provinces, including all of yours, Mayor Wayse. But we rely on local infrastructure to solve the problems of everyday life whenever possible. Be grateful that we are here now."

The High Prince Hatreth was best known for his political acumen, through which he controlled nearly half the vote in the Ellyrian Senate. But he was also known for his stature. He stood a head taller than anyone else in the hall, and though his frame was too thin to mistake for that of a fighter, his physical presence was naturally intimidating. The angles of his face were hard, his dark eyes piercing, and his bearing lordly.

His stare was never easy to return for long.

"Of course, Highness," the mayor muttered, dropping his eyes.

"Let us hear the petitioners. Jadon, the court is yours."

"Mine?" Jadon repeated, thinking he had misheard.

The high prince gestured for his son to precede him onto the platform, a rebuke in his eyes, and Jadon surmised that he had not misheard after all.

If he didn't want me to act surprised, he could have chroming well told me what to expect, Jadon grumbled internally.

"Right," he said. "With me, then." He went up the steps, and the high prince followed, trailed by Zar, the priests, and the half-dozen soldiers of their honor guard, all of whom took up positions behind Jadon.

Jadon strode to the front of the platform and surveyed the townspeople. More were still coming in, jostling those in front and trying not to crowd against the soldiers who lined the walls.

"People of Shenn," he began. "My father and I realize that the uprisings in your city have created difficult times for you all, and you are anxious to know what we intend to do about it. In a moment I will begin hearing petitions, and at least half of you will have to wait outside due to the constrictions of our present establishment. However, I gather Shenn is having a food shortage, and this is the issue of most importance to you all. Am I right?"

The room erupted, most of the noise taking some form of agreement. "Our children are starving!" someone yelled over the general uproar.

Jadon raised a hand. Silence was a while in coming. "We are agreed about the food shortage, then. And yet, when we rode into the city, I saw a half-dozen fields of harvestable crops lying idle. I would like to know the meaning of this, and you are all welcome to remain while it is discussed. Who can answer?"

Another chorus of shouting rendered the conveyance of any real information impossible. Jadon raised a hand again.

"One at a time, please. Mayor," he said, locating the man near the steps. He had forgotten the man's name, so the title would have to suffice. "Perhaps you can explain."

"Certainly, Your Grace. Half the farmers' guild is being held for questioning, as they have been for the last several weeks." The mayor avoided looking at Captain Gregol, who stood next to him. "We've sent as many hands from the city as we can to help save the harvest, but times are hard on all of us, and every man has to consider his own livelihood. We fear we may lose much of the crop, as we did last year."

"Captain Gregol, can we expect the release of the guild men anytime soon?"

"I'm afraid not, Your Grace. They've been working with the Elteressi, and though they're a stubborn lot to crack, their information helped us capture the rebel leaders. We may have to keep them until every last outlaw is brought to justice."

Jadon nodded slowly. "Captain, on the way in, we passed a field where all the wheat had been burned down. Was that part of your campaign as well, or the work of the Elteressi?"

"That's a matter of interpretation, Your Grace." This provoked a stir of angry mutterings from the townspeople. "The men there were harboring Elteressi. The burning was a necessary measure to drive them out."

"I see," Jadon answered, though he could not imagine the circumstances under which burning a wheat field during a food shortage would seem like a necessary measure. This captain, though, had been hand-picked for the job by his father, and there was a limit to how far he could go in rebuking the man without getting overruled.

Jadon hated getting overruled.

"However, judging by the gauntness of the townspeople alone," Jadon continued, "it seems to me that bringing in this harvest should be a Hatreth priority. You and your men may be well fed, Captain, but you perceive that full rations will be insupportable if this harvest is lost. Therefore, while discipline by fire may have been within the bounds of your mandate originally, you will find other methods of punishing these people than burning portions of their food supply in the future."

"Very well, Your Grace," the captain said, taking the ruling in stride.

"And the guild shall have all the hands it needs to bring in the rest of the crop – from among our soldiers stationed here. However," Jadon raised his voice, cutting over the crowd's enthused reaction, "because farm work is not part of their mission here, nor in any way Hatreth responsibility, any crops harvested with our assistance will become the property of House Hatreth. You will have to buy the food back from us at a price, which will be set at the discretion of Captain Gregol."

That quieted the crowd, though no one raised any objections. The only people who would be ruined by it were the ones accused of abetting the Elteressi. The rest of them would have had to pay out of pocket anyway, though probably not as dearly as the captain would make them.

"Nothing too steep, Captain," Jadon advised. "I expect there to still be a populace here come the spring, and will hold you personally accountable if they starve."

"Very well, Your Grace," the captain repeated, though in a less equitable humor than before. He glanced at the high prince before responding. Jadon was pushing the boundaries of his father's forbearance with the warning, and the captain suspected it. But the high prince said nothing.

"Such is my ruling," Jadon finished, feeling rather proud of himself as he scanned the room. It was not a perfect solution, but no one would have guessed that he had been blindsided in having to produce one. "You are all witnesses. Now, if you would be so good as to disperse and reform in a more orderly manner, we can begin hearing petitions."

Most of the townspeople brought accusations against individual soldiers. The Hatreth men had immunity from the local justice system, so complaints against them had to wait for royal justice unless their officers deemed the offense unacceptable. Judging from the number of petitions awaiting Jadon's judgment, Captain Gregol had given his men significant leeway.

Jadon denied most of the petitions. After the first accused guard admitted to forcing himself on a serving girl and Jadon dishonorably discharged him from service and turned him over to local authorities, the rest of the captain's men claimed innocence of all charges. Theft, unjustified beatings, and careless destruction of property: all were met with flat denials, or – when there were too many witnesses to call liars – with claims that the victims had been aiding the Elteressi or speaking out against Hatreth rule. Jadon sided with his soldiers in most of these cases, too. Although he did not doubt that the men had gotten carried away, it was easy to establish that their victims really had voiced Elteressi sentiments.

Jadon was tired by the time a middle-aged man stepped forward, pulling a young pregnant woman with him. With some relief, Jadon saw he was almost through the petitioners. Only a woman and her young son waited after these two.

"Your name, petitioner?" Jadon extended the query for what seemed like the hundredth time that day.

"Tagreff."

"And what would you ask of the Crown, Master Tagreff?"

"Justice, Your Grace," he said hotly, "for my daughter, Chadrie. She was abused and raped and is now with child – a child she did not ask for and cannot support. By that Hatreth there." He pointed to a big, burly soldier who stood with his unit against the wall. "Sergeant Halomish. While that one looked on and laughed," he added, pointing to the dark-haired youth who stood next to him. "Private Kyl, he's called."

Jadon summoned the accused soldiers, keeping his gaze emotionless and away from the man and his daughter. Rape was an awful crime, but justice was not something to be found in any War House court – not against War House soldiers, at least. He had gotten lucky when the first accused rapist admitted to the crime, but that had been before the soldiers wised up and started claiming innocence of everything. He did not expect to get so lucky again.

Halomish and Kyl denied the charges, though their impassive stares and surly attitudes did nothing to convince Jadon of their innocence. Of course, Chadrie was the only eyewitness, and she seemed so scared she probably wouldn't have found the courage to answer Jadon's questions without her father's urging. But she confirmed what her father had said, and she named the exact day and time of the assault, four months before.

She was so young – younger even than Jadon, who, at seventeen, had just reached majority himself. That made it worse.

Jadon asked the accused for their alibis, and they claimed to have been playing cards in the barracks. Then he asked the rest of the soldiers in the room if anyone remembered their presence in the barracks at the time in question, and one of them stepped forward and said he did. Another obvious lie.

"Why do you remember that specific day?" Jadon challenged. "What were you doing?"

The soldier swallowed and looked away.

Captain Gregol cleared his throat. "I believe that was the evening Sergeant Halomish, Private Kyl, myself, and Private Fren there were playing courts and duchies. Private Kyl beat my houses with a royal seat in the last hand. The rest of us lost a lot of silver – it was a rather memorable occasion."

Jadon flicked his gaze back to the girl, annoyed. He might have been able to poke holes in the stories of common soldiers, but he could not question the captain's word in front of his father. "Have you any proof that these were the men who assaulted you? Are you sure there were no other witnesses?"

"Impossible, because it didn't happen," Kyl interrupted loudly.

"Chadrie, was there anyone else?" Jadon asked again.

She shook her head. "They came at me in the stables, when I was alone," she whispered.

"Lying whore!" Kyl snapped. "She got herself with child from selling herself out. Got no more than she asked for, no doubt about it."

First mistake, Private. Jadon smiled grimly and turned his gaze on the one called Halomish. "Is that what happened, Sergeant?"

Halomish narrowed his eyes, sensing the trap. "I didn't touch her. That's all I know."

Jadon returned his attention to the girl's father. "Is there anyone who can vouch for your daughter's character, besides yourself?"

"I can," the woman waiting her turn to petition answered. Shooting the soldiers an angry glare, she stepped forward to join Tagreff and his daughter, laying a hand on the girl's shoulder. "She works at my inn. Not a harder worker or a more virtuous girl in the princedom. Unless it's a crime to be young and pretty, I'll swear up and down to her blamelessness."

Jadon nodded, turning his attention to Tagreff. "I cannot find these soldiers guilty of raping your daughter. It is her word against theirs, and while her word may be generally trustworthy, they have confirmed alibis. She could have mistaken their identities."

Tagreff said nothing, but his hands tightened into fists at his sides, and he was all but shaking with rage.

"But, Captain Gregol, even though our soldiers might not have been responsible in this case, I want you to issue an official rebuke to your men for their general lack of discipline and remind them that they are to keep their hands off the loyal Hatreth-sworn women of this city. Is that understood?"

The captain nodded, and a chorus of "Yes, Your Grace" echoed from the assembled soldiers.

"Good. And have Private Kyl flogged for unfounded slander against a respectable woman of this town."

Kyl flushed with anger, but this time he had the presence of mind to keep his mouth shut. The captain frowned, but nodded. "It will be done, Your Grace."

Jadon watched as the girl dissolved into tears, tightening his lips in discomfort. Kyl's punishment was not enough, but there was nothing else Jadon could do. Not with his father standing behind him. "Such is my ruling," he pronounced grimly. "You are dismissed." There was a sour taste in his mouth as he watched Chadrie's father lead her from the room.

Jadon should never have had to come here. He should have been partying in Lystra with other Eshtem initiates, not playing mouthpiece for his father.

"Next," he said, ripping his gaze from Chadrie and turning to the last petitioner and her son. "Your name, petitioner?"

The woman introduced herself as Morgaine Haloway, and she accused three soldiers of breaking two tables and a window in her inn. She wanted compensation to restore the damaged property, but Jadon learned from the soldiers that the old innkeeper – Morgaine's late husband – had said the Elteressi had it right and House Hatreth could go to the Abyss. The man had not survived the ensuing brawl.

"It sounds to me like the inn was the property of an Elteressi sympathizer at the time of the damage." Jadon gave Morgaine a flat stare, annoyed that she had bothered him with such an obvious case. "Is this so?"

Morgaine looked away. "Yes."

"Then the property was unprotected by law, and I will not fine these men for damages. Such is my ruling."

She nodded slowly, unhappy. Jadon was unmoved. "You are dismissed."

He looked to his father as she left the room.

"One more," the high prince told him, flicking his gaze to the captain. "Bring in the lieutenant."

Right, Jadon thought. *The one who let the prisoners be rescued.*

He waited impatiently while two soldiers retrieved the lieutenant from prison. He was a tall man with a square face and a solid build, and despite his chains, he held his head high and walked with the dignity of an officer. He met Jadon's gaze before the guards forced him to his knees in front of the platform.

"This is Lieutenant Firhelm." Captain Gregol's voice was laden with distaste. "Three days ago, I took half the company and rode out looking for the Elteressi. We had reason to believe some of the outlaws would be gathered at a place near the mountains, a day's ride from the city. At the time, we had three Elteressi leaders in custody. I left Lieutenant Firhelm in command of the fortress with orders to kill the prisoners if any rescue attempts were made in our absence. Yet when we returned, we learned the Elteressi had attacked and Lieutenant Firhelm had turned over the prisoners unharmed, in direct violation of my command. He awaits the Crown's justice."

Jadon studied the prisoner, trying to size the man up. His father would have sentenced the man to death without a second thought. But the lieutenant would have known that, and where he knelt in his chains, chin high but eyes downcast, he seemed to have accepted his fate. *But if he knew he faced execution, why didn't he kill the prisoners?*

Jadon frowned, unable to work it out. "Lieutenant Firhelm, you stand accused of insubordination and unauthorized surrender to the enemy. In Hatreth lands, that's treason. How do you answer?"

"I do not deny releasing the prisoners, Your Grace."

Jadon's frown deepened. "Have you nothing to say in your defense?"

For a moment the man kept silent, and Jadon thought he would not answer. But when he spoke, his words were clear. "Perhaps what I did was wrong. If so, I regret it. The gods know it was a hard decision. But *traitor* is a black word with which to label a man who has tried all his life to live in accordance with his vows. There were one hundred Elteressi against us that night, and only five and twenty of us to stand against them. They swore to kill every last one of us if the prisoners were not returned unharmed. We had no chance of surviving."

"Was that the way of it, then?" Jadon surveyed the soldiers lining the walls. "Who here would second that assessment?"

There was a pause. Then one of the soldiers stepped forward, and another, and more, until a full two dozen men had stepped out of line. The lieutenant's entire command from that night supported him. *As they should, since his "treason" saved their chroming lives,* Jadon knew. He probably would have given up the prisoners, too, in the lieutenant's position. There was no point in losing half a company just to ensure three outlaws came to justice.

Only he would not have waited around to face Hatreth law afterward, which was painfully clear on the point.

"Well, Lieutenant," he said, "looks like the odds were against you after all. But there's just one problem. Loyal soldiers of War Houses do not surrender. They fight to the death – odds fall as they may. And yet you and all your men remain very much alive."

"I ordered the men to stand down, Your Grace," the lieutenant said, raising his eyes to meet Jadon's. "Their hands were tied by their oaths to Hatreth. Otherwise, every one of them would willingly have fought and died."

So that's why he didn't take off with the Elteressi. Jadon stared at the prisoner, trying to decide what to do with him. The lieutenant had feared his men might be punished in his stead. *Idiot.*

Admittedly, the man's fear was not without precedent. In the days of Jadon's great-great-grandfather, Augame tul'Hatreth, a platoon of Hatreth soldiers had yielded to fourscore Ithacor raiders, allowing them to sack the city the soldiers were supposed to be guarding. The officer responsible for the decision had disappeared, so Augame had had the entire platoon killed in his place. For all Jadon knew, Lord Juaqen might have done the same to the lieutenant's men, had Firhelm gone over to the Elteressi.

In fact, the high prince might still have the entire command executed, for all that Jadon was allegedly presiding in his stead. Jadon's power stretched right up until the high prince disagreed firmly enough with his son's judgment to take over himself.

The silence stretched while the room waited for his ruling, and Jadon decided to push the boundaries. As long as he had the stage, he could at least make the case for a light penalty. Lord Juaqen would overrule him, but if Jadon's presentation was compelling enough, perhaps Firhelm and his men would escape death.

It was his last case of the day, anyway. If he didn't flout

his father's authority now, he wouldn't get a chance to, and his presence on the trip would be completely and utterly pointless.

Lifting his chin, Jadon walked to the edge of the platform, looking down at the prisoner coolly. "Convenient, that. The wording of their oaths to Hatreth, in which they swore to obey their officers, allowed them to save their own skins instead of serving House Hatreth. Because, as you and I and your entire command are fully aware, Lieutenant, the lives of the Elteressi prisoners were in your hands, and Hatreth's interests would have been better served by their deaths than by your command's survival.

"If a company under House Rithadur tried to hide disobedience to the spirit of their oaths behind mere wordplay, they would be executed to a man for treason and cowardice." Jadon's gaze swept over the assembled soldiers, resting coldly on each of the twenty-four who had stepped forward. "We of Hatreth, though, take our oaths more seriously. No Hatreth in history would have considered your men treasonous for following the orders of their lawfully appointed superiors. But under Heraldus..." Jadon stepped down from the platform and approached the kneeling prisoner. "...your men would all have been killed anyway, while you watched, as a punishment to you before your execution and a warning to all future officers that they stand nothing to gain by ignoring Hatreth interests."

Jadon stopped just in front of the man. Then he let his gaze wander to the windows, as if what he was about to say next bored him.

"We've come a long way since Heraldus, luckily for you and your men. When we lose assets like the Elteressi prisoners, we don't compound the loss by throwing away good men like your soldiers in childish rage. And we've learned officers are self-interested enough to take warning from your punishment without seeing your entire command beheaded.

"Yes, Lieutenant, you should consider yourself lucky," Jadon continued, dropping his voice to a quieter level. "Even Lord Augame would have had *you* killed, at the very least. The current High Prince Rithadur would have you burned at the stake for such a complete failure." He spat to the side and then turned and walked back to the platform. Clasping his arms behind his back, he raised his voice. "But that would be messy."

He turned back to the prisoner. "Luckily for you, you live under the High Prince Hatreth, Lord Juaqen, a less wasteful and more discriminating lord than his peers and predecessors. Hatreth no longer deals out death to all offenses alike. The high prince knows the value of three upstart outlaws, and he knows the political and economic costs of keeping officers with abbreviated life expectancies. And the two are not the same."

Jadon took the steps to the platform and resumed his position in the center. "But even His Merciful Highness of Hatreth does not let crime go unpunished. I hereby sentence you to twenty-five lashes of the riding crop at the hands of the Enlightened of the god of justice, should they be willing," Jadon looked to the priests, and the one called Argest nodded, "to be administered at sunset in the public square: one lash for each of the lives you valued over Hatreth law. After which you will be dishonorably discharged from service and banished from Hatreth territories, along with the whole of your family."

Jadon ignored the prisoner's look of surprise, waiting for his father to change the ruling.

"My son has been studying too much of Edrei lore," said the high prince, stepping forward to center stage. "He must be pardoned. It is their standard of negotiation and peace-keeping that leads him to excessive leniency. Make it no less than the full forty lashes – and use the scorpion."

"Of course, Your Highness," answered Captain Gregol.

Jadon avoided looking at the prisoner. A simple death sentence might have been kinder.

The town square was loosely crowded when Jadon and the high prince arrived. Many of the townspeople had come out to see the spectacle, and all of Captain Gregol's company had assembled. They were not in formation, but they stood together on the left side of the square, so the townspeople kept to the right. The Hatreth princes took up positions near the raised platform at the front of the square, and Zar and the honor guard fanned out around them.

Lieutenant Firhelm stood with his arms raised above his head, chained to the whipping post on the platform. He was bare-backed and shivering in the cool evening breeze, but he gave no sign of fear as Argest approached, brandishing "the scorpion," a six-pronged leather whip with barbed tail-ends. Punishments with the weapon were rare and almost always coupled with discharge from service. It took weeks for men to recover from such beatings – when they did recover.

At the high prince's nod, the Enlightened cracked the whip, and the lieutenant gasped.

"One," Argest counted. As he yanked the scorpion back, Jadon could see six long and bloody gashes crisscrossing the man's back, each ending in round gouges where the barbs had dug in. He could not imagine what it would look like after forty.

For a time, he remained standing by his father, watching the archaic practice unfold in silence. But after a few more lashes fell and the lieutenant's grunts became louder while his back disappeared under overlapping slashes, Jadon turned away.

He spotted Captain Gregol near the back of the crowd and walked toward him, seeking to distract himself from the lieutenant's suffering. He earned a glance from his father as he left, but the high prince said nothing.

"Your Grace." The captain nodded.

"Captain." Jadon stopped next to him, and they watched the proceedings in silence.

"Six." The Enlightened drew back for another lash, and Jadon turned his gaze on the captain.

"Do you often join the games of courts and duchies in the barracks?" he asked.

The captain narrowed his eyes. "I do what I have to, to keep the name of Hatreth out of more serious trouble."

"I'm glad you do, Captain. Having our soldiers brought up on multiple counts of rape would lose us face in the Senate, especially among the other War Houses. But I'd hate to think our officers were gambling with enlisted men."

"I hope you're not accusing me of perjury, Your Grace," said the captain, frowning.

"Of course not, Captain. I merely wanted to thank you for your discretion."

The captain smiled. "All in a day's work."

"Very good. But, Captain, I meant what I said earlier, about rebuking the men for their lack of discipline. I'd like the rebuke to stick, and it would especially please me if you were to find some pretext to make an example of Sergeant Halomish. I don't want him in Hatreth colors the next time I visit."

"I haven't found the man to be unruly." Gregol frowned. Jadon waited, and the captain turned thoughtful. "I suppose I could find something against him if I looked hard enough – if that is truly your desire."

"Make it a reason that reflects well on the severity of Hatreth discipline, Captain. I want his punishment to leave an impression."

"Then it shall be so, Your Grace."

"Fifteen." There was a grating sound as Argest pulled back the scorpion. The lieutenant screamed, and Jadon saw that a shard of bone had been yanked away with the barbed tail-ends. Blood gushed from the open wound.

Jadon looked away, and his gaze fell on a boy of six or seven. The boy stood a stone's throw from him and the captain, where the gap between soldiers and townspeople allowed him a view of the platform even though they were near the back. The child stared at Firhelm, mouth agape in horrified fascination. Jadon recognized him as the innkeeper's son.

Jadon walked closer, disturbed that such a young child was watching. He would not have been here himself if he had the choice. "Boy, where's your mother?"

"She had to go back to work."

"Did she say you could watch?"

"She didn't say I couldn't," the boy said, his eyes glued to the beating in progress.

"Eighteen," the Enlightened counted, and the lieutenant moaned. Jadon looked up to see him sagging against his chains, which were now all that supported him.

Disgusted, Jadon fumbled in his money pouch for two coins. The verdict was out of his hands now, but he was still a Hatreth prince. He could do something, if the lieutenant lived long enough for it to matter. "Do you know what the theals herb is, boy?"

"Sure, it's medicine," the child answered, not looking at him. "Elf-blessed, they say."

Turning the boy by the shoulder, Jadon crouched to face him. He held a coin in each hand for the boy's inspection: one silver mark and one gold crown.

Jadon held out the silver. "Run down to the apothecary's and fetch me a jar of theals and a roll of bandages. Bring them back after the people leave the square, and I'll give you another coin to give your mother." Jadon twiddled the gold crown enticingly. "And we won't have to tell her you were here."

The boy nodded and took the silver, eyes wide. He lost no time running off on his errand.

"Twenty-two."

Jadon decided not to return to his father after that, preferring to watch the rest of the beating from farther away. If the choice bothered the high prince, Jadon would hear about it later in private, but he doubted he would. They both knew how to pick their battles.

Dusk had fallen by the time the crowd began to disperse, the beating finally finished. Lieutenant Firhelm had gone silent some time before, and he lay still where he had fallen after the Enlightened released his chains. His skin had peeled off in sheets, leaving a bloody mess where his back had been, and the bleeding had slowed. Jadon could not tell from where he stood if the man was still breathing.

He waited while soldiers and townspeople filed past him, his hands clasped behind his back, as if he had reason to be watching the lieutenant's final moments. The innkeeper's boy reappeared as the last of the onlookers departed.

"I brought them, my lord, sir!" he said, holding out the theals and bandages. Jadon reached into his purse, smiling at the jumbled title. Then the boy leaned closer and lowered his voice, looking concerned. "And Mama doesn't have to know I was here?"

Jadon nodded. "I won't tell her if you don't. Promise." Finding the crown again, he pulled it out. Then, remembering Chadrie, he pulled out three more. The innkeeper would not let her or her child starve if she could help it, he was sure. He gave the coins to the boy, who gasped at the little fortune.

"Thanks! I won't tell!" The boy took off at a run.

Jadon watched him leave, then looked around to see if the square was empty. Seeing no one, he walked to where the lieutenant lay beside the whipping post, stepping carefully to avoid the bloodstains as he mounted the platform. Drawing a dagger he kept sheathed near his sword, he crouched beside the fallen lieutenant, holding the blade next to the man's mouth. In a moment, a light mist covered it.

The lieutenant was still alive.

Jadon began applying ointment to the man's wounds. The sting brought him back to consciousness, gasping in pain.

"Theals," Jadon told him while he worked, his hands getting wet with the man's blood. "It should stop the blood loss and speed the return of your energy. By dawn, you should be strong enough to leave, and it would be best if you lost no time." He started bandaging the gashes while the lieutenant shuddered. He had little practice dealing with wounds, but his work was better than none. "Go to Lystra. There's a man in the city watch by the name of Keistad Tarrow, an old swordmaster of mine. If you tell him I sent you, he'll put you up until you get back on your feet. Maybe find you some work after."

It was a struggle for the lieutenant to respond. "Why... are you... helping me?"

"There wouldn't have been much point to my ruling in place of my father if you're just going to die anyway," Jadon answered drily. "Keistad Tarrow," he repeated, finishing his work and wiping the excess blood from his hands on the whipping post before taking out a handkerchief to clean them further. "Don't forget."

"It seems there is more to Hatreth justice than meets the eye."

Jadon looked up to see a tall, orange-robed figure emerge from the shadows gathered under the pawnshop across from them.

"Or, rather, *less*." Rilad, the second priest, studied Jadon in distaste. "The Most Enlightened shall hear of this."

Jadon rose slowly. "Good." He stepped down from the platform to bring himself eye to eye with the taller man. He wiped his hands a few more times. He could only guess why Rilad thought he cared about the opinion of the Most Enlightened. Maybe Lord Juaqen had invited the priests so they could report to the head of their order about what kind of high prince Jadon would become.

It made no difference to Jadon. "You can tell the Most Enlightened that for now, I may be no more than a pawn in my father's pocket, but one day, I will be High Prince Hatreth. If he expects me to follow blindly in my father's footsteps, he had better prepare for disappointment."

For a moment the two of them remained as they were, taking each other's measure.

Then Rilad nodded. "All pieces must respect the rules of the game, little prince, so have a care how you play. It would be a shame to see you removed from the board before you became a dragon."

Jadon's eyes narrowed. A dragon could have stood for the game piece, Jadon's future as an Edrei, or even the more generically powerful position of high prince, but Rilad's tone carried more cryptic intensity than any of those metaphors warranted.

Jadon did not care. He tossed his handkerchief to the ground and left in silence.

CHAPTER 2

Out of House Noraan

"Christina! Tell your father you want to master dancing. Sword-play requires much of the same grace and endurance.

"It will be a beginning."

– From *Christina of Kilethe*, added to the Rishara oral tradition some years after the Second Binding

Christina sat upright in the carriage, remembering the old colonel's last words to her as she studied the sheer drop to her left. The captain of her guard had assured her the pass was safe, but the height was dizzying. Christina's driver had had to blindfold the horses and coax them forward by hand – as each of her guards and their Edrei guide, Zanner, were doing with their mounts – to get them to brave the stretch. Christina, too, soon looked away.

Her father had hated the idea of her going to Eshtem. Christina had been determined to enroll ever since her mother had first described it to her: the university where the best minds in Ellyrian were trained to join the Order of the Edrei, becoming guardians of magic and dragons, keepers of peace, and servants of justice. Her mother had married young and never been permitted to go herself, but they had both hoped that Christina would follow a different path. After her mother's death, Christina had thrown herself into her studies with little regard for her father's opinion, and he had dismissed the colonel from his post when he found out that the man had been teaching his seven year-old daughter the sword.

The colonel had only been teaching Christina at her own insistence, and his dismissal had racked her with guilt and made her fear she would never make it to Eshtem. But that had been a long time ago. Christina wondered if the years had been kind to the colonel, and whether he would be proud to know she had worn down her father's objections in the end.

After the stretch, Christina saw two men approach from around a bend in the road. Both wore ragged clothing, and the stubble of days without shaving marked their faces. One had his arm about the other's shoulders and favored his left leg. Her captain and the Edrei moved to speak with them before the captain returned to give her the update.

"Your Grace, these men say they were beset by bandits near Lasdrida's Perch. The Edrei says there's another way we could take if they are still there. May add half a day to our journey."

"Is that man injured?" Christina nodded to the stranger with his arm around the other's shoulders.

"A sprained ankle," the captain explained. "Nothing Your Grace need trouble herself with."

"This far from the nearest city, with not a pack of provisions between them?" Christina glanced back at the men. "Nonsense. He must ride in the carriage with me as far as Lystra."

"Your Grace, I don't believe that would be proper. And we have no mount for his companion."

"Captain, what would not be proper would be leaving these men to die on the side of this mountain. Besides, I believe our Edrei's code of conduct would require him to stop and help them if we did not, and I'd rather keep him with us if there are bandits about. Wouldn't you?"

The captain sighed. "I suppose so, Your Grace."

"We shall have to keep our pace slow so his friend may walk along beside."

The captain obeyed her, but Christina saw that he had both strangers searched for weapons before permitting the injured man to limp to the carriage, with one arm each around Zanner and his companion.

"Lady Christina, allow me to present Lozuri Wentridge," said Zanner. He was wearing a green feathered hat that matched his cloak, and it bobbed as he gestured to the man he helped support. "And Friada Krent," he added, nodding to the other. "They were lucky to have crossed paths with us. This one could use the ride."

"I didn't think to sit with a lady," said Lozuri, sounding nervous. He had a wiry frame and dusty blond hair, and his eyes darted from his companion to Christina and back to the ground. He reminded her of a mouse. "Afraid I'm not dressed for it."

"Please." Christina gestured to the seat across from her. "I would be honored for you to join me, Lozuri Wentridge." The words were meant to make him comfortable, but they had little effect. From the tightly wound braid of her raven-black hair to the hem of her velvet and lace riding skirts, Christina looked every inch the noblewoman. The natural formality in her cool brown eyes warmed only slightly when she smiled at Lozuri. Christina was an only child, and she had spent much of her upbringing with only servants and tutors for company. She had little practice setting others at ease.

"We cannot thank you enough," Friada said as he and Zanner assisted Lozuri into the carriage. Unlike his companion, Friada had a strong build and the accent of an educated man, though his crooked nose suggested it had been broken more than once. "My lady..."

"Her Grace Christina tu'Noraan," the Edrei supplied, stepping back as Lozuri settled into his seat. "Daughter of the High Prince Noraan, Lord Illipen."

"A princess." Friada sketched a bow, and Lozuri made to rise from his seat.

"Please, don't injure yourself," Christina told him, and he sat back down, settling for a nod. "Thank you, Drei Zanner," she said, addressing the Edrei with the honorific given to members of his Order. "I believe we are ready to resume."

Zanner swept off his hat and bowed to her, a twinkle in his eye as he did so. He jogged back toward his horse before Christina could comment. She tightened her lips, vexed.

According to the technicalities set forth in *The Ellyrian Code*, Edrei were supposed to rank on a level with whomever they were addressing. Zanner might have been born a commoner, as the deep brown of his skin suggested some Rishara ancestry, but that should not have affected his status now. He had no need to bow to Christina. Because he had, she ought to have responded with a curtsey of equal depth.

Most nobles would not have noticed the impropriety, let alone minded if someone showed them more deference than they deserved. But Christina was not most nobles. She believed in her country's code as firmly as she believed in the Order of the Edrei, and she took very seriously any deficiency in her own ability to live up to it.

"Your Grace, if I may inquire," Friada said as the carriage lurched into motion. It was a slow pace, and he did not have to hurry to keep up. "What brings the Noraani princess up into the Brennels? With such a small entourage?"

"I am on my way to Eshtem, to become a student of the Edrei." The carriage was not very tall, and the window openings were wide and low. It was easy to converse with the man on foot, though Christina found it strange that he would speak to her. Commoners seldom did.

Friada raised his eyebrows. "A Noraani princess seeking to become Edrei? I have never heard of such a thing."

"The last Noraani to apply to Eshtem was a hundred years ago at least, and no one of note," Christina confirmed.

"What inspired you to break the tradition?"

"The Order of the Edrei is the greatest force for good this world knows. I can think of no higher honor than to join, and I hope to be found worthy." The statement provoked a wry look from Lozuri to Friada, and Christina frowned. "Did I say something amiss, sirrahs?"

"There was a day when I hoped to become Edrei myself," Friada said, smiling as his gaze returned to her. "That is all. But it reminds me, I'd like to have another word with this guide of yours. If you will excuse me?"

Christina nodded. The admission had made her curious, but Friada was already moving to walk beside Zanner, so she asked after Lozuri's injury instead. Speaking with her seemed to make the man even more uncomfortable, though, so they eventually lapsed into silence.

When they came to the fork in the road that would take them toward or around Lasdrida's Perch, the party came to a stop, and Zanner and Friada left on foot down one of the paths. The captain explained to Christina that the

Edrei was scouting out the position where Friada had last encountered the bandits.

They were back by the end of the count, and the captain reported that a dozen bandits were still camped over the perch.

"A dozen is more than I'd care to fight off with six," the captain grunted. "Little training as bandits are likely to have. It will be safer to go around, as the Edrei suggests, though by his route we won't be down from the pass until evening."

"That is quite all right," said Christina. "I've no desire to find myself ambushed – nor, I'm sure, do our guests." She glanced at Lozuri, who coughed and looked downward, avoiding her gaze. "Are you certain we'll avoid the bandits, if we follow the detour?"

"We'd skirt the ambush they have set up by at least ten miles. And the Edrei tells me they'll be in a range soon where he can…" The captain lowered his voice, leaning closer and looking a little uneasy. "…use his magic on them."

"You mean he'll be able to mind their position," Christina corrected. Zanner was a Dreamer, also called a Farseer: one of the Edrei gifted with an ability to see far beyond what a normal human could. Not all Edrei were Imagers – their term for those among them who developed a magical talent – and of those who were, most were not strong enough to accomplish much. Zanner was one of the few.

Christina knew because she had asked, and she had thought to ask only because of her studies. Aside from what could be gleaned from legends surrounding the Order's most famous Imagers, little was known – or even rumored – concerning magic and dragons outside the Order. Most Ellyrians considered all things related to the Edrei wondrous but dangerous and were content to leave them well enough alone.

The path the party took around Lasdrida's Perch was less even than the high road, and the ride in the carriage jostled Christina and Lozuri more as the afternoon wore on. Christina's guard kept a slow pace, with the horses' footing uncertain.

Suddenly there was a hiss and a thud up ahead. Christina gasped as the carriage lurched, hearing shouts from the captain over the horses' neighing and stamping. Her guards wheeled to form up around the carriage. There was another hiss, and an arrow sailed through the carriage window and thudded into the opposite door. Christina jerked back in alarm.

"Easy." The word was quiet, but it carried in the sudden stillness. Craning her neck, Christina saw Friada standing next to Zanner's mount with a knife to the Edrei's upper thigh. Figures materialized from the shadows as Friada spoke, some from the ledges above and some from deeper in the rocks to every side. A few of them held drawn bows; the others held makeshift slings.

Zanner lowered his bow slowly, and Christina's heart raced.

"This doesn't have to take long." Friada raised his voice to address Christina's men. "Lower your weapons, put up no resistance, and we'll just take what we're after and leave you in peace."

"Before you go and decide something stupid, you should know one other thing." The man who spoke stood on a ledge in the rocks ahead, and Christina had to tilt her head toward the other window to catch a glimpse of him. He had a bow trained on the captain's heart, and she quickly straightened her head, hiding herself in the carriage. "We already have an arrow trained on your princess."

Christina, heart in her throat, slowly turned her head to the right. She saw a bowman in line with the arrow that had just missed her. He had another arrow drawn and ready, and there was nowhere she could shift to escape his sights.

Then her gaze flicked to Lozuri, who was finally looking at her. He no longer seemed like a mouse. Her guards had searched him, and his hands rested on his lap, empty.

But he did not need a weapon to pose a threat.

"I doubt the High Prince Noraan would prove the most understanding man," the bandit continued, "should you fail to ensure the safety of his only child."

After a moment, the guards Christina could see lowered their swords.

"Good. Get their weapons. And we'll be needing any gold you have, Princess."

The guard closest to Christina looked toward the captain, and she risked another glance out the window. She could not see the captain's face, but she knew he had to decide what to do in the next few heartbeats.

"Please have the men comply, Captain," she said. He would not counterattack unless he was sure he could protect her, but Christina did not know whether the risk to himself and Zanner would factor as strongly. "Gold can be replaced. Lives cannot." She wished she could order him to stand down, but though the captain would defer to a lady in civilian affairs, she was outside his chain of command. Her preference would count for nothing.

"In fact," Christina leaned out the window to address the bandit who had spoken, her voice strengthened by the need to protect her men, "if you lower your weapons, I will give you whatever you request. There is no need for violence."

The outlaws laughed at her.

"A magnanimous gesture, Princess," another of them said. "Glad to hear your possessions mean so chroming little to you. But we'll be taking them this way."

The captain nodded to Christina before surrendering his weapon. The others began doing the same, and Christina sat back in the carriage, breathing a little easier.

"We agreed to leave the Edrei his weapons," Friada said. Glancing toward him, Christina saw one of the bandits had approached Zanner. "He has a right to them."

"A right to carry weapons, but not to be dealt with in good faith by a stranger?" Zanner spoke softly, but Christina could hear him in the tight stillness. "Who are you?"

"I'm a desperate man these days, and desperation breeds compromise." Friada's tone was light and ironic, but the tension in his body language as he scanned his surroundings made Christina believe his words.

Noticing her attention, he flashed her a smile. "I'm sure your Noraani men are worthy of their weapons, too. But even common outlaws know the Edrei work for the people, not highborn gold, and it's harder to justify stealing from them."

The other bandits snickered. "Right, we *common outlaws* have nothing but respect for the Edrei," one of them said. "Strange to hear that fauxsight from you, though, Hezred."

A few of them laughed, but Friada stiffened, and the mirth trickled into silence.

Christina realized that her men were trading startled looks with one another. Zanner stared at Friada in open disbelief, and one of the guards on Christina's right was studying the pile of swords the outlaws had started building with a dangerous glint in his eyes.

"Whatever his name," the bandit on the ledge ahead of them growled, "we still have you surrounded. Now, boys, the gold, and we'll be on our way."

Two other bandits started toward the carriage, and then the Noraani burst into action, rolling off their horses and charging the outlaws as one.

Christina gasped as Lozuri tackled her out of the carriage. An arrow thudded into the wood, missing her neck by inches. Lozuri scrambled to his feet faster than she did and pushed her away from the open carriage door, looking in the direction of the bowman.

Then one of Christina's guards was there, swinging to punch Lozuri in the face.

"Wait," Christina said, her mind struggling to catch up with the action. Her guard neither listened nor hesitated, but Lozuri ducked under his punch and scrambled away.

The Noraani grabbed Christina's arm and pulled his horse closer for cover. One of the other guards tossed him a sword. He caught it neatly and pulled Christina clear as his mount went down screaming, an arrow through its eye. A thrown dagger from another guard took the shooter in the throat, sending him tumbling from the ledge.

One of the other outlaws came after Christina, but her guard cut him down. Shocked, she backed into the rock wall behind her. A stone caught her guard in the temple, knocking him out cold. She dropped to her knees to help, but then another bandit came at her. She grabbed her guard's sword and scrambled backward, bringing it up to defend herself.

"Limn it, Hezred!"

Christina's attention jerked back to the other bowman, whom she had forgotten all about. He was looking in her direction, an arrow drawn, but he did not fire.

The bandit in front of her swung his sword through the empty air between them, inexplicably failing to close with her. Christina stepped back, wary. She had never learned much more about swords than how to hold one, but she did not intend to go down without a fight.

"Enough!" Friada's voice cut through the fighting. Christina's sword trembled as she took in the scene of battle.

The voice had been Friada's, but Christina did not recognize the man holding a dagger to Zanner's throat. His hair had lightened from brown to auburn, and his nose had straightened. On the left side of his face, a scar ran from cheekbone to jaw, visible even beneath the stubble of days without shaving. Zanner had lost his hat and his horse in the fight, and blood trickled from an arrow wound in his shoulder.

"This is over," said Friada – or Hezred, as the other outlaw had called him. Zanner nodded, stone-faced, and Hezred lowered his knife.

Christina's breath faltered as she took in the rest of the scene. All the Noraani were down, their bodies strewn across the pass in pools of blood. Even her driver lay slumped over an arrow.

"Where's the girl?" the outlaw in front of Christina demanded, turning to Hezred.

Christina blinked. She was right in front of him.

"You have no reason to harm her." Hezred's voice was even. "All the men you threatened with her death are dead."

The bowman spoke next. "And a few of our own, no thanks to you."

"I said I would neutralize the Edrei, and I did. Now, are we done here?" Hezred looked around at the other outlaws, and they began lowering their weapons. The bandit in front of Christina snorted when his eyes finally found her, but he turned away.

A Projector. Christina's gaze returned to Hezred, the realization feeling slow and stupid. *The renegade from the Order.* It had been four years since Christina had heard of the expulsion and escape of the infamous traitor Edrei, but this Hezred could be no one else.

"Lozuri, bind this man's wound," Hezred said.

Lozuri rose from his crouch beside the carriage, moving over to Zanner as the others began checking the fallen. His earlier limp had disappeared.

Christina's gaze caught on the guard lying prone in front of her. His face was turned away, but she could see a gash on his temple. Blood trickled down the back of his head to pool on the stones beneath. There was much about the situation that she did not understand, but she latched on to her guard's bleeding with a sudden clarity. *I have to stop it.*

Throwing her sword down, Christina dropped to her knees and fumbled with the man's gray Noraani cloak, trying to tear it so she could use a piece of fabric to stop the bleeding. Her hands were shaking and the fabric refused to yield. She pulled the whole cloak toward the man's head and bunched the fabric against the gash in his temple, trying to still her hands.

"He's already dead."

Christina looked up to see Hezred. She flinched, keeping her hands over the wound. "No."

Hezred knelt on the ground across from her. He took hold of the guard's shoulder and gently pushed him onto his back. The man's head turned with the motion, and Christina recoiled when she caught sight of his eyes. They were open and sightless.

"How could you do this?" Christina breathed heavily as she locked gazes with Hezred, the words more accusation than question. "I took you in." He no longer looked like the man who had introduced himself as Friada, but he seemed to want her and Zanner to live. Christina could not reconcile that with his choice to deceive and attack them.

Hezred reached down to close the dead man's eyes, looking somber. "I am sorry for them, and for your loss."

"Then why?" Christina's eyes moistened, and she dashed her tears away, frustrated. "Is my money really worth their lives?"

Hezred shook his head, and his tone hardened. "Maybe you should ask your guards what life is worth, seeing how ready they were to throw theirs and yours away when they heard my name."

"That's not what happened."

"Isn't it?" Hezred challenged, meeting her gaze.

Her guards had surrendered and given up their weapons. Only then did they attack – after they heard the name Hezred.

They all knew that arrow was trained on me. Christina tore her gaze from Hezred to look at her fallen guard, dismayed. No one could have guessed Lozuri would save her. She should have been the first casualty, but her guards had risked resistance anyway. *They betrayed me.*

"But why?" Christina whispered. She didn't know if she was asking Hezred or herself. More tears leaked from her eyes, and this time she let them run down her face.

"The people who want me dead are very powerful."

"More powerful than my father?"

Hezred did not answer, but after a moment he stood and offered a hand to help her rise.

Christina regarded him warily, no longer knowing what to think.

"It's over," he said. "For my part, I am no longer your enemy."

She had little choice but to hope he spoke the truth. Her guards were dead, and she was at his mercy. *And he and his associate did save my life twice.* Given that they had been partly responsible for the danger, she did not owe them a life debt, or even much gratitude for it – but it was reason to believe they intended no further harm.

She took Hezred's hand and rose, and he led her over to the only other surviving member of her party. Zanner was sitting now, alert with guarded hostility as he leaned against a boulder and watched the outlaws collect weapons, gold, and the horses still fit for riding. His shoulder was bandaged, but he had lost some color. His wariness seemed to mask significant pain. He was not much older than she was – five or six years at most. Guiding her train to Eshtem may have been one of his first assignments.

She wished it had gone better for them both.

"I am sorry," Zanner said as Christina slid down next to him.

"It wasn't your fault," she said. Hezred continued to stand by them, seeming for a moment as if he might say something. Instead, he shook his head and turned away, muttering something about "truth" and "costs" as he moved to rejoin his men.

"It *was* my fault, though." Zanner broke the silence. "I was scouting. It was my job to see the ambush."

"Hezred." The word was two Jeshim syllables strung together – *without* and *name* – and Christina felt foolish for taking so long to piece it together. "'Nameless.' He's the Projector who was expelled from the Order four years ago – whose name they struck from the records. He hid them from you." Projection and Dreaming were a matched pair of Imaging talents. A Projector could hide men from a Dreamer's farsight if the Projector had the stronger gift.

Zanner nodded. "There were rumors he'd joined up with outlaws and started calling himself Hezred."

They fell silent as Hezred returned with two horses.

"It's still three days' ride to Lystra," he said. "That wound will require better attention, so we've agreed to let you keep these horses. If you leave now, you can cover significant ground by nightfall. You'll find fresh linen in the saddlebags to change your bandages with. We'll bury your dead with ours."

Christina blinked at the unexpected kindness. "Thank you," she said.

"How generous of you, to let the princess keep two of her own horses," Zanner said sharply. "Is this supposed to compensate for the gold you took, or the men you killed?" His eyes were cold as he stared up at the bandit with an intensity that defied his obvious weakness.

When Hezred said nothing, Zanner looked away in disgust. "They say you denied your crimes. Yet you ran from justice and became an outlaw, and now you justify robbing from nobles and content yourself with trying to help your victims survive. You're pathetic. I don't know what you did, and I don't know if you're worth the effort they're putting into tracking you down. But you've proven they were right to expel you from the Order." He leaned his head against the rock, closing his eyes in dismissal.

Hezred watched him in silence, his dark expression making Christina tense. A muscle twitched in the renegade's jaw, emphasizing his scar. "Your name, Edrei?"

"Drei Zanner."

"I have no need to defend myself to you, Zanner, nor will I try. As you have made amply clear, you have neither the patience nor the intelligence to hear or understand anything I have to say. The days when I thought I could win back rank or reputation by convincing every passerby of the injustice of my case are quite over. I am outside the law now, and I will live like an outlaw to survive. Judge me as you wish, but none of this presents any reason why you should die on the road to Lystra. So, if I were you, I'd take the horses and get this girl back where she belongs. We've done what we can for your wound, but like I said, it needs better attention. Soon."

Christina watched as Zanner glared up at the man. Hezred returned the look flatly. Whatever the outlaw's crimes, it was hard to argue with his logic. There was nothing for Zanner and Christina to do but take the horses and go.

Zanner eventually dropped his gaze. He started to rise, and Christina quickly stood to help him. He shot her a grateful look and relied on her heavily in gaining his feet.

"Very well, then," he said, taking the reins of the nearer horse. "We will detain you no longer with our idle accusations."

Zanner mounted. Christina watched with concern, but he gained his seat with a straight-backed poise that made it clear he required no assistance. He avoided further eye contact with Hezred.

Christina regarded the bandit uncertainly. She did not share Zanner's ready disgust for the man, conscious as she was of his having protected them when her guards had failed to. He bore some responsibility for their deaths, but he was not without principle – not at all what she would have expected of a traitor hunted by the Edrei.

She wondered at the circumstances that had driven him from the Order. For a moment she hesitated, looking into the outlaw's solemn gray eyes without knowing how she should take her leave.

In the end, she deemed it impractical to ask him any questions and impossible to offer any thanks. Following Zanner's lead, she rode without a backward glance for the man who had spared their lives.

As they made their way down the mountain, Zanner's wound began to tell on him. He sank lower in his saddle as the counts passed and grimaced in pain whenever his horse took an uneven step. Christina grew worried, afraid he might not make it as far as Lystra.

Eventually, though, their descent leveled off. The road became firmer and wider as they left the mountains behind them, and Zanner picked up their pace.

There were two counts left before sunset when the silence was broken by the sound of a hunting horn. Zanner checked his horse and glanced behind them, then up at the sky. Christina stopped, too, watching him. His eyes took on a distant expression, and Christina guessed he was Dreaming, casting his farsight toward the sound. She wasn't sure where the horn had sounded from, but it seemed strange that he would be looking *up*.

"It's a dragon," he murmured, still staring at the sky. "They must be looking for Hezred."

"A dragon?" Christina repeated, stunned. She looked up herself, but all she saw was puffy white clouds in a blue sky, bright with the evening sun. "Here? Is that even legal?"

The Order kept its dragons on a chain of islands just off Ellyrian's eastern coast. From there, the Order flew them around the world on various missions, but it was rare that they came into Ellyrian itself. The creatures were massive and terrifying to behold, and most Ellyrian lords forbade them from entering their territories. The High Prince Hatreth was one of them, and Christina thought they had crossed into Hatreth territory earlier in the afternoon.

Zanner did not answer. His gaze lowered to the road behind them, and then he uttered a curse. He dismounted and adjusted the saddlebags with his left hand, uncovering the knife sheathed beneath them.

"What is it?" Christina asked, turning her horse so she faced the same way as the Edrei.

"He's coming this way."

Christina looked down the road, her brow tight with concern. Soon a rider appeared, coming toward them at a dead gallop. As he drew closer, Christina recognized Hezred.

There was a large shadow on the ground far behind him, east of the road but coming closer. Christina looked up, squinting into the sky. That had to be the dragon.

"Drei Zanner," Hezred called, pulling his horse up hard and dismounting a few spans away from them. "I charge you to do your duty in the name of the state." Glancing back at the sky, he hurried nearer on foot, spreading his hands when Zanner reached for the knife.

"Stop," Zanner demanded. Hezred halted, still a few paces away. "What are you saying?"

"Arrest me." The horn sounded again, closer this time, and Christina looked between the shadow and the sky. There was something up there, rapidly growing larger as it approached.

"Arrest you?" Zanner echoed, incredulous. "What?"

"Yes, arrest me. Please. I want to stand trial. I have always meant to stand trial. I've been hunting for proof all this time, but our witnesses have a habit of turning up dead. Limn it, I should have explained to you earlier." He glanced back at the sky. Christina thought she could make out wings and a neck in the growing blur. "But now there is no time. No time, no case. But I'm not asking you to believe me – only arrest me. Will you? Please?"

"I cannot," Zanner answered, voice harsh. "You have already been tried and convicted. And sentenced to death. That's why you ran."

Christina could make out the dragon now: a majestic, fearsome creature with enormous, batlike wings. There were several little figures on its back that Christina could only assume were Edrei.

"Already tried?" Hezred repeated.

Christina ripped her gaze from the dragon to look at him. He had gone pale, as if the information came as a genuine shock.

How could Hezred not know he has already been tried? Wasn't he there? It made no sense, and Christina's pulse quickened as she looked back at the dragon, still growing bigger and closing with them at a frightening speed.

She could see the Edrei now. One of them sounded another long note on the hunting horn.

Suddenly Hezred dropped to his knees in front of Zanner, head bowed and right fist over his heart, his left touching the ground. The horn cut off when the Edrei saw the posture.

Oaths were sacred, and not to be interrupted.

"I, Hezred, exiled from the Edrei and claimed by no House," he began in a loud, clear tone, "freely pledge my life to you and do beseech you to accept it. I hereby renounce my past, my present, and all former allegiances. May my means, my sword, and my service become yours. I offer you my oath." The words seemed to ring in the air, and as Hezred knelt on the ground, Christina was struck by the regality of the pose, and of the offer. Here, surely, was an innocent man, ready to go to any length to prove his blamelessness.

In that moment, Christina would have staked all the honor of her House on it.

A fierce wind kicked up around them, and Christina's gaze jerked back toward the dragon, now landing just a stone's throw beyond them.

It was bigger than some houses. Its neck and body were covered in emerald-green scales, practically shining in the light of the sun, and its slitted yellow eyes were fixed on Hezred as it extended one of its wings toward the ground, forming a kind of ramp. Six Edrei had been riding on its back, and they walked down the lowered wing toward Zanner, Christina, and the kneeling Hezred.

"Do not accept that oath, Edrei," the leader commanded as Zanner kept staring at Hezred, dumbfounded.

Hezred glanced up at Christina and tapped his ring finger. Understanding him, she turned her ring so the Noraani seal faced her palm.

"That would be a mean way for this recreant to escape justice," the leader continued. He was a tall man with wavy black hair, and he walked closer to Zanner. He frowned when the other man failed to respond. "Do you know me, Edrei?" he demanded.

Zanner glanced up at him and started. "General Anandolf." He saluted.

General Anandolf was one of the Order's highest-ranking officers, below only High General Serend and the Council itself, and Christina frowned as she tried to make sense of it all. Finding Hezred was a priority for the Order, but they had been searching for him for four years. Was he really a high enough priority that the Order's second-in-command would be sent after him? And why would Anandolf have brought a dragon here, in violation of Hatreth law?

"Good." The general's cold blue eyes did not reflect his smile. "So that much is clear. What should also be clear is that this man committed crimes against the Order and fled into the mountains to take up the life of a bandit. For his crimes, he has been sentenced to death, and now that justice is closing in, he is grasping at straws. Offering oaths he doesn't mean to keep, hoping to involve innocent passersby in his troubles. Cruel of him, really, to put that on you. But I'll make it easy for you." He stepped around Hezred and clasped Zanner's good shoulder. "Decline the oath. That's an order." He returned his hand to his sword hilt.

Christina had dozens of questions, but she could not ask them now. The general's short speech had already pushed the bounds of propriety, but as Zanner's commanding officer, he had a right to weigh in on the Edrei's decision.

Now, though, they all had to wait for Zanner.

Zanner tore his gaze from the general to answer Hezred, who looked him steadily in the eye.

Take it, Christina found herself urging Zanner silently. *Take the oath.*

The young Edrei hesitated, his face drawn in dismay, and Christina knew both his options were impossible. To defy the direct command of a superior would stain his honor as irrevocably as the death of an innocent.

But as Christina watched, Hezred shook his head, and the renegade's proud assurance seemed to dissipate. It left only a condemned man, looking up at Zanner in silent resignation.

It was a Projection, Christina realized. The confidence, the regality – carefully crafted to imply innocence. Gone in an instant, just like Lozuri's limp.

Why would he drop it now?

The dragon let out a *whuff* of air, drawing Christina's attention. The animal looked no less terrifying than before, with its massive bulk, armored head, and slitted eyes. But somehow, Christina sensed something like sadness in its posture.

"I–I…" Zanner stuttered. He cleared his throat. Christina had thought his color poor before, but as he struggled with what to make of the kneeling criminal, it drained away even further. He wavered on his feet and narrowed his eyes, glancing between Hezred and the general. "I cannot…" he tried again, voice quavering.

He got no farther before he collapsed.

"Drei Zanner!" Christina scrambled down from her horse to kneel next to the fallen Edrei.

"Do it," the general said, gesturing to one of the others, who drew a sword.

"Wait… what?" Christina said, glancing up at the general. "But Drei Zanner didn't–"

"Don't," Hezred said softly. She was on his level now, and he locked gazes with her as the Edrei with the sword walked closer. "Don't watch."

Hezred closed his own eyes, then, and bowed his head.

"But–" Christina started, but no one listened, and the sword came crashing down.

CHAPTER 3
The Road Through Lystra

Two threes of color
Two threes of light
Three powers of affect
Three powers of sight
Three gods of morning
Three goddesses of night
The Six spokes of forever:
Wheel them fast and they make White.

— From *Compilation of Kilethi Nursery Rhymes*, translated from
Old Noraani by Head Lusse Baraka Festus.

Jenne opened her eyes to the sight of an elaborate sunburst. Hovering between sleep and wakefulness, she realized it was an engraving in the domed ceiling. Around it, six majestic figures danced in abandon, all dressed in beautiful, flowing robes marked with their symbols. A flame for Ignescens, goddess of passion, who was pictured with her head thrown back and one arm upraised, skirts awhirl. A crown for Aurantiacus, a leaf for Virens, a raindrop for Coelestens, a mask for Porphyreus. Xanthinus, sketched larger and in more detail than the rest, stood with arms outstretched, a matching sunburst emblazoned across his chest. This was his temple.

Jenne blinked. *Why am I in a temple?*

Sitting up, she realized in shock that she had been sleeping on the altar. Quickly getting down, she brushed her blonde curls back from her face and studied the large stone altar, trying to remember how she had come to be sleeping on it. *I was...* Jenne blanked on her train of thought.

Her gaze fell on the rolled-up cloak resting where her head had been. Its cerulean color was reserved for Eshtem initiates. *That's mine.*

I'm an Eshtem initiate. Jenne smiled broadly as she slipped on the cloak.

She was on a raised marble platform, and a few steps fell away in a circle around her. Four passageways led away from the hall, a pair of sculptures standing at the entrance to each one. Between them, the walls were lined with stained-glass windows on three sides. The fourth was dominated by tall double doors.

Jenne furrowed her brow, recognizing the chamber. She was in the sun god's temple in Lystra. She hurried toward the doors, anxious to distance herself from the strangeness of waking up here. It felt wrong. *At least I wasn't sleeping on an altar to Aurantiacus or Ignescens*, she supposed. The altars of the sun god had never been used for living sacrifices.

"My lady," a voice called. She turned to see an elderly, white-haired priest in the golden robes of his order hurrying toward her across the marble floor. "Are you leaving us so soon?"

Jenne gave him her most winsome smile, hoping he had not seen her sleeping arrangements. "I am no lady, Illumined One. Just a common-born girl here to seek the sun god's favor on my journey."

His face broke into a kindly smile. "It seems the god of freedom has already granted the favor you sought. We feared for you when you came to us last night and threw yourself onto his altar, crying out his name. Many of the brothers have spent the night in prayer. They will rejoice to hear the sun god has given you relief."

Jenne stared at the priest, eyes wide. She had no memory of the events he described.

"Wha–" Jenne stopped, physically unable to complete a question. *What happened? Why did I do that? Did I tell you? Do you know me?* Her mouth worked in silence.

She frowned, realizing she did not want to ask the priest anything, after all. "Tell them I am grateful for their prayers," she said instead. It was better not to let on how completely disoriented she was. Not until she'd had a chance to sort through it herself.

If something was deeply wrong with her, no one else needed to know.

"Of course," the priest said. "They will be glad for the notice of one so clearly favored by our god." He indicated her sun-gold hair. Then he nodded deeply, swept his hand in the circle of Xanthinus, and rested it on her head. "May the favor of the sun god brighten your way, blessed one, wherever your restless feet may lead."

He bowed to her, and Jenne bowed back, all smiles and politeness. As soon as the priest continued past her, she pushed the doors open and slipped into the bright morning air.

She leaned back against the doors and studied the row of shops across the cobblestone road, her anxiety growing as she tried to think back to the last thing she remembered. She drew a complete blank, and her heart rate quickened.

Instinct prompted her to check for a money pouch. Relieved, she found she had one, and when she checked it, she found four gold crowns, a key engraved with the words "Weary Traveler's Inn, rm 14" and a smithy receipt with a date: 29 Aurant 64 yr. 17 ct.

Why am I carrying gold? Wait – what day is it? The year on the receipt was the current year. Jenne knew that, but not how she knew, and not whether the twenty-ninth of Aurant had yet passed. She knew her name, but not how she had come to be in Lystra; nor did she have any memory of being in the city before, though its layout was familiar to her and she could make a fair guess at the fastest way to the inn and the smithy.

She started breathing faster. *What in the flames of the Abyss happened to me? I know Lystra, but not anything about my own past?* Her head spun.

A wagon clattered on the cobblestones before her, jolting Jenne out of her panic.

Remembering could bring only anxiety and pain. She was suddenly sure of it.

The moment she stopped trying, a sense of normality and calm washed through her. She was uninjured. In fact, she felt good. *Better than I should*, she thought – although that thought, too, was a mystery.

Her reasoning seemed sound enough, but Jenne knew it could not account for her sudden and complete equanimity. She embraced the feeling anyway. *What if Xanthinus really did grant me relief from some kind of distress?* she asked herself. Perhaps he had blessed her by allowing her to forget her troubles. *Why waste the gift?*

She knew her name and her surroundings, and she knew that she needed to get ready for Eshtem. Jenne broke into a grin, latching on to that single strand of memory with enthusiasm.

The past could keep its secrets. She would not let them ruin her future.

Diar squared his new sword in front of his face, hoping it was worth the twenty-five silver marks he had just spent on it. The smith had claimed it was one of the best-made swords in the establishment, and it was certainly sharp.

Diar smiled as he slid it into the new sheath at his side, admiring the depiction of a six-petaled rydar flower that decorated both hilt and sheath. It was the sigil of House Noraan, the royal House that his own House, Jax, owed allegiance to. He had never met any Noraani, but royal-marked swords were of a finer make than the average weapon, and carrying the sigil lent him a certain gravitas. He was starting to feel like an Eshtem initiate.

"Easy there, Diar." Marcellus clapped him on the shoulder. He had to reach up to do so, as Diar stood head and shoulders taller. "Try not to strut like a peacock on your way out the door. You're as likely to knock that thing into the wall as you are to win tournaments with it." Marcellus and Salo, two of Diar's oldest friends, had been excused from the chores of the trading caravan so they could accompany Diar on his errands. Everyone from home had been excited about Diar's acceptance at Eshtem, and Marcellus's uncle, the caravan leader, had been only too happy to take Diar as far as Lystra.

"Can't a man enjoy his purchase for half a second?" Diar objected. "I dare say there would be a strut in your stride as well, if you were headed for Eshtem tomorrow."

"Where I'd be forced to reunite with our charming Lady Trista and rub shoulders with who knows how many of her snobbish noble ilk? No thank you, sirrah, I'm quite content at home."

"But Trista hasn't seen Diar's new tail feathers yet," Salo pointed out, mussing Diar's coal-black hair like a child's. Salo was a big guy, and the movement jostled Diar off balance. "She'll probably take one look at him with his Noraani-marked sword buckled at his side and swoon. Then she'll beg forgiveness for forgetting the common children she used to play with."

"Ha!" Marcellus scoffed. He walked toward the door. "You assume she is capable of human feelings."

"You do remember that we're supposed to have forgiven her, right?" Diar said, following Marcellus outside. Diar and his friends were Rishara-ahn, practitioners of a minority religion that held that the six gods and goddesses worshiped in Ellyrian were all misguided representations of one true God, the White. As such, he and his friends were supposed to hold themselves to the high moral standard of the White Way, which included offering love and forgiveness freely to everyone.

"I have forgiven her," Marcellus grumbled. "I'm just not anxious to see her again. Where to next, Diar? Did we finish the list?"

Diar paused in the roadway, admiring the towering Temples of Ignescens and Porphyreus that stood down the road to their left. It was a bright summer day. It was not so crowded here on the city's outskirts as it had been in Market Square. A few visitors could be seen enjoying the temple gardens, where priests and priestesses tended the plants, and a pretty blonde girl nodded to Diar and his friends as she walked past them into the smith's shop. "Slate, chalk, initiate's cloak, *Nations of the Edriendor Alliance*, sword and scabbard – that's everything. Should we head back to the caravan?"

Marcellus laughed. "What a silly idea! Of course not. Now we tour the city!"

The sound of horses drew Diar's attention. Three riders were approaching from the road that led deeper into the city, and Diar and his friends moved to the side to clear their way. Their embroidered doublets and the decorations on their horses marked them as highborn.

"There they are!" The rider on the left pointed at Diar, and Diar froze in surprise. "That has to be them, right?"

"The dark-skinned initiate in the company of a strapping blond youth and a scruffy dwarf?" The rider in the middle smiled broadly. He was a wiry fair-skinned boy no older than they, and he wore white frilled gloves to complete his outfit, despite the warm weather. "There could hardly be *two* such trios wandering the streets of Lystra."

Marcellus ground his teeth. He was shorter than average, but it was only because both his friends were so tall that anyone would liken him to a dwarf.

Diar cleared his throat as the riders came to a stop. "Can we help you, my lord...?"

"That's Perleyon tu'Sendell, heir to the duke," the rider on the right supplied. He was taller and more muscular than the duke's heir, but their facial features were similar, and the matching trappings on his horse suggested he also hailed from House Sendell.

"We heard you recently acquired a copy of *Nations of the Edriendor Alliance*." The lord called Perleyon smiled. "We'll be needing it."

Diar opened his mouth, aghast. The text was required reading for Eshtem, and books were expensive.

Salo leaned closer to Diar and asked in an undertone, "Can he do that?"

Diar did not know. There were few noble families in Meiveon, where they were from, and Diar had had little occasion to interact with any, besides Trista. But she had been just another one of the group when they were little, right up until the year they turned thirteen and he had never seen her again. Diar was unclear on the proper protocols.

"Find your own chroming copy."

He turned to see that the blonde girl had come out of the smith's shop, a sword now buckled at her side. Her green eyes flashed with anger as she addressed the duke's son.

"Watch your tone, commoner," Perleyon returned, sneering. "Did you not hear I'm the son of a duke?"

"You're an Eshtem initiate. Same as me, same as him." The girl gestured at Diar. "It's his book, and if you think he has to give it to you because of who your father is, you'll find the Edrei think differently. We all have the same station now, remember?"

Perleyon laughed, moving his horse toward the girl. "We're not at the university yet, are we? In Lystra, House Sendell answers only to the lords of Rithadur, and last I checked, the nobles in Rithad can kill with impunity any lowborn foolish enough to get in their way."

"Whoa!" Diar held up his hands and moved between the girl and the nobleman's horse. "Nobody is getting in anyone's way here, right?"

"Well, Perleyon wants your book, and you haven't given it to him yet, so technically, you're in the way," the second Sendell lord pointed out. He sounded oddly bored by the situation, which made Diar wonder whether their lives were not really in danger. *Or maybe he just doesn't care?*

"Perhaps they think we mean to steal it," Perleyon mused. He turned his gaze on Diar. "We're more than willing to compensate you. Generously. But I'm afraid the fact of the trade is non-negotiable."

"I see," said Diar, trying to update his read of the situation. Every possibility ended with his losing the book, but maybe the noble would give him a fair price. "We can work with that. How much are you offering?"

"You don't have to sell it to him," the girl said to Diar. "The scribing establishments have all run out of copies, so you won't be able to buy another. That's why he wants yours."

"Don't let your blonde friend fool you," Perleyon said. "This is not a negotiation."

"How do you figure that?" she demanded, stepping around Diar. "If he doesn't sell, will you start a brawl with other Eshtem initiates the day before orientation? Less than a mile from Edrei headquarters?"

"Not necessary!" Diar interjected. "Really!" The girl was fearless, but the lord was right about the law. None of them were initiates yet, and if Diar did not do something quickly, she was going to get them both into trouble.

He reached into his shoulder bag and pulled out the oak-boarded codex. "See, the book is right here, and I'm happy to sell. I got it for ten silver – does that sound fair?"

The second Sendell lord stepped his horse forward and took the book out of Diar's hands. "There it is." He passed the book to Perleyon. "Let's get out of here."

"Thank you, Dreck." Perleyon slid the volume into one of his saddlebags and started back the way he had come, the other two falling in behind him.

"Hey," the girl called after them. "You said you would pay. Are you a liar as well as a thief?"

Perleyon stopped, turning to look at her. "I said I would 'compensate' you. And I have." He turned his gaze to Diar. "I'm choosing to overlook the comments of your little girlfriend here. Another lord might not have treated you so well." He started his horse again, and as he rode away, he added, "Throw in a couple coins, too, Haf. I'm feeling generous."

The one called Haf took out a handful of coppers. His face twitched in a sneer, and he put half the coppers back in his pouch. He let the remaining three fall to the cobblestones before trotting off after the Sendell lords.

The blonde girl took in a breath, moving to follow, but Diar seized her shoulder. She turned to him with a questioning look, as if surprised that he would let the son of a duke walk all over him like that.

Diar searched for something gallant to say, hoping to save face. "Thank you for standing up for me," he started. There was a light dusting of freckles across her cheekbones. She wore them well, and Diar tried to refocus on what he was saying. "But I can't let you risk upsetting a noble on my account. It's only a book."

"It's ten silver," the girl corrected, sending another angry glare after the lords. She looked at Diar and sighed. "Is this your first time in the city?"

Diar nodded and held out a hand. "I'm Diar Jax, from Meiveon in northern Kilethe. And these are my friends, Marcellus Kerim and Salo Madrige."

"Jenne Kiri," the girl said as she shook Diar's hand. "Sorry about your rough welcome."

"What gave our inexperience away?" Marcellus asked.

"Was it how the mere sight of a noble left us utterly dumbstruck?" Salo suggested.

"Well, none of you seem to be royals, so the Noraani-marked weapon kind of gives you away." Jenne smiled at Diar, and his face warmed.

"Is there something wrong with the mark?" he asked.

"Just that it advertises your loyalty to House Noraan. A Blood House noble could notice and take advantage. Also, Kerim and Madrige are Gold Houses, no? While Jax is a Blood House? It's very unusual for Eshtem initiates to associate with people outside their own House divisions."

"It is?" Diar asked, his brow furrowing. There were three divisions of Houses in Ellyrian: the royal Blood Houses were descended from ancient Kilethi kings; the royal War Houses had seized land through conquest long ago; and the royal Gold Houses had purchased princedoms by funding the government back when the nation was born. Diar knew nobles from different House divisions often feuded, but Blood and Gold House-sworn commoners intermingled freely in Meiveon, and Edrei were expected to discard House and rank anyway. "I thought Houses of origin weren't supposed to matter at Eshtem. Aren't we not even allowed to mention them once we get there?"

"They're not supposed to matter, but they do," Jenne explained. "Just like a noble student isn't supposed to ride by and steal your copy of *Nations of the Edriendor Alliance*, but it happens."

"Wait... but Kiri is a Gold House." Marcellus voiced Diar's next thought. "Does that mean you'll be parting ways with Diar after this?"

Jenne shrugged, glancing at Diar. Her mouth quirked in a mischievous half-smile. "That's what most initiates in our shoes would do. But if he doesn't mind..."

"I like Gold Houses," Diar volunteered, eager to dispel any notion that he might hold her House against her. "Half my friends are Gold House-sworn."

Before Jenne responded, they heard more horses approaching. Looking toward the temples, Diar saw a hooded man and a young woman riding double on a black horse, coming in at a canter with another horse running on a lead rope beside them.

The man was drooping forward. Only the young woman's arms kept him upright. She rode with a straight-backed calm that suggested all was well, but she was dirty, and her black velvet dress held a few small tears and many wrinkles.

Stopping the horses in front of the inn across from them, the woman looked at Diar and his friends. Her eyes fell on his scabbard. "Are you sworn to Noraan, boy?"

"Yes." Diar tried not to make it sound like a question. He was definitely sworn to Noraan, though he did not know what that committed him to or whether he would like it.

Dropping the lead of the second horse, the woman extended her free hand, the other still supporting the man in front of her. In a louder voice, she said, "I am Christina tu'Noraan, daughter of the High Prince Lord Illipen tul'Noraan, and I would requisition your services."

Her tone was clipped and hurried, and Diar realized he was supposed to note her signet ring. It bore the same flower as his hilt and scabbard.

Behind him, he heard Jenne grunt in derision.

"What would you have me do?" Diar asked, hoping the princess was not expecting a more ritualized response.

"Help me with him," she said, sounding urgent as she reclaimed her arm from around the man in front of her. Diar reached out to steady him as the princess dismounted, relieved. She could have just asked; he would have been happy to do that much without being "requisitioned."

Then Diar noticed, with some alarm, that the man's right shoulder was wrapped in bloodstained bandages under his cloak. He was mumbling to himself, too, seemingly delirious, and his skin was pale despite its Rishara-brown coloring.

"Bring him inside," the princess ordered. Seeing that Salo and Marcellus were already moving to help him, she turned her gaze to Jenne. "Fetch a healer for us?" The rise in her tone made it a question, but her gaze brooked no room for disobedience. She did not wait for an answer before sweeping past them on her way into the inn.

"Nobles," Jenne muttered. With a glance at the wounded man, she ran to do as she had been told.

"He's Edrei," Marcellus said as they pulled him down from the saddle. The man's green cloak identified him, though the dirt and wear had made them slow to recognize it.

Diar tried to be gentle with the Edrei's wounded side as he and Salo took him by the shoulders and Marcellus the legs, but the man cried out from his state of semi-consciousness as they moved him toward the inn. His skin was feverishly hot.

"My father will cover all your expenses just as soon as I can get a bird to him," Diar heard Christina tell the innkeeper as they stumbled through the door. "And if you would send a stable hand outside, I have two horses that need seeing to."

"Yes, of course, Your Grace." The innkeeper was a rotund little man, and his hands fluttered in nervousness as he hurried over to direct Diar and his friends up the stairs.

"Your Grace," one of the serving girls gushed to Christina, "if you'll step this way, we'll take your measurements and have you something new to wear as soon as you finish the bath we'll draw for you."

"That can wait." The princess brushed her off, following them upstairs. "Bring me pen, parchment, and sealing wax."

The innkeeper held open the door to the first room on the second level, and with only a little maneuvering, Diar and his friends managed to get the Edrei through the door and onto the room's well-cushioned bed while the innkeeper stammered apologies to the princess.

She silenced him with a wave of her hand. "That will be all for now."

The innkeeper bowed as he backed out of the room, though the princess seemed not to notice. She kept her eyes on the Edrei while Diar and his friends adjusted the cushions behind his head and shoulders.

Then Jenne burst through the door, breathing heavily, and stood aside for the middle-aged healer who came in hard on her heels. His mossy green tunic signaled his station, and he knelt by the bedside to undo the Edrei's bandages.

"Will he recover in your care?" asked Christina. "Or shall I send for the Edrei healers?"

The healer looked over the wound before replying. "This is a dangerous wound, but I believe we have caught it in time. He should make a full recovery with medicine."

She closed her eyes in relief. When she spoke again, though, her tone was only a little less commanding. "I take it you three are not sworn to Noraan," she said, glancing from Salo and Marcellus to Jenne. "And I make no further claim on your service than you have already been gracious enough to extend. You may go."

The serving girl appeared with pen and parchment, and the princess dismissed Diar's friends from her attention. Sitting at the room's other prominent furnishing, an oaken desk, she dipped a feathered pen in the inkwell. "You, I would have wait a moment and deliver a letter for me," she said, presumably to Diar, as the serving girl had left the room.

He shot the princess a surprised glance, but she did not look up from her letter. Marcellus gave him a commiserating shrug. Salo, though, smirked gleefully, and Jenne just shook her head. Diar rolled his eyes at all three of them.

"My life is Noraan's," he answered loftily, gesturing his friends toward the door.

Jenne bit her lip to keep from laughing as they left.

The healer finished cleansing the wound before the princess completed her letter, and he promised to return in a few counts to check on the Edrei's progress. Christina nodded vaguely and waved the healer away, intent on her work.

Diar kept standing there while she scratched away at the parchment. The silence stretched, and he shifted uneasily. He had no idea how to replace *Nations of the Edriendor Alliance* by tomorrow, and now he was stuck running errands for who knew how long.

Jenne was right about the royal mark. It had been a mistake.

After what seemed like forever, Christina laid her pen aside. Tearing a smaller piece of parchment from the bottom of the sheet, she frowned before scrawling a few sentences on it. Then, brushing back a few strands of hair that had escaped her long, dark braid, she turned to him with a considering look. He waited for her to break the silence.

"We are a long way from Noraani lands," she said.

"Yes, indeed," Diar offered in a commiserating tone.

"And unless I miss my guess entirely, you are no swordsman," she continued as if he had not spoken. "You are on your way to Eshtem."

Uncertain of how to reply, Diar settled for a nod.

"So am I," she said, pursing her lips. Rising to her feet, she took the parchments and blew on them to dry the ink.

Folding the larger twice, she rolled her ring in the sealing wax and pressed it against the parchment. The other, she rolled like a miniature scroll and secured with a string before extending both to Diar. "It is unfortunate that we have crossed each other under these circumstances. But I trust you will not fear that your House's being sworn to mine will in any way affect our acquaintanceship at Eshtem, should we happen to form one. When next we meet, it will be as equals, and you may call me Christina."

"I'm Diar. Of House Jax." It was a reflex answer, and Diar decided it was a rather stupid one as soon as it was out of his mouth. She had not asked for it, and they were not equals yet.

The princess narrowed her eyes, as if confused as to why he would speak, and Diar gave her a smile full of contrition for his backwardness.

She knitted her eyebrows and lifted her chin. "Diar," she said, then nodded to herself. "So I will call you at our next meeting. For now, I need you to take these letters and have them sent to my father in Kale. The smaller should go by pigeon, immediately, with the other to follow."

Realizing with vast embarrassment that she was still holding the letters out to him, he took them and bit his tongue on the apology that leaped to mind. He stepped toward the door.

"The renegade. What... what happened?" The voice from the bed – weak but lucid – arrested him. Diar turned to see the Edrei's eyes were open, locking gazes with the princess. "How did it end?"

The princess's hands tightened on the back of the desk chair, turning the knuckles white as she met the Edrei's gaze with eyes that clearly wanted to look anywhere else.

Her composure began to melt as she faced him. "They killed him," she said, and a few tears leaked from her eyelashes as she blinked furiously. As the Edrei closed his eyes, fading back into semi-consciousness, she looked very young and alone.

Realizing that he did not belong in the room any longer, Diar put his hand to the door, hoping to slip out unnoticed.

"Diar Jax," Christina stopped him, brushing away her tears, "Noraan thanks you for your service."

It seemed an oddly formal thing for her to say in such a vulnerable moment, but Diar's heart went out to her all the same. "My pleasure," he said. Since that did not seem like enough, he bowed to her. He had little practice bowing and was sure it looked silly, but it felt like the right thing to do. "Your Grace."

She smiled and nodded her dismissal.

Pocketing the letters, Diar left the room and went down the stairs, feeling not a little ashamed that he and his friends had been so quick in their judgment of the noblewoman. She had been trained to command, and whatever she had just gone through had left her far out of her depth. And they had helped her save a man's life only grudgingly.

By the time Diar reached the ground floor, he realized he had no idea how to send letters to Kale, but he no longer regretted his Noraani-marked sword.

Luckily, Jenne was still waiting outside with Marcellus and Salo when he reached them, and she *did* know where to find both a pigeon-keeper and the post riders. She seemed less willing to forgive the princess for "requisitioning" Diar's services than he was, noting that such an errand could more appropriately have been assigned to one of the inn's serving girls. But when Diar insisted he did not mind and wanted to deliver the messages himself, Jenne was gracious enough to show them the way. She spent most of the afternoon with them, and before they parted ways, Diar made sure to confirm that she, too, would be riding out with the Eshtem caravan at noon the next day.

Not even his friends' merciless teasing could keep him from smiling about it.

CHAPTER 4

Initiation

Jadon and I may have been born to the same rank, but he will not be my equal in the Initiative. I have cultivated my reputation and earned the respect of the other War House boys over time, and I have seniority. Jadon cares nothing for the opinions of others and will not surpass me in their esteem. He poses no threat to our plans.

– Initiate Rindarin, in correspondence with his father, Lord Harral tul'Rithadur, on the eve of his second year at Eshtem

Jenne's time with the Eshtem caravan passed in a happy blur. The Edrei who led the caravan were welcoming and friendly, and she made half a dozen new friends before they left Lystra. One girl with honey-yellow hair and soft blue eyes introduced herself as Liana tu'Adagal, forgetting that House affiliations would be effectively dead once they passed the Dragon Gate and they were no longer supposed to reference them. Since they had not crossed the gate yet, though, the slip was inconsequential, and when pressed, Liana had admitted that Vorsand ti'Adagal was her uncle.

Since waking up in the temple, Jenne had done her best to catch up on the national gossip. She expected all the highborn students would know who was who at Eshtem from their shared time at court, and Jenne did not want to be disadvantaged – nor did she wish to clue anyone in to her missing memories. From chatting with the Lystran locals, she had found out that Drei Captain Vorsand was widely regarded as a hero for his exploits at Eshtem and afterward, despite hailing from one of Ellyrian's lowest Houses – so low that the high seat of House Adagal was not even a baron, and though the prefixes in their names marked Liana as his daughter and Vorsand as his brother, none of them were nobles.

The initiates had a grand time pressing Liana for the true stories behind Vorsand's legends, and Jenne enjoyed the occasional flirtatious exchange with Diar along the way. The dark-skinned boy was easy on the eyes, and he seemed to like her, though her banter sometimes threw him off guard. It was cute to watch, and it felt as though hardly any time had passed before they reached the university.

The sight of it took her breath away.

The Eshtem campus was situated on a plateau, contained by sheer cliffs on all four sides and accessible only by dragon in times of war. The Dragon Arch was an engineering marvel: a bridge spanning over twenty lengths across and wide enough for a pair of wagons to cross abreast. Made of margarette – a radiant silver-white material strong enough to withstand the weathering of centuries – the bridge was breathtaking in its delicacy, as if a spider had spun it of silk on the wind. The sun was beginning to set when they arrived, and its rays caught the metal filigree on the guardrails, releasing jewels of light.

At the crest of the arch stood the Dragon Gate. Never breached, the gate's locking mechanism and design had been the subject of debate among scholars and engineers for centuries. It could be opened only from the inside, and its secret had never been revealed outside the Order.

"Welcome to Eshtem!" a voice boomed from nowhere, and the gate slowly opened to admit them.

"Resonation," Jenne whispered to Diar, grinning. "So this is it."

Up ahead, a majestic complex of white buildings and towers rose from the plateau, walls and arching skyways forming connections between them. The silvery spires of the tallest towers sparkled orange in the setting sun at the four compass points of the university.

Jenne felt as though she were walking on air as she passed through the gate. Somehow, she felt becoming an initiate was something she had wanted her entire life.

Her euphoria lasted all through the tour of campus and the evening meal, and only began to be tempered when the initiates were asked to seat themselves in the Eshtem Arena for orientation. Only a fraction of accepted initiates ever progressed to full Edrei; most of them were sent home in the first two years of study. The curriculum was demanding and the code of conduct uncompromising, and Jenne would have to work hard to keep up with it.

The second largest stadium in Ellyrian after the War Games Coliseum in the nation's capital, the arena was built to allow for over ten thousand spectators. As the first of the night's stars began to twinkle through the gathering dark, twin beams of white light shot up from the stadium's floor to illuminate a giant, shell-shaped platform between the benches on the southern side of the arena. A Drei Master stood there, regal in his black robes of instruction. Light caught the gray in his receding hairline and reflected in his earth-brown eyes, painting him as older and wiser than his years.

"Initiates," he began when the stillness was complete. Jenne knew only Resonators could use the shell to enhance their voices. That meant this was Garadil, the only Resonator among the Drei Masters.

Many details about Eshtem and the Order's history had been part of the inexplicable knowledge base Jenne had woken up with, but she did her best not to notice. She did not like being reminded of the gaping holes in her memory, and she was uninterested in speculating about why she retained the things she did.

She would have liked to forget, in addition to her entire past, the fact that she had forgotten it. Maybe if she ignored it long enough, she would.

"Today you join a tradition as old as this nation." The master paused, his eyes sweeping the arena. He had their full attention. "Seventeen hundred years ago, the War of Shadows raged across this continent. The great armies of Jeshimoth and Alterra, each seeking the promises of greater wealth and prestige, and each spurred on by the unrecognized, insidious abuse of the Imaging powers of nine High Wizards, poured into our country from the south and the north, clashing from Telron to Kale. At that time, Ellyrian was nothing but a handful of divided tribes spread across the territories of Kilethe and Lanimshar, oppressed, exploited, and at times driven from their homes by first one and then the other of their more powerful neighbors.

"But sixteen hundred sixty-four years ago today, Aander tul'Noraan returned from the Hahiroth, and elves and dragons came with him. The Jeshim and Alterran armies were cowed and the warmongering Imagers among them exposed, contested, and defeated. The peoples of Kilethe and Lanimshar were delivered from their enemies, and on the battlefield at Helos, fourteen tribal leaders pledged to unite their peoples and territories, to become strong enough to stand against their neighbors should war ever break out again. Thus the nation of Ellyrian was born, and the elves safeguarded its peace with dragons."

Here the master paused again. Jenne knew the story – every man, woman, and child in Ellyrian did – but tonight, she was becoming part of the Order's legend. She hung on the Drei Master's words.

"But the dragons were a power like nothing this world had ever known. The elves could not entrust them to just anyone. The dragons could stand against armies, level cities, defeat the supreme Imaging powers of even the nine High Wizards. In the wrong hands, they could be used to conquer and enslave the world.

"Their handlers, then, would have to be selfless, wise, and just – more intelligent, more skilled, and more honorable than their peers, with the capacity to rise above their fellows, yet incorruptibly dedicated to remaining the servants of all.

"Knowing this, the elves did not construct this university or design its curricula with an eye for what would make its initiates feel distinguished, seem impressive, or bring easy points of honor to their Houses. The training you will undergo here will, consequently, be unlike anything you have experienced before. Those of you sitting before me have already distinguished yourselves among your peers. Most of you are accustomed to being praised for your successes, held up as examples for your peers to follow, and accorded greater honor than the other youth of your Houses and cities.

"That ends here. You will not, here, be praised for your successes. You will not be made to feel proud of your strengths. You will not be coddled when you fall behind, and your failures will not be waved away or reframed as partial successes.

"This is because you are not being groomed, here, to take high positions in society. Here, you are not leaders. You are not nobles. You are not the heirs of your Houses, your family estates, or your masters' businesses. You are no longer the first in your classes.

"As of tonight, you join a new class, where you are among equals – many of you for the first time. Tomorrow you will begin a rigorous process of training in which you will be made to confront weaknesses you may never have known that you had. You will be pushed to perform to a standard higher than anyone has heretofore required of you. Before the process is over, hundreds of you will have been sent home to your Houses, steeped in disgrace, and many more of you will, more than once, rightly fear yourselves to be on the brink of such dishonor. This university was not intended for personal advancement, and very few of you will feel yourselves to be advancing during your stay."

Jenne doubted any initiate needed the reminder. Although there was a system of demerits and rankings that determined most cuts, expulsion could happen at any time, for any slip in adherence to the university's expectations. Stories were told of initiates expelled for coughing at the wrong moment during a lecture – stories that contributed to the perfect silence kept by over a thousand new initiates as they waited for the master's next words.

"Sixteen hundred sixty-four years ago today, this university was conceived in the midst of violence and bloodshed wreaked by whole nations of powerful individuals, each seeking his own advancement.

"This university was intended to be something else entirely: a place where individuals would be equipped to pursue the good of every nation and people. To stand against the senseless spread of selfishness and destruction. To dedicate themselves to the enlightenment of the ignorant, the sustainment of the impoverished, and the defense of the powerless and oppressed. This university was founded to create peace in the midst of the storm."

In the silence that followed, the words reverberated faintly throughout the arena, sweeping Jenne up in the vision they painted. She knew that not every initiate had come here because they believed in the university's dream. Perleyon and his highborn friends were proof of that. But Jenne wondered if, in this moment, everyone could sense the ideals embodied in the university that had forged and protected a nation.

Resonation could have that effect.

"Seventeen hundred years ago, a storm raged across this continent with a ferocity we have not seen since. To bring that storm to an end, kings and armies needed to be defeated. Imagers of unsurpassed strength needed to be destroyed. Assassins, conspirators, and lords of crime and corruption needed to be ferreted out and brought to justice. Sixteen hundred sixty-four years ago today, elves, Imagers, and dragons took their stand and brought that storm to an end.

"The War of Shadows is over now," Garadil continued, his voice falling to an intense quiet that was still audible to all, "its horror and destruction faded to little more than a rumor. But every now and then, the winds still blow, the seas rear up, and darkness and evil arise once again to threaten our world's tenuous calm.

"Today there are no elves left to stand against them. We do not know how or why it was that they left us to face these latter-day squalls alone.

"But we do know..." The master paused, and when he spoke again, his voice was louder. "...that they did not leave us undefended.

"This university still stands, their legacy among us, and the foundation of the Order they built to ensure that no War of Shadows would break this continent again. This university may not be easy, but it has proven strong enough to stand against each and every threat this world has ever brought against it.

"And tonight, Initiates..." The master swept his eyes across the assembly, then slowly smiled. "...it becomes yours. Rise, students of the Order, and be welcome at Eshtem!"

Somewhere a cheer began. As happened every year, it spread across the whole assembly, until over a thousand initiates were on their feet, Jenne among them, all yelling together in celebration. Tomorrow they would train, study, and compete, and many would eventually fail. But for now, they let themselves revel in what they had already accomplished. The highborn, the lowborn; the rich, the poor; the idealistic, the ambitious, and the dutiful; the naturally gifted and the tirelessly hardworking; from Gold Houses, War Houses, and Blood Houses alike: all cheered together, and for one timeless moment, all divisions among them disappeared.

Only Jadon tu'Hatreth was not among them. Instead, the Hatreth heir was riding down the road from Lystra in the deepening dark. Glancing up at the sky, he supposed Drei Master Garadil would be finishing up his speech soon, if he had not already.

Jadon had heard the speech before. In his role as Senator-Liaison, Lord Juaqen had visited campus several years ago to review the university's quality on behalf of the Eshtem Oversight Committee in the Senate. He had taken his son along, and the Drei Masters had invited them to experience the orientation ceremony with the incoming class. The speech was pretentious and obsolete, and Jadon had no real desire to hear it repeated. But he was annoyed, all the same, to be missing it at his father's behest.

The Dragon Gate was glowing faintly in the moonlight when Jadon reached it.

"Who goes there?" The challenge came, as sourceless and unnerving as it had been on Jadon's last visit.

"Jadon tu'Hatreth," he answered. "Initiate."

The gate slowly swung open, revealing a cloaked figure on horseback. "Just 'Initiate Jadon' now. Your House name stays at the gate," the man said, his face drawn in disapproval. "I am Rastilap, administrative aide to the headmaster. I'm to escort you to your dorm." The aide turned his horse and started down the bridge. "The orientation ceremony in the arena is an extremely important part of this university," he continued as Jadon drew alongside. "Experiencing it together with the other initiates is what sets the tone for the entire program of study here. But I suppose you think you're above all that."

"No, sir," said Jadon, not sure how he was expected to respond. "Here I am just the same as any other initiate."

"And yet, all the other initiates were here on time and sat together through the orientation speech." After they crossed the bridge, Rastilap turned left to follow the latticed stonework path that connected the outer buildings of the university. They were set in a nearly circular ring around the central area of campus, where the library stood in a lawn dotted with trees in full summer foliage.

Jadon did not bother to answer. The aide knew why he had missed the speech. Lord Juaqen had sent word ahead and cleared Jadon's absence – so why the reproach? *Am I supposed to think they might punish me anyway?*

They rode in uncomfortable silence as far as the west complex, where the boys' dorms were housed. The central building was twelve stories high, measuring little over half the height of the towers that bordered the area to the north and west. Walled walkways connected the central building to shorter structures on either side, and four lesser buildings formed a square around this central construction. A tall, silver-white wall, adorned with deep green climbing vines, encircled the complex.

Rastilap told Jadon how to find his room and left him at the gate, taking both horses. When Jadon reached his room, on the third floor of the northwest building, he found another initiate reading a codex by rushlight. The boy smiled and stood to greet him. "I take it you're my roommate?"

"Jadon." Jadon extended a hand.

"Diar J–" The other initiate hesitated as he shook Jadon's hand. "I suppose it's just Diar now, actually."

It seemed Jadon's name had not rung any bells for his roommate, which meant he was either unusually forgetful or extremely out of touch. Jadon could not remember the last time he had introduced himself to someone unfamiliar with his name.

Abruptly, the door opened again, revealing a third initiate. He was several inches shorter than the two of them, but athletically built, and the lazy confidence in his dark eyes suggested the room would be as much his as theirs if he bothered to claim it.

Jadon knew him. "Chase. Small world."

"Jadon." Chase nodded to him. "Rindarin wanted someone to come back for you, when he realized you weren't with the others."

Jadon and his roommate glanced at each other. "How nice of you to volunteer," Jadon told Chase.

It was War House Initiative business, he supposed. The Initiative was a student group for War House-sworn that was founded around after-curfew forays off Eshtem grounds for drinking, gambling, and practice for the combat trials. Rindarin tu'Rithadur, a second-year War House prince and the group's current leader, had mentioned he would invite Jadon the last time they spoke at a court function – and of course, Chase, being from House Entaren, was also a member. Jadon had just not expected his own involvement to begin so soon.

"If you call drawing the short straw volunteering." Chase shrugged as he opened the door. He was in his third and final year at the university, if Jadon remembered correctly, and though Chase was not a prince, Entaren was a royal House. Jadon doubted anyone would have asked Chase to do anything against his will, but if he did not want to admit to volunteering for Jadon's escort duty, that was his own business.

Jadon took a step after him. Then he paused and asked his roommate, "You coming?"

Chase frowned at him. Bringing his dark-skinned roommate to an event meant for War House nobles would certainly irritate some, as Diar's obvious Rishara heritage made him unlikely to be either noble or War House-sworn. Hundreds of years ago, the Rishara people had lived in Blood House territory and worshiped the White God, making them heretics to fair-skinned Ellyrians who worshiped the Six. Since then, many Rishara had married into the northern Houses, and most had left their old religion behind. Still, few dark-skinned people had married into noble families, and in War House territory, intermarriages were rare even in the lower classes.

Jadon sized up his roommate, wondering how much of a splash he would make with the Initiative. Diar was taller than Jadon by maybe an inch or two. Despite being broader of shoulder and considerably taller than Chase, though, Diar did not look as though he would be the one to win in a fight. He lacked Chase's sleek athleticism.

And at the moment, he looked incredulous. "You guys are going out?" he asked. "Weren't those the curfew bells that just tolled?"

Jadon shrugged. "Suit yourself," he said, following Chase out the door.

The elves had taken some precautions with the boys' dorms when the campus was built, barring the windows on the first and second floors of each building and lining the top of the west complex's wall with shards of glass, but the measures were woefully inadequate to contain the War House Initiative. Chase and Jadon let themselves out a third-story window, used the climbing vine that adorned the outer wall to scale it, and laid cloth strips over the glass to protect their hands as they crossed to the other side.

Chase led Jadon north and east through the pine forest that bordered the complex. When the trees began to thin, they saw Rindarin standing in front of the canyon dividing the campus plateau from the next one over. Upwards of threescore initiates sat facing him, all dressed in the standard Eshtem issue of pale blue tunic, brown hose, and cotton shirt. Rindarin, in contrast, wore his own attire: a War House-style doublet with the Rithadur lion emblazoned across the chest.

Jadon was often compared to Rindarin. Rindarin was a few inches taller and Jadon's facial features were sharper, but the court spoke well of the handsomeness of each. They were both the heirs of royal War Houses, and now they were both Eshtem Initiates.

Jadon had never much cared for the other prince.

"When he saw that he could shake the Drei Master in no other way," Rindarin was saying as they drew into earshot, "Lathew Entaren did not slow his run, but leapt down onto the ledge you see before you, sprinted the last few steps to the edge of the cliff, and threw himself over the canyon in a desperate attempt to reach the neighboring plateau."

Rindarin paused, and Jadon could see his gaze sweeping the assembled group, using the silence to build their suspense. His showmanship reminded Jadon of Garadil's, though there was something more self-satisfied and almost indolent about the way Rindarin commanded attention.

As Chase moved toward the clearing, Jadon caught up and put a hand on his shoulder.

"Wait just a second," he suggested, nodding toward Rindarin. "Let's not interrupt." It was with some interest that Jadon noted the other first-years were dressed in their uniforms. Chase had not been, so it had not occurred to Jadon to change.

"The Drei Master," Rindarin continued, "not daring to follow, and still not knowing who it was that he had chased, left to rouse the other masters and begin a count of the initiates to discover who was missing. With the aid of Filip Sendell – with whom he'd just been dueling – Lathew returned to this plateau, and the combatants successfully sneaked back into their rooms. From that day to this, the War House Initiative continues to meet in secret on Eshtem grounds, preserving the ideals of strength, honor, courage, and ambition prized by our Houses. And tonight, we invite you to join us by attempting the same leap as our predecessor.

"Which of you dares to jump first?" Rindarin's gaze challenged each of the invitees.

"What are the rules for this jump?" Jadon drew the attention of the group as he approached.

A good entrance was all about timing.

"Rules?" Rindarin smiled to himself. "This isn't a Blood House event, Jadon." Raising his voice, he said, "Everyone, meet Jadon – the last of our invitees for the evening." Looking back at Jadon, he added, "No rules. Just jump."

Jadon nodded, then walked past Rindarin to the edge of the plateau. Though most of the face was sheer, a small lower portion of the cliffside curved outward beneath where they stood, jutting out over the canyon to form a depressed ledge. The drop to the river on the canyon's floor was only fifty or so lengths here, though the waterfalls a few miles west would increase its depth to over a hundred lengths before the river turned to flow under the Dragon Arch.

Hopping down to the ledge, Jadon walked up to the edge and studied the distance to the next plateau. It was much too far for any human to make unaided.

The point is for all the first-years to look like fools, he deduced, twisting his mouth in annoyance. The challenge was all show and no substance – exactly the kind of thing that made Jadon despise court functions. Well-bred politicians like Rindarin and Jadon's father always expected Jadon to keep his head down and play along.

Chrome that. As a War House noble, Jadon would lose face at court if he failed to participate in the War House Initiative. With all the other initiates shut away in their dorms, there was nothing better to do anyway, but since he was going to spend his first night at Eshtem playing Rindarin's game, he intended to beat it. "Define 'jump.'"

"Really?" asked Rindarin.

"Indulge me."

"All right, then." Rindarin stepped to the edge of the plateau proper, so that he stood about four lengths higher than Jadon as they both assessed the gap. "The kind of 'jump' we're looking for here," he said, keeping his words slow and clear, "involves both feet leaving the ground and your body sailing out through the air over the chasm." He glanced back at the other initiates with a small smile, sharing his amusement over Jadon's density with them. "Are there any other terms you'd like defined?"

"That will do," said Jadon, turning his attention to the ledge itself. It was maybe seven lengths long – not enough to get much of a running start. "For now," he added, tossing Rindarin a smile.

Somewhat belatedly, he noted that Chase had never followed him out of the forest. *Lookout duty?* he wondered. A group like this would need at least one scout, in case any Drei Masters wandered into the vicinity. As far as Jadon knew, it was rare for them to stumble across an Initiative event by accident. They turned a blind eye to the group as far as they could, and related expulsions usually occurred only when a third party was able to establish that members had violated campus rules. However, if a master chanced to walk by, initiates would be expelled on sight for breaking curfew.

"Is this series of inane questions your way of volunteering to jump first, Jadon?" The expectancy in Rindarin's tone made it something other than a question.

"On the contrary," said Jadon, scuffing the ground of the ledge with his foot, "I am more than willing to surrender that honor to someone else."

He pulled himself back onto the plateau.

"I'll do it." One of the initiates stood as Jadon regained his feet. He was shorter than Jadon – probably shorter than Chase, too, and of a slighter build than either of them. There was nothing slight about the hard stare he gave Jadon, though. He did not approve of backing down from a challenge.

"Very well, Fendi," Rindarin said. Stepping to the side of the ledge, he swept his arm open in invitation. "The Initiative salutes you."

Since he was still standing in the way, Jadon mimicked Rindarin's gesture as he stepped to the other side, doubling the invitation. Fendi ignored him, walking back toward the forest. After removing his sword belt, Fendi stripped off his outer tunic and boots, and the circle of invitees parted to clear a path for him.

Turning back toward the chasm, Fendi rolled up the sleeves of his cotton shirt. Then he started to run, working up a good speed by the time he sailed past Jadon and Rindarin.

He did not slow for the drop to the ledge, absorbing the impact with bent knees and not a trace of a stumble as he continued to the edge of the chasm. His jump carried him almost halfway across the divide.

He flailed a bit as he started to fall, arms turning circles in the air as he plummeted toward the river below. He regained his composure before hitting the water, going in feet-first at a near-vertical angle. The invitees crowded close for a better view as they waited for him to reappear.

His head broke the surface moments later, a couple spans downstream.

As Fendi started swimming for the far side, Jadon broke away from the onlookers. He used his sword to cut down one of the taller, thinner pines that had fewer branches than the others at the forest's edge. The resulting crash drew everyone's attention.

"Were we boring you with all this, Jadon?" Rindarin called, his gesture encompassing the gathered initiates, the ledge, and the canyon. He sounded amused, as though Jadon's interruptions were more a bizarre sideshow than a significant disruption. "Perhaps you require a few hands?"

"Not at all," Jadon answered, waving a hand in dismissal. Most of the initiates were watching him with interest. Some of them had to have guessed what he was up to, though they would not believe it possible to span the gap until they saw otherwise. "Please, carry on. I'll rejoin you in a minute."

While Rindarin continued the ceremony, Jadon used a broken branch to whack at where branches were joined to his fallen tree. It was not a quick process, but there were several dozen initiates waiting to jump. Jadon finished separating the last of the branches from the tree trunk while there were still two initiates left, leaving himself with a very thick, very sappy sixteen-length stick. He dragged it toward the ledge. Both the remaining initiates jumped before he reached it.

"Now would be a good time to abandon this foolishness and follow the rest of the first-years into the river," Rindarin said as Jadon dragged his branchless tree trunk toward the ledge. Chase emerged from the forest to join Rindarin, and they both watched Jadon with skeptical expressions. "What do you think you are going to do here? Build a bridge?"

Jadon snorted as he released his tree and jumped down to the ledge. "Crossing a bridge would hardly qualify as jumping." He drew his dagger and squatted on the ground near the edge. There was a sizable rock buried in the surface there, and he began carving a hollow in the earth near its base. "This will take just a minute."

"I'm afraid we don't have all night," said Rindarin, his blue eyes flashing in irritation. "Go ahead, Chase."

Chase may have been at the school longer, but he clearly deferred to Rindarin. It was not that unusual. Third-years spent a fair amount of time away from campus doing field training, so it made sense for a second-year to shoulder the responsibility of leading an unsanctioned group like the Initiative. The role usually fell to the highest-born War House initiate among the upperclassmen, and this year, that was Rindarin.

It did not surprise Jadon that Rindarin had waited for the other first-years to leave before expressing any displeasure with Jadon's antics. Jadon's rank outside of Eshtem was just as high as Rindarin's, so the other prince had to treat him with tolerance and respect if he expected status by birth to carry weight with the others – at least, so long as the others were around to observe.

"Actually, I was hoping to borrow Chase for this," Jadon said. Rindarin would probably have done as well for what Jadon had in mind, but he guessed the Rithadur prince would prove less than willing. "If you think you can handle it, that is, Chase."

Chase looked from the hollow Jadon was carving to the tree trunk he had dragged to the ledge. He shook his head slowly. "You'll want Alaxis... if you actually intend to do this without any practice."

Chase nodded toward the forest, where another figure dressed in street clothes was emerging from the trees – the group's second lookout, presumably.

Jadon nodded, recognizing Chase's cousin. Alaxis was a second-year, like Rindarin. "He's taller than you two, anyway. Better angle to throw from."

Chase and Rindarin both smirked.

"Yeah, that's why." Chase walked back toward the forest. He doffed his sword belt and boots before starting his run, dodging Jadon neatly when he dropped to the ledge and continuing out and over the edge without slowing. He turned several tight somersaults in the air as he fell, extending his body into a straight line before he hit the surface in a perfect headfirst dive.

Show-off. Given what he was about to attempt himself, Jadon was hardly in a position to throw stones. "My turn," he said, grabbing one end of his tree trunk and pulling it down onto the ledge. He positioned its base firmly in the hollow, so the trunk rested at an angle on the edge of the plateau.

"This is a new level of reckless, even for you." Rindarin pressed his lips together.

Jadon smiled. "It's only dangerous if I mess up." He pulled himself onto the plateau. "Alaxis," he said, beckoning the taller student over. His tree trunk slanted against the plateau at a modest angle, its upper end resting several lengths above the ground. "If you don't mind doing me a favor. I'm going to need you to throw this end higher into the air, on my signal. Think you can do that for me?"

"You got it, Jadon." Alaxis's grin contrasted sharply with Rindarin's disapproval. He was carrying a small pack, and he opened it to pull out a coil of rope. Crouching near the drop to the ledge, he tied one end around the tree.

Jadon frowned.

"In case we want to use it again," Alaxis explained with a wink. "Don't worry, I won't pull until you're clear. On my honor."

"And you just happened to have a coil of rope along?"

"The Initiative doesn't bring tenderfeet to the canyon without any rope. You wouldn't believe the scrapes first-years have gotten themselves into around here."

Jadon shrugged. If Alaxis wrecked his momentum and he shorted the vault, the extra height meant a higher chance of injury on impact with the river – but the glory was still worth the risk. He walked back toward the forest, taking off his sword belt as he went.

"On my signal," Jadon repeated. Then he took a deep breath and prepared to run. This would be nothing like vaulting the outer wall of the Hatreth estate, nor the narrow river that ran through the woods on the property. All the dimensions were different.

The concept, though, was the same, and he was sure it could work.

"Ready," said Alaxis.

Here goes nothing, thought Jadon, stomach turning flip-flops as he broke into a dead sprint.

"Now!" he called, and Alaxis tossed his end of the trunk up, so that the stick reached nearer verticality from where it stood anchored in the hollow. Jadon, pushing off from the ground with all his might, caught the trunk as it was rising. His momentum carried it up to its full height as he arched his body to aid the vault. He let go as the trunk started to fall, experiencing a rush of adrenaline as he sailed over the near seventy-length drop above the river on the canyon's floor.

There was little time to note the view as he plummeted toward the opposite plateau, where initiates were quickly clearing out of the way.

This is going to hurt, was all Jadon could think as he sped toward the ground on the other side, twisting to take the impact on his shoulder.

It did hurt. Moreover, he came closer to falling short of the next plateau than he cared to consider, smashing into the grass mere lengths from the edge. A moment after colliding with the earth, he realized his feet were dangling over the edge of the cliff.

Next time I'll need to grab the tree closer to the top.

It was a useless thought. He doubted he would ever do this again.

A few of the initiates started clapping. Fendi offered him a hand up.

"That was something else," he said as he pulled Jadon to his feet.

"Hey, looks like the upperclassmen are going to try to replicate your stunt." One of the other initiates pointed across the canyon. Alaxis was positioning the tree trunk the way Jadon had had it, resting one end in the hollow. His trick with the rope had apparently worked.

"They would have to be insane," another initiate said. He had a wiry frame and a supercilious manner, and Jadon recognized him as Duke Sendell's son, Perleyon. "No offense," he added, glancing at Jadon.

Jadon walked closer to the edge to see what Rindarin would do.

The Rithadur heir stood at the very edge of the ledge, contemplating the drop to the river. Turning his own gaze downward, Jadon studied the canyon's floor.

He had not noticed before, but the river did not stretch unbroken between the canyon's walls. Sharp rocks broke its surface far below where Jadon stood, continuing a few lengths out toward the river's center. The last few jumpers were reaching them now on their swim to the plateau where Jadon stood. The rocks were too far away from the opposite face to pose a danger to the unaided jumper, who would fall to the river far short of where they began. But if a vault from the ledge fell just short of the next plateau, the danger could prove mortal.

Jadon had risked his life without fully realizing it.

Moreover, he had effectively challenged Rindarin to do the same. Now that he had proven the entire gap could be crossed, attempting anything less would look like cowardice and would undermine Rindarin's position in the Initiative.

Sanity was not a virtue highly prized among War House youth.

They watched eagerly as Rindarin walked toward the forest and removed his sword belt. Alaxis stood near the ledge, prepared to toss the end of the trunk up as he had done for Jadon. Rindarin faced the canyon. Jadon and the others could just make him out from where they stood, as a shadowy form outlined by starlight. Before beginning his run, Rindarin raised his right arm, bent with fingers pressed against his forehead, and extended it outward in a soldier's salute.

Jadon returned the gesture, knowing Rindarin had considered the possibility that he might die.

Maybe next time he would think twice before putting Jadon in a situation where he was expected to fail.

"We should back up," Jadon said. "Looks like he's coming over."

Rindarin broke into a run. Alaxis's timing was perfect, and Rindarin caught the trunk in the air just as Jadon had done and arched his body to propel himself upward and outward.

Then he let go and sailed through the air over the canyon unaided, falling fast toward where Jadon and the others stood.

He made it across with more room to spare than Jadon, but he hit the ground hard and not well, attempting to land on his feet but crashing flat on his face instead. He brought his hands up at the last minute to protect his head, and from the look of it, Rindarin's right wrist took the brunt of the impact. Jadon suspected it was sprained.

A few initiates chuckled at the sight of the second-year spread-eagled on the ground.

"How are you doing?" Jadon asked, offering Rindarin a hand up. "Quite a jump, wasn't it?"

"Quite the idea," said Rindarin, rising on his own. Gingerly, he began brushing dirt off himself, favoring his right hand. "Let's see what Alaxis does with it."

Rindarin turned to watch the opposite side, crossing his arms. Following his gaze, Jadon saw that Alaxis, impressively, had once again managed to reel the tree trunk in without spoiling Rindarin's vault. He stood near the ledge with the trunk resting on one of his shoulders, angling the other end into the hollow. Then, after carrying the tree back a few steps, he came forward again, guiding the trunk into the hollow more quickly.

"Is he really going to try it alone?" asked one of the initiates.

"Impossible," muttered Perleyon as Alaxis backed up toward the trees on the far plateau, still carrying the tree trunk over his right shoulder. "He's going to get himself killed."

Alaxis started running. He lowered the tree trunk as he approached the ledge and must have struck the hollow despite the darkness, because the trunk stayed anchored as he vaulted. He released the trunk as it reached its apex, and this time it fell into the canyon as he sailed toward the opposite cliffside, right on target with room to spare.

He turned a perfect somersault on his landing, using the momentum to regain his feet.

One of the initiates whistled at the stunt, and the rest were equally in awe. They were a sizable group by now, most of the later jumpers having made it to the top and joined their growing circle.

"Nicely done," Rindarin told Alaxis. "Some of these skeptics thought you were going to get yourself killed."

Alaxis laughed at that.

"They'll learn better what to expect from War House elite upperclassmen by the time we finish their education." Rindarin's mood seemed to be improving, now that the first-years had been properly impressed by a second-year.

"Better keep them away from vaulting in the meantime," Alaxis cautioned, still grinning. "The tenderfeet *could* hurt themselves."

"I couldn't agree with you more. Though," Rindarin added, glancing at Jadon, "it was quite the idea. If Lathew Entaren had thought of it, he might have avoided getting wet in his flight from the Drei Master. That is, if he had had time to cut down a tree and trim it while he was running." Rindarin smiled at Jadon, but he got the sense he was being rebuked.

"I admit, it probably wouldn't have worked for Lathew," said Jadon. "Even if he had had the time, the Drei Master could have just lassoed his stick and followed."

A few of the initiates chuckled at that, and Rindarin stopped smiling. He stared at Jadon, and for a moment Jadon wondered if he had made an enemy.

"Spectrum's spitfire." The voice belonged to Chase, who had just made it to the top of the plateau. "You made it. All three of you vaulted?" he demanded. "I thought you would talk yourselves out of it for sure."

Rindarin smiled, finally breaking eye contact with Jadon. "Perhaps you should have had more faith," he said. "But come. The evening is young. We must toast everyone's entry to the Initiative, and the other upperclassmen will want to hear about what happened. It's been a long time since we've had anything so unusual happen during initiation." He nodded to Jadon, easing the tension between them as he led the group into the woods to meet up with the rest of the Initiative's second- and third-years.

Jadon did not mind finding himself restored to Rindarin's good graces as he started to follow, though he knew he had only his bloodline to thank for it.

He doubted he would remain there long.

CHAPTER 5

Debt of Honor

We do not erase information from our records, but neither do we maintain copies of Ellyrian records with the express purpose of preventing the Ellyrians from ever effectively erasing information. We also do not abet Alterran investigations into erased Ellyrian information by allowing anyone with ties to the Lussonne to go through our records.

> — Vaar Merhni, lecturing the apprentice
> staff at Our Library

Christina's first night at Eshtem was long and troubled.

She had wanted to be a student here for as long as she could remember, but when she listened to Master Garadil's speech about the university's founding and its mission to bring peace, justice, and knowledge to a war-torn world, all she could think about was the green-cloaked Edrei parting Hezred's head from his shoulders.

Zanner had never given a proper answer to his oath, but that had not mattered. Her own doubts had not mattered. General Anandolf had given the order, and then it was over.

Was that what bringing peace to the world was supposed to look like?

Hezred had been an outlaw. He had been complicit in the

deaths of her own men. Zanner had very nearly died, too, because of him. Christina kept telling herself that Hezred's death was just, but that had not helped her sleep any better in the inn at Lystra, and now, as she lay in the darkness, listening to her roommate's breaths coming slow and even from across the dorm, she was reluctant to close her eyes. Her nightmares had been vivid the night before.

Instead, she twisted the Noraani signet ring on her finger and thought about Hezred's last moments. He had wanted her to hide the ring from Anandolf. That could only mean Hezred did not want the general to know who Christina was, but why would he care about that?

Why had he used his last words to tell her not to watch? There was so much Christina had wanted to know about him: what the accusations against him were, what he claimed had happened instead, what he meant about his witnesses' ending up dead. She wished he had used that moment to say something that mattered.

His advice had been wasted anyway. Christina had had no time to look away, even if she had wanted to – and that was another puzzle. Rushing the execution before Zanner could formally respond to Hezred's oath was bad enough, but why had Anandolf carried it out right before her eyes? She was a civilian, and even if he had not realized she was a princess, he knew she was a noblewoman. *He* should have been the one telling her to look away.

Once Hezred was dead, the Edrei who killed him had roughly frisked the headless body while Christina stared at the outlaw's lifeless eyes in dismay. His head had rolled near her.

A wave of great sorrow had come over her then, and wind stirred her hair as the massive dragon she had somehow managed to forget moved its wings. Christina looked up and met the dragon's gaze as the Edrei cursed, failing to find whatever he searched for on Hezred's body.

She was numb, just as she had been when her soldiers were killed. The sorrow belonged to the dragon. She had been sure of it at the time, but now, Christina wondered. *Why would a dragon mourn the execution of a renegade?* And even if the creature had been saddened by Hezred's death, how could Christina have sensed it?

Then the general had ordered the group back toward the dragon, and Christina called out to remind him about Zanner. A pair of them came over and looked at Zanner's wound. They used magic to restore him to consciousness, but they said they did not have time to heal him fully and directed him to seek follow-up care in Lystra as soon as possible. Zanner nodded weakly, and the other Edrei wrapped Hezred's head in a cloak, mounted the dragon, and flew back with it toward the mountains.

They left his body lying in the road.

None of it lined up with what Christina would have expected. The renegade had treated her and Zanner with more care and consideration than Zanner's own superiors. Then they had killed him.

And she was supposed to believe that was justice?

Zanner had seemed as troubled by the incident as she was. Neither he nor Christina had voiced any criticism of Anandolf, but the two of them had taken the time to bury what was left of Hezred's body. They did not have anything to dig with, but there had been a copse of trees nearby. Zanner cut down some large, leafy branches while Christina gathered fallen ones, and they managed to roll the body off the road and cover it – a difficult process, and obviously painful for Zanner, who had very limited use of his right arm.

"He died nameless, and a criminal," Zanner said when they finished. "But he didn't let the other outlaws kill us. I'm grateful for that."

"So am I," Christina murmured.

It was not much of a funeral, but at least they had not left Hezred's body lying in the road. Christina wished the Edrei had not taken his head. It should have been buried with him, and she could not fathom what purpose the Edrei might have for it.

When she finally fell asleep, she was back on that road, watching Hezred offer his oath to Zanner. The general's command came next. Christina had seen this sequence replay a dozen times in her nightmares already, but this time, desperate to change something, she burst to her feet and exclaimed that *she* would accept Hezred's oath.

The shock of it woke her, and as she blinked awake in the darkness, Christina realized it could have worked. Hezred had been right in front of her when he had offered his oath, and though it was clear to everyone he had meant it for Zanner, he had not said so. Christina could have jumped in and accepted, and it would have been legally binding unless Hezred had denied having offered it to her.

She could have prevented his death – or at least delayed it until she was sure it was just.

Rolling onto her stomach, she buried her face in her hands, upbraiding herself for her failure. Maybe the outlaw had deserved to die, as the Edrei had claimed. The Edrei, who were supposed to be the representatives of all that was fair and good and true, to whom life was sacred, as it had been to the elves and had never been to the Ellyrian War Houses before Eshtem. The *Edrei*, who brought peace and knowledge and justice to Ellyrian and to the world – these same Edrei had judged Hezred worthy of death, so who was she to disagree?

And yet Christina did disagree. She could not see how the man who had protected her and Zanner deserved to die without a trial. She could have stopped it, but she had not.

Why didn't I think of this then? Her efforts to slow things down had been so paltry, so half-hearted. *How did I let myself do nothing?* She had simply watched as an innocent man was murdered.

A man I thought *was innocent,* she corrected herself, turning onto her side. *Who pretended ignorance of his trial. It might have been an act. Like his Projections.* She was too tired to think straight. *Shouldn't I be having nightmares about the deaths of my own men?* Surely they deserved more of her sympathy and guilt than a renegade Edrei sentenced to death.

After a time, her mind slipped back into troubled dreaming.

"I am sorry... I should have explained... Our witnesses have a habit of turning up dead... Please don't die."

"I offer you my oath." He had declared the truth, and there was nowhere to hide from his truth... Drei Zanner couldn't hide from it, not even behind General Anandolf's cold unforgiveness... Until he let the magic die. *"The truth costs too much..."*

"Don't," he told her, his voice full of warning. *"Don't watch,"* he said, glancing at the general, but that wasn't what he'd meant at all.

Don't make a scene. Don't try to stop them.

Don't make yourself a target.

Christina opened her eyes, coming awake as the puzzle fell together. Hezred's surprise at hearing he had already been tried had been genuine. Which meant that the Edrei law stipulating that a member of the Order must have a chance to speak in his own defense before being sentenced to death had been circumvented... which meant someone with influence in the Order must have been afraid of what he might say.

"Tell no one what happened here." General Anandolf had said that to her and Zanner, just before he and his team had flown back toward the Brennels. Christina did not know why he had said that, but she felt he must not have wanted them to speak of how Hezred had been executed before Zanner answered his oath. It was an impropriety that made sense if someone powerful had wanted Hezred silenced.

And they wouldn't want me spreading stories of that impropriety, lest it lead someone to look into why they'd wanted Hezred killed so quickly – and to uncover whatever he knew. That would also explain why Hezred had wanted Christina to conceal her signet ring; if one of Anandolf's superiors heard his report and wanted to make sure of her silence, it would require more of an effort to figure out who she was and come after her.

It was almost unthinkable that a murderous conspiracy could be at work in the Edrei, but Christina knew she couldn't just let it go. After all that she'd seen, she couldn't just trust that the Edrei general had acted correctly. If Hezred had deserved to die, she needed to know why. And if he hadn't... Well, she needed to know for sure.

There would be no records left in Ellyrian that referenced Hezred or his past, now that his name had been erased, but Christina knew the Alterrans made and kept their own copies of the Lists in a grand library called the Lussonne. Their staff were notoriously disdainful of the Ellyrian practice of altering historical records. Alterran scholars cared nothing for how their own unaltered records sullied the honor of every House that ever happened to produce an undesirable offshoot, calling family affiliations between honorless criminals and upright citizens "the truth," even when all members of the House disavowed the connection.

Christina did not like the idea of turning to such a corrupt institution for help. She might never learn enough to settle the question of Hezred's guilt one way or the other, and attempting to do so could bring dishonor on herself and her House.

But that was nothing compared to the dishonor she risked by doing nothing if Hezred had been framed and she was the only person alive who suspected it.

She could write to the Lussonne and request copies of the Eshtem Lists from between fifteen and thirty years ago. The man who had called himself Hezred must have graduated within that time. His original name would appear in the Lussonne's copies, along with any special honors he had received and the details of his first assignment. If she cross-checked them with the Lists kept on file at Eshtem, that entry would be the sole discrepancy.

It was not much, but it was somewhere to start.

Christina got a little sleep after she made the decision, but it was restless. She kept checking her window for signs of dawn, and when it finally looked as though the sky was starting to lighten, she got up and changed into her new uniform: a white chemise and pale blue overdress. It was a little short for her and much looser than she was accustomed to, given the lack of a corset, but it came with a white sash that Christina tied tightly around her midsection. She supposed there were too many initiates for the uniforms to fit everyone exactly, and she doubted she would miss her corsets once she got used to breathing without them.

Her roommate stirred at the noise but didn't wake, and Christina left the room in silence.

She saw no one in the halls or outside, but the gate to the east complex was standing open. She made the short walk to the north tower, where the mess hall was located. Since she was awake, she figured she might as well eat.

The doors of the north tower opened into an entrance foyer with a large staircase leading up on the left-hand side. The far side of the foyer opened into the mess hall, where lines of tables stretched across the floor from wall to wall. There was not enough seating to accommodate every initiate that had been at the orientation ceremony the previous night – perhaps not even half that number – but when they had gone over campus rules, the Drei Masters had explained that the students were not required to eat in the hall or expected to take their meals at the same times.

Christina was a little surprised to see that she was not the first initiate to arrive. Six others were already eating, three of them talking together in quiet voices and the others sitting alone at various tables. There was no line at the kitchen window yet, so Christina picked up a trencher and received porridge and a morning roll from the kitchen staff.

A few other initiates trickled in while she ate and considered how best to communicate with the Lussonne. Eshtem had its own post, but all the correspondence that went through it was reviewed by the mail carriers for compliance with university standards. Anything going to or from the Lussonne would raise questions that she was not prepared to answer.

"Good morning, Christina." A thin, brown-haired girl

with tightly braided hair sat across from Christina at her table, setting her trencher down in front of her. "What has you up so early?"

"Good morning, Claire." Christina managed to smile for the other girl. Claire was the daughter of a Ryder princess and the Entear commoner she had run away to marry, and she had been adopted back into the nobility by her mother's relatives after the deaths of her Entear family. That made her another Blood House noblewoman, which did not matter now, but when Christina had arrived in Lystra, penniless and alone, and heard that Claire was passing through the city on her way to Eshtem, Christina had sent a message asking if she could ride with her the rest of the way. Claire had responded favorably and been nothing but kind to Christina since.

Christina was not in the mood for company, but she owed Claire some measure of civility. "I could ask you the same," she said in lieu of answering.

"Oh, I couldn't sleep." Claire shook her head. "I don't know how anyone did. Do you think it will be as difficult here as people say?"

"I suppose we can only hope that it is." Christina furrowed her brow as she dipped her spoon into the porridge. Claire gave her a curious expression, and Christina paused. "An Edrei must be learned and competent across a wide variety of domains," she explained, "with a character well tested and above reproach. Do you not wish to be challenged?"

"Oh, no… that is… yes." Claire flushed, dropping her eyes. "I only meant that I hope I prove to be a worthy candidate. That is all."

Christina nodded. "You seem to have an appropriate disposition for it. As long as your skills keep pace, I wouldn't be worried."

The comment was not exactly a glowing endorsement, and it was based on nothing more than Christina's first impressions. She was taken aback when Claire's whole countenance brightened.

"Do you truly believe so?"

Christina was spared the necessity of responding as two other initiates paused by their table, both holding trenchers.

"Claire, is that you?"

"Hello, Lelise," Claire greeted the speaker, a pretty blonde girl with impeccable bearing. "Have you met Christina?"

"So you *are* Christina," said Lelise, her pale green eyes turning a self-satisfied glance toward her friend. "I suspected as much."

"Christina, meet Lelise," Claire said, the introduction sounding rather clipped with both their House names removed. "I'm afraid I do not know your companion." She glanced at the girl standing with Lelise, whose light olive skin and black hair suggested some Rishara blood.

"This is Saleah," Lelise supplied.

"A pleasure to meet you, Christina, Claire," Saleah told them, glancing at Lelise. Her friend continued studying Christina, who nodded to them.

"Indeed," Claire agreed after a moment, glancing at Christina. When Christina said nothing and no one moved, she added, "Won't you sit down?"

Lelise smiled as the two of them sat. If they had been at court, the whole business would have complied with etiquette exactly, except for the point of Claire's having invited them to sit instead of Christina, whose rank was higher.

But they were not at court, and Christina saw no reason for Claire to defer to her.

"We have not met before," Lelise said, "but I knew you were Christina. Saleah doubted me, but I had your description from my cousin Vannes. I believe you met him the last time you were at court, isn't that right?"

"Vannes..." It took a moment for Christina to remember Vannes to'Jinn, the nephew of another Blood House high prince. She had been a child at the time. "Yes, I suppose I did meet him."

"There has been *much* speculation as to what became of you after that," Saleah informed her.

"We're pleased to see you have not turned into a mute or an invalid, as some of the rumors said," Lelise added.

They were both studying her with obvious curiosity, and Christina supposed she had to say something. "My father and I mourned a long time after my mother passed away, and I eventually took on a bigger role managing the estate. Between that and my studies, it no longer made sense for me to travel so far."

The truth was, her father had never gone back to court after her mother's death. After her own last appearance, the eight year-old Christina had insisted that if he did not have to go anymore, neither would she. She had never cared for the empty pleasantries of court people, and their condolences were even worse. Her father had relented when Christina passed his quiz on all the social graces and protocols she was meant to learn, and she had been relieved to spend the intervening years alone with her books.

"Those rumors were all false, then," Lelise concluded. "But there's just one more thing I have to ask. Is it true you were attacked by bandits on your journey to Lystra?"

"Yes," Christina answered, choosing not to elaborate.

"How awful! How did it happen?" Saleah pressed.

"Thank the Six you survived," Lelise cut in, casting a reproving glance at Saleah. "It is dreadful to think that such a thing could befall a traveler on one of the high roads. But we shan't press you for any more uncomfortable details. We are simply pleased you are here. Now you have much smaller problems to concern yourself with, such as the quality of the breakfast fare." She lifted a spoonful of porridge and watched some of the creamy liquid slosh back into the bowl on top of her trencher, frowning at it as if it could not possibly pass for something edible.

"And the cut of these Six-forsaken uniforms," Saleah added, fussing with one of the pins she had added to tighten her bodice. "It will be such a relief to have these things properly fitted."

"Oh, yes," said Lelise. "We are planning an outing to see the tailor in Lystra on Seventhday, as we won't have class and will be permitted to leave campus. Christina, you will come with us, won't you? And Claire, of course," she added, almost as an afterthought. Her attention was keenly focused on Christina. "Vannes and a few of his friends have agreed to escort us."

"I think the purpose of issuing everyone uniforms is to make us look the same," Christina said, frowning. "As not all initiates can afford to have them professionally tailored, I'd prefer not to be among those who do."

"How very noble of you." Lelise's tone and the tiny smile on her lips suggested Christina's feelings were more quaint than admirable. "I suppose we will have no choice but to grow accustomed to living more like commoners in some respects." She returned her gaze to her porridge. Making a visible effort to steel herself, she took a small bite, chewed, and swallowed. "Claire, you will come with us, won't you?"

"I… um…" Claire glanced at Christina, conflicted.

"Don't stay on my account," Christina said. "In fact," she added, turning to Lelise as a thought occurred to her, "I would like to ride along with you when you visit the city, though I will not require the attentions of the tailor."

"I suppose we can accommodate that." Lelise nodded to her. "Perhaps you'll change your mind before we get there. Six days is a long time to wear a dress that fits so poorly."

Lelise smiled at her, and Christina forced a smile in return.

She would not be changing her mind about the tailor. However, an outing to Lystra would give her an opportunity to use the Lystran post to correspond with the Lussonne. If Christina was circumspect, she would be able to do so without alerting the Drei Masters or anyone else about what she was up to.

Making nice with Lelise and her friends would be worth the effort if it meant a safe trip there and back.

CHAPTER 6

The Third Principle of Politics

Just because they have dragons, they think they can rule the world. I claimed a similar right based on my understanding of the needs of the Dophkan people. Unfortunately for me, dragons come in handier in a frontal assault.

> – Phel Naergar, interviewing with Dophkan
> historian Astrella Maelin in the third year of his
> imprisonment at Dreiloch Castle

Jenne was early to her first class. She walked in to find Liana and Telius – a tall, fair-haired initiate that she and Diar had befriended yesterday in the caravan – seated at the third of four long tables facing the podium. A few other early arrivals sat at the first and second tables.

"No Drei Master yet?" Jenne asked quietly, setting her satchel down next to Liana.

Jenne had loved hearing the stories about how Vorsand's accomplishments had put all the highborn in his class to shame, and she was equally delighted to have met his niece. Liana was shy and soft-spoken – Jenne's polar opposite – but Jenne had decided they would be fast friends.

"Not yet," Liana said, keeping her voice down as well. "How does your schedule look?"

"Like I'm training to join the Edrei." Jenne grinned, settling in her chair. "Rhetoric, law, and Jeshim after this. Tomorrow: Alterran, ethics, and weaponry. If only these uniforms weren't quite so hideous, I would be maximally happy."

"Please. You want to complain about *your* uniform?" Telius scoffed. "We may all be stuck in baby blue, but at least you two don't have to worry about being emasculated by it."

Jenne smiled, but then all three of them came to attention as a Drei Master walked into the room.

He was a portly – though not soft – man, tall enough to render his girth reasonable, but not so tall that his stature would be called imposing under normal circumstances. In this moment, however, he was Eshtem, and the class knew repercussions would be swift if he found them lacking. His calculating gaze did nothing to relieve their nervousness as he scanned the room, withdrew a pair of spectacles from a pocket in his robe, and consulted a slate lying atop the podium.

More initiates walked in, finding chairs quickly and quietly as the master continued surveying the room and his notes, making marks on the latter every so often with chalk. Jenne found herself sitting straighter as they all waited for him to speak.

The room was nearly full when the bells of the north tower rang. The master tucked his spectacles away and stepped out from behind the podium, clasping his hands behind his back. He waited for the echo of the bells to fade before breaking the silence.

"Who can tell me what subject matter we are met in this room to study?" His gaze passed over several initiates. "Liana. Perhaps you can."

Liana shifted next to Jenne, licking her lips before answering. "Politics? Master…"

"Ah, yes, a few points of etiquette before we begin. I am Master Porrian. You may address me as such, or as 'Drei Master.' You, in turn, will respond to your given names or the title 'Initiate.' If you wish to be recognized to speak in response to a question of mine or a comment of a fellow initiate's, you may indicate this by making eye contact with me and sitting forward in your seat, factors which I may or may not take into account when choosing whom to select. If you speak without being recognized while class is in session, you will earn a number of demerits or merits suitable to the egregiousness of the interruption or the quality of the contribution, as the case may be. Three merits earned will cancel a single demerit from your record. Ten uncanceled demerits on your record will earn you an immediate expulsion.

"Now, back to the matter at hand. Liana has suggested that we are met here this morning to study politics, in a singularly hesitant and inane response to the question put to her. What she did not tell us is what the term 'politics' is meant to signify. Kiprim, perhaps you can explain?"

Jenne followed the master's gaze to a heavyset boy in the last row who looked positively flabbergasted to have been singled out. "Um…" he said, clearing his throat and beginning to flush under Porrian's observation.

After three beats of silence, the master clicked his tongue. "One demerit for you, Kiprim. Try again."

Kiprim glanced at the initiates on either side of him, nearing panic. "Uh…"

A slight figure in the front row cut in before he got any further. "The interpersonal, intergroup, and legal dynamics and machinations that determine the distribution and potential applications of power wielded by individuals and organizations over and on behalf of a grouping of people or peoples."

"It seems Nefry has read Copronde," Porrian observed, moving to stand directly in front of the outspoken initiate. He regarded the boy with a cool gaze, and the class waited in silence to see if demerits would be awarded for the interruption.

"An astute enough scholar, though his musings were a bit verbose," Porrian concluded, returning to his podium. "It seems you'll have to be faster next time, Kiprim. That will be another demerit."

Kiprim sagged in his seat, though whether from despair at being awarded another demerit or relief that the master's attention had moved on was impossible to say.

Just then, another initiate appeared in the doorway, looking out of breath and disheveled in his ill-fitting Eshtem uniform. His slinking posture suggested he wished to avoid drawing anyone's attention, but all eyes were on him as he made his way to one of the two remaining seats in the back row and sat down.

After an uncomfortably long silence under Porrian's stare, the latecomer cleared his throat. "Apologies, Mast–"

"One demerit, Elad, for speaking out of turn," Porrian cut in, his voice and posture radiating displeasure. "Two more for walking through my classroom uninvited. And since you found the first few minutes of class unnecessary for your education, you must already be familiar with Copronde's definition of politics. Perhaps you'd like to repeat it for us?"

Elad's mouth opened as he searched for something to say, seeming to shrink under Porrian's stare. "N–no, Drei Master," he stammered. "I couldn't find–"

"Three demerits for tardiness," Porrian interrupted. "And another for speaking off topic. That's seven. Would you care to remind the class how many will get you expelled?"

Elad fidgeted. "Ten?"

"Are you sure about that?" The question sounded dangerous, and Elad's gaze flicked around the room, searching for answers.

Telius gave him a small nod.

"Yes," Elad said quickly, returning his attention to the Drei Master.

"No, you were not, which will cost you another demerit. Telius, on the other hand, seems to have an abundance of confidence in his knowledge of this class." Porrian took a few steps to his left, stopping in line with Telius. "Perhaps *you* would like to remind us how Copronde defines politics?"

Telius cleared his throat. "The… um, interpersonal and intergroup machinations… er, dynamics… that determine the power distribution among individuals acting on behalf of a group of people? Or peoples."

"Close enough," Porrian said. "Though it will not spare you a demerit for influencing Elad out of turn."

Telius grimaced, and Jenne glanced at him with a slight shrug. He had brought it on himself by attracting the master's attention.

"Let us move past Copronde," Porrian continued, "as we are not here to memorize his rhetoric. Rather, we are here so that I can impart to you a practicable understanding of that nebulous art, politics. Normally, this will involve your having read about a particular political conundrum in advance of class and our dissecting the situation and debating the best line of action to advise in response. Today, though, we will limit our discussion to the three principles of political power one must bear in mind before attempting to address any political issue.

"First – and you may wish to write this down, you will be expected to remember this…" Porrian paused as initiates all around the room, including Jenne, Liana, and Telius, reached into satchels and shoulder bags to withdraw the slate and chalk they had been advised to purchase for use during classes. "All political power has a source. Second, all uses of political power have repercussions. Third, political power can accomplish only the possible, which does not necessarily include the desirable."

Porrian surveyed the room as initiates furiously scribbled away on their slates. "Elad, would you care to repeat the second principle of political power for us?"

"The use of political power has… repercussions." Elad was visibly struggling to maintain his composure. Alone of all the initiates in the room, he had no slate.

Jenne felt no pity for him. *What kind of fool gets into Eshtem and doesn't bring a slate to class?* she wondered. *This is Eshtem, by the seven sights of the Six's beloved. Did he think he would get away with it?*

"*All* uses of political power have repercussions," Porrian corrected, clicking his tongue in disapproval. "An important distinction, the ignorance of which will bring you to a total of nine demerits."

Another initiate appeared at the door as Porrian spoke, once again drawing all eyes. This latecomer looked more put together than Elad had, though from the angle at which he held his head and the way he squinted as he looked into the sunlit classroom, Jenne guessed he had a headache. There was something about the way he carried himself she did not care for.

"Ah, Jadon, I see you've decided to grace us with your

presence after all. Perhaps you can repeat the third principle of politics for the class?"

"According to Arelis Tesicus, Copronde, or the Jeshim School of Vaars?" Jadon inquired, making a visible effort to open his eyes wider as he focused on the master.

Arrogance, Jenne decided, was what she had not liked about him. He carried himself like nobility. No wonder, since this could be none other than Jadon tu'Hatreth. His father was both a high prince and the Senator-Liaison to Eshtem, and Jadon himself was apparently the most promising young duelist since Merabe One-Strike.

Lystra had been full of gossip about him.

Porrian arched an eyebrow, reminding Jenne of a cat deciding what to do with its prey. "According to the Edrei school at Eshtem, my boy."

Jadon nodded slowly. He peered around the room as he did so, his gaze trailing over the assorted items on the master's desk and coming to rest on the large Jeshim representation of the mapped world that adorned the back wall.

The prospect that he would soon meet with Eshtem justice in the form of many demerits pleased Jenne greatly.

"The desirable is not always possible in politics," he said, raising one hand to rub his forehead as he returned his gaze to Porrian.

He's hungover, Jenne realized. Her eyes narrowed.

Ale had been served at dinner in the mess hall the previous day, but it had been too weak to get the initiates drunk. The Edrei Ideals prized character, and character included moderation. Based on Jadon's demeanor, he had access to his own supply of alcohol, and he had indulged in such a manner as to compromise both his health and his judgment the night before.

As far as Jenne was concerned, he deserved whatever was coming to him.

Porrian tilted his head, then slowly nodded, seeming surprised by Jadon's answer. "Not incorrect. Though next time I'll expect you to stick to the original wording. Take a seat."

Jadon nodded and moved to the last open seat in the sluggish, delicate way that hungover people were wont to move, still the focus of everyone's attention.

"Now, then," Porrian continued. "All political power has a source. What makes this an important principle?"

What? It was all Jenne could do to keep her objections internal. *Is Master Porrian really going to let him off without a single demerit? After just eviscerating the last latecomer with nine?*

The last lowborn *initiate*, she realized suddenly. *So much for purported Eshtem equality.*

"Jenne?"

Jenne's attention snapped back to the master as she tried to put aside the question of how he already knew her name – *and everyone else's* – and recall the question she was supposed to answer. *All power has a source*, she reminded herself.

"Well, in order to be a good politician," she began, her mind racing to come up with a reasonable explanation of the principle, "you would have to understand that all power has a source in order to think about what the sources of your power are."

"True enough," Porrian confirmed, and Jenne started to relax. "If incomplete to the point of meaninglessness, necessitating the awarding of yet another demerit," he added, with a reproving glance in her direction.

Jenne pursed her lips, suppressing a flare of anger. She was supposed to be equal to the highborn here. If Porrian wanted to run his classroom through fear and favoritism, she could not stop him, but she would not wait on the edge of her seat to win his approval, either.

The master continued his lecture, and Jenne did her best to set aside her resentment and focus on what he was saying. He was not easy to follow, and when he called on her classmates, it was sometimes worse. The biggest problems were Nefry and a girl named Saleah, who had elegantly braided black hair and dark brown eyes. The two of them kept volunteering answers that Jenne found indecipherable. Nefry rattled off complex explanations too quickly for her to wrap her mind around them, and Saleah expressed even simple ideas using large words and complicated sentence structures.

It was how nobles spoke at court, and Jenne decided Saleah was highborn. The fact that Porrian took a shine to Saleah, giving her more merits than Nefry even though Jenne suspected Nefry was making better points, supported Jenne's hypothesis that the man was judging them as much for their backgrounds as anything else. It did not help that Jadon, who looked like he was falling asleep in the back row, continued to escape demerits – even when he laughed out loud in the middle of the discussion. Nefry had just explained that people accept the legitimacy of laws because they understand that without them, power would be seized by strength of arms, and when Jadon's chuckle drew everyone's attention, Porrian asked if something had amused him.

"Just the idea that people respect the law because they actually weighed their alternatives," said Jadon, not even bothering to sit up properly. "Always seemed to me such respect was more a culturally indoctrinated reflex."

"Certainly the norms and values of Ellyrian culture play a role in fostering respect for the laws here," Porrian agreed. "An astute observation, worth a merit."

Jenne seethed. Apparently, it was not enough for the Hatreth prince to escape any demerits while flouting any reasonable expectation regarding classroom decorum. He also had to let everyone know that he was just as smart as Nefry when he cared to pay attention. And the Drei Master had seen fit to reward him for it.

The next time Porrian singled her out, Jenne made her answer sound as prissy as one of Saleah's. It seemed to help. The master moved on, and Jenne started thinking that despite her profoundly wounded sense of justice, she would make it through her first class with just the one demerit.

But fate conspired against her. Toward the end of class, Telius asked Porrian if counseling a politician to take a prudent action in lieu of a just action conflicted with the Edrei Ideals, which called for an Edrei to show character "heedless of consequence." Porrian asked Saleah to respond, and the highborn girl argued that in the case of a country's choosing not to go to war to protect one of its allies from an invader, there was no conflict. Jenne did not quite follow her logic, and apparently, Jadon did not either. He jumped in to accuse Saleah of trying to rationalize an obvious failure to follow the spirit of the Ideals.

"A provocative opinion," Porrian noted when Jadon finished speaking. Jenne was no longer surprised that the Hatreth prince earned no demerits for speaking out of turn.

"Saleah's argument was hardly a rationalization," the student seated next to Saleah announced into the momentary stillness, not attempting to be recognized before speaking. He turned around to give Jadon a look practically dripping with contempt as he said it. *Probably a friend of Saleah's*, Jenne deduced. *Definitely highborn*. No one else mastered the drippingly contemptuous stare at quite the same level. "Or would Jadon have us believe," the boy continued in the same tone, "that character heedless of consequence means intentionally sending men to their deaths for no tangible gain?"

"Yes, that's exactly what it means, Jonn," Jadon answered slowly, looking amused. "Well, technically it would mean 'leading' the men to their deaths. From the front. Or anyway, it used to, back when Edrei were elves and the Ideals were more than guidelines. But the elves never counseled Ellyrian lords to adopt such ideals because they knew leaders of men were more pragmatic. Human politicians consider it ethical to protect their own, and if that means an occasional compromise with the forces of evil, so be it."

Did he actually just say that? Jenne stared at the Hatreth prince, her mouth open in disbelief. *He's going to show up late and hungover to his first class at Eshtem and suggest that Edrei need to compromise with the forces of evil? And not get* any *demerits?*

"Something to say, Jenne?"

Of course, Master Porrian would remain silent during that entire unrecognized *exchange*, thought Jenne, *and when he finally chooses to chime in, it's to call on* me. What came out of her mouth, with neither her full awareness nor consent, was, "Maybe that's how Hatreth politicians think, but I'm sure *some* leaders in the world care about doing what is right, even if their people are the ones who have to pay a price for it."

The comment was greeted by perfect silence from the rest of the room. Other students avoided meeting Jenne's gaze, Liana and Telius included.

It took her a moment to realize she had thrown Jadon's House name at him in front of a Drei Master and the entire class. It was an expellable offense.

Her mouth went dry.

"Jenne," Porrian chided, his voice deceptively gentle, "you have just referenced the House name of–"

"Hatreth," Jadon interrupted. "A House which is hardly alone among the many Ellyrian Houses who do not train politicians to follow the Edrei Ideals. Though, as a quintessential War House, Hatreth is admittedly franker than most about the disconnect between its principles and the Edrei's. But no Ellyrian House would have committed troops to die in someone else's lost cause. And no one here is arguing that they should. Jonn and Saleah are simply pretending that failing to do so is consistent with the Edrei Ideals, and I'm saying it's not."

Porrian narrowed his eyes as he listened to this speech, and Jenne felt every one of her muscles tense as she waited for judgment.

"A demerit each," he finally said, "for Jenne and Jonn, for speaking out of turn argumentatively without increasing the enlightenment of the class. A merit, on the other hand, for Jadon, who has made an interesting and unconventional argument demonstrating insight into the matter at hand."

Jenne started breathing again, barely able to process what had just happened. *One demerit* – that was the important thing. *Which makes two demerits. I can work off two demerits.* She was still enrolled at Eshtem.

She shot a glance at Jadon, whose eyes were just open enough to meet her gaze. He gave her a slight nod: a *you're-welcome-I-deigned-to-notice-that-my-smart-alecky-interruption-of-the-sort-I've-been-making-all-morning-happened-to-keep-you-from-getting-expelled* sort of nod.

She would have resented it more if she had not felt so relieved.

Porrian returned his attention to the class at large and started wrapping up his lecture. As he drew near the end, he slowly scanned the room from right to left, his gaze finding every student to ensure that each had listened and understood. Despite her best intentions, Jenne dropped her eyes when his gaze fell on her. She did not want him to be reminded that she existed, let alone that he could still expel her for her slip of the tongue.

But he moved on.

"All political power has a source," the master repeated. "All uses of political power have repercussions. Political power can accomplish only the possible. If you remember nothing else from today's discussion, remember these principles. We'll end there for today."

As if on cue, the bells of the north tower chimed again, signaling the end of class. Elad was the first to rise.

"I have not dismissed the class, Initiate," Porrian informed him coldly. "That will cost you another demerit. Your tenth, I believe."

Elad's mouth opened, but no sound came out of it as he quailed under the master's gaze, stuck halfway between sitting and standing.

"Well? Don't let me keep you," Porrian told him. "You have no reason to stay here any longer. Go home to your House, if they'll take you back. Regardless, you have exactly one count to collect your things and remove yourself from Eshtem premises."

Elad blinked back tears as he stood and walked out of the room under the very silent observation of the class. Porrian waited until his footsteps had faded down the hallway before he dismissed the rest of them, a potent reminder of the fate that could befall anyone who failed to measure up to the Eshtem standard.

Anyone lowborn, Jenne amended. Jonn had been assigned a demerit as well, though, and Jenne was certain he was nobility. Perhaps not all the highborn were untouchable when they chose to court the Drei Masters' displeasure.

Perhaps it was only the Hatreth heir who could do no wrong.

As she gathered her things to leave, she was just happy to have escaped Elad's fate – as much as it smarted that she had only the intervention of that selfsame arrogant, entitled, supremely spoiled son of a high prince to thank for it.

CHAPTER 7
The Hierarchies of Eshtem

When a dragon lands in Jezimkai in Jeshimoth, word of it spreads like wildfire. Crowds flock to the palace to see it, and streets become impassable for miles. Children squeal in delight, bartenders offer rounds of drinks on the house, and no one speaks of anything else for a week.

When a dragon lands in Helos in Ellyrian, the people in its immediate vicinity will stop and stare – how could they not? But word spreads no farther than the immediate witnesses. No one gathers, and by the end of the day, no trace of its visit remains.

This conduct is surely odd, and the Ellyrians themselves seem hard-pressed to account for it. Some warn that idle talk of magic or dragons is sure to attract the notice of angry spirits from the Six. Others dismiss such superstitions and claim the topics are merely uncouth. *The Ellyrian Code*, which is supposed to explicate all their cultural rules, contains no mention of either topic being untoward – yet both highborn and commoners in Ellyrian rigorously enforce upon their children the norm of avoiding any extraneous speculation or gossip on these topics.

> – Bard Hilodez of the Jeshim court, in
> compiled observations on his journey through Ellyrian

Diar's first day contained more information about laws, duties, Jeshim history, and ethical principles than he knew what to do with. He covered every corner of his slate with tiny chalk-written notes, and he knew he would not be able to memorize it all before the next morning. At least he had not gotten any demerits.

Eshtem was everything he had imagined and more, but he surprised himself with how much time he spent thinking about Jenne. She had done him the enormous favor of replacing his copy of *Nations of the Edriendor Alliance*, and he had not yet thought of a suitable way to repay her. She had refused his money, claiming she had gotten the replacement dirt cheap, and they were planning to share the book – but Diar felt he should do something more.

They had agreed to meet up after classes in the central room of the south tower. By the time Diar got there, Jenne was already sharing a table with Liana, Telius, Eridike, and Brinnette – all initiates they had met on the Eshtem caravan. Sunlight streamed in from the floor-to-ceiling windows that lined the room, rendering unnecessary the light from the great chandelier.

"Diar!" Jenne grinned when she saw him, and he ducked his head to hide the depths of satisfaction in his smile. "How were your classes? The rest of us are worried we may not last the week."

"Yes, me too," Diar agreed, resting his shoulder bag on the table and fishing out his slate. "I'm already out of room on my slate, and I was almost late for my first class. My roommate was still asleep when I stopped at our dorm after breakfast, so I had to drag him out of bed before rushing off myself."

"What's your roommate's name?" Jenne asked, eyes narrowed.

"Jadon," Diar told her. "I think he's from a War House."

The group laughed, and Jenne clapped a hand to her face. "You helped him make it to class?"

"Did you say you *dragged* him out of bed? As in *the* Jadon?" asked Eridike. "Literally?"

"Well, no, I just shook him and told him he was going to be late." Diar frowned. "What do you mean, '*the* Jadon'? And what was I supposed to do – leave him there to get expelled?"

"If only!" Jenne rolled her eyes heavenward. "Don't you remember? I told you all about him and how insufferably entitled he would be, and he did not disappoint."

"Jadon?" Diar searched his memory for the relevant conversation. Jenne had shared gossip with him about the nobles who would be part of their class while helping deliver Christina's letters in Lystra, but he did not remember the name Jadon.

"You know, the…" Jenne set her hands on the table and leaned toward Diar, dropping her voice to a whisper to say, "*Hatreth prince?*"

"Careful, Jenne," said Telius, grinning. "A Drei Master already caught you naming that House once."

Jenne settled back in her seat and winked at Diar. "Somebody had to tell him."

Diar's first reaction was embarrassment that he had unknowingly given a prince such rough treatment, but then he remembered that Jadon would have missed class without his help. "That's good to know, I suppose, but it doesn't really make any difference, does it? We still share a room, and he still has to go to class. I'm sure he'd do as much for me if I slept through the morning bell."

"I doubt that." Jenne was still shaking her head, but she smiled as her eyes met Diar's.

Her smile was very distracting, and Diar found himself wondering what exactly she had meant to convey with her wink.

Eventually they managed to settle down and get to work. They realized they could condense everyone's notes for each class on a separate slate. It would mean they would have to meet up between classes and switch slates around, so anyone going to law class would have the law slate, but this way they would not have to erase until the end of the week. If they still thought they could not memorize enough to keep up by then, they agreed they would go to Lystra on Seventhday and purchase some parchment folios so they could keep their notes more permanently.

Diar figured they would make some headway on the memorization today, but by the time they finished sorting out which notes they wanted to keep for which classes and had everything written in tiny letters on the designated slates, the rest of the group had lost motivation. Eridike suggested visiting the shooting grounds, and everyone but Diar latched on to the idea with enthusiasm.

"Have fun studying, Diar," Jenne said as they packed up their things. "Catch you later."

Diar grimaced, displeased that she seemed indifferent to his decision. Truth be told, he did want to see the shooting grounds. Or, more accurately, he did not want Jenne to go there without him. "I'll come too," he decided.

As the four of them trooped outside, Diar craned his neck to keep an eye on the sky. He could still hardly believe his good fortune to be enrolled here, and Eshtem had already presented him with plenty of wonders and challenges to pull his focus, but he was still waiting on one critically important part of life on campus to be revealed: dragons.

Of course, he knew that he would not be training with dragons himself – not as a first-year initiate, and perhaps not ever. Only the fraction of Edrei who were gifted with certain forms of magic could become dragon handlers, and the bulk of their training took place after graduating. However, there was a landing ground for dragons on the eastern side of the campus plateau. The area was strictly off limits to initiates, as the Drei Masters had their residences nearby, and Diar did not know how often it was used, but he was hoping to catch a glimpse of a dragon coming or going at some point.

"What are you looking for, Diar?" Jenne's tone suggested she already had an inkling.

"Oh, nothing," Diar said, dropping his gaze as they followed the campus walkway around to the north side of campus. As someone who had spent his whole life hoping to become an Edrei, he spent a lot more time thinking about magic and dragons than anyone else in his community, but he had learned long ago not to talk about them. At best, people would look at him as if he had suddenly sprouted a horn or a third eye and change the subject. At worst, they would curse him for invoking subjects sure to draw the attention of angry spirits who would rain down terrible misfortune on any meddler who thought he could involve himself in matters that could only safely be left to the Edrei.

As Rishara-ahn, Diar believed that, like everything else in the world, magic and dragons were created by the White. He did not give any credence to the idea that merely discussing either would attract angry spirits or bring down misfortune, but there was nothing to be gained by ignoring the broader public's sensibilities. Now that he was in the company of other Eshtem initiates, perhaps the rules would change – but old habits were hard to break.

"I think we can all guess what Diar is looking for," Telius said, taking a moment to scan the horizon himself.

"You're not going to see any," Liana murmured, keeping her words quiet. "When the Master Imagers come and go from Renasche, they fly through the canyons at night and never fly high enough to be seen over the wall around the landing grounds. The only other time dragons come here is when they fly in all the proctors for the Eshtem Tourney."

"You mean we're not going to see any dragons until the tourney?" Eridike asked, keeping his voice just as quiet.

"We're probably not even going to see them then," Jenne said at a normal volume. "The landing grounds are off limits to first-years, remember? The Order doesn't want us knowing anything about magic or dragons until they have a better idea about which of us are likely to graduate and which aren't."

"We might see something," Liana said, sounding oddly confident.

"What does that mean?" Diar asked.

"I don't know, exactly," Liana admitted. "But sometime during the tourney, I'm led to believe we might see something."

"Something like… what we saw at orientation?" Eridike asked, frowning.

"Something like… a dragon?" Brinnette suggested, sounding more excited.

Liana shrugged. "No one would tell me, and I probably shouldn't even be telling you. But I think it will be a bigger deal than orientation."

"Do you know which day of the tourney?" Diar asked. The Eshtem Tourney was the combat trial that all first-years participated in toward the end of the academic year, and it was seven days long.

Liana shook her head.

"Probably the last day," Jenne suggested. "That's when everybody gathers to watch the championship."

"That would be my guess," Liana agreed.

"Well, thanks for telling us," Jenne said, taking Liana's arm. "Now I'll really be looking forward to it."

The shooting grounds stood outside the circle of buildings making up the central campus, encompassing perhaps a third of the forested area on the plateau's northern side. Most of the trees in the area were broken and dead, what remained of their trunks seldom reaching higher than a man – the result of a long-ago fire, perhaps, or an unruly dragon's having once wreaked havoc among the trees. More sunlight reached the forest floor here than in the rest of the pine forest, allowing the undergrowth to flourish. Moss and flora covered the ground and decorated the tree stumps. Frequent visitation and some upkeep by the Eshtem groundspeople kept the area from succumbing entirely to the underbrush, but footing could still be treacherous.

The entire area was roped off and used for exercises during some of the second- and third-years' classes and combat trials. Outside of those times, students of any year were permitted to use the grounds for personal training and play. Bows, arrows, quivers, and armor were kept in a storage shed that stood just outside. Two suits of armor – no more than pairs of wooden boards joined by adjustable ties, meant to be worn over the shoulders – were missing from the racks when Diar followed Jenne and the others into the shed.

"Hey, is anybody out there?" Jenne called, walking out to survey the grounds.

"Yeah." A figure stepped out from behind one of the taller tree stumps, his armor blending in with the greenery around him. He waved at them with his bow. "You'll have to come back la– *oof*." The initiate staggered forward as an arrow struck him from behind, turning his armor solid brown as Diar watched. Another figure materialized from the underbrush several spans more distant, her own armor still camouflaged.

"Hey!" the first initiate exclaimed, turning to face his assailant. "That does not count!"

"Don't be a sore loser, Cardos," the second initiate told him, lowering her bow.

"You guys don't mind if we join you, do you?" asked Jenne. "Four on four will be a little more interesting than one on one. And it looks like you're between rounds anyway."

"Actually, we're saving the grounds for Ramich and his friends," said Cardos, carrying his bow back toward the shed. "I don't think they'd appreciate it if we let you take them over." He hopped over the rope between them, nodding to them as he leaned his bow against the shed and walked in, taking off his armor. He hung it on the rack, and Diar watched in fascination as it changed color again, from the solid brown that it was to a darker, subtler shade that matched the rest of the suits of armor and the wall where they all hung.

It had to be magic. It was surreal to see other initiates playing with it so casually – let alone to think he was about to do so himself.

"Incredible," Liana said, wide-eyed. "How does it work?"

"Hanging the armor on the rack restores the camouflage," Cardos said as he put it back on. "Some kind of Projection, I guess?"

"Hitting it with an arrow cancels it," Cardos's companion added, having joined him in the shed. She took an arrow from her quiver to show them its blunted point. She struck Cardos's armor, and it changed back to light brown.

"Limn it, Elophine, would you cut that out?" Cardos took his armor off again and put it back on the rack.

Diar could not imagine one day being able to create such magic himself – but he hoped he would. Nearly half the initiates who made Edrei developed a magical talent during their second or third year at the university.

Even if he was not among them, Diar would like to learn how magic worked.

"Ramich asked you to reserve the grounds, did he?" Jenne leaned back against one of the posts supporting the rope that marked off the shooting grounds, already having dismissed the magical color changes from her attention. "How long ago was this?"

Ramich, Diar remembered from Jenne's gossip, was from House Tarix, a royal Gold House. He was one of the highest-born initiates in their class.

"Does it matter?" Elophine asked.

"I'm just wondering how long he expects you to wait for him, and what you're getting out of the arrangement."

Cardos snorted. "What do you think we're getting out of it?"

"I don't think you're getting anything out of it, which is why you're perfectly free to indulge yourselves with a game of four on four. If Ramich wanted the grounds so much, he could have come down here himself." Jenne put a hand on her hip, tilting her head to one side, and Diar's attention caught on how the pose accentuated her beauty. She was so confident, so utterly unintimidated by Ramich's station. It was not an attitude Diar shared, or even fully approved of – nobles were nobles, after all, lawfully and socially entitled to respect, and Jenne would only get herself into trouble by trying to change that – but he admired her spirit.

Cardos and Elophine traded glances.

"Unless you'd rather keep shooting each other indefinitely." Jenne shrugged. "It just seems like a lot of walking back and forth to the shed for not very much action."

"How about we play with you just until Ramich and his friends get here?" Telius suggested.

"Yes," Diar agreed, leaping at the suggestion. "We'll clear out right away when they come. We have to get back to studying anyway."

"Fine. Why not?" Elophine shrugged. "How should we split teams?"

"Girls against boys," Jenne suggested.

Telius chuckled. "I don't see how our side would stand a chance."

"Well, then, we'll just have to go easy on you," said Brinnette.

Diar shook his head, thinking this division of teams ridiculous. "Really, girls, I'm sure there's a more equitable way to divide ourselves."

"You think you can take us just because of your gender?" said Jenne. "Please. *You* are on your team, Diar. My money's on us." She shot Diar a look equal parts mischief and invitation.

Diar eyed her up and down, letting her notice his attention. For a girl, she was probably a competitive athlete, but with Liana, Brinnette, and Elophine on her team, he did not see how she hoped to match up against Telius, Cardos, and Eridike, to say nothing of himself. "Let's put them in their place," he said to Telius.

"Good luck with that." Jenne pushed his shoulder playfully on her way past him, scoffing. She tossed him a smile as she helped herself to some armor, and Diar grinned.

He did not regret taking a break from his studies.

A few minutes later they were suited and arrayed across the grounds, the boys starting from the south side and the girls the north. After a few moments of creeping toward the enemy while trying to stay concealed in the underbrush, they were interrupted.

"Cardos! Elophine! Who are these imbeciles eating up space on our grounds?"

Diar turned around to see a group of students coming from the shed. Dirty blond and well formed, the speaker stood a couple inches taller than the other boys with him, and though he was not the most thickset or muscular, he was no one Diar wanted to cross. Ramich ti'Tarix, he assumed. And at his side, prim and proper in an initiate dress that had been perfectly fitted to accentuate her curves, with her sandy hair done up in a braided twist that must have taken at least a count to secure, was none other than Trista to'Rinton, his one-time noble friend from Meiveon

"We were just killing time until you got here," Cardos called back, still concealed in the underbrush.

Hearing motion ahead of him, Diar ducked behind a tree trunk, narrowly avoiding the arrow that whizzed past a moment later. "Don't worry, we were just leaving," he said. Pulling back an arrow, he stepped out from cover to aim at the girl who had just missed him, hoping to get in a hit. He caught sight of Jenne and loosed, but he missed and she disappeared into the underbrush. He ran up to the next tree and ducked behind it.

"Why don't you all arm up and join us?" Jenne's voice was close ahead and to the right.

From where Diar crouched to nock another arrow, his back against the tree trunk, he had a fine view of Ramich as the Tarix noble hopped over the rope and started striding toward them, a fistful of arrows in his hand and displeasure all over his face. His friends fell in behind him.

Diar set down his bow and stood, hands raised to placate the scowling nobility. "As much fun as that would be, I insist you guys keep the grounds to yourselves. We have to get back to studying anyway."

Jenne rose from the underbrush, bow still drawn, and loosed at an unseen target. "Oof," came Eridike's voice from that direction. Jenne turned to face the nobles, looking highly pleased with herself. Telius and Elophine, both surprisingly near, then materialized, and Liana, Brinnette, and Cardos appeared more slowly, farther away.

"Still keeping the same dynacomb company, I see," said one of the other boys, looking from Diar and Jenne to Telius and back. Diar thought he recognized him from the Eshtem caravan. Diar was not wearing his Noraani-marked sword anymore, but "dynacomb" was a derogatory term for Blood House-sworn, so the boy must have remembered it and assumed everyone in Diar's company was from a Blood House.

"What are you lot doing with these stock-possessed?" Another Blood House slur from another one of the boys, apparently addressed to Cardos, Elophine, and Telius.

"Always a pleasure, Gossem." Telius nodded to him with a tight smile. They must have known each other outside of Eshtem.

Ramich laughed, clapping Telius on the shoulder as the others came closer to the discussion. With a look that took in Diar, Jenne, and the rest of their group, he said to Telius, "Fallen in with the wrong crowd already, have you? Why don't you stay and play a round with us? Cardos and Elophine will be happy to teach you the rules."

"You think you can boss them around just because you happen to know their Houses are sworn to yours?" Jenne demanded, stepping closer. "Well, I'll have you know that despite what you assumed, I am not Blood House-sworn. I'm a skinflint, just like you lot, sworn to Tarix. And I'll associate with whomever I please," she added, covering the remaining space to take Diar's arm, still scowling at Ramich.

"And so will I!" said Brinnette, stepping forward and crossing her arms. Eridike and Liana moved to stand with them.

"Some of us left our affiliations at the drawbridge," said Telius. "Like we were told."

Ramich took a step forward, bringing himself close enough to make Diar and the others conscious of his superior height. Eyes narrowed, his gaze swept over their little tableau, pausing on Jenne and coming to rest on Telius. The two of them were almost toe to toe, the air between them thick with tension.

Suddenly Ramich feinted forward. Telius flinched, and Ramich began laughing as he turned back to his friends, a deep laugh of genuine amusement that lasted much too long. Diar watched Trista, who avoided his gaze but did not appear in the least embarrassed by the display.

"Those affiliations will be waiting right where you left them as soon as you're finished with the Order, you realize," said Ramich when he finally caught his breath, facing them again. "Which could be much sooner than you anticipate."

"An empty threat from a power-drunk bully who's just realized his position isn't what it used to be." Jenne stepped closer to say it right to Ramich's face. The look in his cold dark eyes made Diar nervous, and he put a hand on Jenne's shoulder to pull her away.

"Is there a problem here, Initiates?"

Diar looked up to see Estilend, their Jeshim instructor, approaching. He breathed a sigh of relief as the Drei Master unhooked the rope from one of the posts, letting himself inside.

"Yes, in fact," said the one called Gossem, just as Diar assured him, "No, not at all."

Estilend looked at them in question.

"These ruffians are refusing to surrender the field," Gossem continued.

"See, that's not true," said Diar. Jenne and Ramich were still staring murder at each other, so Diar gave her shoulder a little tug. "We were actually just leaving, weren't we, Jenne?"

She broke eye contact with great reluctance, looking to the yellow-haired master.

"Surrender the field?" Estilend addressed the question to Ramich, who also turned to face him – albeit even more slowly. "I take it they beat you here, then?"

"We were here first," Elophine hastened to explain. "Me and Cardos. We were supposed to be reserving the grounds for Ramich, but we just thought we'd let these others play a quick round while we waited."

"'Supposed to be'?" Estilend was smiling. "Has Ramich been ordering you about, then, or was this duty born out of the goodness of your hearts?"

"Nobody made them do anything." Ramich crossed his arms, shooting a look at Cardos and Elophine that dared them to suggest otherwise.

"Uh, a mutually agreed-upon arrangement, really," said Cardos.

"And we were just leaving!" Diar broke in. He took off his armor to emphasize the point, offering it to Ramich. No one else moved, but Jenne looked from him to Ramich to Estilend and then sighed.

"Yeah." She took off her own armor and handed it to Trista, who accepted it wordlessly. Since Ramich still had not moved to touch Diar's, he offered it to Gossem instead. Gossem took it and stepped past Diar to grab his bow, jostling him as he did so.

"I guess if they want to leave, there's no dispute here," said Estilend. "But reserving the grounds is not technically permitted. The space, the armor, and the bows and arrows are strictly first come, first served. I can take care of that for you," he added, taking Eridike's armor. His armor was light brown, but under Estilend's touch it quickly regained its camouflage quality. He handed it to Ramich, who was scowling again.

"Thank you, Drei Master," said Jenne, no small amount of satisfaction about her as she smiled at Ramich. "We'll be sure to keep that in mind for next time." She nodded to Estilend and led the way back toward the campus buildings.

"You have a nice game," Telius told Ramich as he walked past.

"And do remember to put the equipment back when you're finished," Estilend told the highborn students before nodding and walking toward the storage shed.

Diar turned to follow Jenne and the others.

"Diar." Trista's voice stopped him. She was still standing next to Ramich, her expression cool and unreadable. "Where's your other Rishara friend from Meiveon? Would not she make safer company for you?"

Diar narrowed his eyes, taking a breath to calm himself. She could mean no one but Adara, the Storyteller's daughter and one of their mutual friends – back from the time when Trista had counted any of them friends. Adara had studied hard for the Eshtem admittance exam and passed it, same as Diar, and it had never sat well with him that she had been unable to come. Trista had no right to raise the topic. "If by 'your other Rishara friend,' you mean Adara, whose name I expect you remember perfectly well, she's not here. University tuition isn't just an afterthought for everyone."

Trista blinked, and Diar turned and hurried after his friends, immediately regretting his tone. Trista may have been a friend once, but they were not children any longer. She was a noble. Despite Jenne's bravado and the university's policy, he was not her equal. If Trista or any of the nobles with her took offense, they could find ways to punish him – easily so, if he was cut from Eshtem. If a noble initiate's lackeys beat up a commoner who happened to be an expelled former student, the Order might frown on it, but they would have no grounds for disciplinary action.

Diar's friends seemed unbothered by the possibility when he raised it on their way back to the south tower.

"They wouldn't go that far," Jenne asserted, confident. "Not because they have any human decency, mind you, but because of how petty it would be. They'd lose face."

"Don't you think a noble could find ways to punish us without having it traced back to them?" Diar asked.

"What would be the point?" Telius shrugged. "If people think we disrespected them at Eshtem, our meeting with consequences much later in secret would do nothing to restore their reputations."

"But aren't your families under Gold House rule?" Diar pressed. "Couldn't Ramich take it out on them if he really wanted to? I mean, hopefully he wouldn't for what happened today, but if we push them too far?"

"Not if he doesn't want to be known as childish and unjust," said Jenne. She stopped on the path to the south tower. "Anyone want to go riding? That break was altogether too short."

"I've never actually ridden before," said Liana.

"Then we should," Brinnette said. "We'll teach you. Edrei have to be able to ride."

"White help me, no," Diar said. Maybe he was more worried about crossing the nobles than he needed to be, but he knew he needed to study. "We agreed – one *quick* round at the shooting grounds and then back to studying."

"Did you swear by the White?" Jenne asked, surprised. "You're Rishara? I mean, I see you have some Rishara blood, but you're a practicing Rishara?"

The term "Rishara" could refer to the race of people or the religion they had historically practiced. Over the many hundreds of years since a small group of elves had intermarried with Ellyrians to found the original Rishara line, many of their descendants had married back into Ellyrian Houses. Dark-skinned Ellyrians loyal to the Six had long since come to outnumber true practicing Rishara, so the question was not surprising.

"I don't belong to the Rishara people group, no," Diar explained. In addition to keeping the White Way, the Rishara people group lived in traveling clans and kept themselves separate from mainstream Ellyrian culture. "My grandmother did, but she left them to marry my grandfather. There's a Storyteller in Meiveon, though, and a group of us who follow the White. Technically, we are Rishara-ahn, as we have adopted the Principles of the White Way without the lifestyle of the Rishara people group – though, in my case, it gets confusing because I also have the heritage."

"Interesting." Jenne cocked her head, and Diar was encouraged to see her smile. Most Ellyrians held his religion in scorn.

"You sure you don't have time for one quick ride around the track?" Jenne laid a hand on Diar's arm, coquettish. "For Liana?"

It took a supreme effort for Diar to take her hand and remove it from his arm, and she kept watching him with that smile, making things no easier. "I would love to," he admitted, releasing her hand. "Another day. For now, I need to get started on memorization, so I'll be in the south tower with the law slate if anyone wants to join me."

Jenne quirked her mouth and shrugged. "Your loss."

Diar frowned at her, but she just smiled and turned to leave. His resolve to go back to studying faltered.

"We'll come join you really soon," Liana promised.

Diar took a deep breath as the rest of the group headed off toward the stables. *I can't afford to let Jenne become a distraction*, he told himself. *Or a bad influence.* He was here to become Edrei.

That had to be his priority.

CHAPTER 8

Traces of Intrigue

I understand that, by now, the chances of recovering Vilinora alive are faint indeed, but with every passing day they grow still more remote, and the likelihood her abductors will evade justice increases. If there is anything you can do, or anyone to whom you could speak on my behalf concerning this matter, I must ask that you do so without delay.

– King Gahon of the dynasty Renard, in
correspondence with Drei Master Tamar

Christina wondered sometimes, afterward, how those early days at Eshtem would have felt, had they not followed so hard upon the heels of her recent attack. Liberating, she imagined. Since the death of her mother eleven years before, Nor had been something of a prison to herself and her father. She, as much as he, had preferred the seclusion of their grief to the empty socializing she might have found at court, and it had been her own choice to spend the intervening years in relative solitude, studying diligently under her tutors, reading of elves and the Order, and doing her best to keep her father from mismanaging their House in his distraction.

Eshtem was a radical change. It was as though she had spent most of her life in a small room without realizing it, and now the doors of existence had suddenly been thrown open. She interacted with more people daily at Eshtem than she would have in an entire season back home. And even after only a few days, it was apparent that her studies had more than adequately prepared her for the competition here, despite the conviction she had felt for many years that her preparation was suffering on account of her father's reluctance to secure her the proper tutors. On the contrary, it seemed she was ahead of the curve, fielding questions that left other initiates stumped and breezing through material others found difficult when the Drei Masters assigned them reading from the library to complete outside of class.

More importantly, she was now where she had always wanted to be: outside the realm of her father's influence and training to join the Order of which she had read and dreamed for so many years. But every night that first week she woke, sweating and anxious, from troubled dreams, and sometimes, when she passed a master in the hall, she felt her pulse quicken and dropped her eyes, as if the entire Order were to blame for what had happened and could not be trusted.

She was impatient to learn what she could from the Lussonne's records. Her trip to Lystra to send her request went smoothly. Lelise and her cousin Vannes went out of their way to make Christina and Claire welcome in their group of friends, and Christina managed to evade all of them long enough to deliver her letter to the post riders and ask that any reply be held for her under a false name.

Time dragged by while she waited for a reply. She enjoyed her classes, but they were not quite what she had expected. The Edrei Ideals were a large part of what had attracted Christina to the Order: *Strength to protect the weak. Character heedless of consequence. Light to shine in the darkness. Life to lay down to serve life.* Those words had inspired Christina to something bigger than herself, her House, or even the nation of Ellyrian. Those were words upon which to build a world order of selflessness, honor, and justice.

The way the masters taught them, though, made it sound as though their meaning could be ambiguous when applied to specific situations. Ambiguity left room for compromise, and Christina did not approve. Moreover, the contributions made by her fellow initiates left her feeling as though the finest minds of Ellyrian were neither as sharp nor as disciplined as she had anticipated.

When the leaves changed color and the crisp bite of autumn chilled the air, it was finally time to return to Lystra to check for answering correspondence. This time, Christina went alone.

The decision went against everything she had been taught and practiced as a highborn girl living under the watchful eye of House Noraan. A princess went nowhere without an armed escort, and Christina's recent brush with bandits had left her feeling vulnerable.

However, in the weeks between her two outings, Christina had learned that most of the commonborn girls did not think twice before venturing alone as far as Lystra. By the Edrei's Peace, it was anathema to lay hands on anyone dressed in the garb of an Eshtem initiate, and if the commonborn girls trusted the policy to protect them, Christina decided she would as well.

The bandits had never been after her, anyway. They had wanted easy gold, and Christina did not carry any with her to Lystra. She could not quite keep herself from glancing over her shoulder and starting at every unexpected noise, but in the end, her logic proved more reliable than her emotions. The post riders had received a package with copies of the Lists Christina had requested from the Lussonne days earlier, and Christina retrieved it from their office without incident.

The Eshtem Lists were kept in the northwestern wing of the library's ground floor, and Christina headed there when she returned to campus. The final Lists from the last three years were kept on display: some six hundred names encased in glass stands that stood in front of the shelves lining the wall. The shelves held the Lists from previous years, filed chronologically from Eshtem's opening to the present. They stretched the length of the entire wing.

Christina started with the shelves that held the newest Lists and worked her way back fifteen years, her movements sounding loud in the otherwise empty wing. Books and files that initiates might need to reference for class were kept in the library's central area, and this wing had no study tables. Students had no reason to be here.

"What are you looking for?"

Christina started at the sound of a male voice. She whirled to find another initiate leaning against the glass display, studying her with a quizzical expression.

"What are you doing here?" Christina returned, flustered. She had thought this wing empty. "Were you hiding on purpose?"

"No." The initiate scoffed, a faint smile on his lips. "I've been standing right here."

"Why?" Christina demanded. She was being rude, perhaps, but she could not conceive of any reason for him to be there and felt his presence to be an invasion of her privacy.

His build did not help. He was taller than her, and his lean, muscular form made him look more like a soldier than an Eshtem initiate. The sharp lines of his face, though well formed, made him seem threatening, and the derisive expression in his dark brown eyes did nothing to relieve the impression.

"I came to look at the Lists," he said. "What are you doing?"

"I–I…" Christina stammered, glancing at the shelves that held the section of the Lists she had wanted to look at. There was no good reason for her to be perusing them.

But he was just another initiate. She did not have to explain herself to him. "That need not be any of your concern," she said.

He raised his eyebrows. "Next time, try, 'I came to look at the Lists.' I don't actually care why you're here." He shook his head and walked away.

Christina watched him go, taking a few steps after him so she could see the door. She wanted to make sure he left, but the door opened before he reached it, and Porrian walked in.

"Jadon." The master nodded to the initiate. "Always a pleasure. I hope we'll see you on time for politics tomorrow morning. The class could use more of your input."

Jadon. Christina recognized the name as belonging to a War House prince who was part of her class. His House of origin should not have mattered here at Eshtem, but it did go some way toward explaining why their interaction had been so uncomfortable.

Except… is he the only War House student I've interacted with outside of class? Christina frowned. Theoretically, Eshtem was a place where students of all Houses were free to intermingle. But Lelise was a cousin of Vannes's, whom Christina knew was a Blood House noble, and the fact that her friendship with Saleah seemed to predate their time at Eshtem suggested Saleah must be the same. So was Claire.

Christina had not pursued friendships with anyone else. Perhaps she should start.

"Fear not, Master Porrian." Jadon made a little bow. "I shall endeavor to be punctual, and if, despite my best efforts, the bells somehow manage to ring before I arrive, I'll be sure to make up for it with enthusiastic participation during the time in which I am present."

"Be sure that you do." Porrian chuckled softly, shaking his head. "And remember, you're responsible for everything presented during the period, even if some of it happens before you arrive."

"I would never imagine otherwise, Drei Master."

"Very good. Along with you, then." Porrian waved a dismissal, and Jadon nodded to him before exiting.

Christina frowned, wondering if she had misinterpreted their exchange. It sounded as though Jadon was habitually late to class, and Porrian was fine with it as long as Jadon kept up with the material.

No one in her classes had ever been late, so she did not know how the other masters handled tardiness. Still, Porrian's chuckle seemed inappropriate. He was a hard teacher in class, and if he did not care about punctuality, Christina hoped he at least grilled Jadon on the material as mercilessly as he would anyone else.

The master's gaze turned to Christina, and she tried to smooth away her frown. "Christina!" he said, walking toward her. "Just the initiate I was searching for. What brings you to this wing of the library?"

Christina swallowed, the satchel holding the package from the Lussonne feeling heavy and conspicuous at her side. "I came to look at the Lists," she said, glad Jadon had left.

"Anticipating the moment when the display might include your own name?" Porrian asked with a knowing smile.

Christina nodded slowly, scanning the shelves. "It's been a long time since any names from my House were included here."

"Decades," Porrian agreed, his gaze sweeping the length of the Lists on display. "Should you succeed here, you will mark the dawn of a new era."

Christina drew her lips together. Becoming the first Noraani initiate in a hundred years had meant so much to her less than two months ago.

It still meant something, but Hezred's death had cast a shadow over the accomplishment. She wondered what would happen if Porrian discovered her with Lists from the Lussonne. "You said you were looking for me?"

"Yes." Porrian clasped his hands behind his back and turned to regard her. "I have spoken with Drei General Anandolf and Drei Zanner, who is currently assigned to our outpost in Lystra. From their accounts, I gather that Drei Zanner traveled there as a guide in your employ, and that on the way, your party was attacked by bandits. One of those was a man who formerly belonged to the Order and was trained as a Projector. Shortly after this individual robbed you, he met you again on the road while fleeing from Drei General Anandolf and his team, who then caught and executed him."

"Yes," said Christina, her heart beating faster. *Could he know that I wrote to the Lussonne? Is that why he's here?*

"Drei Zanner told me that you seemed troubled by the incident when the two of you parted ways, which would hardly be surprising. Is this true?"

This man was Hezred's enemy. The thought sprang unbidden to Christina's mind, with such clarity and force it made her blink. *He is the one Hezred meant for me to hide my suspicions from*. Keeping steady eye contact with Porrian, Christina tilted her head to one side. She narrowed her eyes. "If by 'had reason to speak to,' you mean that this renegade led me into an ambush, killed my guards, and stole from me, then what you say is true. And yes, despite all this, I was initially troubled by his claims, but after further opportunity for rest and reflection, it no longer seems in the least bit strange that a criminal would lie and manipulate to cast doubt on the accusations against him. I wonder only why his execution has not yet been made known to the public. I wish that all of Ellyrian might rejoice in this triumph of justice, as I do."

"It does not trouble you, then, that the renegade offered a life oath to your companion, and that his execution was carried out before he made a formal response, as *The Ellyrian Code* requires?"

Christina blinked. When Anandolf had ordered her and Zanner not to speak of Hezred's execution, she had assumed he wanted to keep the detail of the interrupted oath from becoming part of the official record. She had not thought either of them would share it with Porrian.

If Anandolf had done so – and it must have been him, as Zanner would have faced consequences for breaking a command – it could mean he was a less shady character than Christina suspected.

Keeping her features composed, Christina said, "Drei Zanner had already begun to refuse it in any case. He had his orders and could have made no other choice. Though I admit, I found the breach in propriety curious."

"Christina, you already know more about this than you should," said Porrian, shaking his head. "But because that cannot be undone, and because you seem a trustworthy citizen, I will tell you just enough to explain this 'breach of propriety,' as you call it. Though this is, as you know, a delicate topic. Let me see..." He tented his fingers in front of him, thinking. "Back when the crimes that culminated in the execution you witnessed were committed, an object was stolen from the Order. In the wrong hands – hands well practiced, shall we say, in the art of abusing magic in order to win personal power and popularity – this object could prove very dangerous. Now, recovering this weapon was of the utmost importance to the Order at the time of the execution you witnessed, especially because we believed the weapon could have been in just such hands and used against everyone present at any moment. This does not excuse what happened. Propriety should have been observed. But the breach... was understandable. Do you understand?"

Christina frowned as she considered his account. "Was the weapon recovered?"

"No, unfortunately. We think it was passed to another outlaw – which, incidentally, is the reason we are keeping news of the execution quiet. If this renegade's companions believe he is still alive, they may search for him. Such inquiries might expose them to our intelligence network. This may be our only chance of recovering the weapon, since we know nothing of the outlaws he was with or where they might be now. So, you see, this whole affair must be kept close, with the utmost discretion."

"I see." Christina nodded slowly. She could not have said why, exactly, she did not believe Porrian. His story made sense, but his bothering to talk to her at all reinforced her suspicion that he had something to hide.

"Which brings me to the other matter I wanted to discuss with you," he continued. "You may be one of the only people alive to have witnessed this renegade while he was in the company of his associates, when these bandits attacked you. Do you remember anything about them? Names, numbers, or descriptions, perhaps?"

Well, that would be a good reason to talk to me. Christina sighed and shook her head, deciding to trust her gut anyway. He was hiding something important, and she would, too. "I'm afraid I don't remember much at all. I was so frightened... I didn't think to take notice of anything. I remember thinking that we were outnumbered and expecting my men to surrender, but there could have been anywhere from seven to twenty, and as to what they looked like, I couldn't say. The renegade held most of my attention, before and after. You might ask Drei Zanner. I'm sure he would remember better than I."

The last thing Christina wanted was for Porrian to ask Zanner this specific question, because then he might obtain the name he was looking for: Lozuri. Christina was sure that if Hezred had given anything to anyone, it would have been to Lozuri. If she ever found him again, perhaps he could shed more light on the situation, but she doubted that would ever happen if Zanner gave his name to Porrian.

Porrian, though, would think to ask Zanner on his own – if he had not done so already – and it was better to appear helpful.

"That is most unfortunate." Porrian eyed Christina suspiciously, and she did her best to look regretful. "It seems the trauma of injury and dealing with persuasive Projections, together with two nights of delirium, erased his memory of the incident even more thoroughly than yours."

"I am truly sorry, then," Christina said, shaking her head. "I wish now I had paid better attention. If I remember anything more, you will be the first to know."

Porrian nodded slowly, as if he did not quite believe her. Christina gave him a tight-lipped smile, the package from the Lussonne still weighing heavily at her side.

He sighed. "It may be difficult to think back to such unpleasantness, but I must ask that you try to remember. Even the smallest detail might be of use. You know where my office is?"

Christina nodded. All first-year instructors had offices in the south tower.

"Good. You may come to speak with me at any time, about this or any other matter. For now, I will leave you to your contemplations."

"My thanks, Drei Master." Christina bowed her head as he took his leave. She waited for the doors of the wing to close behind him before leaning back against the shelves with a sigh of relief. Only then did she allow herself to contemplate the gravity of what she had just done.

In addition to his post as Drei Master, Porrian sat on the Edrei Council, and Christina had lied to him about an active investigation. If Hezred had indeed stolen a dangerous weapon and given it to Lozuri, and if Lozuri used it or gave it to someone who could use it to commit any more crimes, Christina had just made herself an accomplice. Every day she continued to sit on her information was a day that made her guiltier, a day the weapon remained beyond the reach of the Order and might be used against it or the civilian populace. If Christina was wrong to be suspicious of Porrian, her deceiving him could be dangerous not only for herself – as she would likely face charges if she was ever found out – but for the rest of the country as well.

Christina, though, did not think she was wrong.

Something was off with Hezred's case and the way Porrian had described it, and she needed to find out what it was. Until she did, she could not rule out the possibility that someone in the Council had wanted Hezred silenced and ordered his wrongful execution on purpose. *And I watched General Anandolf carry it out and did nothing.*

Christina closed her eyes and took a deep breath. Then she blew it out, opened her eyes, and began removing files from the period she wanted. She could not change the past, but maybe one of the files had an answer that could help her make peace with it.

She checked out a few years' worth of Lists and took them to the north tower. In the back of one of the study rooms on the third floor, there was a balcony overlooking the forest. A tasteful arrangement of glowing lanterns kept the balcony lit and warm, and it was Christina's favorite spot to study on campus.

Quiet voices were drifting through the balcony window when she reached the study room. Pursing her lips, she set her satchel on the table nearest the balcony door. She unwrapped the package from the Lussonne and turned the parchment pages until she reached the section that matched the Eshtem files. Taking a quill from the ink jar on the study table, she began checking off each name on the Lists from the Lussonne as she found them in the Eshtem copies, hoping the people on the balcony would leave soon.

"I don't see what you expect me to do about it, my dear," a man said. "They are taking this matter very seriously. Everything that can be done is being done, and as soon as there is anything to report, your friend will be apprised. That there have not yet been any results is a source of great frustration to everyone."

"Then you could at least persuade them to let Luc Amand join the team. He has some experience tracking these people. Perhaps he could find something we missed." Christina cursed silently, recognizing this voice as belonging to one of her teachers: Master Tamar.

Christina had heard the stories about Tamar, the initiate whose talent for Intuition had manifested at the beginning of her second year, allowing her to train with Drei Captain Vorsand's team of Master Imagers for two full years instead of the usual one and a half. She had gone on to become the youngest ever auxiliary Drei Ambassador to Alterra, where an attempted coup had resulted in the death of the lead ambassador, the poisoning of the king, and the kidnapping of the crown prince. Tamar had singlehandedly tracked the kidnappers through the Hahiroth wasteland and rescued the crown prince from them, despite having been abandoned by her dragon along the way. According to rumor, she had contracted the White Plague in the wasteland and lost her sanity for a time, but not before Vorsand flew to their rescue and Prince Gahon ascended his father's throne.

Christina doubted she would be able to conceal anything from Tamar if the master became suspicious of what she was doing. As silently and swiftly as she dared, she put the quill back and began repackaging the Lists from the Lussonne.

"I sincerely doubt that," the man was saying. "Though I suppose the gesture might serve to placate your friend."

"At the very least."

"Well, I will speak to the Council for you, but I cannot promise anything. You know how they like to keep these matters within the Order." There was a drawn-out pause before he spoke again. "Is there something else?"

"Vilinora was an Imager," Master Tamar said, "a Prophet, like the Jeshim Vaar who disappeared last year. I think we should consider whether someone may be targeting them."

"Targeting Prophets? Come. Two instances do not a pattern make. Who would do such a thing? And to what end?"

"Rogue Imagers with an interest in discerning the future. If Imagers were involved, that may explain why both investigations stalled."

Finished putting away the Lists, Christina hesitated. *Rogue Imagers? Is such a thing even possible?* The idea that Imagers might exist outside the Order and be using their talents for nefarious purposes had never occurred to her, and it made her uneasy. She glanced at the door to the hallway, which stood propped open.

She did not want any masters to find out she was corresponding with the Lussonne, but she knew there was no love lost between Tamar and Porrian. The two of them were unlikely to share information, and now that the Lists were safely tucked away in her satchel, Christina felt she could risk listening to the conversation on the balcony a little longer.

The man laughed, then sighed. "I should not laugh, I suppose. Your instincts are generally impeccable. But the improbability... Is it possible that your desire to train students to combat Imagers is making you imagine threats from that quarter? You know that since your return, your Intuition has been subject to clouding. And I sense no connection."

"If that is what you think, then why do you assure the Council that I am still the best choice for Master Imager? My Intuition feels clearer than it ever has, even in the matters where it departs from yours. If it is truly the case that my illness has clouded my instincts so far that I can no longer discern the difference between Intuition and bias, how can I be fit to train new Imagers?"

"We both know that, even now, you remain the stronger Intuiter. And I have never sensed any clouding in you except in matters that touch on the delusion your illness inspired, as this does. In any other use of the gift, you are the stronger talent. And therefore, the appropriate teacher."

They are both Intuiters, Christina realized. She had already overstayed. She stood and hurried quietly out of the room.

Her eyes were still turned toward the balcony, alert for signs of the masters, when she reached the hallway and collided with another initiate.

"I'm so sorry," he said, catching Christina by the elbow as she stumbled backward. The jolt made her drop her satchel, and she watched in horror as the Lists from the Lussonne spilled across the floor.

She dropped to her knees and gathered up the pages as quickly as she could, but the first page – the one with the letter to her *signed by the Lussonne staff* – had fluttered past her, and the boy picked it up first. "Is this from the–"

Desperate, Christina reached up and clamped a hand over his mouth. Their eyes met – his wide with surprise – and Christina snatched her hand back, feeling herself flush at the inappropriateness of her behavior as she held his gaze, her other hand closing around the page he was holding while she silently implored him not to say anything.

She recognized the boy from Lystra, Diar Jax.

Within the study room, the door to the balcony opened. "What is happening out here?" Tamar demanded, closing the distance between them with quick steps.

"I'm so sorry, Master Tamar," Diar said, letting go of the letter from the Lussonne as his gaze turned past Christina. "I was just trying to find a quiet study spot and wasn't looking in front of me, and I nearly bowled Christina over. Entirely my fault."

Christina bit her lip as she tucked the letter into her satchel with the rest of the pages, her eyes fixed on the floor. It seemed Diar was willing to cover for her, but her own behavior had probably already given her away.

"Christina?"

Christina turned to face the master. Sandy-haired and slender of frame, Tamar was neither tall nor beautiful, but there was something in her bearing reminiscent of the stories that had made her a heroine. Something noble, but also cold, and sad, and hard.

"I'm sorry. I was hoping to do some research on the balcony, but then I realized you were already out there…"

Christina trailed off as Tamar's companion joined them. He was a lithe man with wavy, graying brown hair, brown eyes, and an amiable smile. Like Tamar, he was dressed in the black robes of a Drei Master, though Christina did not recognize him.

Her guilt and trepidation were surely obvious, but the man smiled.

"Go right ahead, my dear," he said. "We were just leaving."

He started forward, and Christina and Diar hurried to move out of the way as Tamar walked with him into the hallway. Tamar gave Christina a second glance, and Christina dropped her gaze, her whole body tensing. But the masters both continued on.

Maybe they had attributed her unease to the fact that she had heard more of their conversation than she should have, rather than the satchel at her side.

"Are you all right?" Diar asked after a moment.

Christina glanced up at him and then down the hall. The masters had turned a corner and were out of sight, but she could still hear their receding footsteps.

"Was that letter–"

Christina held up a hand, which – mercifully – silenced Diar, and gestured for him to follow her into the study room. She walked straight to the balcony and held the door open. He walked through uncertainly, and she followed him outside and closed the door firmly as she considered what to say.

It was poor luck that she had run into him, of all people. She had ordered him to carry letters for her at their last meeting – a regrettable necessity, with the two of them poised to become equals – and now she needed something from him again.

"I suppose I owe you an explanation." She moved to the study table, set down her satchel, and sat on the cushioned seat that lined the wall shared with the study room before meeting his gaze. "I am carrying some correspondence from the Lussonne."

Diar frowned, looking perhaps even less comfortable than Christina felt. "Well, I... I suppose that's your own business. It's not illegal, or even against our code of conduct, as far as I know."

"Even so, I'd appreciate your silence on this matter."

"Understood."

"This isn't an order," Christina felt pressed to clarify. "I cannot order you to do anything, here at Eshtem – nor would I wish to. I am simply telling you, as one initiate to another, I would appreciate it if you did not mention this to anyone."

Diar returned her gaze for a moment, and then he nodded. "I understand."

Christina's relief was short-lived, as the door abruptly opened again. At least it was another initiate this time, and not one of the masters returning to question her.

"Hey, you're Christina, right? First-year? Do you come here a lot?" He was short and thin and asked the questions with a great deal of energy. He noticed Diar as he closed the door behind him. "Oh, there are two of you! Who are you? Do you come here a lot?"

"My name is Diar. This is the first time I've been here."

"And you?" He returned the question to Christina. "Do you come to this balcony often?"

"Yes," Christina said, though she was starting to think it wasn't nearly private enough. Perhaps she wouldn't come back.

"You'll probably be an Intuiter, then," he said matter-of-factly, helping himself to the study table's single chair and pulling it back so he could see both Diar and Christina. "Though you, if it's just your first time, hard to say," he said to Diar. "I'm Nefry, by the way."

"What makes you say that?" Diar asked.

"Well, I've been thinking," Nefry said. "It turns out that anyone, anywhere, can develop an Imaging talent, but the frequency is much higher among Eshtem initiates, and even higher among Drei Masters. But even most Eshtem initiates who develop talents tend to remain weak, so that for every real Projector we get, there are five people who can sometimes deflect enough light to be distracting. The exception, of course, is with Intuiters. Every one of them can tell truth from falsehood reliably, and most of them can do more. So, I thought, what if there's something that happens at Eshtem that makes Imaging talents grow stronger, and what if Intuiters instinctively do it more?

"So, for the last few weeks, I've been following the four Intuiters on campus to see what they have in common. Then I followed a few controls to see how much of the overlap was attributable to the common demands of being at Eshtem. And, after eliminating the points of convergence common to each set, I found one commonality unique to the Intuiters: visits to this balcony. And if you come here a lot, too," he added, turning his gaze on Christina, "it stands to reason that you could be an Intuiter. You're lucky if you are – you know Intuiters get to train with dragons after we graduate, right? You could even become a handler one day."

Christina frowned. Everything she knew aligned with what Nefry was saying, though it surprised her both that he seemed to know more about magic and dragons than she did and that he would discuss them so openly. Neither was considered a polite topic in Ellyrian society; one had to seek out a Storyteller or backroom gossip to hear the rumors about how exactly new Edrei were trained or what they could accomplish.

I suppose we're Eshtem initiates now, and there's no reason he shouldn't talk about it. She hoped she did get to train with dragons one day, though she was hardly able to focus on that now. She took out her copies of the Lists – taking care to leave the letter signed by the Lussonne staff in her satchel – and set them on the table in front of her, hoping Nefry would pick up his cue to leave.

"I know four Intuiters is not a very large sample," he said instead, seeming oblivious to her signal, "but so far only two second-years have been identified with Intuition, and Master Tamar and Master Miraj are the only Drei Masters.

The third-year magic users have been off campus for the last few weeks with the Master Imagers, but maybe I can run it again when they get back. Although, the earliest second-years to be identified are always the strongest anyway, so if they are doing something that makes them stronger, I'm pretty sure it's visiting this balcony. But then again, this is the first time Master Miraj came here, and it might just have been because he saw Master Tamar and wanted to talk to her."

So, Tamar had been speaking with Miraj, which made sense. The Edrei Council was the governing body of the Order. It consisted of twelve members, three of whom held simultaneous positions as Drei Masters at Eshtem: Porrian, Derrak, and Miraj.

Christina turned her attention to the Lists, turning the pages in each copy to the place where she had left off, and Diar cleared his throat. "Maybe we should leave Christina to her work," he said. "I'm sure she'd appreciate the quiet."

He really was being nicer to her than she deserved.

"Well, if you'd like," Nefry agreed, glancing between Diar, Christina, and the stacks of paper on the table. "Say, what are you working on? Are those files from the Eshtem Lists? Wait... How did you get two copies? There's only one in the library, and why would you even want a second copy? It would be just the same as the first – unless it was from the Lussonne, and the only difference would be..." His eyes lit up as he reached for the Lussonne copy. "This *is* from the Lussonne, isn't it? You're looking for the name of that renegade, aren't you? Why?"

Christina opened her mouth, dismayed that he had put it together. Realizing she had no idea what to say, she closed it and put her hand down on the Lussonne Lists as her gaze turned to Diar. "Would you shut the window?" she asked, unable to suppress the note of desperation in her voice. "Please don't tell anyone about this," she said to Nefry.

"Well now, it sounds like you should sit down," Nefry said to Diar after he closed the window, waving him toward the table. "I will tell, if you don't say why," he added to Christina.

Christina brought her hands to her face, wondering what she would tell them.

"I take it you're not on a special assignment for a Drei Master, then," Nefry noted.

"It's not really any of our business." Diar sounded more conflicted now than when all he knew was that the papers were from the Lussonne.

"You may as well sit," Christina said, waving a hand absently to the length of cushioned seat that angled toward the railing. Diar moved past Nefry and sat down slowly. "If I tell you why I'm looking for the name, will you both agree never to speak of this?"

"If you tell me why, I agree not to tell anyone *why* you want his name," Nefry returned promptly. "Whether I tell anyone that you're looking for it will depend on the reason."

Diar's brow furrowed as his gaze turned from Christina to Nefry. "Look, she's clearly distressed about this," he said, "and it has nothing to do with us. Maybe we should just let it go."

"*She's* the one trying to uncover erased information," Nefry returned. "Of course she's uncomfortable. But maybe the Drei Masters ought to know."

"Very well, then," Christina said, perceiving that Nefry wasn't going to let it go. "I met him. That's my reason."

"What?" Nefry's jaw dropped as both sets of eyes snapped to her. "The renegade? You *met* him? How? When?"

"When my escort was attacked by outlaws on the way here. Perhaps you heard?" The boys nodded. "Well, he was working with them."

There was a moment of silence as they took that in.

"So why do you want his name?" Nefry asked.

"You promised not to say why, even if you do decide to tell what I'm doing," Christina reminded Nefry, and he nodded. "Does that go for you too?" she asked Diar.

"Of course."

"Then I may as well tell you. He said he was innocent of the charges against him."

"He did?" Nefry's eyes widened. "And you believed him?"

"And I decided I would like more information." Christina folded her hands on the tabletop. "There. Now you know. What are you going to do?"

Nefry thought for a moment, then grinned. "Well, I'm going to help you, that's what. You've got a pretty big stack there."

"In Lystra – at the inn," Diar said, studying her. "You told the Edrei they killed the renegade. That must have been hard, after you met him."

Christina's breath caught. "I cannot speak to that." She inwardly cursed herself for her carelessness. Anandolf had given her an order, and she had not meant to reveal anything to Diar. She was so accustomed to servants' blending into the background that she had not given any thought to his presence in the room. "I have to ask that you say nothing of it either, though I have no right to do so."

"They killed the renegade already, and they didn't tell us?" Nefry's eyes lit with curiosity. "And *you* can't speak of it, either? Why not?"

"Wait… You don't really think he might have been innocent, do you?" Diar asked. "I can only imagine it was hard for you to go through, if you were there," he said to Christina. "And I understand why you might want more information. But this is the Edrei Council we are talking about. They must have had good reason for judging him the way they did, and I'm sure they have their reasons for keeping his death a secret, too. None of which is any of our business," he repeated to Nefry.

"Well, maybe. Probably," Nefry agreed. "But I still want to help you find his name," he said to Christina, reaching for the Lists. "It will take you forever to look through all these entries by yourself."

Christina held up a hand. "If I let you help, I'll need some assurance of your silence."

Nefry clasped his right fist over his heart. "I, Nefry Carril," he said, dropping his voice to a whisper on his House name, "do solemnly swear not to reveal to anyone through word, indication, action, or careless indiscretion that we have Lussonne copies of the Lists, what we are doing with them, or why we wanted to consult them without the prior authorization of Christina tu'Noraan, for so long as we both are living and the Six guard me able to fulfill my vow. Nor will I repeat anything I've inferred about the renegade or his execution." He dropped his hand. "Will that do?"

The oath would bind him to the best of his ability, and since he did not strike Christina as stupid or inept, that meant it would keep him from betraying her confidence unless he was tortured beyond his ability to endure.

She nodded, turning her attention to Diar. "You certainly need not involve yourself with this any further, but I would appreciate your oath of silence, if that is something you are willing to give."

"I'll help you, too." Diar repeated Nefry's oath, replacing mention of "the Six" with "the White."

"You worship the White?" Nefry asked, surprised.

"Is that a problem?" Diar asked.

"Of course not," Christina returned. The Rishara people were descended from elves who had also worshiped the White, after all, and those same elves had saved Ellyrian from High Wizards and founded the Order in the first place.

She glanced between the two boys and sighed – part in relief, and part in resignation. She had not wanted anyone else to know what she was up to, let alone become involved, but the fact that they knew could hardly be undone.

Besides which, she had just been thinking she ought to spend more time with students outside of Lelise's circle. Carril and Jax were both Blood Houses, but at least they were not noble Houses. She would never have met either of these boys at court, and that had to count for something.

"Let's split these up," she said, glancing at the stacks beside her. "Like Nefry said, there are a lot of entries to go over."

CHAPTER 9

Learning the Sword

Long battered, weakened, fragmented the shield
Which assembled, a weapon, one hand could yet wield
Before him the whole of the world would yield.

— From Ocifem's Prophecy, as uttered in
a closed session of the Edrei Council

Of all the classes at Eshtem, Jadon found weaponry the most mind-numbingly dull. He had been training with the sword as long as he could remember. Half his classmates had never held one before arriving on campus. It was a recipe for a poor experience all around, and Master Halce, the weaponry instructor, seemed uninterested in keeping his advanced students entertained. The class met in the Eshtem Arena, and week after week, the master lined them up in rows and called out basic forms for them to fall into.

The forms were all second nature to Jadon and his friends, who handled the boredom by staying in the back row and chatting whenever Halce was out of earshot. The girls on campus were a frequent topic of conversation, especially after Rindarin announced the Initiative would be throwing a mock tournament the night before the Eshtem Tourney began and that girls would be invited to attend.

The class became increasingly unpleasant as the weather grew colder, and it was a particularly crisp fall day when Dreck announced in the middle of form work that Trista to'Rinton was the prettiest girl on campus and he intended to bring her to the Initiative's party. Jadon and Fendi chuckled quietly. Trista was pretty, but she was also the niece of a Gold House high prince.

"I don't see why you would bother, cousin," Perleyon said to Dreck. "It couldn't last, and if anything happened between the two of you, you'd find yourself in a world of trouble with her relatives. Besides, there are plenty of prettier War House girls – like my Idarri."

"Pass right and lunge," Halce called from the front of the class, and they all stepped forward and ended with their practice swords straight ahead.

"As if Trista would ever be willing to go anywhere or do anything with you anyway." Fendi smiled as he held the pose. "Never mind attend a War House event. Besides which, I suspect you'd have to fight Ramich." Ramich was from another royal Gold House, and Jadon had heard that he was one of the most promising duelists in their class.

Jadon looked forward to beating him in the Eshtem Tourney.

"I'm not worried about Ramich," Dreck scoffed. "He tried to commandeer the shooting grounds from a group of lowborn initiates a while back, and they just laughed in his face."

"Retreat right to switch guard," Halce called.

"Did they really?" Jadon asked as they made the retreat. Technically, anyone could use the shooting grounds, but if highborn students wanted to use the area, the lowborn usually cleared out of the way.

"I remember hearing something about that at the time." Perleyon wrinkled his nose. "It was that same blonde girl who tried to start something with us in Lystra, wasn't it? No respect for her betters."

"Cross-cut up, retreating left to gathered thrust high."

"Jenne, some of her Gold House commoner friends, and their Blood House associate Diar, whom we also met in Lystra." Dreck nodded as they all stepped backward and raised their weapons to the level of their shoulders.

"Diar? As in, my roommate Diar?" Jadon asked, surprised. "*He* laughed in Ramich's face?" He was impressed. Sometimes, when he overslept the morning bell, Diar woke him up before leaving for class himself, but aside from that they interacted little, and Diar was always deferential when they did. Diar had not struck Jadon as the type who would stand up for himself.

"Retreat three in ready position," Halce called, and they all shuffled three steps backward.

"Exactly my point," Dreck said to Jadon. "I like my chances in a fight with Ramich. Besides, Trista has not been associating with him as frequently since then. A lot could happen between now and the tourney."

"Care to place a wager on that?" asked Fendi. "Two silver marks apiece against her coming with you to the party. That gives you three-to-one odds."

"Advance three, same position."

"Make it three marks around," said Dreck as they shuffled forward.

"Safest money I ever staked," said Perleyon.

"At ease," Halce finally announced.

"Looks like you have yourself a wager," said Jadon as they all lowered their practice swords and fell into parade rest.

"Pair off," came the next command. As Jadon squared off to face Fendi, something told him they were not about to spar.

"Some of you," Halce said, "are still making your cuts from the wrist, or, at best, the elbow. Not only would such cuts prove weak and ineffectual in actual combat..."

Jadon's mind drifted as Halce continued. He had received another letter from his sister Anna the previous day that was full of questions about how his training was going and whether he had caught sight of any dragons yet. He could imagine the hushed tone she would have used asking the questions, and it was almost enough to make him smile. He had given up his own curiosity on those matters society conspired to keep secret from him around the time his third inquiry about dragons in front of a visiting lord had earned him his first – and only – whipping, as well as a full watch spent writing out *Lords do not speak idly of magic or dragons* over and over again. Anna had been a more discerning child, far better attuned to which topics could safely be raised with which audiences. The curiosity had never been whipped out of her.

Jadon imagined she would be disappointed when he finally got around to penning his response. No, he had not seen any dragons, and aside from the orientation speech and the booming voice at the Dragon Gate, he had seen little evidence of magic either. Training mostly consisted of the masters' droning on about material familiar from all the studying he had done prior to matriculation. Anna had all the same tutors that he did and would probably be as bored here as he was, if their father agreed to let her enroll when she came of age.

She wanted it so much more than he did. It was really a shame that Jadon was the one who carried all Lord Juaqen's expectations.

At least when he wrote her back, he would be able to confirm that Lord Brell had not finished nearly as high in the Lists for his year at Eshtem as he had claimed. The man had been bragging at a recent dinner party, and Anna had asked Jadon to fact-check his claim, which had led to his encounter with that strange girl in the library the other day.

Fendi turned to face him and took up switch guard, and Jadon belatedly realized that everyone around them was pairing off. He hurriedly took up the ready position as Halce ordered them to strike.

The clatter of wooden blade on wooden blade filled the space as each of the pairs made contact and froze.

"Right-hand partner, switch guard. Left-hand partner, ready position."

The exercise continued for some time. Jadon's muscles started to ache from holding the static poses, which he supposed meant his body was involved in some form of work.

When they moved to parry a cut from force guard, one of the initiates' practice swords clattered to the ground.

"Liana?" Halce inquired, pausing in his rounds to address her from the front of the class. "What did you do wrong?"

"I'm sorry, Drei Master," she said as she bent to retrieve the weapon, flustered and shivering. She brushed some errant yellow hair from her face, quite fetching despite her incompetence. "I... I'm not sure."

Halce considered her for a moment, then said, "Come here, Liana. You too, Brinnette."

"You'd think Liana would be better at holding on to her practice sword by now," Fendi said as Liana and her partner joined Halce at the front of the class. "Isn't she the niece of the legendary Vorsand?"

"Maybe that's why Master Halce is not giving her any demerits," Dreck speculated. "Anyone else drops their weapon, easy demerit. No question."

"Vorsand has a niece in our class?" Jadon asked. "Why would that matter to Halce?"

"You didn't know about Liana?" said Dreck, none of them paying any attention as Halce asked Brinnette to repeat the stroke. "Surely you have heard that Master Halce and Vorsand graduated the same year and were close personal friends."

"I heard that Vorsand and Master Tamar were lovers," Jadon countered.

"That is just a rumor," Dreck rebuked him. "Whereas it is an established *fact* that Vorsand and Master Halce have each been visiting the social functions of the other's House ever since they graduated from Eshtem. Not to mention that he was once engaged to be married to Master Halce's sister. Before she died."

"I don't see why anyone should be expected to know all these trivial details about Vorsand's life," said Perleyon. "At the end of the day, he's still only a captain."

"And Lead Master Imager," Jadon added.

"People give him far too much credit," Fendi agreed with Perleyon. "There are dozens of Edrei with records at least as impressive. And yet everyone talks only about *Vorsand*."

"I imagine that has something to do with the fact that he was a nobody before Eshtem," Jadon noted.

"Exactly," said Dreck. "He gets all the glory, and for what? For being lowborn, when you come right down to it. That's the only reason anyone cares about him. It's ridiculous."

"Well, and he's the most powerful Dreamer to pass through Eshtem in a hundred years," said Jadon, playing devil's advocate. He had always liked the idea of Vorsand, and only partly because the legends surrounding him irritated Lord Juaqen. "And he singlehandedly prevented a minor war, among other things."

"Look, the point is," said Dreck, as if in summary, "I don't like him either. But these 'trivial details' are having a direct impact on our lives. Look." He nodded toward the front of the class, where Halce was dismissing Liana and her friend. "No demerits. And why? Because Master Halce wants his best friend's niece to make Edrei."

"You're right." Perleyon narrowed his eyes, quieting his voice further as Halce continued his lecture. "Anyone else drops a practice sword, automatic demerit."

"I'm sure being Vorsand's niece counts against her often enough," Jadon pointed out. "Even I know he has enemies among the staff."

"Vorsand has enemies?" asked Fendi.

"Sure thing," said Dreck. "Master Derrak petitioned the Board of Masters on four separate occasions to have him removed as Lead Master Imager. And the two of them have not attended the same social function since Master Derrak dramatically walked out of the Grand Festival Ball the year Vorsand made full Edrei, right after Vorsand arrived."

"Then there's Master Verizah," Jadon added, "who formally requested Vorsand be charged with insubordination and theft when he took that dragon to rescue Master Tamar and Prince Gahon. Master Felade has accused him of everything from cowardice to corruption before the Eshtem Oversight Committee in the Senate. And he's still just a captain only because Master Porrian has been blocking his promotion for years."

"With good reason, no doubt," said Perleyon. "A man who attracts that much animosity must have done something wrong."

Jadon wondered if Perleyon really believed that statement made sense, or if any reason to disparage Vorsand would have done as well. "Or people resent him for glorifying the lower classes, and make up reasons to justify their dislike," he suggested, smiling. "Like you lot."

"Jadon!"

Jadon looked up to find Halce staring at him from the front of the class, frustration clear in his gaze.

"Why don't you come and demonstrate with Lelise?"

"With pleasure, Drei Master," Jadon returned, walking to the front of the class. Lelise, a petite, blonde Blood House noble, was already standing there, rubbing her free hand against her sword hand to warm them both. She had probably volunteered for this. The girl rarely passed up an opportunity to earn a merit, and Halce was generous with his volunteers regardless of their level of skill. In fact, Jadon got the sense that being a skilled swordsman usually counted against him where Halce was concerned – though he supposed if he was really interested in getting the Drei Master to dislike him less, paying attention in class would be the obvious place to start.

In fact, paying attention might have conferred any number of benefits, not least of which would be knowing what he was supposed to demonstrate.

Lelise dropped into gathered thrust low, shooting a look at her Blood House friends in the first row that spoke volumes of her disdain both for Jadon and for having to face off against him. Jadon, amused, took up the ready position.

"Whenever you're ready, Lelise," Halce told her.

She lunged, thrusting the point of her weapon toward Jadon's chest. He turned sideways as he stepped into the contact, allowing her weapon to strike empty air beside him. Then, noticing that she had leaned too far forward, he tugged her extended wrist with his free hand, using her momentum to jerk her off balance.

It was almost certainly not the maneuver Halce had asked him to demonstrate, but Jadon smiled as Lelise stumbled forward, tripped, and fell.

"Jadon!" Halce rebuked him as one of Lelise's friends took a step forward, spitting mad. He was Vannes to'Jinn, Lelise's cousin. Like Ramich, Vannes had a reputation at court for being a fine duelist, but his contributions during class had so far left Jadon unimpressed. "I asked you to demonstrate a simple deflection. Nothing more."

"Apologies, Drei Master," said Jadon, offering Lelise a hand up. She took it, but quickly snatched her hand back once she regained her feet, the gesture having placated her not at all. "I noticed Lelise had overextended and thought she could use the reminder to attend to her balance."

Fendi, Dreck, and Perleyon were chuckling in the back row. Jadon avoided looking at them, but his own grin broadened as Lelise shot him an indignant glare.

"That will cost you a demerit, Jadon," Halce told him. "In the future, I trust you will remember that I am the teacher here, not you. That said, Lelise, his observation was correct. You leaned too far forward, and that was why Jadon was able to make you fall. Attacks on your balance will prove ineffectual if you maintain a secure base. Show us the lunge again, please."

Lelise brushed her dress a few more times to clear it of sand, then dropped into gathered thrust low. With a contemptuous look for Jadon, she stepped into the lunge, this time achieving the perfect degree of extension.

"Is this better, Drei Master?" she asked, knowing full well that it was. She was quite good with the forms most of the time. Though, most of the time, they worked the forms alone. Lelise would likely benefit from sparring.

"Quite." Halce frowned. "Try striking at Jadon again. Jadon, deflect only."

"No more tricks," Jadon agreed, winking at Lelise as he resumed the ready position.

She scowled and lunged. Jadon, deflecting the stroke to his opposite side this time, noted that she had overextended again.

Some people were just too easy to rile.

"Freeze," Halce told them, walking closer. Taking Lelise's sword hand, he pulled her forward, and she took a step to correct her balance. "I shouldn't be able to do that," he noted. "Don't forget to mind your balance when you strike at a real target. The distribution of weight should be the same as during the forms. Once more."

He backed away from them, and Lelise struck again. Jadon yawned as he batted away her strike. It seemed to upset her further. Then again, everything Jadon did seemed to upset her further, regardless of whether he intended it.

This time when Halce pulled her wrist, she kept her balance.

"Better," he told her.

"Master Halce?" Vannes inquired, stepping forward from his place in line.

"Yes, Vannes?"

"Perhaps I might step in for Lelise?"

Jadon lifted his practice sword, grinning. Vannes was obviously itching to get back at him for embarrassing Lelise. It should make for an interesting demonstration.

But Halce shook his head. "That will be all for demonstrations. Pair off again. But Jadon, this time I want you with Sayler."

"Who, now?"

"Sayler." Halce frowned at him and indicated a boy in the second row with short, springy hair and skin a shade or two darker than Diar's. *As if I could reasonably be expected to know the names of* all *the other initiates in the class*, Jadon grumbled inwardly.

Lelise shot Jadon a smug look that was mirrored by her friend Saleah's. He winked at them as he walked past. Vannes, standing next to them, glowered and took a step in Jadon's direction.

"Vannes," said Halce. "Why don't you partner with Matt."

That sent him to the opposite end of the front row from where Jadon found Sayler in the back. It seemed the score Vannes wanted to settle would have to wait for another time.

Halce asked partners on the right-hand side to attack from any of the forms at half speed while left-hand partners focused on parrying. This put Jadon on the offensive. Dutifully, he began to attack Sayler at half speed, watching the other boy's defensive technique for any errors that could be exploited at the reduced pace. He found none. Sayler met him stroke for stroke, his parries solid and his footwork impeccable, anticipating Jadon's moves almost before they began. Jadon started varying his offensive in ways that would have made no sense if Sayler were free to strike back, to see if they would catch Sayler off guard. They did not. Gradually, Jadon began increasing his pace of attack.

"You're pretty good at this," he said after a while. He had reached about three quarters of normal attack speed, and Sayler had yet to make any mistakes.

"And you are no longer at half speed," Sayler noted.

"You think I couldn't double this pace if I really wanted to?" Jadon pressed his attacks just a hair faster.

"Not sustainably. Not without messing up." Sayler frowned as he matched Jadon's pace. "But that isn't a challenge. I'm not interested in sparring with you. Just in doing the exercise."

Jadon rolled his eyes and slowed down. "Don't tell me you wouldn't rather be doing something more interesting. If Master Halce did let us spar, I expect you'd do well. You might even be able to best somebody as trained as Vannes. Who did you learn from?"

"At the moment, I am trying to learn from Master Halce." Sayler gave him a look that was decidedly unimpressed as Jadon pulled another of his variations, moving effortlessly to parry the blow that came from the new direction. "And believe it or not, I don't care how good you think I am or who I might be able to beat in a contest right now."

"And switch!" said Halce, cutting over the sound of practice swords. "Left-hand partners, attack at half speed. Right-hand partners, parry."

"All right, then." Jadon fell into the ready position as Sayler took up high guard. "I guess I will keep all future compliments to myself."

His attention drifted as Sayler began attacking. His movements were equally well coordinated on the offensive, but they were also slow and predictable and hardly required an effort to parry. Jadon surveyed the rest of the field, wondering whether the other initiates were as committed to the constraints of this exercise as his opponent.

They seemed to be. All the pairs that he could see were diligently striking and countering away, as slow as sap dripping out of a tapped sugar maple. To call the pace half speed was too generous for most.

Jadon's gaze fell on Liana and her partner, who stood next to him and Sayler and worked at perhaps a quarter of Sayler's monotonous pace. Liana had a look of deep concentration on her face. Despite each of her strokes having already achieved the speed of a particularly sluggish snail, she paused after each one to adjust her form.

As Jadon watched, Liana's sword hit her partner's flat to flat, and the other girl's blade slid under the cross guard to hit her thumb. Liana grunted in pain, clasping her injured finger.

"You know," Jadon told her, warding off Sayler's strikes with perhaps a fifth of his attention, "if you slide your thumb closer to your knuckles when you thrust, so that it rests straight up and down under the cross guard, you can protect it from that kind of injury."

"Oh." Liana moved her thumb as Jadon had suggested. "Thanks." She struck at her partner, who blocked without incident. They continued, putting in about three strikes in the space of Sayler's seven.

After a few more moments watching the supremely effortful struggle to remember everything play across Liana's face, Jadon could not help himself. Someone ought to help the poor girl. "But if I were you," he said, earning a frown from Sayler as he continued to parry, "I'd stop trying to think so hard. When you get the forms right, they should feel right. Try to learn them with your body, not your mind."

"What's going on here?" Halce cut in, having worked his way over to them in his slow pacing of the rows. "Something to say, Jadon?"

"Jadon was just giving me some advice, Drei Master," said Liana, full of contrition. "I keep messing up the forms."

"Jadon." Halce's tone was dangerously cool. "I seem to remember having this chat with you once already today. Remind me, who did we say was the teacher here?"

"That would be you, Drei Master." Jadon lowered his practice sword.

"And who, then, is responsible for these initiates' education in swordplay?"

"Not me. I overstepped in thinking I could help." Jadon folded his hands over the hilt of his practice sword and tried to look contrite as he met Halce's gaze. "You have my apology."

"You did overstep, again, and an apology will not spare you another demerit. I hope this one inspires you to correct your behavior before you meet with a worse consequence. Resume." Halce turned away, clasping his hands behind his back as he continued stalking down the line to visit his wrath on the next unruly initiate.

Jadon grunted in annoyance as he resumed the ready position. That brought him to five demerits. Some of them he really had deserved. Halce would find no argument from him there. This one, though, he disagreed with. Liana, he saw, was already improving, her movements a little more fluid than before.

If she's really the niece of his best friend, you would think he'd be grateful that I offered some advice, Jadon thought. *But no. It's not "my place." Better to let her keep reinforcing the same bad technique until a properly qualified master has time to address it.*

Jadon sighed. It did not matter. All the masters knew how many demerits everyone had, and he was convinced that some of them purposefully assigned him more merits on days when his number of demerits was higher. He suspected the whole system was their way of arguing with one another about which students ought to succeed and which should be thrown out, and Jadon had concluded that most of them were on his side.

Halce, though, was not one of them, and perhaps that was the real source of Jadon's complaint. He did not usually care about the sort of impression he made on other people, but today it bothered him, just a little, that Halce disliked him so much. If the man was a close friend of Vorsand's – whom the stories had always painted as someone Jadon thought he might respect – then Jadon felt he and the master could have gotten along under different circumstances.

Then again, perhaps Halce would have despised him regardless. Jadon would never know.

What he did know was that Halce taught a dull weaponry class, and he could hardly be blamed for keeping himself entertained enough to avoid falling asleep in the middle of it. If that cost him Halce's lasting dislike along with a few demerits every now and then, so be it.

CHAPTER 10

The Noraani-Marked Sword

Though Eshtem initiates are asked to leave behind their clans and Houses and think of themselves as servants of worldwide peace, they have never succeeded in doing so. After all, Eshtem initiates are still Ellyrian – and in that culture, personal honor is not easily set aside.

– From *History and Practices of the Edrei*, penned for the collections of the Lussonne by Guizarre Arus

"Diar, could you stay a moment?"

Diar winced and sat back down, watching his classmates file out the door. Master Tamar had called on him twice to answer easy questions, and he had fumbled them both. She had not assigned him demerits at the time. Probably, she would now. *Or maybe she'll cut to the chase and expel me*, he worried.

Why did I let Jenne convince me to stay at the shooting grounds all evening? He furrowed his brow, dismayed at his weakness of will. *I knew I didn't understand the Alterran subjunctive.*

It was impossible to say no to that smile. The more time Diar spent with her, the harder it became for him to remember that his primary purpose here was to become Edrei, rather than to win more moments of affection and approval from Jenne. His priorities were confused, and his self-control was slipping. It was not a pattern he could allow to continue.

He stood as the last of the other initiates left the class, approaching Tamar's desk with promises to do better ready on his tongue.

"Close the door, please." Tamar gestured to the door that was still propped open, forestalling Diar's speech. He pulled it closed.

"Are you keeping up with your other classes?"

"I am so sorry, Drei Master. The truth is, I have an interrogation in ethics after this, and I spent most of the week studying for it," he told her, the words coming out in a rush. "And then last night, I spent the rest of my study time going over rhetoric because Master Garadil tends to assign more demerits. And I know that's no excuse, I owe this class equal attention, and I will make it an equal priority going forward, I swear."

"You will swear no such thing," Tamar informed him, a smile playing at the corners of her mouth. "You have five demerits at the moment, do you not?"

"Yes," Diar agreed, confused.

"That number is high for my comfort. I would like to see it go down, but I can't help you if you can't answer any of my questions during class. That said, earning merits is only a third as helpful as avoiding demerits, so if you find yourself in a position where you must choose between course loads, I expect you to continue prioritizing those classes in which you are more likely to earn demerits. So long as you understand that you'll need to be caught up with Alterran on interrogation days."

Diar chewed on that for a moment, utterly nonplussed.

He had noticed that Tamar assigned him fewer demerits than other masters, but he had thought that a result of her assigning fewer demerits in general, rather than her wanting him to succeed. She had, after all, assigned him at least one demerit that he remembered, though he had earned more than enough merits from her to make up for it.

"Right," Diar said. "Can I ask why you're telling me this?"

"At the beginning of the year, all the new initiates are divided among the Drei Masters, who are expected to ensure any who graduate are ready to become Edrei." She smiled. "You are one of mine, and it seems to me that you have the ability to learn what Edrei are expected to know. I'd hate to see you waste it through a poor allocation of time and resources."

"Oh." Diar was still berating himself for having fallen behind. Tamar deserved better from him. He *would* come prepared to her class in the future. "That's very kind of you."

"What I do, I do not for your benefit, but for the Order's. Should you underperform on your finals or be deemed unworthy of making Edrei for any other reason, I will strike your name from the enrollment lists myself." She considered him while he thought about that, and then she said, "Suppose three Ellyrian citizens are taken captive when their ship is seized by pirates. As an Edrei, you have been tasked with procuring their release. You track the pirates to their base, but they become aware of your presence. They offer to trade the prisoners for you and threaten to begin killing them if you do not comply. You have reason to believe they will kill you if you do, but you know them to be men of their word. Do you make the trade?"

"Master Shiell would call that a gray area," said Diar, assuming Tamar was trying to assess whether he was ready for his ethics interrogation. It was, however, not the sort of question Shiell was likely to ask; his interrogations tended to consist less of practical dilemmas and more of theoretical discrepancies between the duties of an Edrei and those of an Ellyrian citizen. "He would say that a decision to turn oneself in would require bravery and selflessness. However, he would argue that a trained Edrei is a greater force for good than three untrained Ellyrians, and that others would benefit more from an Edrei's preserving himself than from the liberation of three other Ellyrians. He would say the Edrei's duty in such a case would be unclear, and each would have to exercise his own judgment if placed in such a scenario."

"He would say that," Tamar agreed drily. "But if it were you, what would you do?"

Diar frowned, realizing she must not be interested in his ethics preparation after all.

He thought for a minute. "I suppose I can't know for certain until I'm tested," he said. "But I hope I would turn myself in. I think that would be more in keeping with the spirit of the Ideals than letting three innocent people die when I could prevent it." It was also the choice Diar believed the White would approve. The Edrei Ideals had much in common with the Principles of the White Way – which made sense, since both ethical systems were handed down from the elves.

"I expect we will all be tested before the end, in some manner or other," Tamar said. "Do not forget what I said about prioritizing. It will become even more important as finals approach."

* * *

As the first semester drew to a close, Diar felt he was drowning in information about duties, virtues, codes of honor, and the Edrei Ideals and that he had certainly missed something somewhere. He was proven right when Shiell posed two questions to other initiates during the ethics interrogation that he would have had no idea how to answer. Luckily, though, he knew the answers to his own questions and escaped the ordeal unscathed.

He met up with Jenne and the others at lunchtime, and as they finished eating, she announced her intention to study ethics in the south tower when afternoon classes were over. She had her interrogation tomorrow, and though there was little point in Diar's reviewing that material again, he was tempted to say he would join her. Luckily, though, Telius, Eridike, and Cardos had already had their interrogation, too, and they were of a mind to do some training with real weapons in the arena. Halce wanted them all comfortable handling the weight of real metal as the Eshtem Tourney drew closer. Though they would use practice swords during the tourney, he did not want them to forget that their training was meant to prepare them for actual life-or-death situations.

"I'm for weapons training," Diar decided. His weaponry class met tomorrow, and he needed to do a better job of showing up prepared at lesson time.

"Diar, may I have a word?"

Diar looked up to find Christina had paused by their table, drawing stares from the rest of his friends. They all knew who she was. Jenne had recounted their brief meeting with the princess in Lystra more than once.

"What do you want to talk to Diar about?" Jenne's tone was pleasant enough, but Diar could tell her guard was up.

"A private matter. If you do not mind stepping aside?"

Diar shot to his feet, feeling silly for his delayed response. "Of course." His portion of the Lists was sitting in a chest in his dorm room, where he had almost forgotten about it in the busyness of the last few weeks. He gathered his shoulder bag and picked up his empty trencher. "I'll return this to the kitchen."

Christina walked with him to the kitchen window, waiting to speak until they were far enough away to keep their words from carrying back to his curious friends. "Nefry has finished checking through his whole section," she said as Diar put his trencher in a stack of others gathered by the window, waiting for attention from the kitchen staff. "We are curious how yours is coming along."

"I'm afraid I have quite a bit left," Diar admitted. "I haven't had as much time as I expected."

"Of course, that's not a problem," Christina said. Another initiate came to return her trencher, and Diar and Christina moved out of the way before she spoke again. "I have not finished mine yet either, but I am close, and I thought perhaps we could get some of the records back from you since Nefry is eager to keep looking."

"Oh." Diar had mixed feelings about doing less than his share, but with how thinly stretched he was already, he supposed he was in no position to object. "Of course. I can give some of them back. When should I get them to you? Or... Nefry?"

"Is now a good time? I can walk with you."

"Um... sure, they're just in my dorm. I need to stop there before my next class anyway."

Christina nodded, and they walked together toward the exit. Diar glanced at his friends as they passed and found Jenne was staring at him with an inquiring look. He gave her a small shake of his head.

"I've made your friends quite curious, haven't I?" Christina said quietly as they continued outside and were struck by a gust of cold air. It had snowed the night before, and though most of it had melted, small patches remained in pockets of shade near the buildings and the trees that dotted the campus's central lawn. A few shriveled leaves still clung to the branches, but most had already fallen.

"They'll have questions," Diar agreed. "But if I tell them I gave you my word not to speak of it, they'll have to respect that. Would it be all right to tell them that much?" he asked, suddenly unsure.

Christina paused before she answered, and Diar worried she would ask him to lie instead. The Principles discouraged lying except in the service of a greater good, and he did not know if lying to his friends would be justified in this case. Besides which, he wasn't much good at lying, and he had no desire to practice.

"I don't see why not," Christina eventually said, and Diar breathed a small sigh of relief. "But perhaps it would be best if I take *all* the Lists back," she added. "I never meant to burden you with my secrets, and it may prove more difficult for you to keep them if your friends have become curious."

"It's not a burden," Diar hastened to say. "I wanted to help you. I still do." He was not sure if he wanted to help so much because he had seen her cry when she spoke of the renegade's death or because he knew that, outside of Eshtem, she was his princess. That engendered a certain loyalty even in the absence of obligation, and more so because he respected Christina more than any other noble he had met so far. That made him proud to be Noraani-sworn – though he would never admit as much to Jenne.

"I believe you, and I thank you for it. But things change, and you have less time than you expected. You have helped me already, with your oath of silence, and that is more than I had any right to expect. Nefry and I can take it from here."

Diar wanted to argue, but he knew it would be a mistake. Though he was curious about Christina's interactions with the renegade and would have liked to help her find out more, he still felt a bit guilty whenever he handled the Lists from the Lussonne. The information was erased for a reason – and he did not have the time to involve himself, anyway.

"All right," he conceded. "I'll get them all."

Diar stopped by his dorm again after afternoon classes to retrieve his sword and his initiate cloak. It was cold enough now that everyone wore them while training outside, and special training gloves were available at the arena. After he made his way there and collected some, he found that two rows of wooden blocks had been set up for the students to use in practicing their cuts.

"Diar!" Telius waved him over to where he, Eridike, and Cardos were already cutting away. A few other initiates were engaged in the same activity farther down the row, and a few additional pairs with wooden practice swords were sparring farther out on the sands. Like Diar, most of them had their hoods up, protecting their ears from the cold, but some of those sparring kept them down. "Have you seen these blocks work?"

"First time." Diar drew his sword and assumed force guard.

"So, what did Christina want to talk to you about?" Cardos asked.

That didn't take long. Diar grimaced as he swung at the block in front of him, thinking to slice it in half with a downward cross-cut. Instead, his sword bit through only a few inches before getting stuck. "I can't say," he said as he pulled his sword back. "I gave her my word I wouldn't talk about it."

"Keeping secrets for a princess?" Telius shook his head. "Looks like Diar is moving up in life."

"Soon he won't have any time to spare for us commoners," Cardos agreed.

"Oh, come on. It's not like that." Diar swung at his block again. He grunted as his sword was again caught in the wood.

"It won't part unless you lead with the edge exactly," Eridike told him. He demonstrated with his own downward cross-cut, slicing the block neatly from top left to bottom right. The upper half fell to the sands, and Eridike set it back on top of the lower half. Diar watched as the wood knit itself together.

"Seven sights," he said. He had thought Imaging powers influenced only perception. It was startling to see a physical object rebuild itself.

Maybe these blocks were spelled by the elves, he guessed. The elves had been able to accomplish far more with their Imaging than was currently possible.

More initiates entered the arena, and Diar recognized Vannes to'Jinn among them. He was a sinewy, sandy-haired Blood House noble, and he was the only one in the group walking in with his hood down.

Vannes and his friends took up positions uncomfortably near the blocks as they broke into pairs and started sparring with practice swords. Vannes made short work of each of his friends in turn.

"Any other takers?" He turned to address their group and the few other initiates who were training within earshot. "You," he said, his eyes narrowing as they fell on Diar's scabbard. "Is that a Noraani weapon you carry?"

Uh-oh. "What's it to you?" Diar asked.

"Let me see," Vannes ordered, walking closer.

Diar reversed his sword, offering it to Vannes hilt first. "Be my guest."

Vannes took the sword and inspected the flower on the hilt. Stepping back, he took a few experimental swings, then squared the blade in front of his face, inspecting the steel. "With a weapon like this, you should be keeping better company," he noted, sparing a glance for Diar's friends. "Come spar with us."

"Thanks, but I'll pass," he said, reaching to take his sword back.

Vannes shifted, moving the sword out of reach. "A quick contest here, then. To prove yourself worthy of carrying such a mark." He tossed Diar the practice sword he had been using.

Diar caught it by reflex. "Why should it matter to you?" he asked as Vannes handed the Noraani sword to one of his friends and helped himself to the other boy's practice sword. "You're not even from House Nor–"

Diar started as Vannes swung at him with his newly acquired weapon, moving to block with the practice sword in his hand. "I told you, I'm not interested in sparring," he objected as their weapons met. "And I'd like my sword back."

"After we spar," Vannes insisted. He swung again and followed with two quick blows while Diar gave ground and defended himself. His hood slipped off his head in the process, and Vannes's fourth strike saw Diar's practice sword knocked out of his hands.

"I never said I would spar with you." Diar crossed his arms, making no effort to pick up the fallen weapon or pull up his hood, though he was very aware of the cold that now bit at his ears. "Give me my sword back, please."

Vannes raised his practice sword instead, ready to attack, and Diar regretted letting the noble handle his sword in the first place. The gesture had obviously done nothing to keep them on friendly terms.

"Give him his sword," Telius said, moving between them. "He said he didn't want to spar."

"Surely you are not backing down from a friendly challenge?" said Vannes, looking past Telius to Diar.

Diar put a hand on Telius's shoulder, moving him out of the way so he could address Vannes. "You can't challenge me. This is Eshtem."

"Not officially," Vannes agreed, still holding his practice sword ready. He smiled as he said it, knowing that Diar would not refuse him.

Diar stared at the other boy, his mouth tightening in annoyance. Vannes had been training with swords his whole life, and Diar could not hope to beat him. Sparring with him would be pointless. If he was not just idly curious about Diar's level of skill, Vannes probably meant to use the match to punish him for associating with initiates outside his House division, and Diar was in no mood to be humiliated – particularly not while his sword was being held hostage to force his compliance.

But official or not, Vannes had issued a clear challenge, and backing down from it would shame Diar in front of his friends.

"You don't have to do it, Diar," said Telius.

"Yes, I do," Diar disagreed, moving to pick up the practice sword.

"Excellent." Vannes waited as Telius backed up to join Eridike and Cardos. Then he attacked at full speed.

Diar barely managed to deflect the thrust. He had time enough only to be shocked by how close he had come to getting a stake of wood driven into his abdomen – Vannes's blows were *much* faster and more powerful than those of his usual sparring partners, and the practice sword may have been blunt, but it would still hurt – before he found himself reeling from a blow to the head. He had been so intent on blocking the thrust that he had not even seen Vannes's free hand coming in for the punch.

Vannes tripped him before his head cleared, and Diar found himself on the ground with the point of Vannes's practice sword hovering above his face. His ears were ringing.

"Do you yield?" asked Vannes. "Or is there yet enough fight in you for another bout?"

Diar glared up at the noble, beyond annoyed to find himself in the same situation he had been in beforehand: fight and lose with the possibility of injury and certainty of embarrassment, or let himself look like a coward. *What will it take to satisfy this guy? Two bouts? Three? Seven?*

"Vannes!" The shout came before Diar had a chance to respond, from the nearest rows of arena seating where two initiates were standing, one of them waving a flask in the air. Diar recognized Jadon and Fendi, whom he had seen around campus in Jadon's company before. Neither of them wore cloaks or training gloves.

Jadon hopped over the barrier between the benches and the arena sands. Fendi, who also carried a flask, followed and staggered a bit on the landing. Jadon paused to take a swig before they made their way over.

Diar pulled up his hood as they approached, the sight of them making him feel colder. Neither of them seemed to have noticed that it was winter.

"Jadon." Vannes greeted him coolly, lowering his practice sword and pulling his hood up.

"I recall your volunteering to spar with me the other day during class." Jadon's words ran together a little as he spoke. "Since Master Halce so regretfully denied you the opportunity, perhaps you'd care for that contest now? I mean, *if* you're interested... in facing someone who didn't first pick up a sword three days ago."

Fendi burst out laughing, and he and Jadon sipped from their flasks.

Vannes regarded the War House boys with an expression of deep distaste, but Diar could tell by the glint in his eyes he was interested. "I'd hate to engage in such with you at a clear disadvantage."

"*Engage in such*," Jadon repeated slowly. Then he grinned at Fendi. "Is the arena full of courtiers that need impressing? Or do you think he always talks like that?"

Fendi drew himself up straighter and swept his arm to the side, indicating an imaginary crowd. "Were you to skewer yourself in front of *such*, it would be most unfortunate." His impression dissolved into chortles.

Jadon walked closer and extended his hand to Diar. Diar took it and rose, not sure what to make of his roommate's intervention.

Jadon frowned and patted Diar's shoulder. "You're

welcome, I guess," he said. "But I was reaching for the sword." He held out his hand again, and it was Diar's turn to frown. Jadon took the practice sword from him before he had decided whether to hand it over.

Jadon turned to Vannes, weapon raised. "Come. A quick bout. If it goes poorly for me, these boys can approve... can agree..." Jadon frowned again, the word he wanted proving elusive. He eventually settled on, "...can *say* that I gave full free consent to the match." He tossed his flask to Fendi and dropped into the ready position. Fendi backed up to stand with Telius, Eridike, and Cardos, offering the three of them drinks before helping himself to another instead.

Vannes surveyed the group, considering. "And will they further *attest* that your consent was valid, given the state you were in?"

"I hereby vow to so attest!" Fendi shouted, lifting his flask into the air. Holding it high above his head, he tilted it, trying to pour its contents into his open mouth. Instead, he splashed his face and the arena sands. He doubled over in laughter.

Vannes stared in disgust, but he took his cloak off and tossed it to one of his friends. Then he lifted his practice sword and turned to Jadon. "It will be my pleasure to remind you why gentlemen don't spar when they've had too much to drink."

Fendi laughed uproariously. "This guy! Never heard of a War House," he jeered as everyone backed up, forming a loose ring around the combatants.

Diar was not sorry that his own confrontation with Vannes had been interrupted, but he was thinking that the match could not possibly end well for Jadon when Vannes attacked.

The blades met twice in a flurry almost too quick to follow, and then Vannes lunged. Jadon deflected, pulled his opponent's arm forward with his free hand, and spun, a bit clumsily, while reversing his sword to strike Vannes's back with the weapon's hilt as the Blood House noble staggered past.

Vannes turned quickly, eyes narrowed. It did not count as a touch. Only an insult.

"Whoops, I suppose I could've had you there," Jadon apologized, staggering for effect as he reassumed the ready position. "I just wasn't expecting you to fall for the same trick I pulled on Lelise."

Fendi chuckled. Vannes spared him a glance, now coolly furious.

Jadon seized the moment to attack, swinging wildly from middle guard. Vannes parried the onslaught with ease but was unable to penetrate Jadon's defenses. Jadon's parries came faster and cleaner than his offensive strikes, which made Diar wonder whether he might be exaggerating his level of drunkenness. Then he tripped while retreating, turned the fall into a graceless roll that barely evaded Vannes's downstroke, and reversed his weapon to deliver a sharp blow to Vannes's sword hand – again with the hilt. Vannes dropped his practice sword and Jadon snatched it up as he regained his feet. He pointed both weapons at Vannes, smiling broadly.

It was just possible, Diar supposed, that Jadon was enough the superior duelist to defeat the Blood House noble while less than fully sober.

"Yield," Jadon suggested, still smiling.

Vannes scowled, his mouth working in frustration. Then he lifted his chin, glancing at their little audience. "Fine.

This match is yours. You will not find it so easy to face me should we cross swords again in the Eshtem Tourney." Still facing Jadon, he reached an arm out to his side – a gesture which mystified Diar until Vannes's friend placed his cloak in his open hand.

Fendi laughed and tossed Jadon his flask. Jadon dropped the practice swords in an attempt to catch it which failed. He chuckled as he bent to pick it up.

"I think you'll not find it so easy to face *him* next time," Fendi told Vannes, still chortling while Vannes put his cloak back on.

Vannes narrowed his eyes and pulled his hood up as he turned away, trying to muster some grace in his defeat. The other Blood House boys fell in behind him.

"Just a minute, now," Jadon said, stopping the initiate with Diar's sword. "I'll take that."

The initiate looked to Vannes, who gave a curt nod before he released the sword, and then the Blood House boys continued toward the arena's exit.

Diar found himself grinning.

Jadon turned to Diar, reversing the Noraani-marked sword to offer it hilt first. "Yours, I think." He frowned. "Your name is… Diar, right?"

Diar was only mildly surprised by Jadon's uncertainty. The Hatreth prince spent almost no time in their shared room. "Yeah. I'm your roommate."

"My roommate!" Jadon laughed. "Fendi! Meet my roommate! His name is Diar and he carries a Noraani-marked sword."

"Enchanted," said Fendi, sketching a clumsy bow in Diar's direction.

"But, Fendi, let me tell you a secret," Jadon said, waving him closer. Fendi started over, tripped, and caught himself on Jadon's shoulder. "All his friends are from Gold Houses," Jadon said in a stage whisper as he steadied his friend, gesturing to Telius, Cardos, and Eridike.

"Have you got a problem with that?" Cardos demanded.

"No, not at all," Jadon assured him. "Well, actually, Diar, here's my problem," he corrected himself, pressing his flask back into Fendi's hands before scooping up one of the practice swords from the ground. He gave it a considering look. "The sword combat trial is coming up fast, and you are not prepared."

"How is that your problem?" Diar asked.

"Because you're my *roommate*," Jadon said, as though this accounted for everything. "Can't have you embarrassing me with a poor showing. Fendi, give us some room, please." He pushed his friend away. "Come here," he told Diar, waving him closer as he assumed the ready position.

"You want to spar with me?"

"Look, we appreciate that you got Diar his sword back," said Telius, moving to stand next to Diar. "But we've had quite enough sparring for today."

"Shame." Jadon considered his practice sword, then glanced at Diar. "Not even one quick bout? In service of your education?"

"To education!" Fendi toasted, moving to take another swallow from his flask. Finding it empty, he turned it upside down to make sure. Then he tossed it to the ground and drank from Jadon's instead.

Jadon slowly moved his practice sword forward. Diar smiled and shook his head, moving Jadon's weapon aside with the Noraani sword. "It's fine," he told Telius, handing off his sword. He picked up the second practice weapon.

"All right, match on!" Fendi cheered. Jadon grinned, striking up gathered thrust low. Diar moved into the ready position as Telius retreated.

"Ready?" Jadon asked.

"Yes." Diar had barely finished the word before Jadon lunged, much as Vannes had, and he felt a moment of shock as he once again barely managed to turn the blow from his body.

Then he found himself, once again, on the ground, disoriented from a blow to the head.

Jadon offered him a hand up. "Thought you said you were ready."

"My mistake," Diar grumbled as he took Jadon's hand and stood.

"You watch the sword," Jadon noted, studying the sword in question with a look of profound contemplation. "Good. But while you watch the sword, you can still see the hand and react. If you don't let the sword consume your attention."

Diar considered the advice. Considering the semi-intoxicated state of the advisor, he was not sure how profitable this lesson was going to be. But if Jadon was sober enough to defeat Vannes, perhaps he still had reasonable things to say. "All right. Ready."

This time he dismissed Jadon's sword from his attention as soon as he moved to block it, and he finally saw the free hand coming in for the punch. He ducked under it. As he straightened, he realized that the tip of Jadon's sword was pressing against his chest.

"Better," said Jadon, withdrawing his weapon. "But you stopped watching the sword. Focusing *too* much on any *one* move will make you miss the next."

"I think your friend here could use some water," Eridike noted, looking at Fendi. The War House boy had finished off both flasks and was now lying on the ground, peering up into the flask he held upside down above him. "Though I don't know if he can make it to the spring."

There was a spring of fresh water a few miles south of campus. Getting there required a hike, as it was lower down in the ravine that separated the campus plateau from the next one over. Ale from the mess hall was easier to come by.

"Pshh," Fendi dismissed him. "Water weak. More brandy..."

"Oh, he'll get there." Jadon handed his practice sword to Telius and hauled Fendi to his feet over his friend's mumbled objections. "Time for a refill." This cheered Fendi considerably. "Since you drank all mine," Jadon added sternly, stooping to pick up the other flask.

"Thought it was a present," Fendi said as the two of them started to leave, Jadon's steps significantly steadier than his friend's.

Jadon stopped as he passed Diar, giving him a considering look. "You know, roomie," he said, tilting his head to one side. "If you're not stuck to the Blood Houses, you should give the Initiative a try. The night before the tourney opens, we'll meet a half-count after curfew in the woods northeast of campus. Bring a girl if you like. Just tell Enna who."

"See you there!" Fendi raised his empty flask in salute, swaying dangerously.

Diar smiled. Though Jadon did drink too much on campus and apparently failed to make note of other people's names, he was hardly the egotistical beast Jenne had made him out to be. He seemed free of the House prejudice and classism that plagued the rest of campus, at least, inviting a lowborn Blood House boy to an Initiative event.

"I'll think about it," he said.

"Don't hurt your head," said Jadon, nodding a few more times than necessary. Turning, he pulled Fendi's arm around his shoulders. "Let's go get that refill," he said, guiding his friend toward the exit.

"Are you really going to think about going with them?" Eridike asked when they were gone. "After curfew?"

"Spitfire, I would go if they invited me," said Cardos. "You really are moving up in life, Diar. Keeping secrets for princesses and getting invitations from princes."

"The party sounds like the kind of thing Jenne might be interested in," Telius noted, a hint of a smile on his lips. "If she can put her hatred of nobles aside."

"Well," said Diar, thinking about it more seriously now, "I don't know who Enna is. That might be an obstacle."

"She's a second-year War House noble," Telius told him. "I can point her out to you some time."

"But you know they're just going to drink hard liquor and spar with each other. Like just now, but *after curfew*. If you were caught, you'd be expelled on sight," Eridike reminded him.

"The War House students do it all the time." Cardos shrugged. "The Drei Masters haven't done anything to stop them yet, so I doubt they'd expel everybody the one time Diar went."

"But they could!" Eridike insisted. "Why risk it?"

Telius was smiling broadly now. "It's only a small risk of getting expelled. And there's a girl involved."

"So, I'll think about it," Diar repeated.

Eridike was right, he knew – it was a bad idea. Going out after curfew was against the rules, and mixing hard drink with sparring sounded irresponsible, unwise, and very far from Diar's idea of a good time.

But Telius was right, too. When Jenne had first told him about the War House Initiative and the noble students who led it, she had wistfully mentioned that it sounded fun. Not that she would want to go, given that the group consisted of Jadon and his highborn friends. *But if she did...*

He did not know what he would decide.

CHAPTER 11

The War House Initiative

It is simple enough to erase the past from matters of public record, but the process of erasing memories from living minds is far more involved. One must use Intuition to connect to the memory in question, Dreaming to visualize where it sits in a map of the mind, Reading to correlate this map to living matter, Projection to wall the memory off, and Resonation to make the mind accept the wall. Prophecy should also be used to prepare the subject's mind for alteration and again to seal the change. Moreover, the living mind is not a static structure, but is constantly shifting and forming new connections. Even the best-made wall cannot guard against some novel stimulus opening a pathway to walled-off material, so it is best to drench everything to be forgotten with an aversive Resonation, discouraging the subject from exploring far if any such back doors are opened.

A talented elf could learn the art through long and careful study, but human Edrei are limited to one talent each. It requires a team of five or six highly skilled human Imagers to accomplish the same. It is no wonder the practice was discontinued soon after the elves departed.

> – From *What We Know of the Elves*,
> written for the records of the Eshtem Library
> by Drei Master Legreve

Jenne kept wondering about Diar's mysterious conference with Christina all afternoon. Her distraction earned her a demerit in Master Tamar's class, and it took all her self-control to keep from tracking him down at the arena afterward instead of studying ethics as she had planned. It helped that she shared her last class of the day with Liana, who also needed to study ethics and was somehow able to keep Jenne on task.

She could hardly wait to get back to the mess hall for dinner. She was early, but most of her other friends showed up before Diar did. Cardos, Eridike, and Telius tripped all over one another in their haste to tell the girls about Diar's reluctant sparring match with Vannes to'Jinn and how it had somehow ended with an invitation from Jadon to a post-curfew War House Initiative party.

When Diar finally arrived, he announced that he had decided against it.

"It's not like you to say no to a noble," Jenne quipped, still determined to get to the bottom of the Christina matter.

"Oh, please, Christina's being a noble had nothing to do with what she wanted to talk about," Diar returned. "And before you ask, I can't tell you what it was. I promised not to tell anyone."

"Are you sure her being noble had nothing to do with her *asking* you not to tell anyone?" Jenne pressed. If Christina was taking advantage of Diar, she doubted he would recognize it.

"Yes. In fact, she didn't even really ask me to do that. I offered."

"Why?" Jenne was perplexed. Diar seemed far too eager to serve Christina, just as he had been in Lystra. Besides being noble, Christina seemed like a generally disagreeable person, so if Diar did not feel some misguided obligation to her, Jenne did not understand it.

Unless it was just that Christina was pretty.

"Come on." Diar gave her an impatient look. "You know I can't answer that. I'm sure that if I could explain the whole situation to you, you wouldn't worry about her exercising any undue influence."

Jenne pursed her lips, still dissatisfied. If Diar had really sworn himself to secrecy, though, there was no use in pursuing the matter any further. She would not really want him to break his word, anyway. An oath was an oath and ought to be respected as such, no matter the circumstances under which it was given.

"Back to this Initiative party," Elophine said after a moment. "You're really not going to go?"

Diar sighed, glancing at Jenne while the others started arguing about whether he had made the right decision. Jenne looked back at him, and he dropped his gaze to his trencher, suddenly seeming interested in his food. She narrowed her eyes, puzzled by this reaction, but she refocused on the conversation when Telius let slip that Jadon had said Diar could bring a girl to the Initiative party. She started smiling.

Jenne had no fondness for Jadon or any of his War House friends, but she was not one to pass up an excuse for a little daredevilry and excitement. "I think you should go," she told Diar.

"You do?" Diar narrowed his eyes. "Why? Would you want to break campus rules with a bunch of War House nobles we don't like, who certainly don't like us?"

Jenne shrugged and fluttered her eyelashes. "I wouldn't say no if you asked me."

Diar shook his head, grinning. "Well, I suppose I can spare one night for poor choices."

At least Christina didn't make him smile like that.

* * *

Campus was covered in a light layer of snow the night a girl came to collect Jenne from her dorm for the Initiative party. They exited the building together by way of a first-floor window. None of the windows in the east complex were barred, as they were in the west complex, and there were no shards of glass atop the east complex wall. Not all the girls invited to the Initiative hangout were strong enough to climb the vine unaided, though, and it was slippery and wet with snow, so when Jenne and her guide joined the rest of the invitees outside, she saw that they were using a rope. Under the direction of two upperclassmen, they tied each climber to the girl who had reached the top before her so each could use the other's body weight to aid her climb or descent.

Two girls named Kerci and Cyla elected not to wait their turn in line for the rope. They climbed over the wall unaided, and after a moment, Jenne did likewise.

They were disappearing into the forest when Jenne reached the far side, and she hurried after them, using the noise of their passage and what she could see of their tracks in the snow to guide her. The moon was full and bright tonight, and that helped. When the trees thinned enough to allow a view of the canyon, she caught sight of Kerci, who was crossing a fallen tree that spanned the gap. Cyla had already gained the far side.

Kerci turned her head as Jenne emerged from the forest, meeting her gaze.

"You should wait for the others," Kerci called. "They'll use the rope to make the crossing safer."

Jenne approached the fallen tree, looking down into the canyon as Kerci continued across. The drop to the river was only fifty or so lengths here.

She stepped onto the tree. It was snowy and a bit slippery, but underneath, the wood felt solid. Bringing her other foot onto the makeshift bridge, she crouched to keep her center of gravity low and continued after Kerci.

Kerci smiled back at her before she and Cyla disappeared into the woods on the next plateau. Jenne followed, and soon they reached a clearing where nearly threescore War House boys were talking and drinking around a fire.

Cyla and Kerci's entrance was greeted with whistles and catcalls. The two girls threw themselves into cartwheels and a series of back handsprings that set their cloaks whirling and ended with the girls' heels mere inches from the fire. Some of the boys cheered and tossed them flasks, which the girls caught neatly and chugged. They threw the flasks to the ground to general applause.

Jenne hung back by the trees, wondering if she would need to replicate the stunt. She thought she could, but perhaps it was just Cyla and Kerci's thing.

"Jenne!" Diar appeared at her side and offered her a hand. "Shall we join the party?"

Jenne smiled. "By all means."

Diar lifted her hand as though they were courtiers and led her to the fire, where they stood for a moment, taking in its warmth. Jenne glanced sideways at him, smiling.

"What are *you* doing here?"

Jenne turned at the question, releasing Diar's hand. She recognized Perleyon.

Oh, sights. She smiled up at him, remembering their last encounter in Lystra. His same two friends – Dreck and

Haf – were with him. At least they were all equals now, and the War House boys had lost the advantage of their horses.

"Jadon invited us," Diar told them, crossing his arms.

"Jadon! You invited these dynacombs?" Dreck called across the fire to where the Hatreth prince was chatting with Fendi. Jadon looked at them and shrugged.

"Still a skinflint," Jenne corrected.

"Flames of the Abyss, but yeah," said Fendi, raising his flask in salute as he and Jadon made their way over. "I think he did. We might have been less than sober at the time."

"Less than sober?" Jadon challenged. "*I* was less than sober. You, my friend, were thoroughly intoxicated."

Perleyon regarded Diar and Jenne coldly. "There, you see? You are not War House-sworn, and your presence is not welcome. I suggest you hurry back to the dorms before the Drei Masters discover you missing."

"Easy, Perleyon." Another voice interrupted before Jenne had a chance to grow very angry. The speaker was taller than the other boys and broader of shoulder, with an air that was both more laid-back and more commanding than Perleyon's. His hair was dark brown, but his eyes were light blue, and they fixed Jenne and Diar with an amused gaze. Unlike the other boys, he wore his own cloak and clothing rather than the standard Eshtem issue – a right reserved for upperclassmen, Jenne guessed. She had seen him around campus before, and Telius had told her he was Rindarin tu'Rithadur, heir to the Rithadur High Seat. "Any friends of Jadon's are welcome here. As much liquor as that man imbibes, I'd be surprised if he met anyone while sober." Rindarin gave Jadon a measured look, then handed Diar the flask he carried. "Drink up. And welcome to the War House Initiative."

The other girls were beginning to arrive, and Rindarin walked off to greet them.

"You know, it's the funniest thing," said Perleyon, his gaze returning to Jenne and Diar. It had not softened. "That book I bought from you in Lystra. It was stolen from my bedside table later that same night. And in its place, the thief left three copper coins."

Jenne smiled at Perleyon and fluttered her eyelashes. "The idea. Someone took such a valuable and important book and left only *three copper coins* in its place?"

Perleyon's eyes narrowed further. "Haf, how much did you leave them in exchange for the book?"

"Seven sights of the Six's beloved." Fendi's gaze was arrested on one of the newly arrived girls. "Is that *Trista*? Who is *she* here with?"

"If you'll excuse me, gentlemen," Dreck said, clapping Fendi on the shoulder, "I've got a date. And I believe three of you owe me money." He jogged off toward Trista, dropping into an elaborate bow when he reached her and offering his arm. Jadon, Fendi, and Haf followed more slowly, exchanging looks of amazement when Trista took the offered arm. After shooting Jenne one more dark glance, Perleyon moved off to join them.

"And Trista is here, too, of all people. How about that?" Diar looked back at Jenne and lowered his voice. "Jenne, did you steal that book from Perleyon's bedside table? That's the copy we've been using?"

"You're welcome." She smiled as his eyes widened. "Did you want me to let him keep it?"

"Seven sights, Jenne. And now we're showing up to a party with *his* group of friends?" Diar shook his head. "You left him his three coppers? I guess I can stop worrying about how to repay you."

"I told you you didn't have to do that, silly," Jenne chided. "But bringing me here would have been more than enough repayment in any case." She winked. "We're not here for them."

"Oh?" Diar smiled back, his gaze intent. "Why are we here, then?"

Jenne tilted her head, her eyes full of mischief. Diar could have brought her here for only one reason, but now was not yet the time. "Let's try whatever this is." She took the flask that Rindarin had given Diar, drank, and passed it back. It had a pleasant burn to it.

"You are a terrible influence, you know that, Jenne?" Diar took a sip and sputtered.

She giggled. "You've never had hard liquor before, have you? You're cute."

"It's not against the Principles, but the White Way doesn't exactly encourage it." Diar took another sip and frowned. "Did you call me cute? I think you meant dashing."

"I'm certain I meant cute."

"Ladies and gentlemen!" Rindarin called, drawing everyone's attention. "Initiative and guests. As you know, the first-years' first combat trial begins tomorrow, and it is none other than the famed Eshtem Tourney. The tourney will determine the first set of rankings published in the Eshtem Lists and subject the first-year class to its first round of systematic cuts. In recognition of this, and to help them prepare, tonight we graduate our tenderfeet to full-fledged Initiative members through our own combat trial.

"The first two combatants will be chosen by lot from our assembly of tenderfeet, who will fight to three touches with practice swords. Winner stays on. Loser..." He held up a wooden goblet. Setting it on a tree stump near the fire, he filled it with brandy from a flask he was carrying. "...drinks." The boys hooted in response. "When all the first-years have fought, the standing victor may challenge an upperclassman. Then we will transition into exhibition matches, for which anyone may challenge anyone. Afterward, any of our female guests who wish to participate in their own tourney may do so." Cyla and Kerci whooped. "Same rules apply.

"So then, first-year boys, approach Chase and draw your straws. The two short straws fight first. Let the games begin!"

Rindarin bowed as cheers broke out. Diar and Jenne watched as Chase made his way around the first-year boys, offering straws.

"So, this really is all about drinking hard liquor and sparring with each other," Diar noted. Most of the boys carried their own flasks, and they were not waiting to lose in the mock tourney to start drinking.

Perleyon stopped by them on his way to take a straw. "If you intend to remain here, Noraani-sworn, you had better participate. I trust you would not impose yourself upon this gathering and then deny us the honor of facing you in combat."

"Wouldn't dream of it," Diar said with a tight smile. Perleyon continued past them, and Diar sighed. "Guess I'd better go get a straw."

"I guess you'd better," Jenne agreed. Her own smile was quite genuine. "It'll be great practice for the tourney."

"You mean for the part when we chug large goblets full of brandy to avoid elimination?"

Jenne laughed, pushing him in Chase's direction. "Go get a straw, Noraani-sworn."

"Anything for you, kind mistress." Diar bowed with a little flourish and dutifully went to draw.

Jenne smiled as she watched him go. He did have his dashing moments.

He came back without a short straw, but he groaned when the first two initiates entered the impromptu dueling ring. "Oh, no. They're taking their cloaks off."

"They are a little cumbersome for fighting, don't you think?" Jenne asked.

"No. I think it would definitely be worth it to keep them on."

Diar did not draw a short straw until they were a dozen matches in, and despite his proclamation, he did take his cloak off and hand it to Jenne before he went into the ring. Dreck had just defeated a taller, bulkier War House boy by the name of Hectibald, and he went on to make embarrassingly short work of Diar. Diar chugged the brandy in the goblet handed to him like a champion, though, and made it most of the way back to Jenne before it hit him.

She hurried over to assist as he staggered away from the ring, dangerously near the fire.

"You were right, Jenne. It's not so bad. Kind of grows on you. Whew. Am I drunk now?"

"Possible, but unlikely," Jenne told him, laughing as she helped him put his cloak back on. This was a side of Diar she had not seen before. "There probably weren't more than four shots in there."

"But I feel it's affecting me."

"Yeah, that would be enough to affect you. Want some more?" Jenne offered the flask Rindarin had given them, curious.

Diar took another sip and made a face. "*Such* a bad influence."

"Who do you think will win the next match?" Jenne asked. Dreck was getting ready to face a boy named Wrayland. Jenne smiled, gesturing to the brandy. "Pick wrong and you drink. Pick right and I will."

"Spectrum's spitfire. War House culture is really rubbing off on you, isn't it?"

"You said yourself, it's not so bad."

"Fine, then, I accept. And I choose Dreck. It will salve my pride if he turns out to be better than most of these guys."

Dreck won the next match easily. And the next. And the next. Then Jadon drew the short straw.

"Looks like Dreck is pretty good," Jenne noted. "How's your pride feeling?"

"Somewhat salved. And it would be *so* salved if it turns out he can beat Jadon."

"You staying with Dreck, then? Or are you going to switch?"

"I'm staying."

"You are so cute." Jenne chuckled, shaking her head at Diar's ignorance. He had seen Jadon beat Vannes while drunk, but he must have failed to deduce that Jadon was a dueling prodigy. Dreck never stood a chance against him, though the match turned out to be closer than Jenne expected, at three touches to two.

"Staying or switching?" Diar asked as the next short straw was drawn by Perleyon.

"Oh, I'm staying," said Jenne. "Prepare yourself to be drinking for a while. They say Jadon's really good at this."

"Maybe he's not as good as they say."

Diar's hypothesis came to nothing as match after match went to Jadon. Eventually he was the last first-year standing.

"Let's give it up for Jadon, champion of the tenderfeet!" Rindarin saluted him, and a ragged cheer broke out among the assembled War House boys. "Now, for the symbolic graduation of your class to full-fledged Initiative members, to whom among the upperclassmen would you like to issue your challenge?"

Jadon smiled, raising his sword. "Let's make this a symbolic contest between the first- and second-year classes, shall we?" Some of the first-years hooted in appreciation. "I challenge the reigning champion of the second-years, Rindarin himself!" More cheers.

Rindarin narrowed his eyes, displeased. But all he said was, "Very well. Chase, if you would take over the judging duties?"

"Staying or switching?" Diar asked Jenne as Rindarin took off his cloak and retrieved the other practice sword.

Jenne chewed her lower lip. Jadon was good, but he had been drinking more than Rindarin. Rindarin had already proven himself to be the best of the second-year class by winning the Eshtem Tourney the year before. And she really wanted to see Jadon lose. "Switching."

"Ha, finally!" Diar exulted. "Get ready to drink, darling."

She glanced over at him, amused.

Thus far, Jadon had been openly drinking between matches, but any unsteadiness Jenne thought she had detected in his gait disappeared as he squared off against Rindarin. His tolerance must have been remarkably high.

They closed, and Jenne realized after they traded a half-dozen hits that she had chosen wrong. Rindarin had the advantage of reach and was, perhaps, stronger, but Jadon was faster and had the superior technique. The first bout ended in a touch for Jadon.

"What did I tell you?" Diar gloated as Jenne huffed in annoyance. "This has got your name written all over it." He jiggled the flask. There was still a decent amount of brandy left.

Jadon scored the second touch as well. Rindarin's expression was darker when they closed for the third bout. It ended in a double touch, which Chase judged a three-to-one victory for Jadon.

Jenne took the flask from Diar and drank.

Rindarin picked up the wooden goblet from the tree stump and raised it to Jadon. "An engaging match. The Initiative salutes your graduation." His smile did not reach his eyes. He downed the goblet while the onlookers cheered. Jadon bowed, clearly enjoying himself.

"For our first exhibition match," Rindarin announced, refilling the goblet on the tree stump, "would anyone care to challenge our newly minted champion?" He was looking, Jenne noticed, at the taller Entaren cousin, Alaxis.

"Sure," said Alaxis. "I'll knock him down a notch or two."

"We'll see about that, shall we?" Jadon lifted his practice sword.

"Staying or switching?" Jenne asked Diar.

"Staying." She was not surprised by his confidence. "And let's say loser finishes off the flask," he added. That part was a surprise.

"Now who's the bad influence?" Jenne nudged him with her shoulder, grinning. "Remember, the tourney starts tomorrow. We'll want our wits about us for whenever we see whatever it is that Liana thinks we're going to see."

"But *you* didn't think it would show up until the last day. Remember? And since I've already had so much… it's only fair, don't you think?"

"All right," Jenne agreed, stepping closer to Diar as she turned her attention to Jadon and Alaxis. Diar took her hand again, and she let him keep it.

The first bout was over almost before it began.

"One for Alaxis," Rindarin counted. He was smiling smugly.

"Whoa," Jenne said, squeezing Diar's hand. "You might be in trouble, cutie."

"Come on, Jadon," Diar encouraged. "Don't let me down now."

The second bout lasted longer but also ended in a touch for Alaxis. Diar groaned, and Jenne giggled. She had not known Alaxis had Reading magic, but watching him fight, she decided he must. His movements were too perfect to explain otherwise.

"I thought Rindarin was the best of the second-years," Diar grumbled.

"No, Alaxis has always been the best of his class." This comment came from Chase, who was standing close enough to overhear. "And mine. And yours, too, it looks like."

"But didn't Rindarin fight someone else in the final round of the Eshtem Tourney?" Jenne asked, curious. Alaxis could not have been as good the year before as he was now, since his magic must have grown in the meantime. If he had always been the best among the second-years, though, it was odd that he had not done better in the tourney. "What happened to Alaxis?"

"He got sick when the tourney started." Chase frowned. "Just a cold, it seemed, but he grew steadily worse, and by the seventh day he could barely stand. Lost to some nobody. When the tourney was over, he fully recovered."

They fell silent as the third bout began. Jadon held his own this time and managed to sneak in a touch, but Alaxis finished him off in the fourth.

Jenne laughed. "Drink up, loser," she told Diar. He made a face, releasing her hand so he could finish off their supply of brandy.

"Guess the crown goes back to the second-years," Jadon announced. He swayed on his feet as he made his way over to the wooden goblet. "It was nice while it lasted." He slurred this phrase a little, and some of the upperclassmen jeered. Jadon lifted the goblet, saluting Alaxis. He looked at Rindarin before he drank. He took no more than a swallow before he dissolved into a coughing fit, spitting most of it back up.

There were more jeers.

"And now he can't even hold his liquor!" Dreck complained, walking toward him. "Jadon, you're making our class look bad. Give me that." He took the goblet and finished it off, a few of his classmates cheering him.

"I'm sorry, I can do better." Jadon took a few unbalanced steps toward the onlookers. "Who has a full flask?"

Somebody tossed him one, and he chugged it until it was empty, shaking it upside down to demonstrate that there was nothing left. Then he bowed and tossed the flask back where it had come from. "All right, Rindarin, what's next?"

Rindarin, Jenne noticed, had fixed Jadon with a dark expression. It took him a moment to shake it off and respond. "Now any of our female guests who wish to participate in their own tourney may. Approach Chase for straws."

Diar patted Jenne's shoulder. "'S only fair," he mumbled. Jenne grinned.

There were only a handful of girls interested. Jenne bested two of them before losing to Remni, a third-year. It was obvious to Jenne as soon as their swords crossed that Remni, like Alaxis, had Reading magic, but the defeat vexed her anyway. *I used to be faster than this*, Jenne was sure. Her movements felt sluggish and strange – but then again, she had been drinking. If not for that, she was confident she could have beaten the older girl.

As it was, Remni went on to win their little tourney. She chose to challenge Dreck from among the boys, who by this point was having trouble standing upright. Jenne noticed that Rindarin flirted with Trista while they fought. Apparently, the Gold House girl had lost interest in her intoxicated date.

"You want to ditch these bloodhounds?" she asked Diar while they watched Remni beat Dreck. Jenne's face was flushed, and only partly from the brandy she had downed after losing.

They had put in plenty of time at the party, and Jenne was ready to give Diar her full attention.

"I'd say 's about time," Diar agreed. He wobbled as he took a step in the direction of the woods, and he put an arm around Jenne's shoulders to steady himself.

"Still think I'm a terrible influence?" she asked as she began leading him toward the woods. It had started snowing sometime during the mock tourney, and she snuggled closer to Diar for warmth as they left the heat of the bonfire behind, his arm still around her shoulders.

"The abs'lute *worst*," Diar agreed. "But that 'laxis. He was so *fast*. And so *tall*. It was incred'ble. Have we got–" He hiccupped. "S'more brandy?"

"No, Diar, you drank it all," Jenne reminded him. "And I think you're quite drunk enough already, wouldn't you agree?"

"Thought you said I wasn't drunk yet!"

She laughed. "That was *before* you finished the rest of the brandy, brainless."

Diar stumbled over a fallen branch. They had reached the seclusion of the woods, with the sounds of the party now distant in the background, and Jenne let his fall pull them both to the ground, giggling.

Her laughter trailed off as she noticed he was staring at her, their faces inches apart as they sat on their knees on the forest floor.

"You're beautiful." Diar blinked, utterly sincere.

Jenne smiled, entranced by his gaze. She had been careful with him, until now. Flirting was always fun, and so was the give and take of being pursued, but she had not intended to let her guard down. He was the kind of boy that could break her heart, and she had no interest in finding herself heartbroken.

But now, looking back into his deep brown eyes, feeling the whole of his attention focused on her and remembering how he had barely glanced at any other girl since they met, Jenne felt it would be safe to relax her defenses, just a little. She leaned closer, and after a moment's hesitation, Diar kissed her. She kissed him back. In a moment they were stretched out against the ground, her hands reaching to remove his cloak and then his tunic.

He covered her hands with his, stopping her. "Wait," he gasped between kisses.

"You don't have to worry," Jenne said, pressing her body against his. "I won't get pregnant." She kissed him deeper.

"No, wait," he insisted, pushing her away. "Stop."

Jenne sat up, breaking all contact between them. "What?"

"Whew." Diar sat up, too, scooting back to maintain space between them, though he was breathing heavily and he looked as though space was the last thing he wanted. "'M sorry, Jenne." He rubbed his forehead with one hand, as though trying to sober himself up. "Didn't mean t' give you the wrong idea. This…" He waved a hand to indicate the whole situation. "I can't do this. Not just because of… I mean, even if you don't… sights. Get pregnant."

Jenne leaned back on her hands and tried to keep all emotion off her face and out of her voice. "You mean you don't want to."

"No… I mean, yes, I mean…" Diar knocked his head against the tree behind him, upset with himself. "Not *now*. Not like this. 'S not… right. Not–"

"I get it. I'm fine to look at, but not to touch." Jenne stood up, brushing pine needles off her hands. She had thought he really liked her. *When will I stop going for the good boys?* She needed to restrict her fun to men who were shallow and emotionally unavailable. There was a lesser chance of getting hurt that way. "You have standards." *Just like Akarlis.*

Jenne blinked, surprised by the thought and the wash of half-remembered pain it inspired. For a moment, she remembered Akarlis. He had been fair-skinned, but no less tall or beautiful. She remembered rejection. Then she returned to brushing pine needles off her clothes, pushing the memory back into whatever dark, forsaken corner of her consciousness it had escaped from. She did not want to know the rest.

"No…" Diar frowned, searching her eyes. She had puzzled him. "'S not like that. It's–"

"Fine then, Diar." She was not about to wait on a drunk to figure out how to explain himself. "We'll say now is not the right time."

"But really, Jenne. 'S not you. It's the Principles."

The words ran off Jenne like rain off an oiled leather coat. "Of course. You're Rishara, Rishara-ahn, whatever. I can respect that. Let's get you back to your dorm."

Jenne knew enough about religious men to know that if Diar had truly wanted her, he would not have stopped himself, no matter what his Principles were. She had misread him; she was not his type. Perhaps he genuinely thought he liked her – but his mind would eventually catch up to what his body had already told her, and she knew better than to wait around for more rejection.

She gave him a tight-lipped smile. Feeling like a martyr, she took his hand and helped him rise. He was in no state to find his way back to campus by himself, and despite what had just passed between them, she was not about to let him get caught out alone after curfew.

Getting Diar back across the tree bridge to the next plateau was no easy task, and it did not help that the snow was coming down faster and Jenne's mood had soured. She managed to keep him from falling, though, and after that, walking him to the west complex was easy. It was not until they stood looking up at its vine-covered walls, Diar's arm around her shoulders with her supporting most of his weight, that she realized how much trouble they were in. He was not getting over that wall by himself, and even if he could do it with her help, she had no idea where his room was, and he was not going to be any help in finding it.

"Your hair smells nice." Diar, still leaning on her, took in a deep breath, oblivious to their current problems. Jenne turned his face away from hers with the hand she was not using to support him, ignoring this comment as she had all those that preceded it.

"Chroming, self-obsessed, Six-forsaken son of a high prince," she mumbled to herself, finding Jadon a convenient target to blame for their predicament. He had invited them, after all. He had invited them, ignored them the entire time, and was nowhere to be found when his roommate could use his help.

"Is that my roommate you've got there?"

Jenne started and turned. Jadon had emerged from the forest.

"Keep it down!" she hissed. "There could be Drei Masters around."

"Jadon!" Diar's greeting was louder than Jadon's question. "Alaxis was very *fast*, did you see? You were good, too," he added as an afterthought.

Jadon came closer, smiling. "Thanks, roomie." He took one of Diar's arms and pulled it around his shoulders, nodding to Jenne. "Run along. I'll take it from here."

Jenne scoffed. "You've drunk at least twice as much as he has. I doubt you can make it over the wall yourself."

"Appearances can be deceiving, my little blonde book thief." Jadon's brown eyes glinted with moonlight as he studied her, his expression unreadable.

"'S what they say," Diar agreed, nodding too many times as he let go of Jenne and patted her shoulder. "It's the boys' complex, you can't come with us."

Jadon chuckled and pulled out a flask, offering it to Diar. "Drink some of this."

"Are you serious?" Jenne objected, intercepting the flask.

"Relax." Jadon sighed. "This one's water."

Jenne took a sip. He was not lying. She handed it to Diar, who made a face. "Water?"

"Drink it," she told him, and he did.

Jenne frowned at Jadon. Somehow, the fact that he was not as drunk as he had made himself seem only made her more upset. "Not that I would expect you to know or care, but my *name* is Jenne."

"Everyone knows your name, Jenne. Even me. Now, honestly, we're good here."

"Good here, Jenne," Diar echoed. He burped.

She frowned at him, then turned to narrow her eyes at Jadon. "If he gets in any trouble for this, I'm holding you responsible." She turned to go.

"That's two you owe me, book thief."

She turned back, indignant. "I think you mean that's one less *you* owe *him*." If Diar hadn't been waking Jadon whenever he slept through the morning bell, he surely would have missed class by now and been expelled. "And how in the name of Xanthinus would it make two?"

"You think I pretended not to notice that you called me a Hatreth in front of our entire politics class for my own sake?"

Jenne opened her mouth to retort. Then she remembered their first day. She had indeed branded him with his House name. Master Porrian had nearly expelled her. *But Jadon was just taking the opportunity to make a smart-alecky comment…* She closed her mouth.

"You have a good night." Jadon smiled.

Finding herself without an appropriate comeback, Jenne walked away. She did not turn around when Diar called goodbye.

* * *

Jenne slept very little after making it back to her dorm, her mind constantly returning to moments she did not want to revisit. The heat of Diar's mouth against hers, the press of his touch. His rejection. Akarlis.

Somehow, feelings about that other boy – whoever he was – had become entangled with her recent experience, and it pulled Jenne's attention toward something she wanted to ignore even more than her hurt feelings: her lost memories. She did not want to know why or how she had forgotten everything about her life before that day in Lystra. Even just acknowledging to herself that it had happened made her feel sick with dread and anxious to escape into any other line of thinking – but that brought her back to Diar. Which led to Akarlis. Which led right back to the missing memories, in a circle as inescapable as it was vicious.

So, she rose early. No one else was awake. In fact, the main door of her building was still locked when she left her room. The locks were on some kind of magical timer that started at curfew and ended some time before breakfast – not this long before breakfast, apparently – so Jenne left through her dorm room window and climbed over the east complex wall, the process made only a little harder by the fast-falling snow. She followed the main walkway that circled campus and took the branch that broke away to the east, not really thinking about where she was going until she reached a sign standing in the middle of the walkway. By the light of the moon and stars, she was just able to make out the text:

INITIATES PERMITTED NO FARTHER
WITHOUT SPECIAL AUTHORIZATION

A few spans past the sign, the walkway ended in a gate set in a wall that much resembled the east complex. The residences of the Drei Masters were behind that wall.

So was the landing ground for dragons.

Jenne paced to the edge of the walkway and took a good look at the wall, her feet just even with the boundary demarcated by the sign. If she was caught one inch farther east, she would surely be expelled. Even standing here was a risk, given that she was still supposed to be locked in her dorm for curfew.

But the landing ground was tantalizingly near, and she knew that dragons would be using it today. The Master Imagers had probably been using it on and off all year, but true to Liana's prediction, Jenne had yet to catch sight of anyone coming or going. Today, though, was the first day of the Eshtem Tourney. That meant the tourney proctors would be flying in, and their arrivals might not be as circumspect as the Master Imagers'.

It would be incredibly stupid for Jenne to risk her very real chance of being able to train with dragons one day just to catch a glimpse of the creatures now.

But she wanted to see a dragon.

I don't have to be stupid about this, she told herself, striking out from the walkway toward the edge of the nearby forest. The snow was falling fast enough that most of her footprints had already been covered, and the rest should be by the time any masters left their residences. She kept a straight line to the north, straying no closer to the wall. Some of those trees were tall enough that she might be able to see over it without technically violating the boundary.

Jenne's excitement grew as she climbed up one of the pine trees. The needles scratched at her face and her uniform, and she was practically soaked from the snow now, but she didn't care. She hastened toward the top and nestled into a perch near the trunk that let her peer over the wall, her view partially obstructed by the outer branches as she waited for something to happen, all thoughts of Diar and her lost memories forgotten.

Past the wall, she could make out a row of cottages. The walkway continued past the gate, splitting the row in two, and ended in an empty stretch of snow-covered ground that ran to the edge of the plateau.

There was more than enough room for a dragon to land there.

The bells of the north tower sounded the wake-up call, nearly startling Jenne from her perch. Then the muffled sounds of opening doors reached her, and soon she could make out the forms of three black-robed masters moving outside the cottages.

Jenne eased herself lower in the tree, disappointed that they had made their appearance before any dragons. She could not afford to stay here much longer. Some of the masters were Imagers, and if they happened to cast their magically enhanced senses about, they might discover her in her hiding spot, even with the wall blocking their view. They might not expel her, now that the bells had sounded the end of curfew and considering that she had purposefully stayed on the safe side of the sign that cordoned off the area.

But they might. It was obvious she was out here to catch a glimpse of something she wasn't supposed to see, and they wouldn't look kindly on that.

Jenne had almost convinced herself to climb down and go back to her dorm when she heard it: a gentle whooshing sound.

The sound of enormous wings?

Jenne's gaze jerked up and eastward, but she could not see past the wall from her new position, and above it, the sky was still moonlit and empty of dragons. She bit her lip and reached up with her hand, determined to risk one more glance over the wall.

Fernuala, nimlyr.

The words froze Jenne in place. She was not sure if she had heard them or thought them – but why would she think them? She did not even know what language they were from, but after her initial confusion, she realized she did know what they meant: *I see you, human.*

Her eyes grew wide, and she whispered back under her breath, "Who are you?"

Lathnaurest, the voice responded, and it was a command: *Flee.*

Jenne shimmied down the tree and took to her heels, obeying the voice at pace. She did not slow until she reached the main campus walkway, and a grin spread across her face.

She may not have seen a dragon yet – but she was fairly sure she had spoken to one.

CHAPTER 12

The Eshtem Tourney

Ellyrians love to keep score. Not only does every educational institution and professional guild routinely calculate and publish rankings for each of its members relative to every other – the most famous example of this being the Eshtem Lists – but the Ellyrians have also managed to systematize the very notion of "honor." All the ways of gaining and losing what they call "points of honor" are enumerated in that extensive and inscrutable document, *The Ellyrian Code*. They keep track of the points of honor won and lost by each House through a system involving post riders, scribes, and the Edrei Order, but it seems impossible that every transfer of points by every member of every House could be reported in a timely manner. Yet every quarter, they release an updated version of the "House listings," the master record in Helos purporting to measure exactly that.

> – From *Ellyrian Culture*, penned for the
> annals of the Lussonne by Guizarre Arus

The sword combat trial for first-year initiates, or the "Eshtem Tourney," as it was more commonly called, was one of the most anticipated national affairs of each year. Initiates were expected to lay aside their House affiliations, but Houses did not relinquish their claims on their students. The House listings in Helos were heavily affected by points of honor students won at the tourney. Since true dueling had fallen out of style, the contest was one of the few remaining ways to determine which of Ellyrian's Houses' sons were best with the sword.

Currently, Rithadur held the distinction of First House. Jinn, Entaren, and Ilsad were in close contention. Of these, only Jinn had a promising contestant in the tourney this year: Vannes to'Jinn. Many Houses that were a little lower in the listings, such as Tarix, Sendell, and Hatreth, hoped to displace the leaders.

The distinction of First House was largely symbolic, but it was highly coveted. Every trueborn Ellyrian smiled to see his House move higher in the listings, and, rare though dueling had become, quarrels still sometimes turned deadly where House honor was involved. Ellyrians were nothing if not fiercely loyal to their clans, and they relished every opportunity for their Houses to compete.

One would never know it by surveying the Eshtem campus the day the tourney began. First-year classes were canceled to accommodate the tourney schedule, but initiates not participating in the early rounds were busy, either still honing their sparring technique or studying for final interrogations. Excepting the last day of the competition, which took place on a Seventhday, the tourney was not a holiday on campus.

The real celebrations took place in Helos, the nation's capital, where Ellyrians gathered all week to watch reenactments based on the blow-by-blow reporting delivered over the communication system that linked the Eshtem Arena to the War Games Coliseum. The elves had designed the link to facilitate quick communication between the Drei Masters and the Senate in times of emergency, but its entertainment value the week of the tourney had since become its primary utility. Helos was jammed with nobles and commoners alike, and drinking, betting, and celebrations would carry on all week long. Every year, jeers and insults were exchanged, and fights broke out among the commonborn when matches at Eshtem resolved in undesired outcomes. Sometimes these fights escalated into full-scale riots that the Helos Watch, the Senate guard, and Edrei peacekeeping forces combined were hard-pressed to control. But such things were a small price to pay for citizens to come together every year and remind themselves that they were Ellyrians.

Christina was aware of all this, and she knew she was the only initiate Noraan had had in the Eshtem Tourney in over a hundred years. Try as she might to remind herself that, as an Eshtem initiate, she should not trouble herself over Noraan's place in the House listings, she could not help but think of the Noraani who might be cheering for her in Helos this week. There would not be many of them, and those who were there would probably be more interested in the performance of the sons of other Blood Houses than they would be in her own. Female participants in the tourney had precious little impact on the House listings, after all. They never won, and most years none of them finished within the top one hundred.

Christina was determined to do well, all the same. So far, the Lists had yet to reveal Hezred's former name, and Christina was beginning to wonder if it had somehow been removed from the Lussonne's copies as well. She and Nefry had a few years left to check. Even if they found the name, though, there was no guarantee it would lead to definitive answers, and Christina had grown discouraged. Training with the sword was a welcome distraction.

She had asked Vannes and his friends to work with her in the weeks leading up to the competition. Vannes thought she should practice with other girls, but Christina was convinced sparring with partners as skilled as possible was the fastest way to improve. The boys were willing to indulge her. They did not fight to their full ability when they faced her, but it was enough to press her, and since they all thought of it as more of a lesson than a contest, she received much advice.

It was a headache to be constantly patronized by her opponents, made even worse as she lost to each of them time after time. Eventually, she was forced to recognize that she was hopelessly outmatched by all of them. It did not matter how many watches she put into perfecting her technique, nor that she had devoted so many years to mastering dance, which allegedly involved a similar skill set. Her blows remained weaker than theirs, her footwork slower, and her stamina less. Not to mention the boys had all been training with the sword for years. Master Halce had taught them only the basics of swordplay; it was not enough to give beginners a chance against students who had trained all their lives. For Christina, doubly disadvantaged by inferior training and the physical limitations of her sex, practicing with Vannes and his friends was like throwing herself at a brick wall. She eventually lost hope that winning the tourney – or even finishing in the top one hundred – was possible for her.

Nevertheless, she met with Vannes and his friends for another practice session at dawn on the first day of the tourney, before the arena was closed for the competition. It had snowed heavily the night before, but the Eshtem staff must have started shoveling well before dawn, because most of the ground had already been cleared of snow by the time she arrived.

Vannes was in a mood. Because Halce had arranged the matches so that more skilled students would not compete until the later rounds, Vannes would not enter the tourney until the seventh day, but he would be one of those to feel the pressure most acutely.

This made him impatient in his practice with Christina. His attacks came faster and harder than usual, and she quickly gave ground. She thought she was matching his strokes well until he suddenly stopped, and Christina realized she had backed out of their dueling circle. This counted as a touch for her opponent.

Vannes was shaking his head. "You should never retreat for so long, circle or no circle. Don't let your opponent control your position."

Christina nodded and fell into the ready position. Vannes came at her again. This time she turned out of the way of his thrust and tried to press an attack of her own, but he dodged neatly and brought his weapon around to tap her on the shoulder.

"Better. And a girl's attacks wouldn't come this fast anyway."

"Assuming I can best the girls, I'll have to face a boy eventually," she reminded him.

He shrugged. "By then, you'd have already done extremely well for yourself. Everyone loses eventually. Everyone but the champion."

Christina narrowed her eyes, tired of the implication that she was wasting her time.

"Again," she said, raising her practice sword.

Vannes shrugged and attacked. After trading just a few blows, Christina missed a parry and gasped in pain as his strike connected with her ribs.

"Sights, I'm sorry. Are you all right?"

"I'm fine." She tightened her lips and resumed the ready position. They both knew the risks of sparring well enough, and if she had been a boy, Vannes would not have asked. "Again."

"I think that's enough for today, don't you?"

"Christina!"

Christina turned to see Nefry approaching with two of his friends, his eyes alight with excitement. "I was hoping you would be here. Remember that thing you were looking for? Well, I found it!"

Christina thanked Vannes for his time and moved to join Nefry. "I don't believe we've met," she said to Nefry's friends. Nefry must have finally found Hezred's name. She was impatient to hear it, but they could hardly discuss it here.

"Oh, Christina, this is Sayler, and that's Kiprim. Sayler, Kiprim, Christina. We can talk later, since these two aren't in our law class and would probably be bored to tears if we tried to explain the disagreement to them, but I just wanted to let you know I figured it out when you're ready to hear about it, because, well, it was kind of a big moment for me."

"Pleasure," said Sayler. The Rishara brown of his skin contrasted with Nefry's pasty white. He and Kiprim nodded to Christina.

"All mine," Christina returned. "Were the three of you about to spar?" she asked, wondering if she could pull Nefry away.

"We're not good enough to challenge Sayler, so he's here to coach us," Nefry explained.

"I hope you're a better teacher than Vannes," Christina noted wryly.

"Does he think you're wasting your time out here because you're a girl?" Sayler asked. "A good teacher would tell you anyone can beat anyone with the right strategy and a little luck. Otherwise I wouldn't be wasting my efforts on these two."

Christina smiled. Nefry was scrawny and would not match most of his opponents for strength, while Kiprim was overweight and looked like he would struggle with speed. It was comforting to know that some initiates had not given up on their friends' chances in the tourney on account of their physical limitations.

"Speaking of Vannes," Nefry said, lowering his voice and casting a furtive glance across the sands to where Vannes was now practicing with another one of his friends. "Did you hear about what happened between him and a certain initiate named *Diar* a few weeks back?"

Christina frowned. "What do you mean?"

"She hasn't heard," Kiprim noted, sounding surprised.

"Oh, this is a great story," Nefry said, warming to his topic. "Apparently, Diar was doing some block cutting with a sword marked with the Noraani sigil – don't look at me like that, he was wearing it openly, so I think I'm allowed to say it, it's not the same as naming his House."

Christina had not been aware of giving Nefry any particular look, but the mention of her House's name had certainly surprised her.

"Anyway," Nefry continued, "Vannes challenged Diar to a practice duel over the sword, which Diar, predictably, lost–"

"But then Jadon showed up and challenged Vannes," Kiprim cut in. "And Vannes lost, and Diar wound up getting the sword back. I saw the whole thing."

Christina's brow furrowed. The idea that Vannes had challenged Diar for any reason did not sit well with her. For one thing, initiates were not allowed to challenge one another to duels – real or practice – and for another, Diar did not strike Christina as someone who would have done anything to provoke a challenge.

The fact that Nefry had mentioned the Noraani sigil as a contributing factor made her worry that she was in some way responsible.

"And after that, Jadon invited Diar to an Initiative party," Kiprim was saying.

"I have it on good authority that he actually went, too," Nefry added. "I told you all that I know Diar personally, right?"

"Yes, you mentioned," Sayler agreed, sighing. "More than once."

"But why did Vannes challenge Diar?" Christina asked, unable to work it out.

"Vannes wanted him to prove he was worthy of carrying the Noraani mark," Kiprim explained.

"He probably thought he was defending your honor, in a way," Nefry suggested. "Vannes really didn't mention this to you? Well, I suppose he wouldn't have wanted to bring it up, considering how it ended."

Christina glanced over to where Vannes was practicing, suddenly feeling ill. Houses of origin were not supposed to matter at Eshtem. Christina had already noticed their influence on her own choice of acquaintances, but she wondered if she had grossly underestimated their importance to the people around her. If Vannes thought Diar had to prove himself worthy to carry the Noraani sigil – a royal Blood House sigil, even though it was not

Vannes's own – was it similar thinking that had driven Lelise to seek Christina's friendship in the first place?

Did they *all* think that the Blood Houses ought to stick together and observe the hierarchy of birth, even here at Eshtem?

The idea was abhorrent to Christina, but now she worried she had been implicitly condoning it by accepting friendship with the other nobles.

Part of her wanted to confront Vannes about it, but perhaps she would only make a fool of herself by displaying how long she had taken to recognize what was going on. "I'll be studying on the balcony if you want to find me when you're done," she told Nefry.

"You should stay and spar with us instead!" he suggested. "I bet Sayler could help you too!"

"Is that so?" Christina directed the question to Sayler. It seemed she would have to wait to talk to Nefry regardless, and she needed practice for the tourney more than she needed to study.

Besides which, Sayler was probably not a noble. Perhaps he was not even from a Blood House. Christina did need to broaden her circle of friends.

Sayler shrugged. "Well, if you were looking to *beat* somebody like Vannes, rather than merely improve your technique, I'd recommend a different approach than the one you've been taking."

"What would that be?"

"Great, so you'll stay!" Nefry grinned. "You work with Sayler first. Kiprim and I have a score to settle from last time." He jogged a few paces away and raised his practice sword.

Sayler stood next to Christina as Kiprim moved into position. "Watch Nefry," he said. "Of the two of them,

Kiprim has the better technique, but Nefry wins more often than he loses. You'll see why."

Nefry took up middle guard to Kiprim's gathered thrust low and began the match with a mad rush. The bigger boy took a few steps back as they met stroke for stroke for the first five, then he deflected a thrust to the side and moved in for a counterstrike. Nefry ducked past him, ran a few steps, and then tripped and fell.

Kiprim made no move to follow. "I am not falling for that again. You're going to have to get up and face–"

Nefry, who had twisted onto his back, threw his practice sword at Kiprim while he was talking. It struck one of his legs.

"Ouch!" Kiprim complained. "You know if we were in a real fight, I could kill you now."

"In a real fight, you would be wounded, and Nefry might have another weapon," Sayler corrected. "Or an ally coming to lend aid. And in the tourney, that's one touch for Nefry."

Kiprim groaned as Nefry scrambled to his feet and retrieved his practice sword, grinning.

"Interesting technique," Christina noted as the two of them began another round. "What's the lesson? I should pretend to trip and throw my sword at my opponent?"

Sayler chuckled, shaking his head. "It's usually a terrible idea to give up your footing. Nefry got away with it only because Kiprim expected something else. And that's the lesson here: surprise. When you face somebody better than you, you can't win if you stick to the forms. You have to change the game. Do something unexpected."

This was something Halce had mentioned in class, Christina remembered: "In a real contest, technique doesn't always matter. If you are less skilled than your opponent, you may still outsmart them." He had been too busy training up their skills to expand on the idea, though, and she had not thought much about it.

"Such as?" she asked.

Sayler shrugged. "I noticed you usually take up the ready position and wait for your opponent to attack first. If someone you face later in the tourney has observed that's been your habit, you might trip them up by coming off the mark swinging. If you can hold back in the early rounds, you might make later opponents underestimate you. But the higher up you progress, the more creative you have to be if you want to keep winning."

"All right, then." Christina raised her practice sword. At this point, she was ready to try anything that might give her the edge she had been unable to attain through practice. "Ready?"

"When you are," Sayler agreed, taking up middle guard.

Christina attacked before he was finished speaking, though he was too skilled and too prepared for her to win a touch. But eventually they changed partners, and she fared better against the other two. She never tried throwing her weapon at her opponent, but she did file away some of the tricks she saw Nefry employ for possible use in her matches.

It gave her a glimmer of hope that she might be able to win against someone who mattered, and it seemed like a short time before staff came to clear the arena to prepare for the day's matches.

"You should work with us again some time!" Nefry said as the four of them walked toward the exit. "But you all go on ahead. I need to talk to Christina about that other thing." He slowed to let Kiprim and Sayler outdistance them. "You see, I was looking through the archives in the southeast wing of the library, and I found that before Qaznaboth united Ithacor, the city of Istar was under Hazmash control like you said, but the second ruling of the Hazmash Council was adjusted by Mabirus, the City Prelate at the time, to account for–"

"I think they're out of earshot," Christina noted. "What have you got for me?"

"Hazzar ti'Rimgard," Nefry told her, dropping his voice to an excited whisper. "His first assignment was a reconnaissance mission in Jeshimoth. I marked the entry for you and Diar. Would you like to see it now? The Lists are in my dorm – I can get them for you."

"Yes, thank you. Jeshimoth is good," Christina said as they left the arena and took the walkway toward the west complex, their boots crunching in the snow. The paths had not been shoveled yet. "The Vaars will have a record of it. I'll write to Our Library."

"There aren't any students from Rimgard here this year," Nefry said, his voice full of disappointment, "though I guess they wouldn't have admitted anyone from the same House as a renegade for a dozen years at least. But if anyone from Rimgard turns up in Lystra on a Seventhday, I'll buy them a drink and see if they know anything about him."

"Really, Nefry, you don't have to do that. No Ellyrian is going to respond favorably to questions about a renegade from the Order, particularly if they were House kin."

"But you've got me all curious now! Don't worry. Probably none of them will come through anyway. Rimgard territory is pretty far from here."

Christina sighed and hoped the Rimgards stayed away from Lystra. "Have you mentioned any of this to Diar yet?" she asked.

"No, I just found the name this morning."

"I don't think we should draw him back into this unless he asks," she said. "He has a lot going on."

"I suppose you're right." Nefry sounded a bit disappointed. "Dueling with Vannes. Partying with Jadon. The whole thing with Ramich and Jenne. The man does have a lot going on."

Christina did not know what Nefry meant by that last bit, but she was glad he agreed to leave Diar out of it. She believed Diar would hold to his oath of silence, but their investigation into the renegade's past seemed like more of a burden to him than it was to Nefry – and besides, a secret was always safer with two than with three.

After Nefry retrieved the Lists for her and eagerly pointed out the entry, Christina lost no time penning her letter to Our Library. It was a relief to be able to use the university post this time, since Our Library was a respectable institution and nothing in her letter should raise any suspicions among the staff who reviewed initiate mail.

She took lunch alone on the balcony, successfully avoiding notice from Vannes and Lelise. She knew she could not ignore them forever, and she was not sure that spending time by herself served the purpose of being free from House and rank any better than sitting with the other Blood House nobles, but it did not seem right to impose herself on Nefry or Diar and their other friends just to make a political statement.

Anyway, with the tourney now under way, they all had more pressing things to worry about.

Diar's intention to spend the first few days of the tourney watching the competition, catching up on his studies, and sparring every moment the arena's practice swords were available was derailed by a vicious hangover. The first morning, he was shocked to be awakened by his notoriously late-sleeping roommate. Jadon had brought him a mug of the vilest concoction Diar had ever tasted, laughed when Diar tried to reject it and go back to sleep, and announced that the tourney had started and that lunch would be served in less than a count.

Then he put the mug on the room's sole table and left.

The combination of Diar's pounding head and his rising panic drove him back to the mug, and it helped far more than he expected. By the time he made it to lunch, his headache had started receding, and even though he'd missed a morning practice opportunity and his friends teased him mercilessly about how long he'd slept, he hoped he could get back on schedule without having paid too big a price for his late-night excursion.

But Jenne was behaving oddly. Diar's worry about oversleeping was quickly replaced by worry about having made a fool of himself the night before. His memories grew a little hazy at the point where he had downed the rest of Rindarin's flask, but he remembered that he had kissed Jenne and somehow managed to restrain himself from exploring her body any further. She had seemed understanding at the time, but she was unusually quiet at lunch, and he worried that he had misread her.

After lunch, he caught up with her on the walkway, happy to seize a moment apart from their other friends.

"Jenne," he said. She glanced at him but kept walking, and he hurried to keep pace while he tried to figure out what to say. The snow was almost as deep as his boots were tall, and some of it fell inside, promising his socks would be wet soon. "About what happened last night."

"We don't have to talk about it."

"Look, if I overstepped–"

"You didn't. It's fine."

"I didn't?" Diar repeated, trying to study her face. She did not slow down or make eye contact. "You're sure? You're not upset? Because I like you, Jenne, and I should have told you that before–"

"I'm not upset. You didn't need to tell me anything." She finally looked at him, and Diar was encouraged by her smile. It was brief, but it transformed her face – just like her smiles always did – and Diar's breath hitched in reaction to her beauty.

But there was still some distance in her eyes.

"Well, I don't want you to think it didn't mean anything to me," he said. "You mean a lot to me, Jenne, and I know we're not in a position to make any promises to each other just yet, but–"

"I couldn't agree with you more," Jenne said. "Look, I really don't need any promises, or speeches, or anything. We kissed. That's all that happened. Maybe it meant something, maybe it didn't. I'm sure that will all sort itself out eventually."

"It definitely meant something to me," Diar said, his concern growing. He wished she would slow down. It did not feel right having this conversation while rushing through snow, especially considering how wet his feet were.

"Right. Sure. What I mean is, we can't just stop our lives to dwell on it right now." Jenne finally stopped and turned to look at him, her brow wrinkled in concern. "This is going to be a big week for me. For all of us. I have a lot of studying to catch up on, and I want to do my best in the tourney. Does that make sense?"

Diar nodded. "Me too. Of course." Neither of them was scheduled to compete until the fourth day, but Liana and Elophine were starting this afternoon, so they would have friends to cheer for when they weren't studying, practicing, or assessing their future competitors. It would be a busy week even without classes, and Diar was glad Jenne wanted to give more focus to their work than to the feelings that were growing between them.

But he wanted to explore those feelings, too, just as soon as was reasonably possible, and he hoped she felt the same. But Jenne had already resumed walking.

"I left some books I need in my dorm, so I'm going to get them," she said as he followed, and Diar realized they were coming up on the gate to the east complex. "But I'm sure I'll see you around, all right?"

"Yes, of course," Diar agreed, hesitating in the walkway. She gave him another brief smile before proceeding through the gate.

It was not exactly what he had been looking for, but it was something. He sighed and turned around to retrieve his own books, supposing it would have to be enough for now.

Christina's first match took place on the third day of the tourney. When she reported to the arena, she found that the ground had been partitioned into twelve regulation-sized dueling rings spaced far enough apart to allow proctors and participants in and out. The sand had turned a bit darker in color, courtesy of the snow it had absorbed, and it was hard-packed and cold, but almost all the visible snow had been removed. Large patches of it remained on the stairs and benches, though, as those had not seen as much use in the intervening days.

The proctors were all junior Edrei – recent Eshtem initiates who had not yet completed their field training. The ability to fairly arbitrate a duel was considered one of the classic functions of an Edrei, and the Eshtem Tourney gave all new members of the Order occasion to practice it. There were fourteen of them on site, dressed in Edrei green with orange stoles to symbolize their dedication to justice in their role as proctors.

Most of the initiates competing today were girls, though there were a few boys among them. Master Halce had determined everyone's starting position in the tourney based on his evaluation of the strength and skill they had displayed during class. Christina's starting on the third day meant that Halce had ranked her in the fifth tier, which put her slightly below average relative to the class, but how far she advanced from here depended entirely on whether she won her matches.

Christina watched a few of her potential competitors while she waited for her own match. When the time came, she stopped by the table two proctors were keeping at the entrance and checked in before proceeding to her assigned circle.

Her opponent had just bested another girl to win the opportunity to face her, but Christina had seen the match and thought both girls' forms left much to be desired. She did her best to mind Sayler's advice and held back as much as she could. She won easily, but she was not as successful in avoiding Lelise and her friends Riara and Adelay, who watched Christina's match and came to speak to her as soon as it was over.

"Good work, Christina." Lelise greeted her after Christina reported her score to the proctors at the exit. "Saleah won her match, too. She accompanied Claire to watch her next opponent. If Claire defeats her, all four of us will keep advancing. Vannes promised to attend our next matches if we survived past the dinner break."

Riara sighed. "I wish I had done as well. Or that the gentlemen might have come sooner, if they were planning to come at all."

"It is not necessary for us to impress the gentlemen, Riara," chided Lelise, "but rather for them to impress us. Wouldn't you agree, Christina?"

"I think Riara is entitled to her own opinion," Christina said.

"Oh, Lelise is surely right," Riara hastened to say. "Though I do wish I was still in the competition."

"What do you think, Adelay?" Christina asked.

Adelay's eyes widened in surprise, and she darted a look at Lelise. "I look forward to watching the gentlemen compete," she said.

Christina pressed her lips together. This was not the first time she had noticed the deference that Lelise's other friends typically showed her, though now that she realized it was almost certainly because of their relative rank outside of Eshtem, it troubled her more.

She was just not sure what to do about it. Riara and Adelay seemed entirely unwilling to assert themselves – and if either of them did have any opinions worth sharing, Christina had yet to see any evidence of it. She could not relate to people who seemed to care so much more about how they came across to the "gentlemen" than how poorly they had done in the competition.

Christina had three more matches that day and won them all. Lelise and her friends watched her matches and kept her apprised of how everyone was doing. Christina was the only one who won through to the next day. She was distant in her interactions with them and kept her replies brief, but that did not seem to faze anyone. She was beginning to think she would have to be openly rude to shake them off, but that was a line she was unwilling to cross.

They had been nothing but friendly to her, after all.

Her first match the next day was against a fourth-tier opponent, and it took all of Christina's skill to defeat the other girl. She watched her potential competitors face off while she waited for her next match.

Christina knew the boy who won his way through to facing her. His name was Gossem, and he was from a royal Gold House. They were in the same ethics section. Christina cared neither for him nor his take on ethics, which only fanned her determination to win a surprise victory against him.

Gossem had been ranked in the fourth tier, which put him below most of the other boys, and after watching his match, Christina could see why. He was heavyset and slower than his opponent. He won only through brute force, overpowering his opponent's parries to win touches.

On the last touch, he had broken his opponent's ribs. The healers on duty had been summoned, but even with their attention, the initiate would take days to recover. Dueling with practice swords was safer than dueling with metal, and it was made safer still by the presence of so many Edrei, but it was still dueling. Injuries were frequent and sometimes severe.

Christina was more intent on winning than avoiding injury, but a single strategy could accomplish both. *Don't try to parry*, she told herself. *Dodge*. To think of Gossem as below average for his sex while she was above hers would be a mistake. He was still favored to beat her.

"To your marks," the proctor instructed. "You have three minutes."

Christina took a deep breath, willing herself not to shiver as she watched Gossem warm up. He had watched her last match. She had maintained the ready position during the warm-up period then, too, and though she had not held back during the match, she had won without resorting to any unusual trickery.

"Right. You are the one who likes to study the opposition rather than warm up," Gossem noted, putting a little flourish into his cross-cut. He still had his cloak on, which Christina interpreted as a sign of disrespect. Hers was waiting for her by the proctors' table, though she had dressed warmly enough to be nearly comfortable without it. "What are you learning?"

"I saw you fight and think I understand your style already," Christina answered. "I'm merely waiting to begin."

"If you saw me fight, I'd think you would want to use all the time you have to prepare to face me." Gossem was grinning. He thought this match was already over.

"Three minutes more or less will hardly affect the outcome."

"You have that right." Gossem swung his sword up into force guard. From it, one could deliver the most powerful downward cross-cut, and Christina doubted she would have the strength to parry such a blow. "We're ready to begin, Proctor."

"Very well. Ready, begin."

Christina coughed, using the motion to disguise the fact that she was drawing her sword in to gathered thrust low. Gossem closed to strike at her, smiling. Christina ducked as she sidestepped and delivered her thrust.

"One for Christina."

"What…?" Gossem scowled. "Lucky trick, that." He stalked back to his mark and resumed force guard. "Enjoy your touch. You won't get another."

"Probably not," Christina agreed, striking up middle guard. *Still cocky.* That could only work to her advantage.

"Ready, begin."

Christina advanced off her mark at the same time as Gossem, making as if to meet his swing with one of her own. At the last second, she dropped to the ground instead, feeling the wind of Gossem's strike move her hair as she extended her sword to catch his foot.

She had learned that one from Nefry.

"One for Christina."

This time Gossem was silent as they moved back to their marks. Christina took up high guard, and Gossem assumed the ready position.

"Ready, begin."

Christina attacked. Gossem parried and riposted. Once again, Christina elected to duck rather than parry, but this time Gossem's sword followed the movement and caught her while she was down.

"One for Gossem."

That was the trouble with a strategy wholly dependent on surprise. It was hard to fool somebody more than once or twice.

In the next bout, Gossem patiently waited to parry Christina's opening attack before pressing a counter. She managed to stay out of reach a little longer, but the bout was depressingly short.

"One for Gossem."

They resumed their marks, and Christina racked her brain for something new to try. This was the fourth day of the Eshtem Tourney, and she was fighting a highborn boy. That meant that a substantial audience in Helos would be watching a reenactment of her match, and Christina knew that every Blood House-sworn among them would like to see her put this posturing imbecile in his place. She had no intention of letting them down.

Gossem took up the ready position, and Christina assumed force guard.

"Ready, begin."

Christina fixed her gaze on the horizon behind Gossem, lowering her sword as she took a step forward, eyes wide. "By the Six," she whispered.

"What?" Gossem frowned. He flicked his gaze over his shoulder, but he did not turn far enough to see behind him. His attention was still on her.

Christina dropped her sword. "It's a dragon!" she exclaimed, doing her best to sell her harmlessness and amazement.

Gossem turned to look, and she kicked her sword across the distance between them. He whipped around at the noise, but the blade knocked against his shin before he could move out of the way. "What–"

"One for Christina. Which closes the match three–two for Christina."

Some applause and laughter broke out among Christina's audience in the stands. Gossem's contingent jeered, some of them getting to their feet, though none were as angry as Gossem himself.

"Wait – no!" Gossem stuttered, face flushed with anger. "That doesn't count. She tricked me!"

"I'm afraid that's not against the rules," the proctor told him. "Christina, carry the score back to the table, and they'll tell you when to report next. Dismissed."

"But she cheated!" someone in the stands objected.

Gossem strode toward the proctor, shaking his sword. "What do you mean, *not against the rules*? How is that fair?"

Christina turned her back proudly as she headed toward the scoring table. She knew the dueling section of *The Ellyrian Code* by heart, and she had not broken any rules. If she had had the luxury of being a well-trained male, she might have chosen to rely on skill alone, as the Gold House boys seemed to think more honorable.

But where was the honor in fighting on terms that would ensure she never won?

Her next match would be against an even more skilled opponent, and likely one who had witnessed this match. She would have no new tricks to try and would almost certainly lose. But she had already done what she had set out to do, and for now, that was a source of great satisfaction.

Diar continued to find Jenne's company elusive during the first few days of the tourney. She practiced sparring when the arena was open, but not with Diar. They took meals together, but other friends sat between them, and Diar had trouble catching her eye. They both studied, but not the same subjects, and sometimes not even in the same group.

It was only a few days, but it was so different from how they had been spending the year until then that Diar felt her absence. He could not help but worry about it.

Once he entered the competition, his matches helped keep him focused. He started in the fourth tier, which put him below most of the other boys and made sense, given his lack of prior training. Diar was not unrealistic about his chances, but he supposed everyone had visions of upending all expectations and finishing high in the Lists. His first few wins buoyed his spirits, and when he won through to the third tier, he was so excited he nearly forgot his concern about Jenne for the rest of the night.

But he lost his second match on the fifth day, so that was the end of his climb. Jenne outlasted him, which might have injured his pride if she had not been besting him in their practice sparring all year. He had long ago given up the idea that his gender should have given him an edge.

Instead, he was surprised to find out that, by evening on the fifth day, Jenne was one of only two girls remaining in the entire competition. By some unfortunate twist of fate, the two of them faced off against each other in one of the day's final rounds.

The other girl was Cyla, whom Diar remembered from the Initiative party. The match was taking place in one of the dueling circles closest to the stands. He and his friends found out the circle assignment and got to the stands ahead of time, so they had a good view, but when the time for the match drew near, they were crowded by an influx of War House boys. Diar noticed Jadon among them, but there were too many people between them to exchange greetings.

From the first flurry of strikes and parries, Jenne and Cyla appeared evenly matched. Jenne had the more aggressive style and spent most of the first round on the offensive, forcing Cyla to retreat. But Cyla never lost her cool, and she seemed to have a preternatural awareness of the circle's edges. More than once, she let Jenne push her to within a single step of the boundary, only to execute a surprising evasion and counterattack at the last possible moment.

Jenne won the first touch, but Cyla won the next, and the cheering of the War House contingent made the support of Jenne's friends seem paltry by comparison. It had to be a terrible distraction to all the other proctors and competitors trying to carry out their own matches at the same time, but when Jenne won the third touch, Diar forgot his concern for them and roared his support right along with Brinnette, Eridike, and the others. They might have been outnumbered by Cyla's supporters, but Jenne's crowd was there, too, and they were not silent.

The War House boys seemed to take it as a challenge, increasing the volume of their own cheers when Cyla won the fourth touch. A silence that felt even deeper by comparison settled over their portion of the stands as Jenne and Cyla squared off for the final bout. The noise of the other matches was still going on, but it felt muted and distant to Diar, whose attention narrowed to just the two competitors before him.

It was the longest bout yet. This time, Jenne and Cyla took turns on the offensive, and Jenne proved just as elusive and aware of the circle's boundaries when she retreated as Cyla had been. But on her last assault, when she had driven Cyla to the edge of the circle for the umpteenth time during their match, Cyla somehow threw herself out of the way in a somersault that repositioned her to swipe at Jenne's feet from behind.

Jenne leapt over the swing in a reaction almost quicker than Diar could process, but then the proctor called the match. It was not until the War House boys began cheering that Diar realized it was because Jenne had landed with one foot crossing the circle's boundary.

It was a disappointment, but still an impressive achievement for Jenne to have made it so far in the competition. Their group hurried around to the arena's exit to meet her and tell her so, but she brushed off congratulations and condolences alike.

"Thank you all for coming to watch me," she interrupted Brinnette, who was lamenting how the last bout had finished. "I appreciate it. Really, I do. But right now, I need to process this alone." She walked off toward the east complex.

Diar took a step after her, but Telius stopped him with a hand on his arm. "Let her go," he suggested. "There will be plenty of time for commiseration later."

That was true enough, but Diar worried as he watched her go, and he felt her absence keenly when she failed to show up for dinner.

CHAPTER 13

The Final Rounds

I saw many things during those hellish days in Gysalt that were not real. The White Plague has that effect, and when I returned, I knew the illness lingered in my bloodstream. I was willing to accept that others might be better suited to distinguish truth from illusion for a time.

But the illness is gone now. My gift is returned to full strength, and it tells me that one thing I saw was not an illusion. There is no one who believes me, no one who will listen. I alone understand the import of what happened, which means it is incumbent upon me, and me alone, to prepare the Order for what must follow.

How our elven founders would despair if they could see how difficult such a task has become.

– From the journals of Drei Master Tamar

The seventh day of the competition was the day many felt the true tourney began. Drei Masters, students of all three years, proctor Edrei not on duty, and distinguished guests by special invitation from the Order all gathered in the arena to watch the final rounds. In the morning, the thirty-two contenders who had fought their way to the top of the second tier each fought one of the thirty-two tourney favorites who had been ranked at tier one. The victors of these matches were then re-ranked first to thirty-second and entered in a seeded tournament to finish off the tourney. Vannes won his qualifying match, was seeded seventh, and won his first match after the midday meal. After that he faced Cyla, whose morning victories had come as a shock to the entire campus.

The last of the other girls had been eliminated two days before, only a few counts after Christina herself. Christina was torn about who she wanted to see win between Vannes and the last girl left standing. In the end it did not matter, since Vannes defeated Cyla quickly. This in no way diminished the enthusiasm of her War House spectators, who applauded her at the end as though she had won both the match and the entire tourney.

Lelise and Saleah shot cold looks at the War House contingent for making so much noise, but Christina found herself smiling.

Vannes faced Sayler next. Until then, at each of the matches Christina had watched involving Vannes or one of his and Lelise's friends – and she had gone to most of them, since they had come to her matches and she felt obligated to return the favor – she had been acutely aware of the gap left between their group and the spectators who came to support the other combatant. When Christina knew the other combatant's House affiliation, she noticed only students of the same affiliation in the other group of spectators. Usually, the other group treated Christina's company with a certain amount of deference, but when the combatant was a War House noble, the groups instead regarded each other with equal measures of disdain.

Today, though, when Vannes squared off against Sayler, Sayler's supporters broke the norm of keeping separate from Lelise and company. Nefry saw Christina, came over, and sat down right beside her, oblivious to the disturbed looks cast his way by Lelise, Saleah, and the rest.

"Christina! You're here to support Vannes, of course, so we'll have to agree to disagree, but it should be an exciting match either way. Oh!" He dropped his voice to a whisper to say, "Did you hear back from Jeshimoth? No, of course not," he interrupted himself, back at regular volume. "That would take far too long. In fact, they probably haven't even gotten your—" Here he returned to a whisper, interrupting himself again to ask, "Have you written them yet?"

"Christina, dear," Lelise cut in, speaking loudly to be heard from where she sat in the row above them and well to the right, as most of the posse sat between them, "would you come here, please? I must show you something."

Christina suppressed the urge to roll her eyes, settling for a few measured blinks as she turned to address the other girl. "I would be happy to come and look at the conclusion of my conversation with Nefry. Perhaps after Vannes's match."

Lelise blinked a few times herself. "But after the match, it will likely no longer be there. Do come now."

"If that should prove to be the case," Christina rejoined, facing forward, "I hope you would be so generous as to describe it for me."

Nefry watched Lelise a moment longer, but she did not speak again. "I think you made her angry," he said in a hushed tone. "I could just leave, you know. We can always talk later."

"No, stay," Christina insisted. "Lelise has no reason to be angry."

"One for Vannes," they heard the proctor call.

Nefry winced. "Come on, Sayler," he urged. "You can fight better than that."

"Perhaps he's holding back," Christina suggested.

"He must be!" Nefry agreed.

Sayler went on to win the match three touches to two. Nefry jumped to his feet and started clapping, elated.

"Perhaps we should find another vantage point from which to view the rest of the competition." Lelise addressed the company, eyes narrowed at Nefry. "One a bit less noisy and crowded."

"My lady, I could not agree with you more," said Jonn, also glancing at Nefry. "Name the spot, and we would be most pleased to accompany you."

Lelise nodded and straightened her cloak, starting to walk away. She paused when she perceived Christina was making no move to follow. "Christina? You'll come, won't you?"

"Just now, I find the view quite to my liking from here, but thank you. Perhaps I will rejoin you later."

Lelise smiled, though it cost her a visible effort. "I hope you'll be able to find us later."

She led the group away, and Nefry gave a low whistle. "She might not *want* you to find them later. Sorry if I got you in trouble."

"*I* might not want to find *them*. Ever," Christina said shortly. "And don't apologize. Lelise has no right to control my associates."

Now that the rest of the highborn were gone, Nefry's friends wandered over to join him. One of them looked from Christina to Lelise. "What was that all about?"

"Nothing of note," Christina assured him.

"Oh, Christina, Matt. Matt, Christina." Nefry nodded to the speaker, who was a head taller than him with fine brown hair and a focused demeanor. "You've met Kiprim."

Christina nodded to them.

"Who will Sayler fight next, Nefry?" Kiprim wanted to know.

"Ramich, probably. Assuming he won in circle two. There will be a break first, though, as soon as the other matches finish, so that the proctors can rearrange the arena. The last three matches will be fought one at a time, each in the center."

"Just two fights to go for Sayler, then," said Kiprim. "He's so close!"

"Since he just eliminated my contestant," said Christina, "let's hope he wins it all."

Jenne had never been the world's most gracious loser, but her defeat on the fifth day of the tourney had been particularly hard to swallow. It did not help that Cyla went on to finish in the top sixteen. Jenne watched some of the other girl's matches, and it appeared that until Vannes, Cyla had an easier time in all of them than she had had in her match against Jenne.

Clearly, they were *both* good enough to have finished in the top sixteen, and Jenne seethed at the injustice of their having had to fight against each other so early.

Even so, she should never have lost. Something had been off about her movements that day, just like during the mock tourney at the Initiative party. She had been sluggish. Reactive. Remni and Cyla were both good, but neither was better than Jenne.

She had spent most of the week more distant from her friends than usual out of a desire to avoid Diar without making a big deal out of it, but after losing in the tourney, she kept away from everyone equally. It would not feel right complaining to any of them, given that her friends had all finished lower in the tourney than she did. And she knew her conviction that she should have done better would only raise uncomfortable questions. Questions like: what made her think she was slower than "usual"? Why should she belong in the top sixteen, when she had no memory of having ever practiced or been trained before arriving at Eshtem?

Why did she think she should have beaten Remni, who obviously had Reading magic?

These were questions Jenne could avoid only so long as nobody spoke them out loud. It was the same reason she had said nothing of her exchange with a possible dragon. Jenne knew enough about the Order to puzzle out that the dragon had probably used words from Command, the special language the Edrei used to communicate with the creatures.

But how could Jenne possibly know Command? *Only* Edrei used that language, and they started teaching it to initiates only during their third year at Eshtem, when graduation was all but assured.

The questions lurked at the edges of Jenne's awareness whenever she spent too much time dwelling on adjacent topics, but for the most part, she was able to avoid letting them cross into conscious consideration. She had no answers, and she did not want any answers. She wanted to keep herself distracted.

The day before, she had hidden herself in the library and spent the whole day catching up on her studies. The material seemed endless, but studying was not an effective outlet for her frustration and restlessness. She had considered sneaking back for another glimpse of the landing grounds, but instead she had reminded herself that Liana thought they might "see something" during the tourney and convinced herself to wait for that instead.

On the last day of the tourney, she had risen before dawn and taken a place in the arena stands. The air was so cold it stung, and the hard stone benches were no better, though at least they had finally been cleared of the previous week's snowfall. She was not the only one to arrive early. In fact, by the time the first matches started, the arena was fuller than she had ever seen it. Jenne noticed when Edrei arrived who were neither proctors nor masters that she recognized, and she saw that some of them escorted senators and foreign dignitaries. She wondered if the Master Imagers were among them.

Liana would know, and she would be able to point out Vorsand if he was there. Jenne spotted Liana, but she was in a larger group of their friends. Diar was with them, and Jenne kept her distance, hoping none of them noticed her in the crowd.

She kept her attention on the matches – especially on Cyla's matches – but all her senses were primed, ready to reorient the moment anything unusual started to happen. As the morning wore on, Jenne grew impatient. The lunch break came and went, and still there was nothing.

It was not until after another break in the competition to prepare for the semifinals that something finally happened.

It was worth every second of waiting.

While Christina watched the proctors erase the twelve dueling circles and draw a new one, twice as large, in the center of the arena sands, a strange hush fell over the gathered crowd. Nefry was in the middle of describing some of the techniques he hoped to see Sayler use in his next match when he abruptly cut himself off mid-sentence, and

Kiprim gasped. Christina glanced at them, puzzled, and followed their gazes up and to the east.

There were two dragons flying toward the arena. They were just as big as the one she had seen at Hezred's execution, but these were flying slowly – lazily, even – and each carried only one rider. The one on the left sparkled red in the afternoon sun, and the one on the right was gold, brown, and black, the colors swirled across its scales in random patterns. The dragons glided apart as they approached, each turning a neat half-circle so that they entered over the arena from opposite sides.

The red one sailed directly above them, and Christina had a close view of its underside as it descended toward the sands. She could see no chink or weakness in the scales that paraded across its belly, varying in shade from deep burgundy to bright ruby. Its four legs each extended into three toes with wickedly sharp claws that might more appropriately be called talons. An additional claw poked out the back of each foot near the ankle joint.

The creature's wings were much darker in color – almost black, though still with a red tint – and they were each at least twice as wide as the dragon's body. Each tapered to a single point on the rostral side that extended into yet another talon, and the caudal side curved into four folds like a bat's wing.

The wind of their passing was the only sound in the arena, where the audience sat breathless with awe – and perhaps terror. A single fiery exhale from the creatures could have ignited half the stands. They continued to descend at a glide until they had nearly reached the sands. Then they flapped their wings in tandem to control their landing, and wind whipped across the arena, tearing Christina's hair loose from its braid and sending a number of poorly secured sashes flying away from their owners.

Somehow, the sand stayed in place while the dragons landed, and the dueling circle in the center was undisturbed. It had to be magic, but Christina could not guess what kind.

The dragons each walked in a slow half-turn about the arena, their wings still outstretched as they took mirrored paths that spiraled in toward the dueling circle. They stopped on opposite sides of it, settling back on their haunches and lowering their wings so their riders could dismount.

It was not until both the riders had dismounted and the dragons had folded their wings closed that the silence held by the audience began to relax.

"Did you know dragons were coming?" Kiprim whispered to Nefry, the first in their group to find his voice.

Nefry shook his head mutely, still staring.

"Do you think this happens every year?" Matt asked, his voice subdued.

If it did, it was a well-kept secret. With all the excitement that surrounded the Eshtem Tourney, Christina had never heard a whisper of dragons' attending the event.

A proctor and two initiates – Ramich and Sayler – walked out to meet the dragons at the dueling circle. The proctor's stride was quick and confident. She must have known this would happen.

The proctor took up a position at the head of the circle, equidistant from the two dragons and the Edrei who stood beside them. Ramich and Sayler walked into the circle more slowly. It was hard to tell from a distance, but Christina guessed they were both staring at the dragons as they moved. After they reached their marks, they each bowed to each dragon, the coordination of it suggesting they had been instructed to do so. They struck their opening poses.

Then the crowd gasped as the combatants suddenly quadrupled in size, becoming even taller than the dragons.

The match began, and Christina watched in breathless fascination as giant versions of Ramich and Sayler traded opening blows.

The illusion was imperfect. The figures were translucent and much less detailed than the actual combatants, with blurred lines for clothing and indistinct facial features. Christina caught glimpses of the two much smaller, real people fighting inside their illusory counterparts. Their movements matched, and so did the arcs of the real wooden swords and the giant ones. It made the battle easier to see.

"So that's why they came," Christina murmured. When it came to magic, dragons had an order of magnitude more power than any Edrei. A Projection this large, well coordinated, and sustained must have required their strength.

"I bet this does happen every year," Nefry said. "They wanted to shock us. Remind us what we're training for."

It was an incredible spectacle, and when Christina tore her gaze away to survey the crowd, she could see it was having the desired effect on the first-years around her. Their eyes were all as wide and fixed on the display of magic as Nefry's were.

But it wasn't just about them. The arena had a section marked off for distinguished guests. Some of the people seated there wore Edrei green, but others were dressed in rich foreign styles, and two wore white tunics with the six-colored bands stretching from shoulder to hip that marked them as senators.

The Edrei were servants of peace. They seldom brought dragons inside Ellyrian or performed any magic in front of civilians. Nothing about the dragons or the illusions would be mentioned to the audience in Helos, though the proctor Edrei in the shell was still narrating the match for them. The Edrei had no interest in frightening the audience at Helos.

But this spectacle was a potent reminder of just how much power they had at their control, for anyone who needed – and could be trusted – with that reminder.

Sayler was behind, one touch to two, by the time Christina managed to pull her focus from the spectacle of it all to follow the match. The next bout lasted a long time, and the combatants covered a lot of ground in the enlarged circle. Sayler's offensive forced Ramich to retreat almost as far as where the proctor stood, but then Ramich regained the offensive and pushed Sayler all the way to the opposite end. Just when Christina feared Sayler would be forced out of bounds, though, Ramich overcommitted to a swing. Sayler ducked and lunged forward, winning a touch as Ramich's practice sword met empty air.

"That's it, Sayler," Nefry encouraged him quietly.

The last bout was the longest. Up until this point, the combatants had managed to keep their distance from the points of the circle nearest the dragons, but in the final bout, Ramich changed tactics. Each time he gained the offensive, he tried to drive Sayler toward one of the dragons. Christina caught her breath every time the distance between Sayler's real form and one of the dragons narrowed to less than a span.

Christina knew the dragons had no reason to hurt the combatants. But everything about the beasts – their spike-rimmed faces, slitted eyes, and the occasional flick of an armored tail or small puff of smoke as they exhaled – screamed that they were natural predators.

Christina had felt a kind of affinity with the dragon she had seen at Hezred's execution, but all she felt watching the red and gold dragons was a kind of awed fear. These were proud beasts, and *very* dangerous.

Ramich had driven Sayler to within two steps of the red dragon, so that his giant figure partly overlapped it, when Sayler managed to sidestep. Just then, the dragon yawned.

If Christina had been focused on the fight of the giant figures instead of nervously fixating on the distance between the dragon and the real combatants, she might have missed it. But as it was, she saw the red dragon's wickedly sharp teeth glint in the sunlight as it stretched its jaws. She understood why Ramich was taking a hasty step backward, his parry almost forgotten, as Sayler's practice sword struck his own and sent it flying out of his hand.

"Get him, Sayler!" Nefry urged.

Instead of pressing his advantage, Sayler and his giant replica gestured at Ramich's fallen sword, leaving time for him to pick it up.

Ramich walked toward it and crouched slowly. The giant version of him did not have clearly defined eyes, but Christina could see that his head stayed up, still focused on Sayler as his hand closed around the practice weapon's hilt.

He rose in a rush, his free hand making a throwing gesture as he closed the short gap between himself and Sayler. Instead of parrying or sidestepping – or doing *anything* – Sayler was recoiling backward when Ramich's practice sword drove into his chest for the final touch. Sayler fell over backward from the force of it.

"What was that?" Matt demanded, leaping to his feet as

Kiprim groaned and applause broke out around them. "He didn't even try to block that!"

Sayler was still lying on the ground when the proctor called the match and the giant versions of him and Ramich disappeared. Christina rose to her feet, nervous for him. It was hard to tell from this distance, but it looked as though his arms were twitching. The proctor and the two dragon riders hurried and knelt next to him.

"Uh-oh," Nefry said. "Looks like he's hurt."

"That'll happen when you take a lunge straight to the chest," Matt noted. Sayler was not the first initiate to be injured during the tournament, though it did feel more dramatic with the entire arena focused on his match.

After just a few moments, the proctor rose and walked over to Ramich. She lifted his arm in a formal recognition of victory, a flourish that had been omitted from the competition until this point. Cheering and applause swelled around them, but Christina kept watching Sayler. The Edrei next to him helped him get up slowly.

Christina was encouraged to see him walk away by himself.

There was enough time between matches that he joined them before the beginning of the next semifinal, which was between Jadon and another War House noble by the name of Regix.

"Sayler, my man, what happened?" Matt greeted him.

"What he means, of course, is a thousand congratulations for making it to the final four," Nefry corrected. "But, well, we had hoped to see you in the final, and it looked like you had an opening that you didn't take, and then–"

"And then Ramich thanked me for that by throwing sand in my face," Sayler said.

"He did *what*?" Matt demanded, shocked.

Sayler shook his head ruefully. "Serves me right for imagining the fight could be fair. I should have paid more attention to the lessons I've been giving these three. Fighting is never fair."

"So why did you let him pick up his sword?" Kiprim wanted to know.

"If I'd been fighting Jadon I wouldn't have," Sayler said. "But Ramich… he's not the same caliber of duelist as Jadon. I didn't think I needed an advantage to beat him."

"At two touches to two, you didn't think it was important to seize every advantage?" Matt challenged.

"It's not like my life was at stake here. Only glory, and I didn't want the glory of a victory over Ramich to be diminished by the accident of a dragon's yawn."

"A what?" Kiprim asked.

"The dragon opened its mouth while we were right in front of it. You didn't see that?"

Nefry shook his head. "We didn't see the sand, either. The giant Projections of you and Ramich and your practice swords were pretty good, but I guess they didn't include everything relevant to the fight."

"What do you mean, giant Projections?" Sayler asked.

Nefry grinned. "Oh, you'll see when the next match starts. It's why the dragons are here."

"I saw the dragon's teeth," Christina volunteered. "It was a shocking sight, even from here. It was good of you to give Ramich a moment to recover."

Christina saw no contradiction between Sayler's actions and the lesson he had given them before. There was a difference between creating the advantage of surprise, as she had done during her match with Gossem, and seizing one that happened by chance or accident. If she had been in

Sayler's place, she would not have wanted to leverage the dragon's actions against Ramich either.

"I respectfully disagree," Matt said. "Now we will have to watch a War House fight a Gold House in the final, and I blame Sayler."

"Oh, look, look, look, they're starting!" Nefry grabbed Sayler's arm in excitement. "Watch this."

There were not many things in the world that impressed Jadon tu'Hatreth – but dragons were one of them. He watched them fly in from where he waited for his match next to the proctors' table by the arena's entrance, and for several long moments, he forgot to breathe. The creatures were magnificent.

Standing on the arena ground put him closer than most to the dragons when they landed. They were easily twice his height at the shoulder, and might have been closer to three times taller when they raised their heads.

The gold dragon walked closer to Jadon as it started its half-turn about the arena, and he caught his breath again as the sun glittered on the golden claw protruding from the upper ridge of the beast's half-extended wing. It looked wickedly sharp, much like the spikes that rimmed its face. Those were a mix of black and gold, the colors swirled together across the dragon's head and neck. Black predominated around the eyes, making their yellows stand out.

Jadon never would have guessed that a reptile's eyes could look intelligent, but these did.

The dragon kept its head high and its gaze forward as it walked, and Jadon started breathing again as it moved past him. Even just half-extended, the wing was longer than the width of the dragon's body, and that was substantial enough to make the rider crouched between its neck and shoulder seem puny. The wings darkened from yellow-gold to burnished bronze at the caudal end, and its scales glittered shades of gold, bronze, and brown with a few lines of black splashed across them.

Despite his lifelong expectation of one day joining the Order, Jadon had seldom imagined whether he might ever ride a dragon. Now, he could not help but wonder about it – and he had to admit, he hoped he would.

Anna would have killed to see this. Even just the description of it would have made for an exciting letter, but of course, Jadon could not write to her about this. She would have the chance to see it herself if she enrolled here, and he was not about to spoil the surprise.

Jadon caught his breath again when the Projections shot up over Ramich and Sayler after they took their places in the ring. The magic was startling, but after a longer inspection, he decided the dragons themselves were the bigger wonder. The Projections had too many flaws, and he wasn't sure that the giant images actually improved his view of the match. They left out too much.

Jadon shook his head when Sayler let Ramich pick up his sword after the red dragon yawned. It was a needless risk – especially given that Sayler had been the lower seed in the competition – but Jadon had to respect it. It would have removed any question of who deserved the victory, had Sayler gone on to win.

Instead, Ramich used the moment to throw sand in Sayler's face and strike the final blow, taking the exact opposite strategy. Jadon's jaw tightened in disapproval, and he was reminded that he did not like Ramich. Ramich had been given the second seed in today's tournament, which Jadon was pretty sure would not have happened had Dreck not been so sick this morning that he had lost his qualifying match. Now, Ramich had secured a place in the final even though Sayler was probably better than him, too, giving the illusion that he had actually deserved the second seed.

Once they cleared the ground, Jadon and Regix were given permission to approach the dueling circle and the dragons who sat tall and proud on either side of it. Jadon could not help but stare as he approached, taking extra time to appraise the red dragon.

It was just as magnificent as its fellow.

It felt right to bow to the creatures, and Jadon was glad they had been told to do so. Ignoring them would have been impossible.

Even after the greeting, turning his back to them and his mind to the contest at hand was not easy. Regix, though, had an even harder time of it. Jadon could see sweat breaking out on the other boy's brow even before they started to warm up, and Regix kept stealing glances at the dragons while they fought.

His distraction was understandable, but there was a fine line between showing leniency and showing disrespect. Jadon kept to the former and defeated Regix quickly. It was a shame, because his opponent was a talented duelist and might have been able to win at least one touch, if he had been fighting at full potential.

Of the final four contestants, Jadon suspected that Ramich was the worst, despite his second seed and the reality that he had won his way into the final. The two of them would fight next. Jadon planned to test whether Ramich deserved to be there.

* * *

"It'll be Jadon and Ramich in the final, then, as expected," Nefry noted. "Come on, we've got to pick one to support. Who should it be?"

"I'd say Ramich, since he bested our Sayler," Matt suggested, "but he's such an unpleasant human being that I can't ethically justify hoping for him to win the Eshtem Tourney. Especially since he won the semifinal by throwing sand in Sayler's face."

"For me, it's less about the sand and more about how hard he hit me." Sayler winced as he ran a hand over his chest. "*That* was unnecessary."

"Did he break a rib?" Christina asked.

"Yes, and collapsed a lung. The Edrei mended it, but they said I'll have a wicked bruise."

"Sights," Matt muttered. They were all a bit stunned.

"So... we'll cheer for Jadon, then?" Kiprim suggested after a moment.

Sayler shrugged. "I'll live. Jadon's hardly any better than Ramich, from a character standpoint."

"Ramich it is," Nefry decided. "Jadon's favored anyway, and it's always more fun to cheer for someone coming from behind."

"Unless it's Ramich," said Matt.

Christina, finding herself indifferent to the outcome, let her gaze wander over the assembled crowd as the Edrei redrew the dueling circle for the final match. After a while, Jadon and Ramich walked out, bowed to the dragons, and took their marks. Their giant counterparts appeared and began to trade opening blows.

Christina's gaze caught on Master Tamar, low in the stands to their left. She was engaged in animated conversation with the gray-bearded Headmaster Regild.

"Ouch," Nefry observed. Christina returned her attention to the arena, where Ramich's giant double was lying on the ground, overlaying his much smaller form. The proctor called a touch for Jadon.

Ramich rose to his feet slowly. The giant version of him did not quite capture the fury that radiated from his small form as he and Jadon returned to their marks. Christina looked back at the masters. Tamar seemed upset.

"I think Ramich is going to lose," said Kiprim. Jadon had just won another touch.

Christina continued watching Tamar as the headmaster walked away, waving a dismissal.

"What's he doing?" Kiprim asked.

"He's toying with him," said Sayler, shaking his head. Christina looked toward the match, seeing that Jadon had lowered his weapon and was merely sidestepping Ramich's increasingly furious assaults. "In front of the entire nation."

Tamar was pacing now, her frustration palpable. Christina noticed Masters Porrian and Felade moving through the stands to approach her.

I have to hear this, she decided. Perhaps their conversation would have something to do with Tamar's theory of rogue Imagers, or the delusions allegedly inspired by her illness. Both were topics Christina was itching to hear more about.

"I'll be right back," she told Nefry.

She kept her eyes on the giant Projections as she moved toward the masters. Jadon was using his weapon now, but while Christina watched, he passed up three opportunities to win touches, choosing to tap Ramich with the hilt of his practice sword or shove him with his free hand instead.

Christina pursed her lips. *War House-sworn.* They did the cruelest things for sport.

"Let me guess. The headmaster refused to reinstate Imaging combat classes for upperclassmen?" Felade was saying when Christina drew within earshot. "This time also? What a surprise."

"Or did this particular dispute have to do with granting Alterrans jurisdiction over Ellyrian investigations?" Porrian asked. "Because I'm afraid the Council would hardly receive that request any more favorably from the headmaster than they would from you or Miraj, even were Regild disposed to ask it."

"There *is* no Ellyrian investigation anymore, near as I can tell," said Tamar. "I sent a message to the Drei officer the Council reportedly put in charge of the matter, and he answered that he had been reassigned within days. No one seems to know who took his place." Tamar turned to face Porrian directly. "Now, why the Council should be content to sit back and let the kidnappers of an Alterran Prophetess disappear into Ellyrian lands is mysterious enough, but what simply defies explanation is that they would stand in the way of anyone else hoping to do something about it. Tell me, Porrian, what exactly is the Council hoping to achieve with this political smokescreen? Are you hiding something?"

"Careful, Tamar," Porrian chided. "You're starting to sound paranoid again."

"Perhaps a few more years in Gysalt are in order," Felade suggested, looking down on her from his superior height.

Tamar smiled. The expression was joyless. "I don't think we have anything further to discuss. Unless you want to give me the name of the new lead officer. If one even exists."

Porrian sighed. "It pains me that you no longer trust your superiors, as you once did. Your plight in the Hahiroth wounds you still, in more ways than one."

"Get me that name and perhaps a measure of my faith would be restored," Tamar suggested, turning back toward the arena sands.

"Enough to convince you to give up your crusade to train combat Imagers?" Felade challenged, his gray eyes flashing.

"I make no promises." Out on the arena ground, the proctor had just called the final touch for Jadon. The Projections disappeared, and Tamar turned and caught sight of Christina watching her. Christina dropped her eyes.

"Nor can I," Porrian returned.

"The tourney is over, and so, I believe, is this conversation." Tamar nodded to the other masters and turned to leave, casting another glance at Christina as she went.

Christina turned away, hoping to escape before attracting Porrian's attention. She did not want him to know she had overheard Tamar's suspicions about the Council. It reinforced her own suspicion that they may have hidden something in the case of Hazzar ti'Rimgard.

If both were true, though, that would mean the Council was even more corrupt than Christina had imagined. The thought was terrifying.

Then again, perhaps Christina should not be giving so much weight to the suspicions of a woman purported to suffer from paranoid delusions. She wished she knew more. Perhaps if she spoke to Tamar, the master would be willing to share her concerns about the Council and how they related to her illness.

It seemed unlikely, but Christina had nothing to lose by asking a few questions.

CHAPTER 14

The High Prince's Shadow

"What lacks the man who has been given everything?"

"The freedom to become what he wills."

— Alleged exchange between a court jester
and King Zerhitak of Jeshimoth

Diar woke up a full count before the morning bell. He had interrogations in Alterran and rhetoric coming up in the afternoon, and had studied himself to exhaustion the night before. After a few minutes, though, he gave up on trying to go back to sleep.

Jenne had been elusive all week. He did not even know how she felt about the two *dragons* that had shown up in the final rounds of the tournament, or about the incredible display of Projection magic. He had broached the topic at dinner with some of the others, but nobody was sure how much they were allowed to discuss what was obviously a closely guarded secret, and the conversation died quickly after a few murmured expressions of remembered awe.

Diar felt sure Jenne would have been less intimidated to speak of it, but he had not been able to catch her alone or engage her in conversation on any topic since the first day of the tourney, when she had assured him that all was well between them.

276

He had believed her at the time, but the interim had convinced him that something was wrong.

Stupid, stupid, stupid, Diar chastised himself as he dressed. *What in the name of the White possessed me to drink so much?* He had never indulged so recklessly as he had that night at the Initiative party. Moderation was encouraged by the White Way, and allowing drunkenness to become a habit was against the Principles. Occasional overindulgences were not uncommon in Rishara-ahn circles, but they were frowned upon. Diar had not meant to get so carried away. Kissing a girl was a serious step, and in his reckless and impaired state, he had obviously botched it.

He had been so sure she was interested in him as more than just a friend. She had even said he had not overstepped when he kissed her. Still, he should have done better – should have asked for permission first, maybe, or told her how serious he was about pursuing a long-term relationship with her. Of course, they were both young, and becoming an Edrei had to be his priority, but he *was* serious about his feelings for her. A girl should have that assurance when somebody kissed her.

Or maybe it was his idiotic behavior afterward that had cooled her interest. *Sights.* He had not even been able to walk straight. *Did I really belch in front of her?*

Diar glanced at Jadon's box bed and stopped what he was doing, surprised. The curtain that closed off the bed had been left open, and the straw tick was undisturbed. Jadon had been out all night.

When Diar got to the mess hall, he saw Fendi and Dreck were up, too. They looked terrible, and Jadon was not with them.

Diar stopped by their table. "Hey – um. Good morning. Have you seen Jadon?"

Dreck turned his head to regard Diar over his mug of ale, the movement costing a visible effort. Fendi did not look up from where his chin rested on his hands, still considering his own mug where it rested untouched on the table.

"Not since Cyla took him upstairs," Fendi grunted, a smile twitching the corner of his mouth. Dreck started to chuckle but stopped, the memory not quite funny enough to distract him from how miserable he must be feeling.

Diar could sympathize. "Upstairs where?"

"At the inn we went to last night. In Lystra."

Diar, alarmed, tried to ignore the absurdity of the fact that the Initiative had gotten it into their heads to go all the way to Lystra to have their festivities. There was a bigger problem at hand. "He didn't come back to campus with the rest of you?"

"I wasn't about to go looking for him," said Fendi.

"Can't imagine he'd have appreciated the disturbance." Dreck sipped from his mug.

"Well, did Cyla come back?" Diar pressed.

Dreck and Fendi traded glances. "Yeah, I think I did see her." Fendi nodded.

"But not Jadon?" *What kind of friends are these people?* Diar was disturbed to see them both so nonchalant. "And you didn't think to check on him?"

"He's not a child. He knows the way back." Dreck sounded annoyed. "What's it to you?"

"He never came back to his room."

Fendi, finally, registered some apprehension. "Aw, sights. You don't think he's still in Lystra, do you?"

Dreck half-chuckled again, then winced. "Flames of the Abyss. He won't be able to squirm his way out of this one."

If Dreck or Fendi were to take a horse and leave right now, they just might find Jadon and make it back on time for class, or perhaps a few minutes late, which would be nothing out of the ordinary for War House boys. But they just sat there.

If anybody was going to save Jadon from getting expelled for missing a whole class period, it seemed it would have to be Diar.

"Which inn, exactly, did you leave him at?" Diar asked.

"Are you going to go get him?" Dreck raised his eyebrows.

"Someone should."

"The Seventh Sword," Fendi supplied, raising his mug. "Just past the Temple of Aurantiacus, inside the east gate. Best of luck."

Diar took a bite out of his roll and discarded the rest of his breakfast, returning his trencher to the kitchen and then starting toward the stables at a jog. If he was really going to do this, he had no time to lose.

But Diar was suddenly glad he had been unable to sleep. He had vague memories of Jadon's coaxing him over the wall of the west complex the night that he had drunk too much. That vile concoction Jadon had brought him to drink the next morning had done wonders for his headache, too, and this was not even mentioning how Jadon had won Diar's sword back before all that. Diar was loath to let the other boy down when he clearly needed a friend.

Lystra was twelve miles from Eshtem, and a horse could cover that in less than a count. There were just under two counts left before class. It would be a near thing, but it was just possible Diar could find Jadon and make it back on time, assuming the stable master would lend him a horse.

As it turned out, the stable master was unwilling to let him borrow one of the campus horses, but Diar was able to talk the man into letting him take Jadon's horse to search for his missing roommate, though Diar did not mention his intention to go as far as Lystra, nor that his roommate had been out partying after curfew the night before. The aide at the Dragon Gate let him leave with just a casual reminder that the gate would not open to readmit him after the first bell of classes.

So it was that Diar found himself riding down the road to Lystra on a royal-bred horse in the uniform of an Eshtem initiate, risking demerits – and even possibly his tenure at Eshtem – for the second time in little more than a week.

At least this time, it's for a good cause, he told himself.

"Jadon! Are you in there? You've got to get up!"

That was Diar's voice. Jadon registered this as he became aware of a distant pain in his head, but most of him was still asleep. The headache promising to intensify when he woke had him convinced it would be better to remain so.

This was not an unusual way for the morning to begin.

There was pounding on the door. "Jadon! Can you hear me? The door's locked. You need to move!" More pounding.

Jadon frowned and opened his eyes. *So bright.* He turned over and hid his face in the pillow.

Then he processed what he had seen.

Spectrum's spitfire. I'm at the Six-forsaken inn. What's the count? And how is Diar here?

"Jadon! Now! We have to go!"

Jadon surged to his feet. His stomach lurched. "Yeah. Aurantiacus. I'm coming." He staggered over to the door and was taken aback to find that not only was it locked, but the desk had been moved in front of it. *What in the...?*

"Today, Jadon!"

Jadon grunted as he shoved the desk out of the way and looked around for a key. "Can't you–"

He heard a click as the door unlocked from the other side. He pulled it open. "Yeah, let's go," he said, moving past Diar and the innkeeper with the master key to lead the way down the stairs. "How much do I owe you? This should cover it," he said, tossing the man a gold crown. "Also, we'll need to rent a pair of horses–" He opened the door and winced at the brightness of the sun's reflection off the snow. Then he noticed his own horse standing saddled and bridled in the roadway. "Oh. You brought mine." He squinted as he started toward it, wishing the sun were less bright.

"I'm afraid we don't keep any horses," the innkeeper said, following him outside. "None but the old carthorse, and she's nearly lame. You might try the stables at center city."

"No time. This will do," said Jadon, already mounting. Judging by the merciless light of the sun, it was the first count of Xanthin, which meant there was less than a count left before class. The horse was in good shape for having already crossed the distance between Eshtem and Lystra once. Still, making it back to campus on time would tax her, especially if she bore extra weight. "Though if you could send a groom with the carthorse along the road to Eshtem to wipe this girl down and walk her back here, there will be another crown in it for you."

"Very well, my lord."

"Jadon." Diar recalled his attention, looking concerned.

As if I would leave him here. Jadon smiled, shaking his head. It was insane that Diar had come all the way to Lystra to get him. And dressed in initiate blue, no less. Initiates were permitted to visit Lystra only on Seventhday, so if anyone reported Diar's appearance to the Drei Masters, he could be expelled. "You didn't happen to bring an extra horse, did you?"

"They barely let me take yours. And you had just the one."

Jadon looked past him to the innkeeper. "You didn't see us here, right?"

"I never do, my lord."

Jadon sighed and turned the horse around. "Come on, Diar. She can take two."

Jadon pulled the horse to a stop a few miles short of the Dragon Arch.

"What are you doing?" Diar asked.

"We're taking the Initiative shortcut," Jadon explained, dismounting. "The bell will sound any minute. They won't open the Dragon Gate after that."

"Great, so we *are* going to be late," said Diar. "We're just leaving the horse here?"

"The groom will find her," said Jadon, breaking into a jog.

He led Diar through the snow and over the makeshift bridge the Initiative had long ago constructed between the mainland and the plateau north of campus. From there, they made their way to the fallen tree that spanned the gap to the campus plateau. The bell rang as they jogged toward the campus towers.

"Limn it," Diar cursed.

Jadon was still content with the time they were making. Being late was nothing new, and it was far less dangerous than missing class. He could always work off a few demerits. "What class do you have?"

"Politics."

Jadon made a dismissive sound. "Just stand outside the room and listen before you go in. Master Porrian will ask you a question he just went over, you'll answer, and then he'll let you sit down. You'll be fine." Being late to politics was an art Jadon had long since perfected. "You keep going," he instructed, angling west as they approached the north tower.

"Where are you going?"

"I still have to change into uniform."

As he made his way over the wall and back to his dorm, Jadon tried to reconstruct the events of the night before. The last thing he remembered was doing shots in the common room at the inn with the other Initiative first-years who had been Seventhday tourney finalists, after they had decided to jog the twelve miles to Lystra to celebrate someplace less miserably cold than the plateau. His memories became hazier after that, but he thought they involved Cyla and Kerci dancing on tabletops. And then, yes, he dimly remembered kissing Cyla.

None of this even began to explain how he had woken up in a locked room, alone. *With a desk pulled in front of the door.* If he had gone in there with a girl – presumably Cyla – she must have exited by the window and taken the key with her, which made absolutely no sense. *Unless she wanted to get me expelled. Or somebody else put her up to it.*

Rindarin. Everyone else in the Initiative liked him, as far as he knew. Rindarin, though, had not appreciated getting bested by Jadon the night of the practice tourney. Jadon had guessed the second-year would seek some form of reprisal, which was why he had not drunk the brandy Rindarin had poured for him after he lost to Alaxis. At the time, it had just been a precaution. It had seemed strange to Jadon that Rindarin had won the Eshtem Tourney the year before, given that Alaxis was so much better. The story that Alaxis had been sick seemed convenient, and when Rindarin had poured the goblet for Jadon, there had been a glint in his eyes that Jadon had not cared for. He had not really thought Rindarin would poison him, but it was better to be safe.

But Dreck had drunk the rest of it. And then Dreck had gotten sick – almost too sick to hold a practice sword, when his time to compete came around. Just like Alaxis.

As disgusting as it was, Rindarin's having poisoned Alaxis the year before made sense. He had removed his strongest competitor and won the Eshtem Tourney, topping the Eshtem Lists and making Rithadur first in the House listings. But Jadon could not figure out why Rindarin would bother to sabotage the tourney favorite among the first-years. The two of them were not in direct competition. Rindarin had nothing to gain.

And now with Cyla. If Jadon was right, Rindarin had used her to try to get him expelled. *All because I bested him in mock combat in front of the rest of the Initiative?* Jadon narrowed his eyes. It made no sense. *I must be missing something.*

Then there was the fact that Rindarin seemed to be getting away with it all, which was also disturbing. As far as Jadon knew, no one had ever accused him of anything.

It was a mark of how little stock Jadon put in authority that the thought of sharing his suspicions with the Drei Masters never crossed his mind. He simply made a mental note that, for reasons he did not understand, Rindarin was dangerous. Perhaps very much so.

That was where he left the matter as he jogged up to the south tower, his thoughts returning to the question of Cyla. He wondered if he had gotten anywhere with her before she left. *Shame I don't remember.* He had never lost time before, and he wondered whether she had slipped him something in addition to the alcohol. She would have had total control over the time at which he passed out, and he could see her choosing before or after sleeping with him with equal plausibility.

It irked him that he had let her into such a position, and it irked him even more that he did not know what she had done with it. But the worst of it was, with or without Rindarin's encouragement, she had tried to get him expelled. *What did I ever do to her?*

It seemed no one in the Initiative could be trusted.

At least there won't be any lasting harm, Jadon told himself, trying to shake off the betrayal. He was now dressed in initiate blue and only moments away from his classroom.

It was all about priorities, this business of violating the rules. Being late would earn him demerits, but their number would not necessarily increase if he was fifteen minutes late rather than ten. Not being dressed in uniform, though, was an additional infraction that would cost independent demerits. Seeing as he currently had six and his first class was Master Tamar's – who, he knew, liked him not at all – he thought it best to show up in violation of one rule rather than two. He did not think she would dare push him over the limit regardless, but it was better not to test her patience.

Tamar did not appreciate his thoughtfulness. She bid him take his seat and two demerits with a look that suggested she would have liked to expel him on the spot.

After he sat down, the crisis of having woken up twelve miles from campus finally resolved, it became difficult to hold to his resolution not to test her. His intentions were good, but he was exhausted, and there was no relief to be found from his headache in listening to the master drone on about the Alterran justice system.

"Jadon?"

Coming to attention with a start, Jadon scanned his memory for the preceding question and came up empty. "My apologies, Drei Master. Would you be so kind as to repeat the question?"

"No, and that will cost you another demerit."

There was a snicker from the back row, where Gossem to'Shale sat with his Gold House friends. He was not usually hostile to other highborn, though Jadon supposed the whole clan would now have a bone to pick with him for defeating Ramich in the tourney.

Tamar frowned. "Gossem, why don't you tell us?"

"Very well, Drei Master. The position is unique because the First Justicer can be replaced by the sovereign at any time, for any reason, and his face is unknown to the court."

"Close, but incorrect, and I have to assign you a demerit for snickering."

Gossem glowered, and Jadon leaned forward in his seat. He knew how to correct Gossem. He also knew better than to speak without being recognized in Tamar's class.

Her gaze rested on him for a moment, taking in his willingness to speak, then flicked past him, unappeased. "Landers, how did Gossem's answer err?"

"The king can replace any official in Alterra whenever he pleases. It's just that he seldom does."

"When a new king ascends to power, he always appoints his own First Justicer and seldom changes any other officials, though it is within his power to do so," Tamar agreed. "What else was misleading?" She scanned the room and again elected not to call on Jadon, instead choosing the Initiative member who sat next to him. "Arzit."

"Uh…"

Jadon covered his mouth and coughed the words "the queen" so only Arzit could hear him. It was too difficult to resist participating, if he was obliged to pay attention.

"Right, the queen." Arzit latched on to the phrase, though he had to think for a moment about what it meant. "The queen's face is always covered when she appears in official capacity as well. So that's not unique to the First Justicer, either."

Tamar narrowed her eyes at Jadon, suspicious. He smiled, trying to look innocent and apologetic at the same time.

"Thus, the original question stands," Tamar eventually said. "How would you answer it, Claire?"

"The First Justicer, rather than a simple judge, investigator, or advisor, serves as liaison between the king and the people. When operating in his official capacity, he wears a mask to meet with the district judges and brings issues of importance to the people to the attention of the king. When the king takes an interest in a case, the First Justicer acts as an anonymous investigator, gathering all the information necessary for the king to act without letting the relevant parties know that he is the king's official representative. One might say the position is unique because it carries all the gravity of royal authority with none of the trappings. I imagine that he and those members of the court privy to the secret of his identity have some difficulty ascertaining his place in the hierarchy."

Jadon turned his attention to the window, hoping the next bell would sound soon so he could tend to his headache. He had run out of the ingredients he usually mixed with water to counteract hangovers, and he was out of water, too. He would have to settle for ale from the mess hall until his next hike to the spring.

"Jadon? Care to weigh in?"

Jadon attempted a smile as he returned his attention to the master. It did nothing to thaw the frostiness of her regard.

He sighed. "Claire has described the position with her customary exactness, though I myself would suggest that the trappings of power are of far more importance to those pretending to it than to those born to it. I doubt anyone of real note in Alterra would be confused about how to treat the First Justicer, though those who come to court later in life might struggle to ascertain the office's place."

Arzit snickered, and Claire stiffened, turning to cast a disbelieving look in Jadon's direction. She bit her lower lip to keep from retorting, then deliberately turned forward. This reaction mystified Jadon. Then he remembered Claire was a commoner by birth. His comment could be interpreted as a personal slight.

Tamar seemed to have interpreted it that way. Her face was cold with anger, and Jadon cringed, wishing he could take the words back. *But she called on me. I had to say something, didn't I?*

The bells of the north tower chimed.

"Class dismissed. Except for you, Jadon."

Jadon leaned forward to rest his head against a fist as everyone else stood to go.

Claire was among the last to leave, and a friend of hers was waiting at the door when she filed out with the others. Jadon heard her ask, "Claire? Are you all right?"

Claire glanced at him, her lips pressed together in anger. He gave her a contrite smile, and she looked away, giving her friend a curt nod before leaving the room.

"Christina?" the master inquired as the other students departed, leaving Claire's friend alone in the doorway. "Do you need something?"

Christina. That made this girl the Noraani princess, which Jadon remembered because his sister had been excited to hear – and to tell him – that Christina tu'Noraan would be part of his Eshtem class. Her application was unusual not only because she was Noraani, but also because she was the daughter of a high prince. Though becoming Edrei was considered a high honor for any man or commoner in Ellyrian, there remained some circles among the upper classes in which it was frowned upon for a highborn lady to display herself in competition with her peers in such a manner as occurred at Eshtem. Christina was not the first princess to do so, but it was a rare event.

Anna hoped to apply to Eshtem herself in two years, when she came of age, but their father had not indicated whether he would permit it. Anna hoped Christina's presence would weaken the stigma against her and sway the high prince toward a favorable decision.

Jadon had seen Christina around campus before and exchanged a few words with her once at the library. He had not known who she was at the time, but he remembered thinking her oddly secretive and self-important. Now that he knew who she was, he decided that, as important as her presence here might be for Anna and other especially highborn women seeking to become Edrei, Christina herself was just another Blood House nuisance.

"I can wait," Christina said with a glance at Jadon. Her

uniform was too big for her through the bust, and the overdress came short of her ankles, revealing a length of white stocking. Her hair was done in a simple braid that reached the end of her shoulder blades, and Jadon wondered if she had styled it herself.

Most girls who could afford it had their uniforms professionally tailored, but Jadon felt he should have marked this one as a Blood House princess from her posture alone. Lelise was the only other first-year girl on campus who made a habit of standing quite so straight and proud. Where Lelise made the pose look supple and haughty, though, Christina was almost rigid, as if, rather than to put on airs, she stood that way because she could conceive of no other postural options.

"He can wait," Tamar said, her tone final. "What can I do for you?"

Christina glanced at Jadon and then out at the hall before taking a few steps into the room, her body language suggesting she would rather have been the one to wait.

Jadon crossed his arms and settled back in his chair, thinking it rather cold of Tamar to deny Christina a private audience simply to make him wait longer.

"Well, Drei Master," Christina began, clearing her throat. "It's certainly nothing pressing, but there's a matter I've been considering which I hoped you might be able to speak to."

"Which is?"

Christina pursed her lips and cast another quick glance at Jadon. "It is commonly said that Eshtem was founded after the Last Aljeshan War to train Imagers to stand against the High Wizards who evaded capture, because the elves were certain these wizards would rise against Ellyrian again."

"So it is said," Tamar agreed, her tone suggesting nothing.

"And yet, the curriculum here..." Christina trailed off.

Jadon yawned, finding the halting pace of the conversation tedious. Christina need not have worried about his overhearing; he was almost asleep already.

"I cannot help but note that the training here does little to prepare one to face such a threat." Christina finally found her words, frowning. "And I wondered how long ago that particular aspect of training ceased, and if it was discontinued on account of a ruling by the Board of Masters or by the Edrei Council, and if it was the Council, I wonder why they made such a ruling, and in particular whether it was to prevent the distrust of Imagers that such training might engender. I furthermore wonder whether the Council continues to make a priority of protecting the reputation of Imaging today, and whether you believe they err in this, given that Imagers have been responsible for at least one war that we know of."

"It seems you wonder a great many things," Tamar noted. She crossed her arms. "No doubt because you heard me speaking with Master Miraj. And then Porrian and Felade, yesterday at the tourney."

Christina returned the master's gaze, silent.

"But you must realize, Christina, that nothing has been seen or heard of these alleged 'High Wizards' in over sixteen hundred years – nor of elves, either. In your next two years, you will learn all you could wish to know of the mythology surrounding the Treaty of Edriendor, including alternative theories about what exactly happened in the War of Shadows. But regardless of whether events unfolded as the stories say, the Order was founded to make and defend peace throughout the world. Today, many threats to peace exist that are imminent and undeniable, and none of them, so far as we can tell, are the creations of High Wizards. The training at Eshtem was long ago adapted to reflect this reality, a decision which would have been within the prerogative of either the Board of Masters or the Council to make.

"As to whether the Council unduly protects the reputation of Imaging, they do not. They only just recently expelled an Imager from the Order and made it known to all that his magic made him particularly dangerous. In any dispute I might have with the Council, I would not impugn them for this, and as to those things I might impugn them for, that is a personal matter – or rather, one for Drei Masters and Consuls. In any case, nothing you need concern yourself with. Is there anything else?"

Tamar's manner was uninviting, and Christina recognized a dismissal when she heard one.

"No, Drei Master. Thank you for your time." Christina nodded and walked out of the room, leaving Jadon alone with Tamar.

The master walked behind her desk and sat down before turning her attention to him, her brown eyes cool and disapproving. Since this seemed rather too far a distance from which to carry on a conversation, Jadon stood and approached, stopping in the aisle that separated the tables making up the first row of seats.

"Do you know how many demerits you have at the moment, Initiate?"

Jadon had to think for a moment, adding the ones she had assigned him to his previous total. The answer came as a surprise. "Nine."

"And, sitting at nine, you chose to slight your fellow classmate for a background that you are not supposed to know, let alone allude to in front of me and my entire class."

Jadon took in a breath to defend himself, but the master held up a hand.

"And yet, you're in no danger of expulsion," she continued, "and I won't insult your intelligence by pretending otherwise. Yes, I could assign you another demerit if I really so desired, and perhaps when the Senator-Liaison came storming onto campus to demand an explanation, the board would uphold your expulsion. Perhaps, perhaps not – it would be a tricky position for Headmaster Regild – but either way, I would lose my post as Drei Master and perhaps even the right to wear green. As much as it irritates me that a highborn boy like you can matriculate in a school that supposedly champions things like justice, equality, and rigorous self-improvement; flout all the rules that would have any less powerful student – anyone lower born, less well-connected, poorer, or female – expelled at the snap of a finger; and get away with it – despite how much this irritates me, I say, and despite how much pleasure I would derive from throwing caution to the wind and going on record as the one to assign you a tenth demerit, the fact is, you are just not worth it to me. I like to believe the work I do here is important, and I'm not going to throw away all the other duties of my post for the fleeting satisfaction of having enforced the principles of this school fairly against even the likes of you.

"This being the case, I'm not going to give you a demerit for your comment to Claire, and in fact I see no reason to go through the charade of attempting to punish you at all. As has no doubt been customary for you all your life, there is no need for you to explain yourself to me or to anyone else." Tamar leaned back in her chair, studying him.

Jadon licked his lips as he considered speaking. What could he say? *I really didn't mean to insult Claire? Even though I did know she was lowborn by birth, I just forgot and spoke without thinking because my head hurts so much, which is on account of the fact that*

I spent the night drinking myself into oblivion miles away from campus – which, by the way, is also why I was late? The excuse was as bad as the offense and would avail him nothing.

"But, Jadon," she continued, leaning forward to steeple her fingers with her elbows resting on the desk, "assuming I and the other Drei Masters continue to turn a blind eye to your offenses – as I expect we will, unless your misdemeanors escalate – you will eventually find yourself wearing the green of the Order. And perhaps one day you will catch sight of your reflection, and you will see the cloak that symbolizes peace, equality, and justice around your shoulders. And perhaps you will ask an explanation of yourself, as to why – and, yes, *whether* – you deserve to represent those ideals. It may be that no one else will ever dare hold you accountable to the standard of the Order, but one day, you might ask yourself the question, and I wonder... what will you say?"

She paused again, and Jadon studied the floor. Through the haze created by exhaustion and the continued pounding of his head, he could discern another sensation contributing to his discomfort: shame. *Shame? For accidentally pushing her to admit a truth we both know? For not holding myself accountable to the "standard of the Order"?* He was not sure that he deserved the emotion, but there it was.

"You are free to go."

Jadon looked up to find Tamar had turned her gaze to the window. She no longer looked angry. Rather, she seemed wistful, as if she would have wished the world a better place but knew it to be unfair and unforgiving.

"You're probably right," Jadon said, more because it was true than out of any hope it might appease her. He was a lost cause in her book, and he had no reason to care what was written there anyway. He started to leave.

"Jadon." He turned to find she was studying him again, her brown eyes steady and unreadable. "Circumstances may have conspired to gift you a cloak, and one day a princedom to replace it. But that doesn't mean you can't still earn them."

Jadon's mouth quirked into a dubious half-smile. "Maybe."

The cloak did not mean what it pretended to anymore, if ever it had in the first place. Jadon doubted whether anyone could earn it in truth and still succeed in an Order as double-minded as the one that required Tamar to spare him a well-earned expulsion in order to keep her post as Drei Master.

Jadon did not see any Initiative members in the mess hall, which meant they must have gone upstairs. There was a study room on the fourth floor that had a dartboard, and they ate there as often as not.

Jadon got only a mug of ale from the lunch line, his stomach too queasy to tolerate the thought of food. Then he headed up the winding staircase in the building's entrance corridor, pausing now and then to take sips and wonder why the Initiative had chosen a room so high in the tower.

As he walked across the landing on the third level, he heard female voices drifting through an open door. Catching the sound of his name, he drew closer.

He paused by the door and saw Christina sitting across from Claire in the back of the room. Claire's back was to him, her cinnamon-brown hair in a twisted braid more intricate than Christina's. A balcony door stood open next to their table, keeping the area brisk. Nefry and another boy were sitting out there, playing kings and dragons with trenchers of half-finished lunches resting near the game board. Sayler played in another match at another table.

The hitch in Claire's voice suggested she had been crying.

Great. Jadon hated unforeseen consequences. If he had meant to slight Claire, tears would not have disturbed him. Since he had not, he found they did.

Sayler looked up from his game. "Can we help you, Your Highness?"

"Actually, only the high prince is 'Highness,'" Nefry corrected, glancing at Jadon before sliding one of his prophets three squares along a diagonal. A glance at the board told Jadon his opponent was finished, though the game would take several moves to resolve. "His heir would usually just be 'Your Grace,' and at Eshtem it's 'Initiate' like the rest of us."

Jadon wondered if Nefry had failed to register Sayler's sarcasm. He took another sip of ale while he considered what he wanted to say here, if anything.

Claire turned to look at him, her tear-streaked face turning angry. "What do you want?"

Christina covered one of Claire's hands with her own. "I'm sure he simply happened to be passing by on his way upstairs." The Noraani princess looked at Jadon, her brown eyes cool and unreadable.

"Look, um… Claire–" Jadon began.

"It really is telling that you would know all the details of her station and yet barely succeed at remembering her name, isn't it?" Nefry's opponent mused, not looking up. "Don't you think you should just leave?"

Jadon narrowed his eyes, trying to place him. The boy was thin, with fine brown hair, and Jadon felt they had at least one class together.

"Perhaps he's trying to apologize," Christina suggested, studying Jadon.

Sayler snorted.

"A fine job he'd be doing," said Nefry's opponent.

"He may not realize apologies work best when the other party can't tell how little you care," said Sayler. Sayler had never liked him, Jadon remembered, though he could not have said why. He himself had nothing against Sayler.

Nefry's opponent moved a pawn one space forward. *Matt.* That was his name. *From weaponry.* Jadon took another sip.

"I wouldn't care if he were." Claire wiped tears away as she turned back to Christina. "I'm just so tired of it. From all of them. It's stupid, really. I know I shouldn't care."

"What's stupid is that he's still standing there with his ale." Matt looked at Jadon, his blue-gray eyes flashing in disbelief. "Can't you tell when you're not wanted?"

"You still can't tell that you've lost," said Jadon, nodding to the game board. "Interesting, for someone who disparages stupidity." The quip was irresistible, but Jadon regretted it after another sip. It had been at odds with his purpose. "But look, Claire–"

"There he is!"

Jadon turned to see Dreck, Arzit, and Hectibald coming down the stairs with empty trenchers. "Jadon!" Dreck grinned. "I see you're still enrolled? Your roommate told us you never came back to campus last night. We were concerned."

"What are you doing with this riffraff?" asked Hectibald, glancing into the room.

"Excuse him, ladies." Dreck sketched a bow toward Claire and Christina. "To be female, by right of birth, is to occupy a position most admired and appreciated in any gathering. The term was directed exclusively toward the males in your company, I assure you."

"Yet only one of them is a lady by birth. You may confuse the other with talk of positions." Arzit was grinning stupidly. "Right, Jadon?"

Jadon used his free hand to massage his forehead, wondering why his friends had to have such abysmal timing. "No, Arzit. I was talking about the *Alterrans*. Nothing else."

Matt had risen to his feet at Arzit's comment and taken a few steps forward when Sayler rose to intercept him. Then Christina stood. After exchanging glances with her, Sayler sat back down, and Matt remained where he was while Christina crossed the room.

She walked right up to Dreck, who stood in front of the propped-open door. "Excuse me," she said, taking hold of it.

"Of course, my lady." Dreck bowed again, smiling broadly as he backed out of her way. "Apologies for my tactless fellows." The man was an incorrigible flirt, though Jadon supposed it was just as well his attention was no longer exclusively dedicated to Trista. The Gold House girl had become more interested in Rindarin.

Christina looked at Hectibald and then Arzit, inviting them to move out of the way as she closed the door. Her eyes met Jadon's last, and he found them as cool and unreadable as when he had entered – beyond the indication that he should leave. That much read loud and clear.

She reminded him of Tamar, which annoyed him as he stepped backward.

It was even more annoying that he found nothing to say as she shut the door. Jadon consoled himself with the thought that he would have been more vocal if not for his headache.

"You do keep things interesting, Jadon," said Dreck as they walked toward the stairs. "What was that about?"

"Initiate Jadon!"

Jadon splashed ale over his hand, startled by the sudden booming. It was Garadil's voice, though the master was nowhere to be seen. *Is this Resonating through the entire campus?*

"Your presence is required off campus. Change out of Eshtem uniform and report to Headmaster Regild at the Dragon Gate."

What in the name of the Six...? Jadon licked ale off his hand, at a complete loss.

"Out of Eshtem uniform?" Arzit repeated.

"Lord Juaqen must want you," Dreck guessed. "I wonder why. They must be granting you Drei Lord leave."

Jadon groaned, annoyed with his head and his ale and his father. Drei Lord leave was a discharge from the Order, usually granted to a male highborn who inherited a lordship or to a female one so she could be married, but with the understanding that the lord or lady could return to the Edrei should their duties to their Houses end. They never did. "That's ridiculous. I'm an initiate, and unless my father is dead, I'm coming back."

"Yes, but Lord Juaqen is Senator-Liaison," Hectibald said. "He gets what he wants."

It went without saying that Lord Juaqen was not dead. There was a formula the Order used for informing loved ones of members' deaths and vice versa, and it did not involve trumpeting a summons across the entire campus.

"Why so glum?" Dreck asked, clapping his shoulder. "It should be nice to get off campus, especially for you. More people to celebrate your tourney victory."

"You wouldn't understand," Jadon muttered. At the moment, he hated life and everything to do with it, his friends included. Sometimes hangovers had that effect.

He took a deep breath and let it out slowly, reminding himself that he really hated only the high prince, and that only sometimes. The rest of the time, it was mere dislike.

"I guess I'd better go change," he said.

His father had left him no choice.

CHAPTER 15

Circles of Influence

"For too long have we endured the yoke of bondage. For too long have we accepted the insults of fate. For too long have we stood idle while those appointed to protect us raided our homes and demanded our sons and daughters as payment for debts they claim we incurred. Are we not also men? Are we not also appointed to protect? If we continue to tolerate this abuse at the hands of those above us, will not our wives and our children continue to suffer the cost of our inaction?"

> – Phel Naergar, in a speech to the people of
> Dophkah City on the eve of the Haliod Massacre

"Phel Naergar was a conniving demagogue who became a conniving dictator and is now just another conniving criminal locked in Dreiloch Castle. Why should we care what he said?"

This comment came from Landers, a friend of Eridike's who had recently joined the study sessions Diar and his friends had in one of the library's lower levels.

"Because, brainless," Jenne returned, fluttering her eyelashes at the new boy, "if we can't understand how to debunk a demagogue's lies, we won't be very effective at convincing populaces to respect the peace, now will we? And then we wouldn't be very effective Edrei – are you following? Or do I need to slow down?"

Diar was quickly coming to hate their new addition.

It was not Landers' fault that Jenne's treatment of Diar had cooled or that she had started flirting with someone else, and it was not in keeping with the Principles to harbor ill feeling toward one's fellow man. But after nearly two weeks of trying, quite fruitlessly, to recapture Jenne's attention, Diar's distress over the situation had morphed into anger. Landers was a convenient target.

"Jenne." Landers laughed. "It's precious that you think you might be able to go fast enough to lose me. Verbally or otherwise."

"You might be able to run faster than me," said Jenne, studying him and then shrugging. "But put us both on horses and you'll be eating my dust in seconds."

"Challenge accepted." Landers smiled. "Name the time."

"All right, you two," Cardos cut in, giving them both patient looks. Diar could have kissed him. "Back to rhetoric. What was the question, Telius?"

"We've been at this for nearly two counts already!" Eridike complained. "These speeches are all the same."

"I'm ready for a break," said Brinnette, standing. "Riding sounds fun."

"I'm in. And I'll back up my claim right now," Jenne said to Landers. "If you think you can handle it."

"You have got to be kidding!" Diar was hard pressed to contain his disgust. "Final interrogations are coming up. And none of us are remotely ready."

"Hey, now," Telius objected. "Let's try not to speak for everyone, shall we?"

"None of us but Telius," Diar amended, shooting the man in question an annoyed look. "And even he could use more time to prepare."

"Exercise helps concentration," said Cardos, beginning to pack up his things. "And we *have* already put in two counts."

"You don't have to come, Diar." It was the first thing Jenne had said to him all day, and she did not even look at him when she said it. She was packing up as well.

"This is a mistake," said Diar, watching as most of the table stood to leave. "Am I the only one who sees that? Liana?"

"Liana, you'll come, won't you?" Jenne cocked her head, smiling.

Liana grimaced. "I'm sorry, Jenne, but I need to keep working. I'm so behind already."

Jenne shrugged. "As you wish. I'll see you at dinner." She left the room with Landers and Brinnette, and Telius passed Diar the leather tome of example speeches before following along with the others.

Soon just Diar and Liana were left.

"Unbelievable." Diar shook his head.

"Are you and Jenne all right?" Liana asked, voice tentative. "Did something happen between you?"

"That's a question for Jenne." He bit back a surge of despair, avoiding Liana's gaze. Something had happened, of course. He had kissed Jenne, and then he had told her he liked her, and nothing had been the same since. "If you find out where I went wrong, please tell me." When he had told Jenne he liked her, she had told him they needed to focus on their studies. Maybe she had been trying to let him down easy. Maybe he had misread her from the beginning.

Diar took a deep breath and tried to refocus on the speech. Going over their interactions again and again in his head was not helping, and Jenne had not offered any further clarification the few times he had been able to question her since. At some point, he had to accept things for what they were and move on.

"Now, where were we?" he said. "How would you break down the argument?"

Liana sighed, a pained expression on her face. "I don't know. I'm not good at this."

"That's why we're practicing." Diar gave her an encouraging smile. "How would you start?"

"Identify the conclusion." Liana frowned, rereading the text. "Men are appointed to protect?"

"He does seem to be implying that," Diar agreed, scanning it again himself. "But that's more of an assumption. I think his conclusion must be that the men should rebel."

"Oh, you're right," Liana agreed, nodding. "Of course. Then, to the premises. Their wives and children are suffering on account of high taxes."

"Yes, and men are supposed to protect their families." Diar felt they were missing something. "If they don't resist the taxes, their families will continue to suffer. Therefore, they must resist taxes? Is that it?"

"I think so?"

Liana was a pretty girl with many admirable qualities. Exceptional helpfulness as a study partner was not one of them.

"Hey, Diar! Are you guys going over the Naergar argument?"

Diar looked up to see that Nefry had paused by their table on his way back from the shelves of reference books that took up most of the floor, a volume under his arm.

"Nefry." Diar nodded to him, realizing that he had completely forgotten about Christina and Nefry and their secret project. He had not spoken to either of them since turning over his portion of the Lists. "It's good to see you again. Have you met Liana?"

"Vorsand's niece, right? I know you're in my politics class, but it's a privilege to meet you officially." Nefry helped himself to the seat beside Liana, setting his book on the table. She nodded to him, but he did not pause long enough for her to speak. "And you, Diar, truth be told, you've become a bit of a legend since the last time we spoke, did you know that?"

"I have?" Diar traded confused looks with Liana.

"Sure! Diar, the Rishara Blood House boy who carries a Noraani-marked sword, runs with a Gold House crowd, and attends War House events. Nobody knows what to make of you. Though, truth is, you're not the only one."

"The only what?"

"The only one in violation of association norms. Trista is fast friends with Idarri, Weza, and Annvar now – all War House girls – even though she herself is from a Gold House. A royal one, in fact: House Rinton. Not everyone knows that, though. Probably because she doesn't go around wearing a royal-marked sword." Nefry was grinning.

"The sword wasn't my finest purchase, I agree."

"You mistake me. I think it's great. And it's not just any Blood House, either. It's Noraan. That ties you to Christina, you know. Which I find *deeply* fascinating."

"Why is that?"

"Because you're roommates with Jadon, and he is the most influential War House noble in our class. You could say he leads that whole clique. You might think the Blood House one belonged to Vannes or Lelise, but Christina is the smartest and the highest born among them, which are both critically important to Blood Houses. And there has been some tension between her and Lelise lately. Right now, the others still take their cues from Lelise, but if you want my guess, that whole clique is going to recenter around Christina because they'll want her help whenever they study. And then there's the Gold House students, who don't follow their nobles. Ramich has a following, certainly, but it's small potatoes next to the crowd that runs with Jenne, and the two of you seem to be joined at the hip. Which makes you, Diar of the Noraani-marked sword, closely connected to each of the three most influential students in our class." Nefry leaned back, folding his hands behind his head and studying Diar with a look of supreme satisfaction.

"Nefry, hello. Did you find what you were looking for?"

The three of them looked up to see Christina approaching.

"I sure did," said Nefry, standing and holding up his book. "Page four hundred sixty-three. But, Christina, look who I found! Diar, and this is Liana, who is Vorsand's niece."

"Hello again, Diar." Christina nodded to him, and Diar stood and nodded back. "And a pleasure to meet you, Liana."

"The pleasure is mine," Liana returned, all smiles and deference as she, too, rose to her feet.

"I have the utmost admiration for your uncle, although, Nefry, you ought not to have told me the connection. It places her in his House."

Nefry chuckled. "Oh, Christina. We're all placed in Houses, and there's no use pretending otherwise. But don't you want to hear why I came down here? I was in Lystra on Seventhday and I found a merchant from House Rimgard, and he told me the wildest story about his brother named Hazzar! But how about you? Any word from Our Library?"

"Nefry." Christina gave him a stern look, glancing at Diar and Liana. "Might I remind you that we are in a public place, where anyone might overhear you?"

"That's the beauty of the Ellyrian system! Nobody knows what it means. Except for the Drei Masters, of course, but I don't see any of them around here, and I don't think anyone will be retelling... um. I see what you mean. Apologies."

"Are you concerned we'll repeat this to the Drei Masters?" Diar asked, looking at Nefry with a quizzical expression.

"Ha ha. No. Why would you repeat this to the Drei Masters?" said Nefry, laughing. His reaction seemed a little overdone. "Why would the Drei Masters care to know wild stories about the brother of some merchant I happened to have drinks with in Lystra?"

"To answer your previous question, Nefry," said Christina, clearly desiring to change the subject, "no, I haven't heard from them yet. Perhaps my first letter was lost. I sent the second only yesterday."

"Wait, does this have something to do with..." Diar trailed off, glancing at Liana.

"The private matter you discussed with Diar way back when?" Liana finished, looking between him and Christina. "You know, I don't need to stay. I could see if Jenne–"

"Please, stay," Christina said, smiling at Liana. "We don't need to discuss anything private."

Nefry cleared his throat. "Well, Diar and Liana were just going over the Phel Naergar piece. If anyone wants my take on how to counter it, I'd say, attack the premises. Are governors appointed to protect the people? Does failing in that appointment mean the duty passes to the men, or are the men still bound by a superior duty to the governors? Or, you might try, is there another way to stop the families from suffering?"

"Slow down, Nefry," said Christina, smiling at the expression on Liana's face. "First, make sure they understand the argument. Can you work out the premises, Liana? Diar?"

"Well, some of them," said Liana. "Governors are appointed to protect the people, but so are the men. If the governors fail to protect the people, the people will suffer. And…"

"And this suffering will constitute a failure on the part of the men," Diar said, piecing it together from what Nefry had said. "So, it becomes the duty of the men to resist the governors when the governors fail to protect the people."

"Good." Christina nodded. "Do you agree with the argument?"

Diar thought about it. "No."

"Why not?"

"Because…" He cleared his throat. "Resisting the governors can't possibly be the only way to protect the families. It's like Nefry said. They could petition the emperor. Or work harder. Or emigrate."

"And if they tried all these things and failed? Would the suffering of the people then represent a failure of the men that could be rectified only by armed rebellion?"

"No. The suffering would constitute a failure of the governors." Diar smiled, the flaw in the argument suddenly making sense to him.

"I don't understand." Liana frowned, disturbed. "The men should do nothing? That's our counter?"

"No," said Christina. "Our counter is that the men are not obligated to rebel. Also, keep in mind that we're looking at the argument academically, but Naergar used it to convince

the Dophkan peasantry to slaughter the emperor's family
and attack the state guard, resulting in hundreds of deaths.
In the end, Naergar merely seized power for himself,
thereafter engineering the systematic slaughter of thousands
of dissidents. If an Edrei could have persuaded that original
crowd to pursue peaceful negotiation, could have warned
them of how following Naergar into bloody revolution might
result, perhaps a better solution could have been found."

"Oh." Liana smiled. "That makes sense. I think I will go
find Jenne and the others and explain this to them. It was a
pleasure to meet you, Christina and Nefry." She nodded to
them both and left the room.

Diar watched her go, feeling conflicted. He did not want
her to feel as if she had to leave, but he did want to ask
Christina and Nefry about the renegade, and Liana's absence
had created the perfect opportunity.

"I don't think we convinced her we have nothing private
to discuss," Nefry noted when she was gone.

"Did you find the renegade's name?" Diar asked Christina.
"Is that why you wrote to Our Library?"

Nefry turned an inquiring look toward Christina, who
pursed her lips in displeasure. "Well, he *is* asking," he
pointed out.

"Which he might not have done, had you not broached
the subject in front of him," Christina returned.

"I'm sorry," Diar said. "You don't have to tell me.
Whatever you might have found, you did it without my
help, and I don't need to know."

"It's not that we don't trust you," Christina hastened to
explain. "I just didn't want to burden you with the hassle of
additional secrets, given that you seemed content without
them."

"Everyone is content not knowing a secret until they realize that there's a secret they don't know." Nefry gave Diar a meaningful look. He was obviously itching to say something.

It was still true that Diar did not need any more complications in his life, but curiosity got the better of him. "If you have something you want to tell Christina, and Christina, if you don't mind my hearing, I'd be honored to hear whatever it is."

Nefry bounced on his toes, giving Christina an eager look, and she reluctantly waved a hand. "Go on, then," she said.

Nefry sat down at the table and waved them closer. "So, the renegade's name used to be Hazzar ti'Rimgard," he said in a hushed voice as Diar sat across from him. Christina came closer and took the spot Liana had vacated. "I was in Lystra yesterday, since it was a Seventhday, and I heard there was a Rimgard merchant staying at the Three Leaves Inn, so I bought him a drink and asked him about his thoughts on the Order.

"He told me that his brother Hazzar was Edrei and that he'd served closely under High General Serend," Nefry went on, turning to address both Diar and Christina, "and that Hazzar's most recent letters had expressed some concern about their missions in Dophkah. Apparently, their unit had come into possession of a magical trinket that Hazzar called a 'shard,' and Hazzar was worried about the effect it was having on Serend and whether the general might have been using it inappropriately. That was five years ago, and he hadn't heard from Hazzar since, but he knew that Hazzar was branded a renegade shortly thereafter.

"Now, I don't know what a 'shard' is, but I knew I'd heard the word before somewhere, so that's why I've been tearing up the library all day. I wanted to find where I'd heard it before I told you what Hazzar's brother said, Christina, and I did, in this book here. But I'm afraid it's not as illuminating as I had hoped." Nefry set his book on the table and flipped it open to a page he still had marked with his finger. He pointed to an indented portion of the text, which appeared to relay a short poem.

"*Seven shards of finest crystal,*" Christina read aloud, her voice even quieter than Nefry's. "*Transparent, light and shining power / Like the Scepter from which they came / In humanity's darkest hour / When God was killed, and the Covenant shattered / But freedom, love, and truth prevailed / But when the shards grow dark with death / Then will his sacrifice have failed.*

"What is this book, Nefry?"

"It's a treatise on poetic forms, and this excerpt is just being used as an example. It doesn't even say what it's excerpted from. Not helpful at all – but I know I've heard that poem before."

"It's a Rishara poem," Diar said, surprised to be able to contribute. "I've heard it before from a Storyteller – it's about the death of the White. He traded himself and his scepter of power – sometimes called the Scepter of the Covenant – to the first High Wizards, so they would give up their control of the elves and humans who had sold themselves into slavery. When he died, the scepter shattered into seven shards that kept some of his power, and the elves and humans used them to defeat the High Wizards. But hundreds of years later, a new compact of High Wizards was formed, and they figured out how to corrupt the shards and use them for evil. But then Aander and Rydara went to Edriendor and found the elves, and... well, you know the rest."

"I've never heard anything about these shards," Christina murmured, turning thoughtful.

"Turns out it's a good thing we brought Diar back into this, isn't it?" Nefry said triumphantly.

"Well, maybe." Christina frowned. "Thank you for your insight. It *is* helpful," she said to Diar. "But we don't really know that the magic 'shard' Hazzar said that Serend had was the same thing as these shards of the scepter from Rishara lore. We don't even know how much of the Rishara lore is true. No offense," she added with a glance at Diar.

"None taken," he assured her. Most Ellyrians believed all Rishara stories were nonsense, though there was enough obvious truth in them that the attitude never made sense to Diar. "But what does it mean if it is the same thing, and High General Serend has a shard of the Scepter of the Covenant? You don't really think he would abuse it, do you?"

"Probably not," Nefry agreed. "That's probably just what Hazzar told himself to justify whatever he did that got him expelled from the Order."

"Maybe," Christina said, but Diar could tell she was not convinced.

"What are *you* doing here?"

Diar turned to see Jenne had re-entered the room with Telius, Brinnette, and Liana. Jenne was staring at Christina, and Liana looked mortified. *Sorry*, she mouthed at Diar.

"Jenne," Diar began. Whatever was wrong between them, it was no excuse for her to be rude to Christina. Before he could rebuke her, Christina interrupted, rising to her feet.

"I came to look something up. This section of the library is open to all initiates, is it not? Did you make a reservation here of which I am unaware?"

"Sure it's open. I just wouldn't have expected you to come yourself when there are so many people around that you could 'requisition' to do that kind of errand for you. Your Grace. Or perhaps that's the very process I've walked in on," Jenne noted, glancing from the book in Nefry's hands to Diar and back to Christina.

"Jenne!" Diar shot to his feet, indignant now, but Christina spoke over him again.

"It's simply Christina, now, thank you. We are equals here, all of us. And if I offended you in some way at our first meeting, that is unfortunate, but I will not apologize for filling the station I held at the time."

"I think none of us finds that surprising." Jenne's tone was ice.

"We've had about enough of your kind telling us what to do and with whom," said Brinnette. "And so has Diar. Given that we are equals now, perhaps you could leave him alone and tell your friends to do the same."

"Don't speak for me, either one of you." Diar's tone was just as hard as theirs. "You left. I've been speaking with Nefry and Christina. It's none of your concern."

"And everyone slow down just a second." Nefry held up a finger. "Let's not assume Vannes and Christina are friends."

"Our apologies," Telius jumped in, addressing Christina. "It's been a long couple of weeks for everyone, and we'd like to get back to studying."

"No apology necessary," said Christina. "Nefry and I were just leaving. Another time, Diar." She nodded to him before sweeping past the others, eyeing Jenne as she went by. Jenne returned the look coldly until Christina left the room, Nefry trailing along behind.

"Spectrum's spitfire! What is wrong with you two?" Diar demanded of Jenne and Brinnette. "She didn't come here to boss me around!"

"So, you weren't discussing more 'private matters' that she made you swear not to speak of?" Jenne returned. "She's taking advantage of you, and you can't even see it."

"She really isn't – but even if she was, why would it matter to you? It's not as though my listening to her would mean you would have to."

"This isn't about me, Diar, it's about *you* and your reckless disregard for your own interests! I cannot *believe* you went all the way to Lystra for *Jadon*. Being their equal on paper means nothing if you keep letting them walk all over you!"

"Who told you that, and – wait. *Why* do you *care*?" Diar wanted to understand her, but sometimes she was so unreasonable he wondered if that was even possible. In moments like these, he felt she was more like a force of nature than a thinking human adult. Like a summer storm that could break out suddenly over open water. *Elemental. Inexplicable. Beautiful.*

Dangerous. Diar stared at Jenne as he completed the analogy. He was desperate for things to return to the way they had been before, but he had no idea how to make that happen. He was still losing sleep over it, and worse, he knew his schoolwork was suffering. *I have to be able to study. Making Edrei is more important than figuring out this chroming girl.*

"You're right," Jenne said after a moment, her voice suddenly cool. "I shouldn't. Let them treat you however you want." She turned and walked out of the room.

The rest of them watched her go with expressions that ranged from confusion to surprise.

Diar himself was aghast. Her leaving was the last thing he wanted, and he still had no idea what he had done to provoke the display.

Liana crossed the room and sank down in the seat across from him. "I'm sorry. I told her they helped us with Naergar. She said she wanted to come back to study. I didn't think she would–"

"It's not your fault," Diar assured her, his eyes still on the door.

If Jenne didn't care to be more than friends – or even to be friends anymore, as the last few weeks seemed to indicate – then why did she care who he spent time with?

Brinnette and Telius traded looks, and then they came and sat down at the table. "I guess she changed her mind about studying," Brinnette noted. "If she ever meant to in the first place."

"Should we get to it, then?" Liana asked, sounding anxious. There was a faint tremor in her hand as she smoothed the pages of the tome in front of her.

Liana was such a gentle girl, and for a moment Diar became upset with Jenne on her behalf as well as his own. It was not fair for Jenne to have an outburst like that and then walk away, heedless of the distress their quarrel had brought on the rest of the group.

Without even bothering to tell Diar what in the name of the White the quarrel was really about. *It can't just be Jadon and Christina. She must be upset about something else.*

Diar tightened his lips, torn between running after Jenne and resuming his studies. But if she had not simply lost interest in him – if he had hurt her in some way – running after her had not convinced her to disclose whatever it was thus far. She was unlikely to be any more forthcoming now, and he could not keep putting off studying if he wanted to make Edrei.

"Yes," he eventually said, sitting back down. "Let's, please." He glanced at Liana as he spoke, noticing the becoming way in which her soft yellow hair framed delicate facial features. He wondered why he had to get so worked up about the temperamental flares of a hot-headed girl like Jenne. *She isn't worth it*, he told himself. *She's reckless, irresponsible, unreasonable, and unkind.*

Once again, he instructed himself to put her out of his mind.

It was no easier this time than ever before.

CHAPTER 16

Jadon's Justice

"Mercy, Your Highness, I beg mercy! They meant no harm!"

"Yet a soldier is dead, madam, and the penalty must be paid."

"A penalty, yes, but not death! They are my sons, not yet of age."

"Only death can answer death. But they are young. Perhaps a measure of mercy may be shown." The high prince snapped his fingers and gestured to the boys in chains. "Release the younger."

"Six bless you and guard your reign eternal, Your Highness." The woman wept as she embraced her younger son, but her eyes were still on the other. "But what of his brother?"

The high prince's face remained as cold as the winter snow. "Only death can pay for life."

– Dramatized excerpt from the court records of
Heraldus the Great, High Prince Hatreth

The High Prince Hatreth had indeed secured Drei Lord leave for his son, which Jadon learned when he reached the Dragon Gate. Zar was there along with Headmaster Regild, though neither said why Lord Juaqen wanted Jadon to leave campus or why the Drei Masters were allowing it.

Jadon listened patiently as the headmaster explained the terms of his leave, which would last until he was called upon to compete in final interrogations. He waited until they left the headmaster to express his frustration.

"What is this about?" he demanded, mounting the royal-bred horse that was waiting for him on the Dragon Arch along with Zar's own. "Flames of the Abyss," he swore as he caught sight of the fifty Hatreth men and two orange-robed priests on the far side of the bridge. They were the same two priests who had accompanied him on his journey to Shenn, he believed: Argest and Rilad. "You brought a whole company? And the priests?"

"This is about Shenn," Zar explained as they started their horses forward. "The situation there has developed a few complications. Your father thought you may require extra hands to restore order, and when you are finished, he expects you to report to him in Hatre."

"He wants me to go to Hatre, personally? To *report*?" Jadon objected. "The terms of my leave won't allow it."

"Your father believes otherwise."

Jadon groaned. Hatre was typically a three weeks journey, one way, and final interrogations were only a month away. It might be possible if he traveled fast.

"Flames of the Abyss," Jadon repeated darkly. *The Senator-Liaison gets whatever he wants indeed*. He would have argued longer if he thought it would make any difference, but his father was not here. The order would stand. "You said there were complications in Shenn? What kind?"

Zar did not answer immediately, and Jadon knew why. Zar was accustomed to shadowing the high prince, and he knew that if Lord Juaqen had been present, he would not have answered questions from his heir on the way to deal out justice. Juaqen would have given Jadon only as much information as he deemed necessary, testing his son's ability to find out the rest. Zar, whose role in House Hatreth could be likened to that of an extra appendage of the high prince's, would have been expected to ignore Jadon's questions as steadfastly as the high prince himself.

"Zar." Jadon stopped his horse. "Were my father present, you would be bound by his wishes and not my own. But he is not here, and unless he gave this company to *you* to command, I am the one in charge, and I will have you answer my questions. Or I can go back to campus, and you can deal with the situation in Shenn without me."

Zar considered him, then nodded. "The command is yours, Your Grace. And I will answer any question you please to ask."

"Good." Jadon started his horse again, taking the lead as they trotted toward the column. "Now tell me about these complications."

The people of Shenn were starving. They had been hungry when Jadon saw them at summer's end, but Zar told him the situation had grown worse in the cold of winter. The children had been thin before. Now they were dying.

Zar's focus in recounting the tale was on the Elteressi. In the first few weeks after Jadon's ruling, Captain Gregol had raided one of the outlaws' hideouts, capturing the three leaders that had previously escaped. Their executions broke the spirit of the Elteressi for a time. Gregol continued holding the farmers' guild in prison and collected Hatreth taxes without incident for nearly two months while the population became further impoverished. Then the Elteressi resurfaced. First, they raided the storehouses where Gregol was keeping the portion of the harvest that exceeded what

the people of Shenn could afford to buy back. Then they
waylaid a wagon carrying taxes to Hatre. Gregol tripled the
guard on the next such wagon, but the Elteressi snatched
that one, too.

According to Gregol, the new leader behind the
opposition was called Drestil Bow. He had thirty
known associates, and Gregol had put prices on each
of their heads and posted notices with their portraits
throughout the town. However, Gregol was certain that
the townspeople were abetting them. Thus far, he had
captured twelve associates and seized Drestil Bow himself
on three separate occasions, but the band had a knack
for pulling off unlikely rescues. Drestil had escaped every
time, and Gregol had been able to execute only three
minor associates to date.

Two weeks ago, however, Drestil had been captured yet
again, and this time Gregol was taking no risks. He had his
full command with him in the fortress where the prisoner
was being held, and he had sent word to the high prince
that he would continue to do so until Juaqen arrived to pass
judgment.

I guess I'll have to do, instead, Jadon reflected. It was strange
to him that his father had chosen not to come. Jadon had
never passed rulings alone before, which meant he had never
really passed rulings. His father had always had the final say,
and he had always used it to overrule Jadon in something. By
not coming, his father was forgoing that right.

It must be some kind of test. That, or his father was busy
elsewhere and considered the situation in Shenn beneath
his notice enough that he did not care how Jadon handled
it.

Probably, it was both.

Jadon elected to make straight for Shenn, though it meant riding well after sundown. They arrived under cover of deep darkness, and Jadon led the men around the city's outskirts so they could approach the Hatreth fortress without alerting the townspeople. If he could, he wanted to keep the dissidents from learning how many men he had brought with him.

From what Zar had told him, it sounded as though the city was in dire straits. If Jadon's rulings here did not immediately resolve the situation, or if the high prince did not like what he heard about the tack Jadon took with the city, he knew that Juaqen would come himself the next time. Jadon would have only one shot at fixing the city's problems his own way: one day in which he could do whatever he wanted. He did not expect to follow a course of action his father would approve of, but he planned to achieve a result that could not be disputed. He needed to, if he wanted his rulings to stand, and if he was to have any chance at success, he would need every advantage he could get.

When Gregol came to greet the column, Jadon told him to clear the fortress of hands hired from the town. "Only soldiers see the horses. Understood?"

"Very well, Your Grace. May I ask why?"

"See it done, Captain. Zar, stay mounted. Enlightened, please do as well, and each of you…" Jadon counted off six men from the column. "The rest of you, dismount, go inside, and stay there. No one sees you but the other soldiers." There was a flurry of activity as the men followed orders. "Dismissed, Captain."

Gregol nodded, looking confused.

Jadon turned his horse around.

"The count is late," he said to the priests as he led his party back the way they had come. Soldiers did not require an explanation, but priests were different. "But not so late that the local inn will be closed for business. I find I could use a drink."

Jadon led them back around to the front of the city and then into its streets, idly commenting that he had forgotten the most direct route to the inn. There were not many townspeople up and about at this count, but those who were took notice of the men in Hatreth uniform with Jadon and the orange-robed priests at their head. They bowed to the Hatreth prince and scurried away.

No one was anxious to hear him pass judgment this time.

When they arrived at the inn, it was mostly deserted, and the few other patrons left when Jadon and his company were seated.

"Mistress Morgaine." Jadon nodded to the innkeeper as she poured him a drink. "Waiting on patrons yourself this evening? Where are the serving girls?"

"Beg pardon, Your Grace," Morgaine answered, keeping her eyes lowered. "I keep only one, now, and I let her go early. Has a newborn to tend to, she does."

"Would that be Chadrie?" Jadon asked, remembering the pregnant girl from his last visit. "How is she?"

"Times are hard all around, for her more than most. Losing her father and all." Morgaine glanced at Jadon, and he caught a flash of disapproval.

"Tagreff? What happened to him?"

She lowered her eyes as she answered, pouring a drink for Zar. "Executed. He murdered that brute Halomish, and your Captain Gregol had him hanged for it. Murder isn't right, so I guess he earned what he got, though it's hard to blame a man for looking to protect his only daughter."

"Protect? Or avenge?" Jadon challenged idly. He rocked back in his chair. "Have you a Snare of the Dragon deck here? Zar and I mean to test the skill of these alleged Enlightened."

"I'll have one brought." Morgaine curtsied before disappearing into the back room. She left the pitcher of ale on the table with them.

It was her son who eventually returned with the deck, breathless as though he had run across half the town to fetch it. "Hello, Your Grace," he said, bowing to Jadon after setting the cards on the table. It seemed he had learned the proper title for Jadon since his last visit, though he still lacked the trepidation Jadon might have expected from a child in a town oppressed by Hatreth soldiers. "Can I ask why you're here?"

"Why do you think I'm here?"

"They say you're just here to kill Drestil, but you won't do that, will you?"

"Drestil Bow, the outlaw who's been killing my soldiers and stealing from me? Why wouldn't I kill him?" Jadon started shuffling the deck.

"He saved Chadrie's baby, and half the town, too, during the outbreak a few months ago. He brought us medicine from Helos. Maybe he stole from you, but that's what you would have wanted the money used for anyway, isn't it?"

Jadon started dealing. "Soldiers are dead, boy. Somebody has to pay."

"Plus, we would have all starved without Drestil," the boy continued, undaunted. "Gregol's been charging too much for the crops, and without Drestil's helping everyone, we wouldn't be eating, let alone paying taxes. He brought Mama–"

"Elrec!" Morgaine reappeared from the back room. "The prince is playing cards. Don't bother him. Your pardon, Your Grace." She curtsied.

"No bother, Mistress Morgaine." Jadon waved a dismissal and Elrec scampered off. Jadon picked up his cards. "Your move, Enlightened."

"Something tells me that boy was about to name people complicit in hiding this outlaw from justice," Rilad noted.

"Whether we know their names is no matter. They'll see justice done tomorrow." It was a brash statement, and Jadon had no idea how he was going to back it up. But the night was young.

"Come to see the man whose blood will adorn your hands tomorrow?"

It was two counts later, and Jadon was standing in the lower level of the Hatreth fortress opposite Drestil Bow, whose face was illuminated in part by the torch Jadon held. The barred door of Drestil's cell stood between them, casting shadows on the outlaw.

Drestil gripped the bars, leaning forward so his face came more fully into the light. "I saved your entire city, you know. You should be giving me a medal."

"You killed Hatreth soldiers," Jadon returned, wondering why he had decided to speak to this man. Nothing good could come of it. "I can't spare you the penalty for that."

"'Only death can answer death.'" Drestil quoted the old War House saying, an odd smile on his face. Then he retreated to the back of his cell and sat down on the hard stone floor. "That's fauxsight, my young lord, and you know it. If you chose to spare me, who could stop you? They tell me the high prince didn't come to see my execution, which makes you the ranking lord here. If you set me free, I'll go free."

"My father would send assassins for you."

"Your father has sent men for me before." Drestil stared up at him. His eyes were barely visible in the shadows, but they were hard to ignore. "I won't beg." He looked away. "What you mean is you can't spare me *and* be taken seriously as a ruling lord, and that's true enough. I wouldn't expect a Hatreth prince to burn his political capital just to see the right thing done."

"Careful." Jadon kept his tone and his gaze utterly neutral, ignoring the strangeness of how this uneducated peasant had come to understand so much of House politics. "Your words border on treason. And I hold your life in my hands."

"I stand condemned of treason already. My life is over." Drestil's focus drifted into the distance, his gaze hard. "Tell me," he continued, his attention returning to Jadon, "if you were to find my men, what would you do with them? Would you kill them, too, for feeding your people? If you do, you realize there will be no Hatreth-sworn alive here after another winter."

"Your men will see justice done, same as you."

"Justice." Drestil snorted. "We lost three, you know. Children. Dead from starvation. After the Elteressi broke apart, before I got my band together. And you speak of justice." Drestil shook his head. "I only wish we'd started sooner. Could have saved three more lives."

"You will all see justice done," Jadon repeated. It was starting to feel like a lie. "Tomorrow."

Jadon handed his torch to the guards at the prison entrance when he left. He paused on the staircase to lean against the wall.

Only death can answer death. The words were ancient, as sound and inescapable as the structure of the War Houses they had helped to shape. Jadon lacked the power to deny them. Perhaps Drestil was right and he could save the outlaw, but the cost was too steep. To let the deaths of soldiers go unanswered would undermine both his reputation and his authority, killing any respect he might have hoped to garner from his people even before he became their high prince. Not to mention how it would inspire Juaqen to redouble the micromanaging of his son for years to come. Jadon would not have another chance at independence like this for as long as the high prince lived.

No, a penalty has to be paid here, Jadon knew. And it could be no less than death.

For some reason, his thoughts turned to something Tamar had said before he left: "Circumstances may have conspired to gift you a cloak, and one day a princedom to replace it. But that doesn't mean you can't still earn them."

It had been a ridiculous thing for her to say, and it was even more ridiculous for him to think back on it. Princedoms were never earned. They were just inherited according to the stupid accident of whoever happened to be born at the right time to the right parents. There were a few things a high prince could do to get himself ousted from the position once he had it, but none of Ellyrian's high princes had secured the position through merit. Jadon would be no exception, no matter how he handled this situation or any other.

But maybe Drestil Bow can be spared. Jadon took the stairs back to the main level of the fortress at a jog, a plan beginning to form.

"Your Grace." Gregol greeted him when he entered the hall, rising from the table he shared with Zar. Off-duty soldiers drank and played cards at other tables, while those on duty watched the exits and windows in parade rest. "Did you find the prisoner's arrangements to your satisfaction?"

"Captain, I believe the last time I was here, I had a word with you about one of your soldiers," Jadon said. "Halomish. What became of him?"

Gregol frowned. "Unsightly business, that. Murdered by one of the townsfolk. Probably an Elteressi. Well after I had him discharged from Hatreth service, of course, which happened shortly after your last visit. Brought him up on charges for conduct unbecoming – closest thing I could find to fault him for. He did well here as a private citizen, though. Became sheriff and then the mayor and was quite helpful in hunting those Six-forsaken Elteressi."

"Did any of the townspeople come to you with complaints about him?"

"Oh, sure, same as they complained about anyone helping the hunt for the Elteressi. Traitors, the lot of them, if you ask me."

"What kind of complaints did they have about Halomish?"

"Well, I don't know as I recall." Gregol stroked his beard. "Though now that you mention it, I suppose a few of them complained about his way with the womenfolk."

"Any women in particular?"

"Some serving maid at the inn, I think."

Jadon pursed his lips and studied the captain, who soon became uncomfortable.

"Why do you ask?"

"Captain, I'm going to need a map of the city. And a man from your company who knows the city and the opposition well. Someone who was there each time the Elteressi broke Drestil Bow out of custody in the past."

"Your Grace, I can assure you we have learned from our failures, and everything has been planned to the last detail. We are taking every precaution, and you need not concern yourself–"

"Have the man and the map brought, Captain. And then you may stand down."

Gregol cleared his throat, concerned by the abrupt dismissal.

As well he should be. Jadon swallowed as Gregol nodded and left. There was a sour taste in his mouth. He walked to the table and sat down next to Zar.

Soon a private by the name of Basicus Wrenk appeared with the requested map. Jadon bid him unroll it on the table, and the three of them began to talk strategy. Basicus walked them through Gregol's plan for the execution, which was to assemble the town outside the Hatreth fortress and behead the outlaw on the roof, thereby ensuring everyone witnessed justice without opening themselves to possible rescue attempts at a less secure location or in transit.

"And what do you think of that plan, Basicus?" Jadon asked. "Would the Elteressi make an attempt?"

Basicus shook his head. "Well, Your Grace, I'm no strategist, but it seems to me that if they could have marshaled enough support to assault all of us here, they already would have. They don't strike unless they think they have an opening, as far as I've seen."

"They've also never forgone an attempt when Bow's life was at stake," Zar pointed out.

"With Bow we've always made mistakes. Same with those of Bow's thirty who got away. They let us kill three without a rescue attempt, though. We kept tight security then, and that's what made the difference. Bow's people would die for him, sure, but not if they don't think they can break him out."

"Tell us about the mistakes they've exploited," said Jadon.

Basicus did. After Jadon and Zar had thoroughly interrogated him about the numbers and strategies they had seen from the Elteressi in the past, Jadon turned his attention to the map.

"We'll stage the execution here," he said, indicating the town square. It had to be the town square. That was where justice was usually administered, and it was the only place to which the Elteressi might believe the Hatreth prince would move the execution without an ulterior motive.

"It's an open area," Zar noted. "Plenty of approaches. Hard to secure."

"Pardon me, Your Grace..." Basicus cleared his throat. "But Bow's people will show up for certain if you take him there. If they see any opening at all, they'll bite."

"I want them to bite, Basicus. I want them all to bite." Jadon studied the map as he considered how best to deploy his forces. "You called them Bow's people. Not the Elteressi."

"The captain still calls them the Elteressi, Your Grace, but they don't style themselves that way anymore. Not since Bow took over."

Jadon digested that for a moment. Gregol ought to have included it in his report. "How many of Bow's people are in hiding?" he asked.

"Twenty-seven, near as we can tell. But up to half the town might disguise themselves and join in if they see a chance to free Bow."

"We can't have that." Jadon frowned.

"They think you have only fifty soldiers still," Zar noted. "Plus seven."

Jadon nodded slowly. He usually enjoyed this type of strategic exercise. Tonight, though, he was playing for higher stakes. People would die.

The weight of it gnawed at him and made him doubt himself in a way he was wholly unused to. "I want the outlaws so thoroughly out-positioned that we don't have to strike a single blow," he said.

He could solve this. He had to.

"Perhaps if you had the cooperation of the townspeople," Basicus suggested. "Bow's men won't fight back if they see they'd only be hurting the townspeople. But the people wouldn't work with you against him."

"Everyone has a price," said Zar.

"What if we took the children hostage?" Jadon said. "Threaten to have them killed if any soldiers die."

"If Bow's people hear about it," said Basicus, "and they usually do, they'll divide their forces and make a play for the children simultaneously. And if they don't think they can save both, they won't try for Bow at all."

Zar was studying Jadon. "And if they do try for Bow, maybe killing a few of our soldiers in the process, you would have a lot of children on your hands and quite a few people watching to see if you're the kind of man who follows through with his threats."

Jadon swallowed. "It's not going to come to that. What makes you so sure they'd make a play for the children?" he asked Basicus.

"They're good people. Um, that is – your pardon, of course they're traitors, all–"

Jadon waved away the error, undisturbed. "What you mean is?"

"They're doing all this for the townspeople," Basicus said, looking chagrined. "They don't want to see any die. Especially not the children."

"You think that will still be true without Bow calling the shots?"

"Yes." Basicus scratched his head. "They'll be answering to Vasil Engus, Bow's right-hand man. He's led these attempts before. And we've tried hostages before. He's been scrupulous to avoid collateral among the townspeople. They all are."

It took a few more counts for them to hash out a plan, and longer for Jadon to summon the soldiers and put it into motion. The work lasted through the night, and it was not until nearly dawn that Jadon found himself with a few spare moments.

Instead of seizing the opportunity for sleep, he helped himself to a greatsword from the armory and went outside to chop firewood. Zar joined him after a time.

"Most people cut firewood with an axe," Zar noted.

"It's late," Jadon said, swinging the blade down onto the log in front of him. It sank only halfway through before getting stuck. "You should get some sleep."

"That blade isn't sharp enough." Zar watched as Jadon pulled the sword out of the wood and swung again at a different point. He cut deeper this time, but not far enough to cleave it in two. "You should use mine."

"Yeah." Jadon drove the point of the greatsword into the frozen ground and turned to Zar, who took off the shoulder strap securing the greatsword he carried across his back. He drew the weapon from its scabbard and handed it to Jadon.

Jadon turned back to the woodpile and selected another log. Positioning it on the stump used for splitting wood, he lifted the greatsword over his head, took aim, and struck. This time he sliced it clean through.

"It's not the same, you know," said Zar.

It was eerie how the man could say so little and discern so much.

"No," Jadon agreed. "I don't suppose it would be."

By the second count of Xanthin, all of Shenn had assembled. It was a warm morning and the snow had already begun to melt, leaving the town square wet and dirty. The raised platform at the front of the square had been turned into a pyre for Drestil Bow, who stood there bound to the whipping post.

A second pyre had been constructed near the shops on the edge of the square, this one enclosed by a fence. About thirty children stood inside, crowding against one another atop the kindling. Fifteen soldiers stood around the pyre, each carrying a lit torch. Jadon noticed Elrec pressed up against the fence. His eyes were fixed on Drestil Bow with a concern that seemed oblivious to his own predicament. The other children ranged from nervous to scared, but none of them were as distraught as the adults who stole glances at them while they waited for Jadon to speak.

Twenty more soldiers, led by Captain Gregol, stood at the base of the platform where Bow was bound, forming a line between the pyre and townspeople. The two priests stood in the center of the line, each holding a torch. The soldiers had their weapons drawn and stood ready for trouble. Eighteen others ringed the square.

Three stood facing the priests with Jadon, Zar included. Jadon wondered if it would be enough to deter assassination attempts. Then he reminded himself that Bow's people had other priorities and there could be no going back on the plan now.

Zar should be enough to protect him, if it came to that.

Jadon drew in a breath and turned to address the crowd. "People of Shenn," he began. He had their attention, though no one wanted to hear what he would say. Their faces were tight with fear and anger. Tears filled the eyes of a few.

Some glared at him in hatred.

He cleared his throat. In all the time he had spent preparing for this, he had not given a single thought to what he would say. *Fauxsight. You idiot*, he rebuked himself. It was more exhaustion speaking than real concern, though. Something would come to him. Something always did.

"For some time now, this city has been the focal point of a rebellion against Hatreth rule." *Focal point? Of a rebellion?* Surely there was a better phrase for that.

Maybe he should have tried to get some sleep before this.

Jadon cleared his throat again and continued. "It began as an opposition of loyalties. The people of Shenn swore loyalty to House Hatreth long ago, but some denied the legitimacy of that oath and of Hatreth's right to rule. They grew tired of the homage and duty their fealty demanded and sought to unshackle themselves from the oaths of their ancestors. They discarded their vows and their honor. They threw off their identity as Hatreth-sworn and put on the title of 'Elteressi,' as if by taking up the name their ancestors surrendered, they could take on an identity older, grander, and more legitimate than their own. As if they could hide under this name that which they really were – oath-breakers, rebels, and murderers. A band of outcast, honorless scum.

"Hatreth responded as any wronged authority should: with the strong arm of discipline. We sent soldiers to enforce the consequences of breaking our commands. As any loving parent would rebuke an errant child, we sought to teach you your boundaries, to be harsh with you in order to restore you to our care and protection. The leaders of these self-styled Elteressi were put to death, and those who abetted them punished.

"There the story might have ended, but there were those among you who refused to be disciplined. Here behind me stands Drestil Bow, one such resister of discipline. He stands accused of treason and fomenting treason. There is no doubt of his guilt. He has been sentenced to death by fire, which you stand here to witness."

Jadon paused, scanning the crowd. Chadrie was openly crying, and she was not the only one. Morgaine looked near to it, though by the glances she kept stealing at Elrec, Jadon supposed her distress was more for her son than the outlaw.

His eyes fell on Basicus, who stood in the back corner of the square. The man saluted.

It was the signal. Those of Bow's people who were coming close to set up shots on the soldiers around the children had been identified and subdued, by the soldiers Jadon had hidden to ambush them. The rest of the outlaws would wait until the last moment to appear and save their leader, but Jadon's soldiers would be ready for them, too.

He nodded to acknowledge the signal.

"You came here to see Hatreth make its answer to the violence that has been done in this town," he continued, trying to ignore the growing pit in his stomach. *Yes, I definitely should have slept.* "Hatreth soldiers are dead. Those responsible must pay, and there can be no doubt that this man," Jadon lifted an arm to indicate Drestil Bow, "is responsible."

Jadon's gaze swept the crowd again. "But he is not alone responsible." He snapped his fingers, and the two soldiers with him and Zar moved to take hold of Gregol.

"Your Grace?" Gregol stuttered.

Jadon turned to address the captain. "Captain Gregol, you are under arrest," he said, his gaze hard and his voice expressionless. "Please surrender your weapon to Enlightened Rilad and remand yourself to Hatreth custody."

Gregol followed his orders, and Rilad accepted his sword, though Argest looked near to objecting. Zar was studying Jadon in open disapproval, and most of the soldiers looked confused.

Jadon had not shared the entirety of his plan with anyone.

But the two soldiers with Gregol bound his hands behind his back, just as Jadon had privately instructed them before they entered the square. No one moved to stop them as they marched him around the platform and then up onto it.

"Wait, what is this?" Gregol panicked. "Your Grace, what are you doing? I've only ever followed my orders!"

"Captain Gregol, when last I was here," Jadon said, taking a few steps to the side so he could address both Gregol and the crowd while the soldiers forced the captain to his knees beside Drestil, "I put you in charge of collecting the harvest for House Hatreth, and I commanded you, in the presence of all those here assembled, to sell it back to the people at a price not too steep for them to afford. Did I not?"

Gregol struggled as the soldiers bound him to the post beside Drestil. Jadon's orders had been specific. Drestil had been bound standing on one side of the post, Gregol kneeling on the other. "Your Grace," Gregol panted, craning his neck to see Jadon, "in all my duties, I have been nothing but faithful to–"

"And I told you," Jadon cut him off, facing forward to address the crowd, "in the presence of all those here assembled, that I would hold you personally accountable if the people starved. And the townspeople, Captain, are starving. Three of them died on your watch, and more would have followed had not the man bound there beside you resorted to open rebellion in order to feed them. His crimes are his own, and he will answer for them, but he will not answer alone. For it is your failure, as much as his, that has brought us here today."

"The high prince would never stand for this!" Gregol was shouting now – shouting and sweating and struggling – but his bonds held fast. "His Grace is overstepping the bounds of his authority here, men. Release me! That's an order!"

No one moved.

"Zar." Gregol craned his neck to find Juaqen's second. "You know the high prince would never allow this. Stop this!"

"Your sword," Jadon said to Zar.

Zar unslung it from over his back and extended the hilt toward Jadon, his gaze tight with concern. Gregol was right. The high prince would never allow this.

Which was why Jadon would not risk ordering anyone else to do this next part for him.

He drew the sword and walked to the platform. "In recognition of your years of service to Hatreth," he said, climbing the steps, "you will be spared the indignity of burning alive." He stopped in front of the kneeling captain. "Any last words?"

"This is about Halomish, isn't it?" Gregol said, trying to meet Jadon's gaze. His eyes were streaming tears, and he was no longer struggling. "Why? I have a family."

"No, Captain," Jadon answered softly, his gaze returning to the crowd. This was not about Halomish. Gregol had miscarried justice there, badly, but did he deserve to die for it? Many a Hatreth officer would have done the same or worse in his place. The real fault lay with the man who had appointed him to this post.

Jadon was under no delusions. This was not about justice. This was about expedience.

Only death can answer death.

"This is about Shenn," he told Gregol. "Your family will be taken care of." He lifted the greatsword overhead and took aim. *Just like I practiced*, he told himself, and then he brought the sword down.

It was nothing like his practice. The spray of blood caught both him and Drestil.

Jadon swallowed, keeping his eyes on the crowd as Gregol's body slumped over. Then Jadon stalked down from the platform and took a position between the priests. He was covered in blood, and everyone was watching him.

He took Rilad's torch with his left hand.

"The sins of the father, however, do not excuse the sins of the son. The deaths of Hatreth soldiers demand an answer, and for that, Drestil Bow is sentenced to death." Jadon tossed the torch onto the pyre.

That was the next signal. Hissing filled the air, and the fifteen soldiers surrounding the children went down, each struck center mass by an arrow. Twelve combatants then materialized in the crowd, drawing weapons and moving to free the children. More ran into the square from behind the shops, trying to reach Drestil before the fire spread.

These were subdued by soldiers Jadon had hidden inside the shops. Those in the crowd were threatened by fathers who stood next to them, whom Jadon had armed with daggers and threats for just this purpose. They knew the fallen soldiers were a hoax. The arrows had been fired by Hatreth archers on the rooftops after Jadon's people had subdued Bow's archers, and they had glanced harmlessly off body armor.

Bow's people raised their hands in surrender.

It had all taken less than the time required for Jadon to clear his throat. He continued speaking as the soldiers around the pyre got up and took control of Bow's people in the crowd. They marched them to the front of the square, where they joined the rest of the soldiers forming a line of subdued outlaws in front of Jadon. The fire slowly spread toward Drestil.

"But this man's crimes are not all that demand an answer. The service he has done for House Hatreth also demands an answer." Jadon nodded to Basicus, and the soldier signaled another, who led a royal-bred horse toward the pyre. "When the citizens of Hatreth were bound and suffering under the yoke of a cruel taskmaster, this man fought to keep their bonds from crushing them. For that, he will not die bound." Jadon took a few steps and leapt onto the pyre, on the opposite side from where he had thrown the torch. The pyre was made of slow-burning tinder, but the fire was already licking Bow's boots when Jadon sliced his bonds with Zar's bloody greatsword.

Drestil staggered forward. He jumped down from the pyre and stamped out a few errant sparks.

Jadon leapt down to join him as the soldier with the horse arrived. Jadon took the reins. "For the means to cheat death which he provided for the Hatreth-sworn who would otherwise have succumbed to disease, we provide him with the means to cheat death." He handed the reins to Drestil, who was staring at him dumbly. "For the time his struggle bought for the Hatreth-sworn who would otherwise have starved, we give him time before his sentence is carried out." Jadon lifted a hand, and Hatreth archers stood from where they had been lying concealed on the rooftops, each pointing a drawn bow at Drestil.

Drestil looked at them, then at the twenty-seven men who stood under guard in a line before him, and then back at Jadon. Jadon gave a small jerk of his head, and Drestil came to his senses. He mounted the horse and kicked it into a gallop, leaving the square.

The road out of town sloped uphill, and everyone watched Drestil ride away. Jadon waited until the shot was difficult, but not impossible, before dropping his hand. The archers fired. They all missed, but one arrow sailed just over Drestil's shoulder. He touched a hand to his neck and reined the horse in, glancing back toward the square. He tossed Jadon a salute before resuming his gallop, disappearing down the far side of the hill.

"And for the many lives he saved," Jadon continued, waiting until he regained the attention of the townspeople, "I grant him the lives of the men who followed him. And full pardons to any who now kneel and swear fealty to House Hatreth."

Soon all twenty-seven were on their knees, taking the vow as the pyre went up in roaring flames. The scent of burning flesh filled the air.

A wave of nausea swept over Jadon as he watched the outlaws take the oath. He clenched his teeth and fought it, unwilling to be sick in front of the people. He had no attention to process what the outlaws were saying, but he could tell from their faces that the words were right. From the gratitude in their eyes, they meant them.

The faces of the townspeople, too, had changed. Some cried in relief or joy. Their children were unharmed, their savior had been spared, and their oppressor had been brought to justice. Some still regarded Jadon with trepidation, but as he scanned the crowd, he no longer read the keen edge of hatred in most of their gazes. What he saw looked more like awe.

"I…" Jadon began when the murmuring faded. He stopped to clear his throat and became conscious of feeling unreasonably warm, even given the blazing fire behind him. He persevered. "I will be recalling half the soldiers stationed here to bolster the forces in Hatre. To replace the deceased in command over those who remain, I hereby name Basicus Wrenk your new captain. And I appoint Vasil Engus mayor in place of the existing one. I will hold the two of you personally responsible for ensuring this town continues paying its taxes. And to preserve the populace."

There was more that he should say, but his nostrils were filled with the stench of Gregol's burning body and the nausea was starting to rise again.

"Assembly dismissed." Jadon turned and stalked out of the square, the priests and soldiers falling into parade march beside and behind him. Jadon raised a fist to halt them as soon as they turned a corner.

"Excuse me for just one moment," he said to the priests, walking toward one of the nearby houses. He went past it, circling around to the back, where, for the moment, no one could see him.

Then he leaned over and vomited into the grass. It lasted a long time, and when it was over, he felt in no way improved.

When he looked up, Zar was there, offering him a kerchief. Straightening, Jadon wiped his mouth and pocketed it.

Zar said nothing as Jadon led the way back to the column. It was the only detail of the morning that Jadon expected his father would never learn or require him to explain.

It would be a long ride back to Hatre.

CHAPTER 17

Conspiracies

Dear Drei Initiate Christina,

Well may you wonder at the delay in our response to your inquiry. The truth is, the Vaars had no intention of answering you at all. I discovered your second letter discarded only this morning. Our records on Hazzar are complete and open to the public here, same as we would have on any other Edrei, so I can only infer the sensitivity is coming from your end. However, the records I've gone through tell the story of a man who reflected well upon the cloak he wore. I've included a copy of his review by our representative at your university as well as the report on his actions here which you requested. I know not why you requested the information or why the powers that be in Ellyrian should desire you not to have it, but I share it with you in the hopes that more information will lead to more informed decisions and superior outcomes, whether for you, a patron and supplicant of Our Library, or for Hazzar ti'Rimgard, who by all accounts was an upstanding Edrei and good friend to this country. Yours in the light of the God of Mystery insofar as he has seen fit to let it be shed upon us,

— Calliope, Apprentice Vaar in the 56th year of King Jazirh

The days stretched into weeks while Christina waited for a response from Our Library. The last of the snow melted, and some of the campus trees began to bud. Nefry asked for an update nearly every day, and he found a few more references to the shards of the Scepter of the Covenant in the library that they puzzled over together. None offered any more clarity than what Diar had already told them, and they were unable to confirm whether the shards were real physical objects, let alone whether the Order had ever possessed any of them. Christina told Nefry what Master Porrian had said to her about Hezred's having stolen some kind of magical weapon from the Order, and they agreed it was likely the high general's "shard" that Hazzar had referenced in letters to his brother – but whether it was a shard of the White's scepter, or whether those could even be used as weapons, they had no idea.

Neither of them saw much of Diar, even in passing. He did not seek them out, and given how upset his friends had become after their last conversation, Christina figured it was for the best.

A response from Our Library came during the week of final interrogations. Because Christina would not compete until one of the latest rounds, she was free to await the post rider's arrival at the posting office in the library three days in a row. On the third day, the post agent barely glanced at the package marked with her name before handing it to her. Christina took it to the balcony on the north tower before opening it up to find the note from the Apprentice Vaar.

That was when she realized how lucky she had been. If the post agent had bothered to open the package and scan the contents, as was normally done with initiates' mail, the note would have triggered a review by the Drei Masters, and they would have learned she was trying to uncover erased information.

Christina breathed a sigh of relief. She had not expected that the Vaars would keep themselves apprised of what information had been erased in Ellyrian, nor that they would show sensitivity about sending such information back in. The name Hazzar ti'Rimgard alone would not have been enough to provoke curiosity from a post agent with no knowledge of the man, Christina was sure, but the nod to the fact that the information had been erased certainly would have. Christina's mistake could have been costly.

But it wasn't, she reassured herself. *I got away with it. And I'll be more careful next time.*

She had forgotten that representatives from Jeshimoth and Alterra were present at the final review of each initiate and were required to sign off on their graduation to full Edrei. The Treaty of Edriendor stipulated as much, though the time when Alterra and Jeshimoth had cared enough to question the Order's judgment had long since passed. Christina had not thought the custom served any purpose, but the Jeshim representative's record of Hazzar ti'Rimgard's review was enlightening.

"Knowledgeable and impressive, with a quality of character reminiscent of an era marked by finer Edrei than the self-involved dross we've graduated lately," Drei Headmaster Regild was quoted as having said of Hazzar, though he was not headmaster then, but Drei Master of Diplomacy and Intelligence. "The strongest of this year's Imagers, and one I'd not hesitate to trust." That was from the Master Imager of Dreaming, Vorsand. "The kind of candidate that makes me proud to train up initiates in the ways of the Order." A master called Kestigon had said that.

Not all the opinions were quite so glowing, but none expressed any serious concern. Of interest to Christina was a quotation attributed to Porrian: "Competent in the basic skills and knowledge base required of an Edrei, certainly; one merely wonders whether he possesses adequate ambition to help guide the actions and opinions of others."

She read the quotation again and double-checked the name.

Her pulse quickened. Everything in the report suggested Hazzar had been a good man, but that Porrian had said *this* – that was the final nail in the coffin of the idea that Hezred had merely been playing a part when Christina had met him.

Her mistakes had been costly indeed.

"Christina!" She started, but it was only Nefry. "My, oh my, look at what you've got! The Vaars finally came through?"

"Not the Vaars. Not exactly." She stood up and moved toward the railing, letting Nefry peruse the papers while she gazed out over the pine forest.

"Sounds like a great guy," Nefry summarized. "Or at least someone who used to be a great guy. Christina, this has been fun and all, trying to figure out if a man might have been expelled from the Order unjustly, but let's pause for a second to make sure we're on the same page." He patted the papers and gave her a dubious look. "We still have zero real information – you do see that, right? And this is probably as much as we'll ever learn. You don't actually think we're in the process of unearthing a conspiracy here, do you?"

Christina turned to face him, settling herself on the balcony's cushioned seat. It was odd to hear him say they would never learn anything definitive, given how enthusiastic he had been about the project in the first place.

But she had always known that what he was saying now was true. "Did I ever tell you what Master Porrian said to me, when he found out I had spoken to Hezred?"

"Other than that Hezred had stolen a magic weapon? No. You've been very close-lipped on everything to do with the renegade. Despite my vow and my invaluable assistance in this investigation, I might add."

"He said – not in so many words, but he directly implied – that Hezred was well-practiced at using magic to win power and popularity. But you see what Master Porrian said about him there?"

Nefry reread the quotation, frowning. "Seems to be saying he lacked ambition. Huh."

"I'm starting to be sorry I involved you in this, Nefry." Christina lowered her gaze, letting it come to rest on the note from Our Library. "You and Diar. I slipped up, using the university post. Who knows what could have happened if I hadn't been there to retrieve the package before the post agents looked over the contents."

"Whoa, whoa, whoa," said Nefry, seating himself at the study table to bring them eye to eye. "First, you didn't involve me. I involved myself, and the same is true for Diar. Secondly, let's be realistic. Sure, maybe we should have thought through how the Vaars might feel about sending us the information on Hazzar, but what's the worst that could have happened if the Drei Masters found out? A slap on the wrist? Maybe a couple demerits?"

Christina sighed. Standing, she turned to look out at the forest again, finding the view comforting. "Or maybe I could have been killed. And you too, if they found out you were helping me. Hopefully Diar doesn't know enough to put him in danger."

"Seven sights, Christina. Why would anyone have *us* killed? We don't know anything more than Diar. Which is nothing!"

Christina turned back to face him. "We know what Hazzar's brother told you about the high general's shard."

"That something about it made Hazzar uneasy? Like I said – nothing."

"We know Hazzar expressed unease about General Serend's use of a shard. We know Master Porrian told me that a shard can be used as a weapon by a talented Projector," Christina returned, ticking off the facts on her fingers. "We know General Serend, like Hazzar, is a Projector. We know Hazzar became Hezred, and that Hezred maintained he was expelled from the Order unjustly and tried for capital crimes in absentia. And I didn't tell you this before, but he also told me that the witnesses in the case he was trying to build kept getting killed.

"Fill in the blanks, Nefry. Porrian and at least a small majority of the Council know what Serend was doing with that shard, and they want it kept quiet. Hazzar figured it out, so they discredited him and erased him, and after he became Hezred and tried to expose them, they killed–" Christina stopped, remembering that she had been ordered not to speak of Hezred's execution. "They killed witnesses to keep it from getting out. What's to stop them from doing that again?"

"Spectrum's spitfire, Christina, I don't know, maybe the fact that *we don't know anything*." Nefry stood and spread his hands, indicating the papers on the table before them. "All you have is a story – and not a very good one at that! We don't even really know what a shard *is*, let alone how Serend could have been abusing one. What makes you think your story is more likely than one where Hazzar really deserved the judgments against him? Is there something you're not telling me?"

Christina gnawed her lower lip and looked away. "I'm not sure how far I should trust you, Nefry. You dropped the name Hazzar in front of Diar and Liana."

"In my defense, the name's been erased for years. Neither of them knew it, and they wouldn't have thought anything of it if you hadn't gone all 'anyone might overhear you' on me." He tilted his head to emphasize the point, then looked down. "But for my part, I am sorry. It won't happen again."

Christina looked out at the forest, moving to rest her hands on the balcony's railing. "Hezred didn't just rob me, Nefry," she said. "He protected me during the fighting. Drei Zanner, too. A few counts later, he caught up to us on the road. A band of Edrei was hunting him, and when they got there, he offered Drei Zanner a life oath, but Zanner fainted before answering. The Edrei executed Hezred before they restored Drei Zanner to consciousness."

And I did nothing. Christina blinked back a few tears, glad she was facing away from Nefry. All this time, she had been hoping to find something that would convince her she had not messed up as badly as she suspected, that Hezred had deserved to die, that his moments of nobility had all been part of an act intended to fool her. That she had not simply watched as an innocent man was beheaded.

"They discredited him. They erased him. And they killed him." Christina took a seat at the table, looking up at Nefry. "Without giving Drei Zanner a chance to answer his oath." She looked down, conscious of a tremor in her jaw. She had been ordered not to speak of the execution, but if that order was part of a cover-up, as she now suspected, it wasn't binding. Nefry already knew the renegade was dead, anyway. "I trust I still have your oath of silence."

Nefry sat across from her and covered her hand with his. "Of course."

She looked up, and he snatched his hand back. He stood and paced the length of the balcony, thinking.

"So the renegade *is* dead, then. And they ordered you not to speak of it? But you've decided we can talk about it between the two of us, given my oath of silence?"

Christina nodded.

"So, the most wanted man in Ellyrian has already been caught and killed, and they decided to keep it secret from the country. I thought so. It seemed a little suspicious at first, true, but Diar was right. There are any number of reasons they might want to keep the news quiet. But you say they killed him before Drei Zanner answered his oath?"

"Master Porrian told me the Edrei broke protocol because they thought Hezred had a dangerous weapon he might use at any moment. And that they haven't made his execution public because they want Hezred's associates to believe he is alive, so they'll keep looking for him and hopefully expose themselves to the Order's intelligence network. They presume Hezred gave the shard to one of them, since it was not on him when he died, and the Order wants to get it back."

"Well, that makes sense. They think he gave the shard to someone else? Probably one of the outlaws you met, right? He realized the Edrei were closing in, so he passed off the shard and led them away from it? Is that what they think?"

"So I gather. Master Porrian pressed me for descriptions of his associates."

"What did you tell him?"

Christina said nothing, and Nefry stopped pacing to regard her. "Christina. You *did* tell him everything you remember, didn't you?"

She remained silent, and Nefry sat down across from her again. "Look, I know you think we're onto something here, but the only thing we actually know is that you're withholding information pertinent to the whereabouts of a magical weapon. You do realize how dangerous that is, right?"

"Of course I've considered it." Christina had not made any of her choices lightly. "But Master Porrian implied that only a Projector could use the shard as a weapon. None of the other outlaws would have been Projectors, but Serend is one. And he's still Drei High General, so who is to say that if the Order recovers the weapon, it wouldn't make its way back to him? Maybe the best place for the shard is wherever Hezred left it."

"What if you're wrong about him? What if he planned for the shard to reach another Projector who would use it against innocent people? Is that really a risk you want to take?"

"Except I'm not wrong about him, Nefry." Christina picked up the note from the Apprentice Vaar and waved it. "Didn't you read the report?"

"So Master Porrian didn't consider Hazzar ambitious at the time of his graduation. So what? People change." Nefry leaned forward, giving Christina a firm look. "You feel guilty about what happened with Hezred," he said, raising an admonishing finger. "He protected you, and you didn't protect him. You weren't convinced he deserved to die, and you think maybe you did the wrong thing. But you didn't. You had every reason to trust the Order at the time, and *nothing we've learned has changed that*."

Christina sat up straighter, setting down the note from the Apprentice Vaar and smoothing it out. "Come on, Nefry. There's no way the man described in this report dishonored himself thoroughly enough to earn erasure and execution and then got so wrapped up in his own ego that he sold an alternate version of events to everyone he met."

"And what are the odds that the Drei High General abused a magic weapon and there's a conspiracy in the Edrei Council to cover it up?" Nefry propped his head on a hand. "It's less likely by far. You're letting guilt cloud your judgment."

"Maybe." Christina took a deep breath and released it. It was true that she had nothing definitive. "But maybe there's a way to be sure," she continued, inspiration striking. "If I'm right, and Master Porrian is covering something up – if he's going out of his way to make sure I'm not suspicious about it – then maybe if I ask him the right questions, he'll contradict the report."

Nefry considered, then nodded, shrugging. "If he has nothing to hide, he would have no reason to do that. But if he doesn't lie, I hope you'll tell him whatever you know about the bandits. I made a vow, so it's your choice. But sitting on that information is dangerous, and I don't think Master Porrian will lie to you."

Christina smiled grimly. "We'll see."

Jenne was slotted to begin final interrogations on the fourth day, which placed her in about the middle of the class. It was not a secure position. Though she had done nothing but study for the last several days, now that she was waiting in the foyer on the highest level of the east tower for her name to be called to go into the testing chamber, she regretted not having done more. Interrogations were not like the combat trials, which eliminated only the worst of the worst.

Interrogations were cutthroat. About half the students who made it this far would be sent home. It was the same way every year, with the cutoff falling a little higher or lower depending on how competent the Drei Masters judged the class. Jenne was in the fourth tier now and would have to advance as far as the third to ensure her safety.

To make matters worse, Landers, Eridike, Cardos, Elophine, and Brinnette had already been tested and eliminated on days two and three. The five of them would certainly be sent home. Liana and Diar had begun interrogations earlier in the morning and were still in the testing chamber. There was no guarantee any of them would survive this round of cuts.

"Initiate Jenne. Initiate Jadon."

Jenne started in alarm. Jadon was brilliant, and she would never have guessed she would have to face him head-to-head in interrogations, let alone during her first round. Moreover, she had not seen him in the foyer. She glanced around again. Just a dozen random initiates, any of whom she would have preferred as an opponent to Jadon.

Maybe it was a mistake? Jenne moved toward the door to the testing chamber, where a third-year was waiting to take her inside.

"I'm Jenne," she told the girl.

"Initiate Jadon," the girl repeated, louder this time.

"He's not in here," Jenne said. "Are you sure he's next?"

"That's what I was told. But if he's not here, he's not here. So much the better for you. Jenne? I'm Psedal." The girl nodded to her, and Jenne nodded back. "I'll be briefing you on your instructions."

Jenne had heard of this girl. "Psedal? As in, niece of Drei Consul Ocifem?" If so, that would place Psedal in Ilsad, a noble Gold House.

Psedal waved dismissively. "It's a big family. I've never met him. And you're Jenne. You did really well in the tourney, didn't you? Second-last female standing?"

Jenne scowled. "I wish I hadn't had to face Cyla so early."

Psedal raised her eyebrows. "Third tier is nothing to scoff at." Jenne shrugged, and Psedal laughed. "Not good enough for you, I see. Fair enough. But enough pleasantries. I need to give you your instructions, so pay attention. If you don't follow the protocol, it will reflect badly on us both."

Jenne waited as Psedal explained the protocol. The Drei Masters would alternate posing challenges to her and her opponent. Eventually, they would choose one to advance to the balcony and one to descend to the floor. The ten initiates standing on the floor might be offered the chance to re-enter the competition if the two being tested both failed to answer a challenge correctly, but if none of them could answer, the masters would have the initiates sitting on the bench behind them replace them on the floor.

There were five benches in the chamber. If Jenne was bumped all the way to the end of the fifth bench and another initiate descended, she would be out of the competition and must leave the testing chamber through the door at the back of the room.

"And when Master Garadil announces a break for the noon meal, stay seated until the Drei Masters have left," Psedal finished. "Then initiates on the floor will leave by the door in the back of the room, and those in the balcony will come down and exit by this door."

"What happens if Jadon doesn't show?" Jenne asked.

Psedal shrugged. "Your guess is as good as mine." She cracked open the door to the testing chamber. "All right. You may go in. Wait until summoned to approach the table."

Jenne nodded and took a deep breath. Then she went in.

The testing chamber was bigger than she'd expected. The ceiling, far overhead, was made of glass, flooding the chamber with sunlight. The room was rectangular, but the edges of the balcony were round, running in a full circle around the room. At the narrower points of the balcony, where the curve of the railing came closest to the line of each wall, it was deep enough to allow only one row of initiates. Several aides were sitting up there along with two dozen initiates, and there was room for many more. The benches on the floor, in contrast, were full. Because they were well spaced and the room was wider than the benches were long, the floor still looked open and spacious. The floor, benches, balcony, platform, and walls were all made of the same white margarette that made up most of the campus, creating the odd impression that the chamber had all been cut from one piece.

The door opened onto the back left of the platform, which ran the width of the room and a fifth of its length. It was a few steps raised from the rest of the floor, and Jenne felt exposed standing on it. Everyone in the chamber could see her, and if she made a sound, they would hear her. Only one initiate in front of the testing table was making any noise, answering the question he had been posed.

Jenne's anxiety grew. The testing table was tall. It, too, was made of margarette, long enough for twelve Drei Masters to sit behind on twelve tall margarette chairs.

She chewed her lower lip, wondering if Jadon would join her. She could not believe they were ranked at the same level. *He's some sort of genius, isn't he? If he shows up, I'm done.* She stopped chewing her lip and tried to develop a more positive mindset. If the masters had ranked him the same as her, it must be because they thought she had a chance of beating him. He did not study much, after all. He missed questions in class sometimes – frequently, even. *Maybe they'll ask us about something he didn't bother to review.*

Jenne fidgeted, scanning the room. She was pleased to see both Liana and Diar seated on the balcony.

"Jenne, Jadon. Approach," Garadil intoned.

Resonation was not considered one of the better magics, but it had its uses. The master's voice carried a regality Jenne had not seen in him since his orientation speech, and she shivered as she walked out in front of the testing table. The setup of the room required her to turn her back to the initiates on the floor in order to face the masters, which was just as well. No need to remind herself how many of them were watching, hoping for her to make a mistake.

"Here is Jenne, but where is Jadon?" Shiell was not a Resonator, but Jenne supposed everyone in the chamber could hear him nonetheless.

"He wasn't in the testing foyer, Drei Master," Jenne explained.

"Very well, then." Regild sighed. "Let us continue."

The masters were at a much higher elevation than Jenne, seated behind the testing table as they were, and there was not a friendly set of eyes among them.

"Challenge." Regosh was the first to speak, his voice sounding deeper and harder in the chamber than it did during class. The burly master had always struck Jenne as an approachable, jovial sort of fellow, but he did not seem so now. "For Jenne. Please recite the third amendment to the guidelines for dueling set forth in *The Ellyrian Code*, as passed by the Ellyrian Senate in the tenth century."

"Complication." Estilend spoke before Jenne could answer. His tone, too, carried the cool and calculating force of a judge, rather than the amiability Jenne had grown accustomed to. "Please do so in Jeshim."

Jenne took a breath. *This isn't so bad.* The languages were the easiest part of the curriculum for her. Most of her friends had spent many watches slaving over Jeshim and Alterran, and they still had great difficulty putting sentences together. Jenne had never had to worry much about it and was glad to have a language be part of her first challenge. She interpreted the amendment without any trouble.

"Challenge for Jadon." Shiell spoke next. He made note of the empty space beside Jenne, and his thin lips drew together in a sudden smile. He leaned forward, a sparkle in his blue eyes as he addressed the empty space. "You and another Edrei have applied for the same post. You are both summoned before the Edrei Council so they may test your aptitude against one another. Your colleague, for reasons unknown to you, does not appear, and the Edrei Council asks for your opinion on how to proceed. How do you respond?"

"Complication." Porrian narrowed his eyes at Jenne. "The other applicant is of higher birth than you and known to be better suited to the post."

This is not like anything we discussed in class. Jenne racked her brain for ethical and political principles she had learned that might be pertinent. Since Jadon was not going to respond to the challenge, she would need to.

There were a few beats of silence, and then the headmaster said, "Time. Jenne?"

She was still coming up dry. *Have to say something now, Jenne.* "I would recommend the Council find another way to test the other candidate if they were able to do so." That seemed altruistic, as an Edrei should be, but it was not enough of an answer or what Jenne actually thought. "But if that would be inconvenient for them, I'd say they should test me alone and award the post without considering the other applicant if they found me qualified. If they found me lacking, then they would need to find another solution, which could involve testing the other candidate or requiring a qualified Edrei who had not applied to fill the post."

Shiell was still smiling. "I find sufficient disparity has been displayed between answers, Headmaster."

"I second the finding." Estilend, too, was smiling, his customary good humor returned.

"Decision has been called," Regild noted. "All for Jenne?"

The vote began at the far left side of the table, where Garadil nodded. Then Estilend, who sat to his right, did the same, and the gesture was repeated by Tamar, Halce, Regosh, Shiell, Verizah, and Miraj – skipping over Porrian, Derrak, and Felade when it came to them.

"All for Jadon?"

No one moved.

"Eight for Jenne. Four abstentions. Jenne advances." Regild nodded to Jenne, and she breathed a sigh of relief as Garadil summoned the next initiates.

As she walked across the platform toward the balcony stairs, she wondered about the abstentions. Porrian's did not surprise her; Jadon was his favorite, and nothing Porrian did to show favoritism surprised her anymore. Derrak and Felade both instructed only second- and third-years, though, and she had not guessed that either of them – or the headmaster – would show such bias. Her answers had been objectively better than Jadon's. It was impossible to argue otherwise, since he had supplied none.

It's the chroming politics. Jenne sighed as she climbed the stairs and took the first empty seat. *They don't want the Senator-Liaison seeing that they voted against his son this early in the competition.*

Eshtem was supposed to be above such considerations, but Jenne had always known it was not. She ought to have been pleased that no more than four had abstained. Fully eight Drei Masters had voted to advance her, after all, ignoring any potential ramifications of offending the Senator-Liaison in their dedication to keeping the competition fair.

The others bothered her anyway.

After a few more matches, a break was called for the noon meal. The masters stood and exited, and then the initiates on the balcony filed down the stairs.

Diar caught up with Jenne as she made her way across the platform, and she suppressed a sigh. Though they had all the same friends and continued to see each other frequently, he had not tried to talk to her since the incident with Christina. The respite had been good for them both.

"Jenne, we need to talk," he said.

"What do we need to talk about, Diar?"

"That day in the library. You yelled at me and then just left, and you've been ignoring me ever since. Why?"

"I haven't been ignoring you, Diar," Jenne corrected. "I just haven't sought you out. You haven't sought me out, either, until now."

"I haven't sought you out because I tried that before, repeatedly, and it hasn't worked. I don't know how to fix whatever you're upset about."

"I'm not upset with you." Jenne had yelled at him, though, so she figured she had better explain. "It was just frustrating for me, watching you bend over backward to serve Jadon and then the same thing with Christina. You think they're your friends, but they're not. They're using you, and it's hard to watch." She did not add that she had been feeling remorseful about leaving Diar and her studies to flirt with Landers, or that hearing about how Liana had left him alone to discuss Christina's "private matter" had been a poignant and painful reminder of how little Diar knew about himself or the way the world worked. "But you were right, of course," she continued. "It's none of my business. I'm sorry I yelled. I'm certainly not still upset."

"Then why don't you talk to me anymore?" Diar's forehead creased, his gaze intent and his voice laden with tightly controlled emotion. "If you don't want to be more than friends, I can respect that. But can't we at least speak every once in a while?"

Maybe he does want me. It was a new thought for Jenne, that maybe Diar's Principles were more than just a smokescreen thrown up to rationalize his lack of desire for her in the moment – but looking at his face, she had to wonder. The boy was clearly suffering.

Sadly, though, it did not matter. If Diar really took the White Way that seriously, there could be no more future for them than if she had been right about his disinterest. Jenne was no Rishara. She was no good with rules of any kind, and though she did not remember her past, she knew she was not the kind of good and innocent girl that a devoted religious boy would be proud to have by his side in the long run. Maybe she was intriguing to Diar now, but when the novelty wore off, she would come to disgust him.

Jenne met his gaze. "We are speaking. I just don't have much to say," she said grimly, wishing he would pick up the cue and leave her alone. She did not owe him her time or affection, and right now, it was too hard.

The testing chamber was emptying quickly, but there was a jam at the door to the foyer. Diar studied her as they slowed down. Jenne, avoiding his gaze, watched the door. Psedal came in as the initiates were going out, in the company of Christina tu'Noraan, of all people. The third-year looked pale and Christina had an arm around her, supporting her.

Following her gaze, Diar noticed Psedal and Christina. "Fine," he said, sounding frustrated, and then, after shooting her another pointed look, he hurried toward Christina. "Is she all right? Do the two of you need help?"

Jenne shook her head as Diar put an arm out to steady Psedal. Diar would not have been Diar if he did not leap to help anyone who appeared to be in some kind of trouble, and Jenne could hardly hold that against him. But the fact that Christina was involved, and that Diar had given Jenne that look, made it feel as though he was making a statement.

"Thank you, I think she needs only a little breathing room," Christina said, disengaging her arm from Psedal as Diar took over. Then, noticing Jenne and a few others watching, she waved a hand. "The rest of you, please, carry on."

Jenne had been going to do that regardless.

When she reached the foyer, she saw that a few of the masters had lingered. They were talking to Jadon.

So he showed up after all, she noted, wondering what they would do with him.

"Psedal?" Christina noticed the other girl's head sag as she and Diar led her onto the platform. The chamber was otherwise empty now.

Then Psedal collapsed; Diar's supporting arm was now all that held her upright.

"This can't be good," he said, looking to Christina in alarm. "We need help now, right?"

"No." It came out more tersely than Christina intended, but Psedal had to stay secluded.

Psedal was the niece of a Prophet, and in the stories that Christina had heard of Prophets, they sometimes lost consciousness on the verge of Prophesying. Christina was certain this was what was happening to Psedal, and that whatever she said next would be important. *The Drei Masters mustn't know about it.*

"Here, let her down. She should lie flat." Christina put a hand on Psedal's head to steady her as Diar lowered the third-year to the floor.

In a moment she was stretched out on the platform, the two of them kneeling beside her.

"Psedal?" Diar asked it this time. Still no response. "I'll go get the Drei Masters."

"No, I'll go." Christina rose to her feet. Diar was right – a master *should* be handling this, and Christina was not sure why she had felt the need to hide Psedal from them in the first place. *Whatever was between Hezred and Master Porrian would hardly have any bearing on this,* she told herself, but the conviction remained just as strong. She did not want Porrian anywhere near Psedal when she started to Prophesy.

There was one master, however, whom Christina was willing to tell, and if she went for help instead of Diar, perhaps she could control the information.

"Stay with her," she said to Diar. "And if she starts talking before I get back, remember everything she says."

Christina ran toward the foyer, slowing when she opened the door. She kept her pace to a brisk walk as she skirted the conversation between Jadon, Regild, and Porrian. She had come here intending to catch Porrian on his way to lunch to ask him about Hezred, but that would have to wait.

Christina resumed running when she reached the stairs, passing initiates on her way down. She drew a few odd looks but ignored them, pressing on until she hit ground level and burst through the door to the outside.

"Master Tamar!" she called, catching sight of her in the group of masters crossing the lawn up ahead. Tamar paused, and Christina hurried to catch up as the others continued on their way, outdistancing her.

"Your pardon, but Psedal is having an episode of some kind," Christina said in a rush. "I thought you should know."

"Where? When did it start?" Tamar started back toward the east tower, walking briskly.

"Moments ago. In the testing chamber. She's there now with another initiate."

"Which initiate?"

"Diar," Christina answered, confused by the question.

"Good." Tamar pushed open the door to the tower and hastened up the stairs, leading Christina against the press of initiates. Soon Regild, Porrian, and Jadon appeared.

"Don't stop," Tamar told Christina quietly.

"Tamar." Porrian greeted her, nodding. "Back so soon?"

Christina continued up the stairs, though Tamar stopped and Christina heard her say, "I desire a word with this young man. Are you finished with him?"

Why does she want a word with Jadon? Christina wondered. *Now?*

"Yes, I believe so," the headmaster said, continuing down. "Consider leaving him time to eat before testing resumes, though. I think he could use it."

"Have a nice lunch, Masters. Jadon, with me, please."

Christina glanced over her shoulder to see Porrian and the headmaster continuing past Tamar, who had resumed hurrying upward, Jadon in tow.

When they reached the top of the stairs, Tamar led them across the foyer. She turned to Jadon when she reached the door to the testing chamber.

He was looking quizzically between her and Christina. "Yes, Drei Master?"

"Jadon, perhaps your lateness today was not entirely your fault," Tamar said, her tone clipped and hurried. "But let the consequences teach you to mend your habits and be punctual in the future insofar as it depends on you. Dismissed."

She didn't want to talk to him, Christina realized. *He was just her excuse for coming back upstairs.* The masters would be more inclined to notice and wonder about one of their own going upstairs than about an initiate doing the same.

"Christina, wait here," Tamar told her.

"But–"

"Wait. Here," the master repeated. She went into the testing chamber.

After a moment of silence, Jadon said, "Care to fill me in on whatever is going on here?"

"I'm not sure that would be appropriate." If Tamar had not wanted Jadon to know that he was merely her excuse to return to the testing chamber, Christina was not about to explain.

The door to the testing chamber opened, and Diar came out.

"This just keeps getting stranger," Jadon noted.

"I've been instructed to go to lunch immediately and never speak of this again," Diar said, frowning. "And she said to tell you the same, Jadon, if you were still here."

"Spitfire." Jadon shook his head. "I don't get it."

"Perhaps the two of you should proceed to lunch, then," Christina advised. "And don't trouble yourselves about it. I doubt it would interest you anyway," she added for Jadon.

"Right." Jadon gave her a dubious look. "Clearly, you have perfect insight into what I find interesting."

"Well, Tamar did say 'immediately,'" said Diar. "So I'll go. Good to see you, Christina. Jadon." He nodded to them and walked toward the stairs.

"Yeah, yeah, I'm right behind you. Enjoy whatever this is, I suppose," Jadon said to Christina, shrugging as he turned to follow Diar.

After their footsteps faded, Christina was left in silence. She crossed her arms and shifted impatiently, wondering what was happening in the testing chamber. It felt like a long time before the door opened again. Tamar stepped out alone.

"How is Psedal?" Christina asked.

"Resting. She'll be fine," Tamar told her, shutting the door. Then she turned to Christina, giving her a critical look. "Let us go over the sequence of events. You came here to the foyer. Why?"

"I knew it was almost time for the break," Christina said, "and I was hoping to speak to Master Porrian when he came out."

"Then what happened?"

"I spoke to Psedal, and she told me there was one more contest before the break."

"And then?"

"We waited a few minutes. Then Jadon arrived. Psedal looked up and saw him, then staggered backward. I steadied her as the door to the testing chamber opened, but she was losing color and did not respond when I said her name. Since everyone was leaving the chamber, I moved her in there where it would be quiet. Diar noticed and joined us. Shortly after, Psedal fainted. We laid her on the floor and I ran to get you."

Tamar studied Christina intently. "Psedal started losing color while the Drei Masters came out of the testing chamber, and you moved her away from us?"

Christina nodded. She had nothing to say to explain it, so she said nothing.

"Then when she lost consciousness, you left to get help. You must have passed Master Porrian and Headmaster Regild on your way, but you kept going until you found me. Why?"

"I thought Psedal would Prophesy when she came to. I thought it would be important and that you should hear it. As a Drei Master and an Intuiter." Intuition and Prophecy were paired gifts. Intuiters were often called upon to interpret Prophecies.

"Why only me? If you had told the first masters you saw, they might have sent for me. And for Master Miraj, who is also an Intuiter."

All Tamar's attention was focused on Christina. It would do her no good to lie.

"I don't trust them," Christina eventually said.

"And you trust me? Why?"

"You don't trust them either."

Tamar held her gaze. Then she nodded. "Perhaps you acted well, perhaps foolishly. Time will tell, but until then, have a care, Christina. Suspicion and doubt make for a lonely road. You are young to embark upon it, and I would wish a better way for you." She turned away.

"Master Tamar?" Christina asked. "What did Psedal say?"

Tamar turned back to her, shaking her head. "It is time for you to go now, Christina." Her tone was a little gentler than before. "Eat, rest. Attend to your studies. See to your friendships. One day, you and your class will become Edrei. Then the weight of the world will rest on your shoulders, and it will matter how many friends you made during your time here, and which ones. That should be your only concern for now."

Tamar went back into the testing chamber, and Christina sighed. Perhaps she would never know what Psedal had Prophesied.

But at least no one else, aside from Tamar, would either. That felt like a victory – though she could not have said exactly why.

"Wait up there, Diar."

Diar paused, letting Jadon catch up with him.

"You're really not going to tell me what that was all about?"

Diar shrugged as they continued down the stairs. "Sorry, Master Tamar said not to. But if it makes you feel any better, I don't know what was going on either. Just that–" Diar interrupted himself, shaking his head. He had never seen anyone pass out like that and was quite concerned about Psedal. But Tamar had seemed to have things under control, and she had given him a direct order. "No, I really shouldn't say anything. Where have you been? You missed your finals slot."

"Shenn. Hatre. The high prince required my presence." Jadon sighed. "You'd think he could have gotten a report from Zar, but no. It had to be me, final interrogations notwithstanding. My studies at Eshtem, becoming an Edrei…

Apparently, these things are trivially unimportant beside whatever game he's playing with me and the orange priests."

"Huh." Diar frowned, shooting Jadon a sidelong look as they reached ground level and continued onto the lawn.

"What?"

"Oh, nothing. Just…" Diar hesitated.

"Spit it out, roomie."

"Just, I wouldn't have guessed you considered your education important. Took me by surprise, is all."

"That's not the point." Jadon narrowed his eyes. "It's my life. I should be the one setting the priorities." He waved a hand in dismissal. "Never mind. You wouldn't understand."

"Because my father's just a merchant?" Diar frowned, thinking he could empathize with Jadon more than the prince realized. "He wasn't exactly supportive of my studies either, you know. He would have preferred to see me in the family business."

"That's hardly the same thing." Jadon glanced at Diar. "And I don't mean that as an insult. It's just reality."

Diar shrugged. Jadon was probably right. "Are you in trouble?"

Jadon shook his head. "After the break, I'll start on the floor, having descended five spots."

Apparently, Jadon did not consider that "trouble."

Our life experiences have been different indeed, Diar reflected as they reached the north tower. "Good luck with that," he said as they went into the mess hall and joined the line for food.

"What about you, roomie? Are you in trouble?"

Diar smiled, surprised that Jadon would ask. Even after the incident with Vannes, the debacle of Diar's visit to an Initiative hangout, and his trip to Lystra to rescue Jadon from missing class, it was odd to find himself chatting so casually with the Hatreth prince. Almost as though the two of them were friends. "Not yet. At least, not in the competition."

"You in some other kind of trouble?" Jadon sounded curious.

"No, just... it's this girl." Diar shook his head, knowing his focus should be on the competition. He could lose his chance at making Edrei, yet here he was, bent out of shape about Jenne.

Diar rubbed his forehead, wishing he understood where he had gone wrong.

"Jenne," he said as their turn came to collect food. "I thought she liked me, but now she doesn't. I think I might have offended her, but I'm not sure how." He glanced at Jadon, realizing he had probably overshared.

But Jadon just nodded, adding more potatoes to his trencher. "My advice? Give it time. If you did something and she decides to consider forgiving you, she'll let you know how to make it right. And if she doesn't... well, the best you can do is try to preserve some dignity."

"Thanks," Diar sighed, figuring he did not have much of a choice. "Oh, there's Christina." He caught sight of her as she entered the mess hall. "I need to talk to her."

"Right. Well, you two enjoy your secrets." Jadon nodded and left, taking his trencher toward the stairs as Diar hurried to Christina.

"Is Psedal all right?"

"Yes, of course," said Christina, moving to join the line.

Diar moved with her. "You saw her? I know we're not supposed to talk about it, but she stayed unconscious for that whole time you were gone. And now she's fine? You're sure?"

"I'm quite sure. She..." Christina trailed off. "I really shouldn't say anything else. But you can be quite confident she's recovered. Thank you for your assistance, and good luck with the rest of your testing."

"Of course, and you too. When your testing begins, I mean." Diar left quickly, feeling stupid.

The mood was no better back at the table with his friends. Jenne got up and left when he arrived, taking Brinnette and Landers with her. All three of them were done eating, so it might have been a coincidence.

This sort of thing had been happening too often, though, for Diar to believe it was just a coincidence.

"What did Christina want this time?" Eridike asked as Diar set down his trencher.

"I thought Jenne left," said Diar, fed up with everyone's opinions about whom he was talking to. "Did you want to go with her too?"

"Take it easy, Diar," said Cardos. "You're not the only one having a bad day."

That's fair, Diar realized, looking around the table. Most of them would be going home soon.

Perhaps he would be, too.

In Jadon's opinion, it was absurd that the masters had called him to begin interrogations on the fourth day. He was too advanced for it, and they were just creating awkwardness for themselves by summoning him before he was back from a leave they had granted at the Senator-Liaison's demand. Jadon had made excellent time to and from Hatre, and if he had been scheduled to compete even one day later, he would have been on time. It hardly seemed fair, and Juaqen would be furious if Jadon was cut from Eshtem as a result.

Regild and Porrian had both taken pains to reassure Jadon that advancing from the sixth place on the floor was quite possible. After the break was over, though, it took three matches before a challenge was opened to the floor. It was harder than the challenges that the initiates had been facing until then, and Porrian had posed it, which made Jadon think he had done so on purpose to give Jadon a chance to get back in.

He was the only one who knew the answer, and in short order he found himself on the balcony among those advancing. He had to wait a long time before he was called on again, and watching other initiates in the meantime was dreadfully dull.

The next time he was called on to compete went smoothly, and he returned to the boredom of the balcony without incident. The time after that, though, he fumbled one of his answers. Tamar had posed the challenge, asking for the name and background of the current Head Lusse. It was not something Jadon had ever had occasion to know or care about, and if they had gone over it in class, he had no memory of it. Perhaps they had done so while he was in Hatre.

He was sent back to the floor, peeved once again with the whole situation. He should never have had to go to Hatre. He sulked as the next match passed without any challenges getting opened to the floor. He moved down a place in line as the loser joined them.

"Diar, Liana. Approach."

Jadon looked up as his roommate and Vorsand's niece made their way down from the balcony.

The match proceeded well enough until Liana was asked to explain, in Alterran, the ethical infractions in the Jeshim slave code. It was hard to tell which was worse – her logic or her Alterran. Or perhaps she was having a hard time remembering the slave code. They had learned it in Jeshim, after all, so perhaps her command of that language was the real problem.

In any case, Jadon was convinced Diar would do better. But after Liana finished speaking, obviously distressed by her poor performance, Diar said nothing. After a few beats of silence, the challenge was opened to the floor.

Jadon stepped forward, but so did the girl on his right, who had descended more recently. She was recognized to speak and performed a fair sight better than Liana. The Drei Masters invited her to the stage, and after the three of them were posed a few more challenges, they voted to send her to the balcony.

Diar let Liana take the rightmost spot on the floor.

"That was stupid, roomie," Jadon said under his breath as Diar joined him. "You can't afford to be chivalrous."

Diar's mouth quirked, but he said nothing. Liana shot a glance at Jadon, then looked at Diar, her eyes full of hurt and accusation. "You should have answered," she whispered.

Diar shook his head. "It was a hard challenge."

"Sure it was," Jadon said, deadpan. The challenge may have been tricky, but a precocious five year-old could have handled it better than Liana.

The three of them fell silent, turning their attention to the current match. After a few minutes, Garadil asked one of the competitors to argue against the logic that had supported Purmaea's invasion into Gysalt in the fourteenth century. Jadon listened as the boy started making his response, then clicked his tongue when he noticed an error.

"Identical logic would have sent them to war with Ithacor a year earlier," he said quietly to Diar. "That's the flaw. But there was gold in Gysalt."

"Oh, that's right, isn't it?" Liana said, just as softly.

"They'll open this to the floor in a minute," Jadon predicted.

"You'll have a chance to answer it, Liana," said Diar.

She shook her head. "I won't. I wouldn't have thought of it."

"She's right," Diar said. "It's your answer, Jadon. You should advance for it."

"But I'm not going to. And if you don't," Jadon jerked his head to indicate the boy standing to his left, who was listening to their conversation, "he will."

The masters opened the question to the floor, and after a moment's hesitation, Diar stepped forward along with the boy to Jadon's left. Diar was recognized, and he did a fair job constructing the argument. He was invited back to the stage, and when the round was over, he advanced. The two original competitors descended and took their places next to Liana as everyone moved down.

Two more matches proceeded without any questions opened to the floor. Then Derrak asked for the difference in legislation concerning blood feuds according to whether the dispute took place on lands controlled by House Kish or House Meretril.

The second- and third-year instructors had been throwing in occasional challenges and complications all along, keeping the material relevant to first-year studies. This, however, was quite the nuanced detail for this stage in the competition. Kish and Meretril were both lower Houses sworn to Hatreth, and Jadon knew the answer.

Jadon leaned close to Liana and spoke softly into her ear while the initiate on stage tried to make up something that sounded plausible. "House Kish allows any first-degree male kin of the victim to retaliate against the killer. House Meretril allows only the closest in line." Jadon would have liked to see Vorsand's niece advance in the competition, at least far enough to protect her tenure. No one would be throwing out challenges that only a commonborn girl from House Adagal would know, however.

The hypocrisy of the whole situation disgusted him. If the masters were going to summon him to testing before he should have been called and then rig the game so it was impossible for him to lose early enough to be cut, there was nothing he could do to stop them. But there was likewise nothing they could do to stop him from giving a few answers away.

"I thought you said we couldn't afford to be chivalrous," Liana returned.

"I said *Diar* couldn't afford to be chivalrous."

Liana shook her head. "Thank you for helping Diar, but I descended fair and square."

"This whole competition is rigged."

The question was opened to the floor, and Jadon stepped forward, jerking his head to indicate Liana should do the same. She would be recognized before him if she did.

But she just lifted her chin, a little tremor in her lip. She would take her chances on her own merit, uncertain as they were.

Shame. Jadon was recognized to speak. He advanced to the balcony shortly thereafter.

Christina was waiting by the door to the testing chamber when the masters filed out for the evening break. This time, there were no surprise magical occurrences to distract her from her purpose.

"Master Porrian," she said. "I was hoping I might have a word?"

"Christina." Porrian nodded to her. "Certainly. Walk with me."

They followed the other masters across the foyer and down the stairs.

"What did you wish to speak about?" Porrian asked.

Christina looked around at the crowded staircase. It did not seem like the best place to begin asking questions about a man whose name and history had been erased. "Could we perhaps speak somewhere more private?"

"Very well." Porrian turned when they reached the first landing, leading her away from the stairs and the other masters. He took her down a narrow corridor and opened the third door they came to on the right, letting her into a room dominated by a large desk and chair. A few smaller cushioned chairs stood to the side beneath an elaborate painting.

Porrian seated himself at the desk. "Felade's office," he explained. "He won't mind if we chat here. Pull up a chair."

The painting on the wall attracted Christina's attention as she moved the chair. A lion and a fieroq were tangled together, the lion with an open mouth and its claws at the fieroq's throat while the fieroq breathed fire toward the lion's eye. A real fieroq, which was a rare kind of dragon-shaped lizard, would have stood no taller than Christina's calf, but in the painting it matched the lion's size, and it was unclear which beast would prove victorious. A smaller, bat-like grestim with two wicked horns watched the contest from above, its wings covering most of its face. Only the eyes peered through.

Christina did not care for the painting, for reasons quite beside the fact that the creatures were the emblems of the three royal War Houses. She sat down, happy to look away from it.

"Now, Christina, what is on your mind? Have you remembered anything about the outlaws you encountered, perhaps?"

"Actually, I had a question for you."

"About the outlaws?" Porrian frowned. "Christina, I will certainly answer insofar as I can, but you understand there is a limit to how much I can tell you."

"Yes, quite." She folded her hands in her lap, trying to decide how to broach the topic. "It's not about the outlaws. At least, not exactly."

"Perhaps it's about just one of the outlaws?" She said nothing, and Porrian nodded, taking her silence as confirmation. "Please, speak your mind. If there is a way for me to address any concern you may have, I will."

Christina took her time before answering. "All my life, I have respected and admired the Order of the Edrei. I thought the Edrei were peace-sworn heroes, guardians of magic and knowledge and dragons, worthy of the faith the people put in them and the responsibility they hold. I thought they were incorruptible." She let that hang between them, watching to see how he would take it.

"You are an idealist." Porrian nodded, either oblivious to the veiled accusation or choosing not to see it as such. "And the idea of the Order... that is a worthy ideal. But Edrei themselves are only human."

"Yes. But for one to fall..." Christina hesitated. "Sometimes I look around at my classmates, and I wonder. I know most of them won't make Edrei, but some of them seem capable and as though they might be worthy. But if someone the Order saw fit to elevate could fall so far, sometimes I wonder... how can any be trusted?"

"The Order is only human, Christina." Porrian leaned back in his chair, now smiling. "It may be hard for an idealist such as yourself to accept, but the process of raising new Edrei is imperfect. Sometimes warning signs are overlooked. Edrei are needed, and compromises are sometimes made. Now, usually such warning signs come to nothing. If you take a potentially dangerous person and surround them with good people and good morals, they will usually straighten themselves out, and such people often prove reliable for the Order. Vorsand was such a case. We took a gamble on him, and now he is a captain, our Lead Master Imager, and a national war hero besides.

"Sometimes, though, taking a risk on a candidate ends very badly. But that hardly means the warning signs were never there for any who cared to discern them, whether instructor or fellow student."

Christina frowned. "Are you saying there were warning signs with He– " She checked herself. The name Hezred may not have been erased as Hazzar was, but the outlaw's existence was still classified, and she supposed it was better to ask about him as circuitously as possible. "Are you saying there are always warning signs, in cases where an Edrei fails the Order?"

Porrian considered her. "I see this has been troubling you."

Christina tightened her lips. "I have had to reconsider much of what I thought I knew."

"In the case of the man now known as Hezred, yes, there were warning signs," said Porrian, choosing to answer her real question directly. "I remember his final review as though it were yesterday." The master shook his head, the picture of grieved remembering. "He had a charisma that drew people to him, made you want to believe in him. He was popular with both his instructors and his fellow students. There were a few incidents, though, in which we believed he had acted dishonorably, with the goal of discrediting his competitors. We knew he was ambitious, and we suspected he was not always honest. We considered barring him from the Order. To my shame, I was among those who argued that we should give him a chance. I liked him, and he had a real talent with his Projection. I hoped that when it counted, he would choose to use it for good. It was the single greatest mistake I have ever made."

Porrian paused, studying her reaction, and Christina marveled at how directly he had just lied to her. *Directly and shamelessly. And needlessly.* She had thought she would have to prompt him much more specifically to get him to contradict something in the Jeshim report, but here he was, casting his web of lies far and wide at the tiniest provocation. *So certain he can't be caught, he's grown careless.* He was talking to a student, after all, about an erased criminal. She would have trouble looking into it, and why would she bother? She had the word of a Drei Master. Surely that would be enough.

"I am telling you this," Porrian went on, "because you remind me of another idealist I once had the pleasure of instructing in the ways of the Order, and this is something I wish I could have taught her sooner. The Order is not the ideal you may have imagined. The Order is human. Humans err. But that does not mean you cannot trust them, or that you can put no faith in the Order. The Order is flawed, yes, but it is still good – perhaps the greatest force for good this world has. Likewise, your classmates, and even your instructors, may be flawed – some more than others – but that does not mean you cannot trust anyone. Keep yourself from trusting blindly, yes, but neither would it be wise for you to keep yourself from trusting at all."

"Is that what she did?" asked Christina, thinking he must be speaking of Tamar. "What became of her?"

"Oh, nothing too dreadful. She still wears the cloak, but it disappointed her, and now she has no faith in it. She believes herself to be alone in her quest to uphold its ideals. I would have spared her that, if I could have found a way."

Christina blinked, finding the words an eerie echo of what Tamar had said.

But this man is a liar who arranged to have a good man thrown out of the Order, killed, and erased. No doubt, it had been lies like his that had broken Tamar's trust and driven her into her loneliness. *And he has the gall to sit there and blame it on her idealism, which he "would have spared her."*

How dare he.

"I did remember something about the bandits. Though I'm not sure how helpful it will be." Christina cleared her throat. Nefry had done a little research for her, chatting up the post riders in Lystra about the bandit situation in the Brennels. There had been a number of bands roaming the area around the time of Christina's attack, including a group of eighteen that styled themselves the Hounds of the High Road – too many to have any connection to the group that had attacked Christina. The Hounds had lost two members over the summer. "I've gone over the attack, and I think – although I cannot quite be sure – that there were nearly twenty of them. I know my men killed one, perhaps two."

Christina dropped her eyes. The memory was supposed to be difficult.

As she had come to expect, Porrian took her at her word. He smiled and rose to his feet. "That should indeed help us, more than you know. I will send word immediately, that our people will better know where to focus their efforts."

She gave him a tight smile and rose as he opened the door for her.

"And, Christina, do feel free to come and chat about anything, anytime. I am glad that you feel you can talk to me. We could use more people like you in the Order."

She nodded and thanked him as she left, and he closed the door behind her. Apparently, he was quite at home in Felade's office.

She was pleased she did not have to walk with him on her way to the north tower. She went through the line for the evening meal and took her food to the study room with the balcony, still contemplating the enormity of Porrian's lies.

Nefry was there, along with Kiprim, Sayler, Matt, and Claire. His eyes lit with curiosity as she set her trencher down next to Claire's.

"Christina! Did you speak with Master Porrian?"

"Yes." Christina glanced from Claire and Sayler to Kiprim and Matt, who were playing kings and dragons next to Nefry at the other table. She did want to talk to Nefry, but not here, so instead of sitting, she hesitated as she tried to think of a reason to leave the room.

"Christina, dearest, we've been looking everywhere for you."

She turned to see Lelise at the door, Saleah by her side.

They entered and seated themselves at Christina's table, though Lelise gave Sayler a measured look as she did so. It was a look that suggested he was beneath her, but he was at Christina's table, so she was prepared to let it go.

It was amazing how much that girl could convey with her eyes.

"Why is that?" Christina asked, still standing.

"The seventh day of final interrogations is coming up, and we need you to help us understand the Wargon Arrangement," Saleah explained, tucking a stray lock of jet-black hair back into her braid.

"If you have time," Lelise corrected. "More importantly, though, we've missed you these last few weeks. You and Claire. I can't help but wonder who is keeping you apprised of the latest news. Did you know Jadon was scheduled to compete today, and that he was late?"

"He's descended to the floor three times already," Saleah contributed, "but finished the day still in the competition. Nobody else has done that."

"Nobody else has *ever* done that," Lelise corrected. "In all the years since Eshtem's founding."

Christina frowned, puzzled as to why they would think she cared. She had weightier things on her mind. "We can talk about the Wargon Arrangement if you like, but if you'll excuse me for a minute, I think I'll fetch myself another cup of ale first."

"But you already have one, dear, and it's full," Lelise noted.

Christina shrugged. "I know talking politics will make me want another." It was a dismal excuse, but she did not need a good one. She shot a look at Nefry as she left the room.

She waited at the stairs, and he caught up with her shortly.

"Well?" he asked.

"He lied." Christina shook her head. "Blatantly. Said he remembered Hezred's review like it was yesterday. He remembered there was some question about Hezred's character then, whether he was too ambitious, too dishonest, but they passed him anyway. He could not have contradicted the Jeshim report more directly if he had tried."

Nefry let out a long breath, his curiosity turning sober. "He spun you a tale." He furrowed his brow. "Is there a reason he might have done that even if Hazzar was really guilty of the charges that got him erased? Master Porrian was ashamed everyone misjudged the man so completely, so he remembered something else instead? Something more palatable?"

"No." Christina blinked, surprised Nefry was still trying to find another way to account for it. The obvious was staring him in the face. "The principle of simplicity, Nefry. Hazzar was framed. And Master Porrian is part of the cover-up."

"Yeah. Probably." There were a few beats of silence as Nefry considered. "This is big. Really, really big. Way bigger than us. And *very* bad." There was another beat of silence. He looked at her, fear stealing across his features. "What do we do with this?"

Christina shook her head, frustrated. The question had been nagging at her ever since she left Porrian's office, but she had known the answer before ever taking it upon herself to investigate the renegade's case, and nothing had changed.

"Nothing," she said. Hezred had not deserved to die, but she had reached the end of what she could hope to learn or do about it, with all the records erased and at least one Drei Master prepared to lie – and perhaps kill – to protect the secret. "There's nothing we *can* do."

CHAPTER 18

One Drink Too Many

Go. If I could, I would send with you my signet ring and a hundred men, but you must travel alone and without my protection. I do not know if your presence there would provoke a war, but it would strain our relationship with Ellyrian to an extent that we cannot afford. Learn what you can. If you find Vilinora, and if she is alive, then you must do whatever is necessary to save her and bring her home – even if it means revealing yourself. However, if she is dead, avenge her; but secrecy must remain our first priority.

– King Gahon of the dynasty Renard, in
correspondence with Luc Amand

Christina was not summoned to compete in final interrogations until the seventh day. Jadon pulled off a momentous upset by defeating Lelise in her first match, knocking her out of the seeded tournament and leaving her spitting mad to be watching her friends compete from the floor. She did not make it back in. The Blood Houses were over-represented in the tournament even without her, claiming sixteen of the thirty-four finalists, and the ratio grew only more dramatic as the day progressed, with more of the Gold and War House students getting eliminated in the afternoon. Vannes's friend Jonn beat Perleyon, and then Nefry faced Jadon and beat him, leaving the War Houses short two competitors. Jadon made it back to the balcony a few matches later when Idarri and her Gold House opponent both failed to remember the Alterran funeral rites, becoming the only War House representative left.

Christina, Vannes, Saleah, Nefry, and Claire all had undefeated mornings. Saleah bested Claire in the afternoon, and Christina defeated Vannes shortly thereafter. The semifinals saw Christina competing with Saleah and Jadon facing off against Nefry once again. Christina defeated Saleah quickly. In the other match-up, Jadon pulled off another surprise victory, having made use of the noon break to straighten out the topic that had gotten him into trouble before. Command of the material was roughly equivalent between the two of them now – or perhaps Nefry had an edge, it was hard to say – but Jadon had a better handle on people and how they were likely to think. The challenge to construct an argument to encourage a collection of townspeople to build a canal eventually won it for Jadon.

This brought Christina and Jadon together for the final match. In terms of national prominence, final interrogations were nothing beside an event like the Eshtem Tourney. There was no reporting on what happened during them, no live reenactments in Helos. No one outside of Eshtem would know who won until the Lists were posted, after the Drei Masters finalized the rankings and determined where the cut would fall. Not even everyone at Eshtem was present to watch the showdown between a Blood House princess and a War House prince for the first-year interrogations championship. Only the sixty students most recently eliminated watched in the testing chamber, hoping for the unlikely event that both these celebrities would falter and allow one of them a chance to get back on the stage.

Even so, the competition's significance could not be overstated. For Christina, it mattered because no Noraani had enrolled at Eshtem in over a hundred years. Before that, Noraan had dominated the academic competition at Eshtem. It was up to her to re-establish that tradition. For Jadon, who had already won the Eshtem Tourney, it was a question of whether he could become the first student since Vorsand to triumph in both combat and academic disciplines.

The match lasted well over a count, with topics covering first-year studies and then reaching well beyond. Decision was called after Christina corrected Jadon on a minor translation error, but only Masters Estilend and Garadil, the two who had posed the challenge, voted for her to advance. The rest abstained, waiting to gather more information. Decision was called again after Jadon disagreed with Christina about how best to mediate between two lords who wanted to duel, suggesting it would be better to let them take their places and feel the imminent danger before talking through the wills they wished to leave behind. Only Masters Halce, Regosh, and Felade felt Jadon should advance for it.

The appointed time for the evening break had already come and been pushed back before a real disparity emerged between the competitors. Estilend called the challenge.

"For Jadon," he said. "You are the advisor to the lord of a War House who is responsible for judging the leader of an outlaw band that has been thwarting the efforts of the lord's military in the area. Money has been stolen and soldiers have died. What do you advise?"

"Complication," Tamar announced. "The military had overstepped the lord's mandate and were oppressing the townspeople to the point that all were impoverished and some had starved. Every action undertaken by the outlaws protected the townspeople, and without them many more of the people would have died."

Jadon stared at Tamar, eyes narrowed. Three full beats of silence stretched in the testing chamber while the masters waited for his response. The sixty students watching from the floor wondered why he was taking so long to speak. Christina, too, turned her head to glance at him – the first time she had done so during their match.

Only Tamar and Jadon himself understood that she was asking him to explain himself regarding the course of action he had taken in Shenn, and he was refusing to do so.

"Time," the headmaster called. "Christina?"

"Well…" Christina blinked. She had not expected the challenge to come to her. "It would be ill-advised for a lord to let the deaths of his soldiers go unanswered, especially in War House lands. Someone would have to be executed. Otherwise, the rest of the soldiers would lose confidence in their lord. At the same time, though, if the criminal's actions were indeed necessary to protect the townspeople, and if he was regarded as a hero among them, he would not deserve to die; also, the lord would lose any hope of recovering the confidence of the townspeople if he put their hero to death." Christina paused, thinking. "Moreover, it sounds as though the criminal in question would not be the one – or at least not the *only* one – to blame for the soldiers' deaths. If the soldiers had indeed overstepped their lord's mandate, and if the deaths were a direct result of the townspeople's having tried to protect themselves from this overstepping, then fault lies also with the soldiers' commanding officer, the one who led them in unduly harassing the people. I would counsel such a lord to pardon the criminal and put this officer to death in his stead."

A wry smile played at the corners of Jadon's lips while Christina arrived at his own solution.

Like all the students and masters watching, though, he knew he would have to find fault with her answer if he hoped to compensate for his earlier silence.

"My competitor's analysis is flawless," he said, "and I would counsel much the same. But I think it would be most unwise for her to offer such counsel herself, being a woman. It smacks of compassion, and coming from a woman, it would be written off by a War House lord as a woman's weakness. Within the Order, we may treat one another the same and see one another the same, but my competitor should know that, looking at her, a War House lord would see a woman first and an Edrei second, and so would any War House-sworn who should happen to overhear her advice. If she wanted the lord to follow the course of action she has outlined, her task would be harder than mine. She would have to advocate a harsher or more merciful approach and lead him to conceive the middle way himself, so that he might be seen to overrule her."

It was a cheeky critique, and not one Jadon expected to salvage the competition for him, but it was the only weakness he could find with Christina's answer. He could not let her walk away completely unopposed.

After a moment of silence, Estilend spoke. "I think sufficient disparity has been shown between answers, Headmaster."

"I second the finding," said Tamar.

"Decision has been called," Regild announced. "All for Jadon?"

A moment passed, and then Tamar nodded. Another few moments passed, and then Felade nodded as well.

"All for Christina?"

Garadil glanced at Estilend, indicating he would abstain once again. Estilend nodded. Halce and Regosh abstained, and for a moment it seemed as though the Drei Masters would be unable to decide once again.

But then Shiell nodded, and so did Porrian, Derrak, Verizah, and Miraj. The vote finished with Regild, who also nodded.

"Two for Jadon. Seven for Christina. Three abstentions. Christina is named champion."

The Drei Masters stood. Garadil, who stood closest to the foyer door, swept his arm to the left, inviting Christina to exit ahead of them. Her footsteps echoed in the chamber as she made the walk, her exaltation contained and almost concealed by the poised regality with which she carried herself. She was not one to grin or celebrate in front of so many observers. But her eyes shone.

"Thus conclude final interrogations," Garadil intoned, his voice echoing through the chamber.

After curfew, the War House Initiative took its festivities to Lystra. For the first-years, the occasion celebrated the end of final interrogations. For the second-years, it served to kick them off. Their own competition would begin the following morning, though no one who had to compete on the first day bothered to show up. The third-years were off campus on some excursion with the Master Imagers.

For those present, the mood was more subdued than at the party after the Eshtem Tourney. Jadon had won the tourney, after all, and the Initiative had been thrilled to claim the victory for one of their own. Final interrogations had gone to a girl from a Blood House, though, and that was less than ideal for those assembled. Moreover, only two Initiative members had made it as far as the seeded tournament on the seventh day, and of those, only Jadon had finished in the top ten. Some had hoped for better.

Moreover, some were tired of seeing Jadon succeed. Rindarin was chief among these.

"A tourney victor and an interrogations finalist." The Rithadur prince approached Jadon as more initiates trickled into the common room, sweating and winded from the run from campus. Most of those assembled had already cooled down. Rindarin, ever one to formalize the beginning of a party, was carrying a shot glass in each hand, and he extended one to Jadon. "Following in my footsteps, I see. You've earned yourself a shot."

Jadon was already a few drinks in and feeling it, courtesy of the flasks he and Fendi had chugged on the plateau next to campus before Rindarin suggested the move to Lystra. It had seemed like a good idea at the time, but running so far on so much brandy had reminded Jadon that he did not like Rindarin or much care for his ideas, and it had not helped that Rindarin had made better time than Jadon and Fendi on the run. That was unusual, and Jadon felt that he must have cheated by stashing a horse for himself somewhere along the way.

He made a point of reaching past the offered glass to take the one Rindarin was still holding close to his chest. The man had tried to poison him once before. "An argument could be made that I've already surpassed you. Considering."

Jadon did not think Rindarin would try to poison him again – at least, not tonight. Interrogations were over, and if Jadon took sick now, it would not affect his placement in the Lists. He had nothing to gain from tipping Rindarin off to his suspicions, though, and if he had been fully sober, he might have thought twice about it.

But just now, he felt he had every right to be irritated, and he wanted to watch Rindarin squirm.

His comment drew a few chuckles. The boys assumed he was referring to having finished higher in interrogations than Rindarin had the year before.

"It's still early in your tenure," Rindarin noted. He was not smiling, though he kept his tone light enough that only Jadon caught the touch of venom in his manner. "Who knows what could happen between now and the time you're where I am?"

Jadon bristled, but Cyla and Kerci burst through the doors to the common room, distracting the rest of the boys. They never expected girls to make the run from campus, though Cyla and Kerci often did.

"Oh, look who showed up." Rindarin smiled. "If it isn't Jadon's greatest weakness."

Dreck jumped to his feet and waved at the bartender. "Will you knock him off his high horse again, Cyla? Put him through his paces, then lock him up in his stall?" The bartender handed Dreck a glass, and he passed it to Cyla. She looked at Jadon as she picked up the drink, expression sultry.

"Not tonight, devil," said Jadon, holding up a hand to forestall her. "I know where you come from. Try somebody dumber."

"Perhaps that one," suggested Rindarin, nodding to Dreck. "He's known to learn slowly."

"I don't mind repeating lessons with a tutor so fine," Dreck agreed, winking at Cyla.

Cyla quirked her mouth in pity. "But a tutor quickly grows bored, when so little progress is made." Dreck laughed along with the other boys as Cyla took a seat at the bar, but the best Jadon could manage was half a smile. Cyla had seduced him, drugged him, locked him in a room upstairs, and left him there to get expelled. Worse, she thought nothing of it.

It smarted.

Rindarin, crossing the room, handed the second shot glass to Perleyon. "For the finalists," he announced. "Perleyon, as the earlier to have been eliminated, why don't you make the first toast?"

"It would be my honor." Perleyon stood. "I'll drink this shot to my co-finalist, Jadon." He lifted his shot glass high, his too-wiry form otherwise the picture of a perfect gentleman. He was even wearing court-worthy gloves, which irritated Jadon. They took Perleyon to a new level of pretentiousness. "For representing the War Houses all the way to the championship match, giving the Initiative hope that one of our fine House banners would finally top the Lists of Achievement for both interrogations *and* the Eshtem Tourney, only to blank out on the final question and let a girl from a Blood House run away with the competition." He drained his glass to the sound of jeers, laughter, and scattered applause.

"And I'll drink this one to my co-finalist, Perleyon," Jadon returned, lifting his own shot. He had had about enough of the War House Initiative and their pretend solidarity for the evening. "For burying his head in his books all year, keeping his nose clean and his reputation unsullied, if unimpressive, and for squeaking into the final thirty-four, only to lose to a guy who lost to a girl who lost to a Blood House girl who *didn't* win the whole Six-forsaken competition."

Jadon drank to more jeers and louder laughter.

"And the toasts turn savage! This calls for another round!" Rindarin moved toward Jadon and waved to the bartender, and the boys cheered as more drinks were poured for everyone.

"Take it easy there, Hatreth," Rindarin said as he stopped beside Jadon. The rest of the Initiative had broken into separate conversations. "Cyla was a prank which you overcame admirably. No reason to lash out at Perleyon or anyone else because of it. We're all friends here."

"Now, why would I blame Perleyon for a stunt you pulled yourself? You are the one who sicced Cyla on me, aren't you?"

"Me and a few others, actually." Rindarin smiled and clapped Jadon's shoulder. "It was a prank pulled on the tourney champion, to remind him of his tender feet. Don't make more of it than it was."

"Is that what you told Alaxis?"

Rindarin dropped his hand. "Be careful what you insinuate, Hatreth. A certain level of ribbing and pranks is to be expected among friends. But there is a line. You don't want to cross it."

Jadon clapped Rindarin's shoulder, leaning closer. "And yet something tells me that you already have. Friend."

Rindarin broke the contact between them, moving across the room to sit with Perleyon. Looking at Jadon, he lifted his glass, then glanced over at Alaxis and back as he took a sip. The gesture spoke a clear message. *Your move.*

Jadon lifted his empty shot glass in acknowledgment. Then he picked up his chair and moved it to the other side of the table. On the way, he knocked it against Fendi's chair and almost tripped over his scabbard.

He was feeling the alcohol as he made to squeeze in between Alaxis and Dreck.

"Make some room," he said, shoving Dreck's chair out of his way. "Interrogations runner-up coming through. And bartender, my glass is empty. Let's get some faster service."

"What's the matter, runner-up?" asked Fendi, who was sitting beside the spot Jadon had vacated. "Does somebody smell on this side of the table? And is runner-up really something you want to advertise? After how that last match went for you?"

"Both of you stink to high heaven." Jadon indicated Fendi and Arzit, who was sliding over to fill the empty spot as the table accommodated Jadon's change. "But the fumes are no better over here. No, I merely grow tired of your conversation." He held out his shot glass as a serving girl appeared to refill it. His eyes met Rindarin's across the room, and he drained his glass. "Dreck, let's talk," he said, holding his glass out for another refill. "Nobody expected you to make it to the seventh day in interrogations, so I'm not blaming you for the fact that Perleyon and I are doing victory shots alone tonight, but let's review. The Eshtem Tourney? After starting in the first tier? What happened? Remind me."

Rindarin's expression grew dark, though he sat too far away to hear. Leaning over, he said something to Perleyon, then got up and walked toward the exit.

"Leaving already, Rindarin?" Alaxis called as he reached the door.

"Please, stay," Jadon invited. "Have another drink with us. In celebration. On me. Dreck was just about to tell us where he went wrong during the Eshtem Tourney."

"Jadon, for a champion I'd stay and celebrate all night, but for the runner-up, I've put in enough time already. Big week coming up for the second-years. We'd probably all be better off retiring early. It's a long way back to campus, and the night is not as young as when we left."

"But we've only just arrived!" Jadon objected. "Is our

fearless leader showing signs of timidity as the end of the year draws near?"

"No, Rindarin makes a fair point," Perleyon announced, standing. "There's not much here to celebrate. I think I'll head back early as well."

"Sycophant," Jadon taunted. "If he's playing the final interrogations card, what's your excuse?"

"With the company so obliging, why shouldn't I care to stay?" Perleyon returned. "Haf, Dreck? Shall we accompany Rindarin back to campus?"

"And they call for an entourage!" Jadon felt he was on a roll. "What's the matter? Afraid that bandits will prey upon you in the streets? Aren't you both from War Houses?"

"Rindarin has established that well enough," Alaxis admonished him. "Winning the Eshtem Tourney and all. He can leave when he pleases."

"Whereas Perleyon didn't even make it to the seventh day in the tourney," Jadon agreed. "There's always been some doubt as to whether he was truly War House-born."

"Watch yourself, Hatreth," said Perleyon, his eyes flashing. "I'll pretend I didn't hear that because I know you've been drinking."

"And are drunk, I'd say," Rindarin noted. "You'll head back to campus soon, Jadon, if you know what's best for you. Perleyon and I are leaving now, and the rest of you would be wise to do likewise."

A few of the second-years stood, and so did some of Perleyon's friends.

"In the Initiative there's always time for another round. And the next one's on me for anyone who stays!" Jadon announced, leaning back in his chair. He was not going anywhere at Rindarin's bidding.

"One more round," Fendi chanted, pounding on the table. "One more round." Several of the first-years joined in, and some who had stood to leave sat back down. The chanters broke into cheering as the serving girls came out to refill everyone's glasses.

"Dreck?" Perleyon seemed confused by his cousin's failure to come with him.

"One last stab at increasing their numbers before they brave the streets of Lystra!" Jadon laughed, standing. Walking closer, he taunted, "Aren't your own swords enough protection for you?"

Perleyon moved to meet him, putting a hand on his sword hilt. "I already warned you once. Walk away."

"Or what? You'll duel me?" Jadon asked, remaining where he was. "Coward."

Perleyon ripped off a glove and moved to throw it at Jadon's feet in formal challenge.

Rindarin intercepted it. "Let's not make any decisions we'll regret," he said, putting a hand on Perleyon's shoulder to move him aside. "You're drunk, Jadon, but that's no excuse. Recant."

Jadon narrowed his eyes at the taller prince. "Coward," he repeated.

Rindarin punched him in the face.

Despite Rindarin's assertions, Jadon was not drunk yet, and he saw the blow coming. But the alcohol was starting to affect him, and he was too slow. The blow, aimed for his nose, took him in the left eye, sending him reeling into the table behind him. He clambered to his feet, clumsy and spitting mad, but Fendi and Arzit grabbed him before he could charge Rindarin. Most of the initiates were on their feet, but Rindarin held out a hand to forestall interference. When Jadon ceased struggling, Fendi and Arzit released him.

He took a few breaths to calm himself, his head still reeling. He was in no condition to fight. Besides which, Rindarin was stupid. Jadon did not need to fight him.

"No offense taken, fearless leader," Jadon said, panting. "I spoke out of turn. All here assembled know your true merit. Or they soon will." He put a hand to his eye gingerly, then lifted it in salute.

"We'll make sure he gets back safe," Alaxis told Rindarin, obviously thinking this would please him. "It won't be long."

Rindarin left without a word, Perleyon and others following behind. More left with them than had indicated they would, the mood in the inn having soured.

But a fair number remained, including everyone at Jadon's table. They were all he required.

"Now, what's this nonsense about *one* more round? We only just got here," Jadon said, easing himself into a chair. "Anyway, Dreck… the Eshtem Tourney. Tell us what happened."

"Oh, Jadon, please," Dreck complained, taking a drink. "We've been over this. I got sick. It happens. Even to tourney favorites. Besides, don't you need to see to that eye? Looks like it'll be a real shiner. Maybe we should head out."

"Nonsense," said Jadon, touching his eye again. It was starting to swell. "Just a flesh wound."

"Tourney favorite." Arzit chuckled. "Pretty sure Jadon was the tourney favorite."

"A correction so obvious it hardly bears mentioning." Jadon waved dismissively.

"Though it does happen to tourney favorites," said Fendi. "I heard Rindarin's win was an upset after Alaxis got sick last year."

"*Alaxis*'s sickness I believe. I've crossed swords with the man and lost, after all. But tell us about this 'sickness' of *yours*, Dreck," Jadon encouraged. "When did you decide it would be your excuse not to face me in the championship?"

"Look, when a man is burning up with a fever so severe he can barely stand, he can hardly be blamed for losing to a significantly inferior opponent. Which would have been the only scenario in which I'd have lost to you, if I'd made it as far as the championship round."

"And this 'disease.' Did it materialize suddenly, just as you were about to compete?"

"No, Jadon, I was sick all week. You remember."

"Oh, you mean with the sniffles you developed the day after the Initiative hangout?"

"In the man's defense, it was hardly just the sniffles," Fendi noted. "He practically needed to be carried to the arena by the seventh day. Don't you remember?"

"What I remember is that by the eighth day, he was completely recovered – just like Alaxis the year before. Must be a bizarre campus disease."

"That strikes one person once a year?" Alaxis raised an eyebrow.

"I guess the two of us just have terrible luck." Dreck took another drink and sighed. "Two tourney champions that would have been. Forced to live in the shadows of our classmates who have thrived in our misfortune."

"Oh, I don't know about that." Alaxis took a long drink. "The shadows aren't such a bad place to live. Makes it harder for your prey to see you coming."

"Exactly what I always say." Dreck nodded emphatically. "Who needs the pressure of being the tourney champion? The fame, the glory, the adoring fans? Why force yourself

to live up to that kind of title? Better to leave that to
figureheads like Rindarin and Jadon. Let the real warriors
lurk in obscurity. To strike with godlike skill, greater than
champions. That's how Alaxis and I prefer it."

"Sure, Dreck." Fendi snickered. "No doubt you'd have
bested Jadon along with the rest of our class if you'd been
scheduled to fight on any other day. Just like Alaxis."

"I don't know about that either." Alaxis shrugged. "Sure,
I could take Rindarin now, but a year ago? It would have
been a near thing."

"Please," Jadon sputtered. "It's a night and day difference
between you two. How much can that have changed in a
year?"

"I'm a Reader now." Alaxis frowned at Jadon. "It makes
a difference."

Jadon opened his mouth, then closed it. He had never
thought about it, but suddenly things that had not quite
added up before made sense. In the Initiative, everyone
liked to posture and compete, pretending they had greater
prowess than they did – but nobody challenged Alaxis in
any physical task. Not even Rindarin. Not ever.

Then Jadon remembered how Chase had recommended
Alaxis assist him in vaulting the ravine on the first night of
the Initiative. Finally, that level of deference made sense,
and so did Alaxis's ridiculously impressive unaided vault,
which he had pulled off on his first attempt.

The man had Reading magic. There must have been
dozens of upperclassmen with magic strong enough to
notice. Jadon felt like an idiot for never having thought
about it or realizing that Alaxis had to be one of them.

"You didn't know, did you?" Fendi started laughing. "And
this is the man who beat the rest of us in interrogations." He

clapped and rose to his feet, and Dreck walked to the bar. "Behold, deductive reasoning at its finest. Jadon tu'Hatreth, everyone."

"I need another shot." Jadon touched his eye, as though the injury could be blamed for his obtuseness.

"Drink up, geniuses." Dreck carried in shots and passed them around the table. "Now we know why the War Houses never take the interrogations final."

They drank the shots, and Jadon felt this one go straight to his head. He had started this conversation for a reason, but between Dreck's humor and Alaxis's revelation he seemed to have gotten distracted. He put down his glass with emphasis. "Have you all ever heard of the yellow serpent's tongue?"

"What now?" Fendi asked.

"It's a yellow flower," Jadon explained. "The petals look like a tongue? Anyway, the leaves are toxic, and if you eat them, you come down with a fever that kills you after three days. But if you just eat the petals, or if they're torn up and mixed in with, say, a drink, it'll just make you a little sick at first, like a cold. And then you get sicker and sicker with fever, and it reaches its highest point on the seventh day. They sometimes call it the sennight's serpent."

"Jadon, you've already revealed your idiocy." Dreck lifted his glass and put it back down, as if in illustration. "You can no longer succeed in cloaking it with random trivia. Nobody's impressed, man! Time to admit defeat!"

"What happens on the eighth day?" Fendi asked.

"Well–" Jadon began, but he was interrupted by the bartender.

"My lords!" he said, bowing. "Your pardon, but it looks as though a party of Edrei is headed this way."

"Flames of the Abyss." Arzit's curse was the only utterance as they let that sink in.

Alaxis was the first to gather his wits. "Edrei!" he announced to the other tables. "Everybody out!"

The warning barely preceded the appearance of six green-cloaked figures in the doorway, and the common room dissolved into chaos.

"Nobody move!" an Edrei ordered, but tables were already being overturned as the initiates tried to conceal their identities. Some made for the stairs, some for the door behind the Edrei, some for the back way out through the kitchen. Alaxis picked up a chair and threw it through one of the big windows next to them, jumped on the table, and led them outside. Someone smashed another window, and soon a dozen of them were in the street.

"Hectibald!" they heard an Edrei say. "This one I don't know. Get them in the wagon." They heard curses and the sound of horses. The Edrei had brought reinforcements.

"Split up!" Alaxis said, picking a direction and running like mad.

Jadon sprinted across the street, got tripped up by his scabbard, and fell into an alley as the horses came into view, cursing the Initiative's habit of going everywhere armed to the teeth.

"There's more back here!" one of the Edrei yelled, grabbing an unfortunate boy to get a look at his face. The Edrei were trying to corral the initiates, but all they really had to do was be able to identify them later in order to enforce the penalty for being out after curfew.

Jadon scrambled to his feet and resumed running, keeping a hand on his sword hilt to avoid tripping. If he was caught, he would be expelled, too, son of the Senator-

Liaison or no. There would be no way around it. He took a turn and then another, the sounds of commotion still loud and not far behind. Then, hearing horses up ahead, he stopped. Edrei riders came into view on the heels of some hapless initiate. They caught him and pulled him out of the shadows.

Jadon recognized Fendi and cursed. He considered charging the group of Edrei, thinking the confusion might allow his friend to get away.

But they had already seen Fendi's face, so he would likely be expelled anyway. Did Jadon really want to risk showing his own? A future at Eshtem was a lot to give up for a casual acquaintance, even one he liked as well as Fendi. If other War House boys had been with him, Jadon might have marshaled them into making a concerted effort to free his friend. More bodies meant more confusion – not to mention more glory in the attempt – and that was a level of risk Jadon might have been willing to accept.

But he was alone, and so far as he could tell, unobserved.

He turned and ran in the other direction.

There were Edrei behind and before him, so he took the first turn he came to. The adrenaline had sobered him some, and he felt he was going uncharacteristically fast, but his movements required extra concentration. It was a heady but unstable feeling, like a baby bird trying its wings for the first time. He turned again and then again, heading deeper into the city. The Edrei would expect initiates to take the most direct route back to campus.

Jadon ran for what seemed like a long time before the sounds of pursuit faded. Only then did he pause to get his bearings and catch his breath. He leaned over, panting heavily, and surprised himself by throwing up in the road.

Wiping his mouth with his sleeve, he straightened and looked around. The streets were empty and the buildings dark. He recognized nothing. Hearing the sounds of a river to his left, he headed that way. If he followed the river, he would find his way to something familiar eventually, and he could figure out the best way back to campus from there. He would have to get back before the Edrei got word to the Drei Masters that there were initiates in Lystra and they called for a count of all the students in their dorms. As far as Jadon knew, the last time they had called for such a count had been scores of years ago at least, but with Edrei hunting down initiates in Lystra's streets, they would have to enact the policy. There was a limit to how much ignorance they could pretend of the War House Initiative's activities.

At most, he had three counts before they discovered him missing.

Jadon grinned stupidly, the whole situation reminding him of hide-and-go-seek tag. He had always enjoyed that game as a child, and now, with his future at Eshtem on the line, it was rather exciting.

He stopped walking when the road dead-ended in a stone wall. *The flood wall*, he realized. He could hear the Sanhivre flowing just beyond it. A long time ago, the river used to flood the lower city during the rainy season, so the Edrei had constructed twin flood walls. They began a few miles south of South Bridge and ran along the banks until the river left the city, protecting the houses that ran up to the river's edges in those areas and forcing the extra water to flood instead the fishing beaches by South Bridge and the plains outside the city limits.

All of this meant that Jadon had gone much farther south

than he had realized. The way north, though, was blocked by a building nestled against the flood wall. He turned around.

A man was walking toward the flood wall on the other side of the street. Jadon started, but he was dressed in gray, not green.

Just a commoner coming back from a late night drinking, Jadon assumed. But the man's movements were full of purpose and fluidity. He ducked into the shadowed area between two buildings. Jadon caught the glint of moonlight on steel. Then five more figures came into view, fanning out and looking around.

"Hello there," Jadon hailed the group, now pleased to be armed. This was a bad area of the city, and these people looked like thugs. All of them sported swords or knives, and none of them were dressed like nobles.

They continued their slow search of the shadows. One of them was about to draw even with the first man's hiding place, not a stone's throw from where Jadon stood.

"Stop there, sirrahs," Jadon advised, adrenaline starting to flow. He put a hand on his sword hilt. One against five was poor odds for the man these thugs were looking for, but Jadon was here, too. If violence broke out, he wouldn't just stand by and watch. "Can I help you find something?"

No one stopped. The man in the shadows made his move suddenly, coming out to bury a dagger in the chest of his nearest pursuer. The thug dropped with a moan. The man in gray twisted the dagger as he pulled it back with his left hand and turned to hold the sword in his right between him and the remaining thugs. Three of them hurried forward, drawing weapons, and the man in gray dashed away.

Jadon also attempted to draw and run, but he had to stop to struggle with his weapon, the draw less fluid than expected. "Stop, in the name of Hatreth!" he commanded, managing to brandish his weapon as the man being hunted ended his dash up short against the flood wall, now just a few steps behind him. There was nowhere for him to go but back up the street. "What is the quarrel here?" Jadon demanded.

"Nothing that involves you, stranger," the figure farthest from the action answered, signaling the other three. They had slowed their rush and now fanned out across the street, knowing their quarry to be trapped. The speaker signaled again, and they stopped, the four of them now in a loose line blocking the way out. "You may pass."

"And this man?" Jadon gestured with his free hand to the man behind him, who was watching the exchange with a grim expression, sword and dagger both still drawn and ready. He had shown some skill in taking out one of his pursuers, but there were still too many for him to have a chance.

"A murderer. What's he to you? Go now. Last offer."

"You should go," the man in gray agreed. "No point in both of us dying tonight."

"This man is under my protection," Jadon insisted, backing up to stand beside his charge, their backs against the flood wall. He felt more brash than he should, with the alcohol and the excitement, perhaps, but his duties as a lord were clear. "If he has killed unjustly, he must have a trial, and as a Hatreth lord, I remand him into my own custody until such a thing can be arranged."

"As you wish." The speaker signaled again, and the four figures began moving forward.

"Watch the two on the left," the man beside him instructed. Jadon caught the trace of an accent in the man's words. *Alterran, maybe?* His *th* sounded more like their *z*. "They're yours. Don't lose track of them." The *r* was wrong, too.

Jadon considered the advice, shelving his curiosity about his companion's mother tongue. The two on the left were hulking men. One held a sword, the other a pair of daggers. Otherwise, they might have been identical. Mercenary tattoos decorated their necks: crossed swords over black roses.

Then suddenly there were a dozen men approaching them instead of four. "What in the flam–" He must have been drunker than he thought.

"The original two. I'll take the rest."

It made no sense, but there was no time to think. They attacked, and Jadon's attention narrowed to the two originals. He could not fight them all, and the man with the sword was swinging at him. Jadon parried. Too late, he saw one of the others also swinging at him, and despite what he had said, his ally did nothing to stop it. The blow landed across Jadon's thigh.

He felt only a vague tingling. *I am very drunk*, he marveled as he kneed the first man in the groin, disengaging his sword just in time to catch a dagger from the second man. *Is any of this happening?* He dodged the second dagger by powering forward into his first opponent, making the man stagger back. More of the figures were landing blows, but he felt only tingling. The two men he was fighting, though, seemed to have substance.

Bad time to hallucinate.

As suddenly as they had appeared, the extra men were gone. Just four figures were left, one of them dead at the feet of the man in gray, one of the two in front of Jadon going down with a dagger in his neck. The remaining two started running.

"That's right, run away!" Jadon yelled, exhilarated. It was his first real battle, and he had won. He took two steps in pursuit before he felt dizzy and remembered he must be drunk, which meant it was a miracle he had survived.

He heard the soft *chink* of something hitting the ground behind him, and he turned around to see his ally pulling the dagger out of the dead man's neck. A black stone had fallen to the street beside him.

Jadon moved to pick it up. On closer inspection, it was more like crystal than stone, and its blackness seemed more like a thing it contained than merely the color it was. Jadon hardly knew how to describe it, but the object felt *wrong* in his hands. "I think you dropped this," he said, holding it out to the man in gray.

And then he saw that the dead body, which he had originally taken for that of a hulking man, belonged to a woman. A thin, attractive young woman, with big black eyes staring senselessly at the moonlit sky. Blood streamed from the wound in her neck to pool on the cobblestones beneath her.

"Flames of the Abyss!" Jadon exclaimed, leaning closer. "What–"

"I owe you a debt," the man in gray said, wiping his dagger on the woman's clothes. "But I cannot pay it now." He sheathed the dagger and stood, taking the strange crystal from Jadon's hands. "This cannot stay in the city." He hurried back up the street.

Jadon barely registered the man's words or his flight. He knelt next to the woman, stupidly feeling for a pulse. She was clearly dead. *I thought she was a man.*

I thought she was fighting me. Had he been wrong about that, too? But no, her right hand was clasped around the hilt of a dagger, and another dagger lay next to her left hand where she had dropped it.

How did I not know I was fighting a woman?

A startled intake of breath made Jadon look up. He saw the black robes of a Drei Master.

His eyes met those of Master Miraj.

"Sights." Jadon looked at the woman lying dead on the cobblestones. He had forgotten all about the search for initiates. He would be expelled for sure. Perhaps charged with the murder of this woman. "This isn't what it looks like." Hearing an approaching horse, Jadon looked up.

Miraj was gone, but an Edrei on a horse was coming toward him, taking in the sight of the two dead men, the dead woman. The blood on Jadon's hands.

"They were fighting us," Jadon started to explain. "There were five of them. Twelve of them. And she was a man. A big hulking man. A thug. And I'm not the one who killed her." He stopped, cleared his throat, looked at the dead woman. It made no sense, and he could make no sense of it through the alcohol that fogged his brain. The Edrei had dismounted and was coming closer, a cold revulsion on his face.

She was a man before, wasn't she? So, she's a woman. But she still attacked me, didn't she? Didn't she?

"I didn't kill her," Jadon repeated, wanting it to be true. He needed it to be true. *Where did the man in gray go? He knows, doesn't he?* "I didn't kill her."

It sounded like a lie.

CHAPTER 19

Jadon's Allies

Adding Psedal's prophecy to the handful of those that speak of the next world struggle makes one thing very clear. The direction the Order takes will hinge on one decision made by a single member – and that future Edrei is a student at Eshtem today. If this person is a War House prince, as some of the other prophecies have suggested, that means the only possible candidates are Rindarin tu'Rithadur and Jadon tu'Hatreth.

Six save us if the fate of the world ever depends on Rindarin.

– From the journals of Drei Master Tamar

Diar did not know what time it was when the bells of the north tower interrupted his sleep, but it was most certainly not morning.

"Initiates!" Master Garadil's voice rolled across the dorm, perhaps across all of campus. "A count has been called. Please exit your rooms and stand beside your doors. Wait for a Drei Master to come down the hall and acknowledge you, then go back into your rooms. Any unauthorized noise or delays to these proceedings, intentional or otherwise, will result in demerits or immediate expulsion."

Diar came fully awake. Getting up, he checked Jadon's box bed. It was empty. *Seven sights. He's in trouble this time.* Growing nervous, Diar took a few moments to pull his uniform back on over his smallclothes, wondering if his roommate would show up in time for the count.

Diar slipped out into the hallway to stand beside his door, noticing that the other initiates on his floor had remained in their smallclothes. Perhaps taking the time to dress had been a mistake.

He heard someone running in the stairwell. A moment later an initiate appeared, stripping off weapons and outer clothing as he hurried down the hall. It was Regix, the War House boy Jadon had defeated in the tourney's semifinal. Diar watched as he opened the door to his room, threw his clothes and weapons inside, and took his place next to his roommate, now also in smallclothes. Over the next few seconds the boy's breathing began to return to normal, but he was still dripping with sweat.

Diar bit his tongue to refrain from asking about Jadon. Garadil had forbidden unauthorized noise, and he did not want to risk expulsion. Not with the Lists not out yet; not when he might have another year ahead of him if he did nothing to jeopardize his standing further.

At the same time, though, he wished he could do *something*. Jadon had risked his own standing at Eshtem to assist Diar during interrogations. But he could think of nothing, no way to cover for Jadon without getting into deep trouble himself.

Then Master Shiell appeared at the end of the hall, coming out of the stairwell. He nodded to each initiate as he passed, dismissing them back into their rooms. He paused in front of the sweaty War House boy.

"Regix." Shiell acknowledged him. "Present, but drenched in sweat." It sounded as though the master was talking to someone else.

Maybe he is, Diar thought suddenly. Maybe the masters were using magic to communicate about the count.

Come on, Jadon, he urged silently, part of him still expecting his roommate to materialize from the stairwell, or perhaps from one of the windows within their room. *You're running out of time.*

"Regix, can you account for your present state?" Shiell inquired.

"I was having a nightmare, Drei Master." The boy sounded like a soldier making a report, and he was standing like one, too. "I get them sometimes."

"Another nightmare sufferer, it seems," Shiell concluded, nodding a dismissal. He continued down the hall.

Any initiate on the floor could have told him Regix had only just arrived, but the masters did not invite initiates to sell one another out. They considered it their job, and theirs alone, to maintain discipline. From what Diar had gathered, they did not care if students got away with breaking a few extra rules as a result.

Shiell paused as he drew level with Diar. "Third floor, fifth door to the right. Diar is present, but only Diar." There was a beat of silence, and then he said, "Jadon's room. Interesting." He nodded to Diar, and Diar went back into his room, dismayed.

Jadon had missed the count.

When morning came, the dining hall was abuzz with gossip. Everybody wanted to know why the masters had called for a count and who had missed it, if anyone.

Unfortunately, those of Jenne's friends who made it to breakfast on time had little information to share with one another. This disappointed her greatly.

"If it had anything to do with the War House Initiative, I bet Diar would know," Cardos suggested. "You don't think *he* missed the count, do you? Could that be why he hasn't shown up yet?"

"Not a chance," Brinnette scoffed. "We all heard him swear them off."

"He's probably just late again," said Telius. "It's not like breakfast is mandatory."

"No need to wait for him." Jenne rose to her feet. "There are plenty of other people who know what happened. Liana, come with me, please. The rest of you, we'll be back with information shortly."

"All right." Liana sounded hesitant, but she stood. Jenne led her to the kitchen so they could both return their trenchers, and then they started up the stairs. "Where are we going?"

"Sometimes the Initiative boys take their meals to the fourth floor," Jenne explained. "I didn't see them on the main level, so we're going up there to check."

Liana furrowed her brow. "Why am I coming?"

"They don't care for me. You are my peace offering." Jenne smiled. "Because you are pretty and famous. Also, I wanted the company."

"Wouldn't it be easier to wait for Diar?" Liana's tone was gentle, but her look was expectant. "It seems like you've been going out of your way to avoid him lately. Whatever is going on, don't you think it's time for it to stop? He might be one of the only friends we have left here next year. Or you might never see him again. What happened?"

He rejected me. Jenne left the thought unspoken. It sounded petty, and childish, and maybe it was. "Nothing happened," she said.

Liana lifted her eyebrows. "Nothing?"

Jenne shrugged. "We kissed, I suppose. That's it."

"That's it?" Liana repeated, incredulous. "Jenne, you have been punishing him for weeks. What happened after you kissed? Did you fight?"

"No, that was it." Jenne's tone was shorter than she intended. "Nothing else happened. And I have *not* been punishing him."

"You've been pretty cold to him," Liana disagreed. "And there was that whole thing with Christina."

"I've already apologized for yelling at him about her, and aside from that, well... I just haven't been as interested in keeping up the friendship, that's all."

"Did you... *want* something else to happen?" Liana cocked her head to the side. "Is that what this is about?"

"Nothing else was ever going to happen." Jenne sighed, annoyed with herself for winding up in this conversation. She had no desire to think about how that had made her feel, let alone talk about it. "He's Rishara, after all. Rishara-ahn. They have views on these things."

"You mean on physical intimacy?" Liana's brow wrinkled in a pretty frown. "Jenne, if he'd been intimate with you, wouldn't you be worried about what might have resulted?"

"It wasn't the right time for me to get pregnant, if that's what you mean."

"How can you be sure?"

"I know my body." Jenne had assumed every girl could feel the difference between her fertile and infertile times of the month, but Liana's wide blue eyes suggested otherwise.

"You're braver than I would be. My family wouldn't survive that kind of scandal." Liana shook her head before looking back at Jenne. "Are you angry with Diar?"

"No." *I'm angry with myself,* Jenne realized. She had been angry with Diar, for making her think they could be something, for letting her get hurt. But it was not his fault that she had not known sooner how seriously he took his Principles, and it was nobody's fault but her own that she had been hurt.

The door was open when they reached the Initiative's room. Perleyon was the first to notice them.

"Are you girls lost?" he asked.

"Liana and I were hoping to have a word with your cousin," Jenne told him, smiling sweetly. Perleyon hated her, but Dreck had thrown a compliment her way once or twice. He had even asked her about Liana, though Jenne had never given him the time of day. "Dreck, right? Is he in here?"

"Liana and Jenne, is it?" Dreck turned slowly. "Looking for me? What for?"

He was hungover. It was a shame. He would have leapt at the chance to talk to Liana otherwise, Jenne was sure. "Everyone wants to know why there was a count last night and whether anyone missed it. We were hoping you might have some insight."

"After me for my gossip." Dreck grimaced. "Figures."

Perleyon smiled. "Looks like nobody wants to talk to you. Beat it."

Jenne scanned the room. Usually the War House boys could be heard making a ruckus from far down the hall, but not today. No one was playing darts. They were lounging about at the various tables, half-heartedly watching the exchange. Several of their number seemed to be missing. "It looks like Jadon's not in here. Can we expect that trend to continue?"

"Out." Perleyon stood up, walked over to them, and closed the door in their faces.

Jenne led the way back to the stairs, unfazed. "I wonder if Jadon missed the count," she said. "Some of them must have."

"Diar would know," Liana noted. "You should talk to him."

Jenne sighed, deciding Liana was right. She and Diar came from two different worlds, and she would never measure up to the standards of his well enough for them to be lovers – but that did not mean the two of them could not be friends. She was starting to miss his company.

Perhaps it was time to make amends.

Probably past time, Jenne admitted to herself, grimacing. If Liana had thought she was punishing Diar, Jenne's distancing behavior may have been more pointed than she had intended. *I might owe him another apology.*

Jenne did not enjoy the prospect of apologizing, and she would have been happy to put it off for a few more counts. When they got back downstairs, though, she saw that Diar was eating with the rest of the group. She and Liana resumed their previous places, which put Jenne at the opposite end of the table from him.

"No, it just took me a long time to fall asleep after the count," Diar was explaining when they sat down. "Jadon missed it. I guess I was waiting for him to come back."

"Did he?" asked Jenne.

He gave her an odd look from across the table, and Jenne realized it was the first time she had addressed him, other than in response to a direct question, since she had yelled at him for going to Lystra on Jadon's behalf. That had been weeks before.

I do owe him an apology. She studied the table, feeling sheepish.

"Good morning, Jenne," Diar said to her. "Good to see you. No, he never did come back to his room. But all his things are still there."

"Why would his things be gone?" asked Eridike.

"Kerci rooms on my floor, and she missed the count," Brinnette volunteered. She had supplied this detail earlier, but it was fresh for Diar and Eridike. "Came back with one of the campus aides sometime during the night. Cleared out her stuff. Left campus."

"I saw Fendi do the same," said Diar. "But Jadon's things are all still there."

"You want to go find out what happened to him?" Jenne asked. "You and I?"

"You mean together?" Diar blinked.

"Yes, you two should go find out," said Liana. "Let us know what you find."

"All right, then." Diar took a few more bites of his breakfast and stood. "I'll just take this back to the kitchen."

"I'll go with you," said Jenne, following him. "The Drei Masters should be coming by soon. We could ask one of them."

"Does this mean you are speaking to me again, then?" Diar asked as they paused by one of the garbage cans on their way toward the kitchen. He emptied his trencher.

"Yes." She turned to face him. "I should not have been so cold to you these last few weeks. It was unnecessary and unkind, and you deserve better. Forgive me and be my friend again?" She offered a hand.

"Few weeks? It's been over a month since the tourney, Jenne, and we've hardly spoken since." Diar started toward the kitchen, lifting his trencher as if to show he had no hand to spare. "If we're going to be friends again, does that mean you'll tell me what I did to upset you?"

"You didn't do anything, really." Jenne brushed some errant curls out of her face and avoided eye contact. They had reached the kitchen window, and Diar set his trencher down among the others. "I just needed some distance."

He turned toward her and stared. "I told you I liked you." His tone was not harsh, but it was not gentle either. "It's clear that you don't feel the same. But you could have just said so. Why did you need so much distance?"

Jenne blinked a few times, suppressing a surge of frustration. *He asked to be friends again the last time we spoke, didn't he? So why does he suddenly need an explanation?* "Look," she began, searching for the quickest and most painless way of explaining herself. "We're friends, you and I. For a minute there, I thought we might be something more, but you didn't want that. I responded badly, but I'm over it now. And I'd like to go back to being friends, if you'll allow it." She held out her hand, offering a handshake again.

Diar took in a breath, paused, and released it. He was still staring at her, though his expression had changed from skepticism to perplexity. "Is that what you think I want?"

"You don't want more now." Jenne pursed her lips, unwilling to explain why that meant they could never be. "And I'm not going to wait. So that makes it friends or nothing."

Diar looked as though he wanted to say something, but there was nothing to say, and Jenne had no intention of dragging this out. She kept holding out her hand. Friendly, but only friendly. Her resolve on that was firm.

She was not one to risk rejection more than once.

"You make no sense, Jenne."

She dropped her hand, exasperated. She turned to the kitchen window. "Have the Drei Masters come by to collect their breakfasts yet?" she asked one of the workers.

"A few minutes ago."

"Come on," Jenne said to Diar, hurrying toward the tower's back door. It was the way the masters came and went. "We'll have to catch up before they get to interrogations. Master Tamar likes you, doesn't she? Maybe we could ask her."

She pushed the door open and put a hand on Diar's arm, slowing him. Tamar stood a stone's throw beyond them, arguing with Regild. The other masters were already crossing the lawn toward the east tower.

"Surely–" Tamar was saying.

"No," the headmaster cut her off. "Interrogations begin in less than a quarter count. If you can send word to the city watch in the meantime, feel free. But if you are not in the chamber on time, I will have no choice but to remove you from your post and find someone who takes the office of Drei Master more seriously."

The headmaster continued toward the east tower. Tamar stood still a moment longer, her frustration palpable.

"You ask her," Jenne whispered to Diar.

"Master Tamar?" Diar said, walking closer.

Tamar turned to face them.

"I'm sorry if this is a bad time," Diar continued. "We were just wondering if you might be able to tell us what happened to Jadon? He's my roommate, and he missed the count last night. We – well, *I* was worried."

Tamar stepped forward, a sudden light in her eyes. "Do you want to help your roommate, Diar?"

"Does he need my help?" Diar sounded bewildered.

"He hasn't been expelled, then?" Jenne asked.

"He has not been expelled," said Tamar. "Yet. An Edrei found him in Lystra after curfew last night, standing over three dead bodies. He appealed to the Redemption Clause in the Edrei Charter, saying that his curfew violation enabled him to save a man's life from a group of attackers, and that he was caught only because he stopped to help this man. He is in the east tower now, pending the Drei Masters' decision. We will meet tonight after interrogations are over to hear his arguments and make a ruling."

"What would he need from me?" Diar asked.

"Do you want to help him?" Tamar studied Diar intently, and Jenne got the feeling she was using her gift to read his intentions.

"Yes," said Diar. Jenne was not surprised.

Tamar nodded. "Then you must go to Lystra. The city watch is investigating the deaths related to Jadon's case. As of now, they believe the victims attempted to rob Jadon and that he fought and killed them alone. The watch released Jadon to us, as they are not bringing any charges against him. However, if the Drei Masters believe he fought them only to defend himself, he will be expelled for the curfew violation.

"The watch has until tonight to produce someone who can corroborate Jadon's story – either the man he says he rescued, or one of the attackers who ran away. They have Jadon's description of the man he rescued, but they do not know that one of the attackers had a prominent tattoo on the left side of his neck. You must tell them. Crossed swords over a black rose."

"Can't you tell if Jadon is lying?" asked Jenne. Everyone knew Tamar was an Intuiter. Jenne thought Intuiters were good at that sort of thing. "Why would you need another witness?"

"Jadon is not lying," said Tamar, turning to look at the sun. "But he was drinking last night, and parts of his story struck some of the masters as implausible. There is some doubt as to whether his memory is reliable."

"Right." Jenne was not surprised to learn Jadon had been drunk.

"Listen," Tamar said, turning back to them. "The watch has little time to produce another witness. I would go to Lystra to aid them myself if the headmaster would permit it, but he will not, and I cannot convince him to delay the hearing. This means the watch must have assistance from another quarter. Since it is your desire to help Jadon, you must go to Edrei headquarters in Lystra and ask for a Drei Jere. He is an Intuiter like me and could speed the investigation. He may prove reluctant to get involved, but you must persuade him to do so."

"How would we do that?" Diar asked.

"Tell him," said Tamar, thinking, "that more than Jadon's fate alone is at stake here. If he will not aid Jadon simply because I ask, tell him he must do so on behalf of the Order itself."

"Why?" Jenne's tone was dubious.

"Such is my message." Tamar ignored Jenne's question. "Will you take it?"

"Yes," said Diar.

"You must do *everything* in your power to aid Jadon in this." Tamar glanced at the sun again. She was running out of time, and she knew it. "Will you?" She returned her gaze to Diar, still intent.

Diar nodded. "I will."

"And you?" Tamar surprised Jenne by turning the question – and that Intuitive gaze – on her as well.

The memory of Jadon's words after the Initiative hangout came unbidden to Jenne's mind: "That's two you owe me, book thief." She realized what her answer had to be.

"I will, too," she said.

She did not like it. But Jadon had kept her from getting expelled, back on their first day of class. She could afford to help Diar carry this message on Jadon's behalf, and she probably owed it to Jadon. Besides which, helping Diar might convince him to let her go back to being his friend.

Tamar nodded. "You will, won't you?" She sounded more confident in Jenne's commitment than Jenne was herself, which was odd.

Jenne did not like the feeling that the master had seen something in her that she herself did not know was there, but she had a hard time shaking it.

"Hurry now," Tamar told them. "Jadon is running out of time."

Shortly thereafter, Diar found himself on a second trip to Lystra riding double on Jadon's horse, a trip once again taken on behalf of the War House prince. This time, at least, he was not risking expulsion himself. There was no need to rush to return in time for class. The academic year was over. The first-years were free to visit Lystra while they waited for the Lists, or to go even farther if they wished; moreover, a Drei Master had all but ordered him to do so.

Yet Diar found the second trip no more relaxed than the first.

He decided two things as he took Jadon's horse to a canter, Jenne riding behind him with her arms wrapped around his waist. The first was that he was in love with the girl whose body pressed so closely against his. Her touch was both exquisite and painful, overwhelming and not enough, and all he could think about was how much he wanted to cross whatever distance had opened between them and kiss her until it was gone.

The second was that she was not for him and never would be.

Finally, he understood why things had changed so much between them. It wasn't because he had kissed her or embarrassed himself that night at the Initiative party. It wasn't because he had told her he liked her. It was because he had told her he couldn't sleep with her. *That* was why she was hurt.

You don't want more now, she had said. She could have meant nothing else, because in any other sense, he did want more. He wanted her attention, her affection, her commitment. Watching her flirt with Landers the past few weeks had been torture, and being so close to her now, riding together, was the most pleasing sensation he could imagine, short of kissing her.

The White Way forbade physical intimacy outside an enduring commitment, and Diar had always intended to honor the teaching. But he doubted he would be able to if he ever found himself drunk with Jenne again. Even despite her repeated attempts to brush him off, even in spite of Landers, his feelings for her had only grown harder to ignore since that night.

I'm not going to wait, she had said. That was a clear message. She did not share his values and would not support him in keeping them.

She could not possibly want to risk pregnancy, but Diar had heard rumors that some girls on campus knew where to buy tonics in Lystra to keep that from happening. He had not guessed that Jenne might be one of them, or that she would want to rush into a physical relationship so quickly. But apparently, if he wasn't willing to give her what she was looking for, she intended to find it with someone else.

He could hardly blame her for that. Jenne was not Rishara-ahn. If she wasn't worried about pregnancy or the risk to her reputation, she had no reason to deny herself. Diar was curious enough about sex himself. It would be thrilling and dangerous – exactly the type of thing Jenne would want. The thought that she might try it with Landers made his stomach turn.

He should have seen this coming. When he had met Jenne, that long-ago day in Lystra, he had known that their values were different, and yet he had let himself hope for something between them. He had refused to put two and two together, somehow hoping that she might prove open to the White, open to the teachings of the Rishara-ahn.

Open to me, Diar finished the thought, narrowing his eyes. *Idiot. Why would she be? They call the White Way narrow for a reason. Why would she want to keep it without even knowing the White?*

Jenne had her own way, her own principles. It was her nature to seek and defend her freedom to follow them as she saw fit, to refuse to bow to the whims of nobles or to bend to the strictures of others' rules, expectations, or opinions. It was part of what made her so exotic, so foreign to Diar, who had spent his whole life doing his best to please everyone around him as far as he could. Jenne represented something he himself could never have or be. It was a large part of what drew him to her, while also being the reason they could never work. Asking her to bind herself by the Rishara Principles, even only insofar as concerned her interactions with him, would be asking her to contradict the essence of what she was.

There was no way around it. He would keep the Way, and she would not. He could have known that from their first meeting if he had bothered to think ahead.

But he had not thought ahead, and so here he was, drawing the obvious conclusion nearly a year later, with a pit in his stomach that his heart had opened by dropping into his gut when he heard her ultimatum of *friends or nothing*. It felt as though her arms around him were all that kept it still inside his body.

She's not for me, Diar repeated to himself, trying to grasp the idea, trying to force his mind and his heart to accept it. She was riding with him only so they could help Jadon.

As they neared the city, Diar made a mighty effort to rip his focus away from her and turn to the task at hand. He feared he would fall to pieces otherwise, and he could not afford that. Not with Jadon depending on him, and not when he had made a promise to Tamar.

They left Jadon's horse at one of the city's stables before walking to Edrei headquarters. Conversation between them was minimal, as it had been on the ride to the city. Jenne had tried several topics without success. Diar did not seem interested in speculating about why Tamar thought Jadon's hearing was important to the Order, or how the Hatreth heir had managed to get himself involved in a killing after curfew in Lystra. She eventually picked up on this and respected the silence between them.

It had taken her over a month to decide the two of them could go back to being friends. If Diar needed a few counts to acclimate to the idea, that was more than fair. She just hoped he would come around eventually.

When they reached headquarters, they were greeted by a Drei Istanosh, who told them that Drei Jere was leaving on an assignment. Diar insisted they had to speak with him right away, and Istanosh told them they might catch him in the stables around back.

An Edrei was saddling his horse when they approached.

"Are you Drei Jere, the Intuiter?" Diar asked.

"I am, though that's not typically part of my title." Jere smiled. "What can I do for you, Initiates?"

"We have a message for you from Master Tamar. She wants you to help the city watch investigate a case – a killing. An Eshtem initiate was involved, and the watch needs your help today if they are to have any chance of finding a second witness before the initiate's hearing tonight. He'll likely be expelled if his testimony about the events isn't corroborated."

Jere stroked his horse's mane as he listened. "Jadon's case, you mean. Master Tamar believes his story?"

"You're familiar with it?" Diar asked.

"Of course," said Jenne. Tamar had mentioned an Edrei had found Jadon at the scene of the killing. As an Intuiter, Jere would have been asked to listen to Jadon's account of what happened before the watch became involved. "You must have spoken to Jadon yourself."

Jere was nodding. "I heard his version of events last night. I told the city watch not to give it too much credit, prince though he may be."

"What?" Diar sounded scandalized. "Master Tamar said he wasn't lying."

"Lying, no," Jere agreed. "But he had consumed a fair amount of alcohol. I sensed no deceit in him, but as far as I could tell, he didn't believe half of what he was saying himself – and no wonder. His story didn't add up."

"How's that?" asked Jenne.

"How much did Master Tamar tell you?" Jere returned.

"Just that Jadon claimed to have rescued a man from a group of attackers," said Diar, "and that the watch has to find that man or one of the attackers, in order to corroborate the story. She gave us a description of one attacker."

"She was pressed for time," Jenne explained.

"True." Jere nodded, studying her. "But misleading. You do not think she would have shared any more with you, even had she had the time." He started walking again, leading his horse around them on his way outside. "But I suppose there's no harm in adding that, according to Jadon's description, the man he rescued was an Alterran lord dressed like a commoner, and the woman he killed was a remarkably strong Projector working with criminals known to the Lystran watch. Implausible, to say the least."

Jenne and Diar traded looks, surprised. Remarkably strong Projectors were rare, and as far as Jenne knew, they did not involve themselves in brawls or work with common criminals.

"Well…" said Jenne, searching for something to say. She had promised to try to help Jadon, after all, implausible as his story seemed. "Master Tamar believed him. Isn't it worth looking into?"

"I have another assignment, unfortunately," said Jere, leading the way outside. He stopped when they reached the road and turned to mount his horse. "The city watch will have to manage without me, though I do hope your description proves useful to them if there is any merit to Jadon's tale."

"There's more to the message," Diar said, hurrying to face Jere from the other side of his horse. He stood close enough that the Edrei could not mount without kicking him in the face, and it did not look as though Diar was about to move. "Master Tamar said more than Jadon's fate alone may be at stake here." Standing eye to eye, Diar was taller than the Edrei and making the other man feel it. He leaned in, and Jenne was surprised by the intensity in his demeanor. "She said to tell you that if you will not help him for her sake, you must do so on behalf of the Order itself."

Jere returned Diar's gaze for a moment, then glanced back at Jenne, a smile on his face. "Did you see anything change in him just now?"

Jenne tilted her head, trying to put her finger on what she had noticed in Diar. "He sounded like a lord there for a second." Normally that would have displeased her, but it was so out of place coming from Diar that she was impressed. Looking at him now, though, it seemed that whatever air he had taken on to deliver Tamar's message was gone. He was back to his unassuming self.

"But did he seem any taller to you?" asked Jere.

Jenne considered their relative heights, and realized that Diar was not as much taller than the Edrei as she had thought. She frowned. "Maybe a little."

"Will you help him?" Diar asked Jere.

"She says I must on behalf of the Order, does she? I suppose she didn't mention why." Jere shook his head, his gaze distant. The sound of approaching hooves snapped him out of it. Another Edrei was riding toward them. "I wish I could. But I have an assignment."

"On your way out, Jere?" The incoming Edrei, a man with skin the same deep brown as Diar's, checked his horse as he reached them. Jenne's attention was caught by his green feathered hat. It seemed an ostentatious choice for an Edrei.

"Yes," Jere told him. "There's been a rumor of Hound activity a day's ride from the mountains. Marsil wants me to chase it down, see if I can find any of them."

Diar was still looking at the newly arrived Edrei, and Jenne, taking another look herself, realized she recognized him.

"Drei Zanner," said Diar. "It's a pleasure to see you well, sir."

The Edrei dismounted. "Have we met before, Initiate? I'm afraid you'll have to refresh my memory."

"Oh, I wouldn't expect you to remember, sir." Diar was smiling. "But I helped carry you off your horse into an inn when you arrived in Lystra last summer."

"Did you? Why then, I owe you my thanks." Zanner swept off his hat and bowed.

"None necessary, sir," said Diar.

Zanner smiled and turned to Jere. "You're riding out now, then?"

"I was about to."

"Is there any way you could delay?" Diar's approach had devolved from injunction to plea. "Jadon's hearing is tonight. We need your help."

"What's this, now?" asked Zanner.

"Remember Jadon?" Jere raised his eyebrows, and Zanner nodded. "Apparently Master Tamar thinks there's merit to his story, but the rest of the board is inclined to agree with me, absent corroborating evidence from the watch investigation. These two want me to help them search."

"Not just us – Master Tamar," Diar corrected him. "She said that it's very important. She asked me to do everything I could to help."

"Me too." It was hardly much of a contribution, but it was all Jenne had to offer. She glanced at the sun. "And the longer we stay here trying to convince you to join us, the more time we lose in the investigation. Sir."

"Maybe I could run down that Hound lead for you," Zanner said, looking at Jere. "Since I'm back early. Dreaming might be more useful than Intuition anyway, if you're looking for them in open country."

"Are you sure?" Jere asked. "You'd be willing to ride out again so soon?"

"Why not? You said yourself, you haven't known Master Tamar to err."

"That was before." Jere's tone spoke volumes.

"Before what?" Jenne asked.

"It's your call," said Zanner.

Jere considered Zanner, and Jenne inferred that he was not going to answer her question. "Yes. I will go with them," he said. "Better not to ignore Tamar's admonition."

"Thank you," said Diar. "Thank you both. And not just for us, or for Jadon, or even for Master Tamar. For the entire Order."

Jenne thought it sounded like a little much. Diar was playing up the "the Order depends on this" angle much more than she would have, given that neither of them knew anything about it. It had helped to convince Jere, though, and that was something.

When they reached the offices of the city watch, they were directed to find Watchman Firhelm, who was the only man the watch commander had put on Jadon's case, and that only because this Firhelm had apparently insisted. *Probably looking to curry favor with the high prince*. Jenne may have come here to help Jadon, but even so, it annoyed her to find he had so much favor from someone in the watch even after the Edrei had told them they could dismiss the case. She doubted Firhelm would have insisted on investigating if any other initiate's future at Eshtem had been at stake.

It took them another count and a half to find the watchman, given they were told only that he was searching the lower city for the Alterran Jadon had allegedly rescued. When they found him, he was having a mug of ale in the common room of an inn. It was past time for the noon meal by now, and Jenne took the liberty of ordering food for herself and Diar while they were there.

"A man matching the description Jadon gave us was in the city," Firhelm was explaining when she returned from the kitchen. He stared straight ahead as he spoke, his expression grim. He acknowledged her with only the barest of nods as she joined them at the table and set down two plates. Diar started eating from his absently, so focused on the watchman's words he seemed almost unaware that he was doing so. "Stayed two nights at this very inn," Firhelm continued. "But he settled his bill late last night, gathered his belongings, and left. Nobody has seen him since. He probably left Lystra. I'd ride after him, but nobody knows which way he went. So, I appreciate the offer, but I don't see that there's anything left to be done. Not even for an Intuiter." He took another drink from his mug, sounding utterly defeated.

Jenne wondered whether he was taking the morning's failure rather too hard for someone merely looking to curry favor from a lord.

"You found a man matching the description?" Jere asked, surprised. "How closely?"

"A hand under five lengths tall," Firhelm recited, "blond hair, dressed like a commoner, talked like a noble with a hint of a foreign accent."

"Was the accent Alterran, like Jadon said?"

"Could have been, but the people I talked to wouldn't have known how to place it."

"But that's good for Jadon's case by itself, isn't it?" Jenne asked, looking at Jere. "You didn't think such a man could be in Lystra, but he was."

Jere was shaking his head. "It is not enough. Jadon might have seen this man, and in fact that would help explain how he imagined such a person. But it lends no credence to the idea that events occurred as he described them. However, you said Master Tamar described one of the attackers? Perhaps he will prove easier to find."

"She said one of them had a tattoo on the left side of his neck." Diar spoke up between mouthfuls. "Crossed swords over a black rose."

"The sign of the Blasted Company? Truly?" Firhelm set down his ale, glancing from Diar to Jere. "Why didn't we have this information before?"

"Jadon was reluctant to describe his attackers. I didn't press him because I had dismissed his tale already." Jere pressed his lips together. "Tamar must have gleaned more."

"This changes things," said the watchman, standing. "Perhaps he can be found at the Company's house, and an Intuiter's help would be most welcome. Thank you." He nodded to Jere. "And thank you for bringing this to us," he added to Diar and Jenne. "We will take it from here." He began striding toward the door, a sudden energy about him.

"Please, can we come?" Diar stood, taking a few steps after Firhelm and looking to Jere when the watchman stopped. "If there's any way we can help, I'd like to be there. I promised Master Tamar I'd do everything I could."

Jenne stood, too, seconding Diar's request with her eyes. She expected them to say no, though, and was already planning another route she and Diar could take to the Blasted Company House.

"The Blasted Company is a rough bunch," said Firhelm. "I wouldn't take initiates to their house, but you can assure your Master Tamar that if this attacker can be found among them, we will find him without delay."

Jere looked from Diar to Jenne, considering. "They can wait outside when we get there," he decided. "I expect they'll only follow us if we try to leave them behind."

"Very well." Firhelm led the way toward the door.

"Thank you," said Diar, hurrying to follow.

Jenne drew alongside Firhelm when they reached the street. "You seem to care a great deal about this case," she said. A light rain had started falling while they were in the inn, and the streets were not very busy. "May I ask why?"

"I owe my life to Jadon tu'Hatreth," he said, surprising her. "My honor demands that I use it to offer him aid as far as I am able. And I am told his enrollment at Eshtem hinges on whether I am able to produce another witness."

"He saved your life?" asked Jere.

"He spared it," Firhelm corrected. "I had committed a treasonous offense in the service of Lord Juaqen. Jadon presided over my case and commuted my penalty to a mere whipping."

Now that makes more sense, Jenne thought. Refraining from sentencing someone to death was hardly the same as saving them, and were she in the watchman's shoes, she doubted she would sing Jadon's praises over it.

"A whipping for treason?" Jere sounded impressed. "That is uncommon. Even more so in War House lands."

"Quite," Firhelm agreed. "Now you understand how deeply I am indebted. But this Alterran, he is even more so. And yet he has not come forward, abandoning his rescuer to face repercussions alone." Firhelm shook his head. "He disgusts me."

They walked in silence after that, and Jenne glanced at Diar. He looked straight ahead, the lines of his face tight with anxiety. She recognized those anxiety lines from interrogation days and the many times she had pushed him into doing something that stretched his comfort zone, but today they were different. Today he would not look at her, and she could do nothing to ease them.

"Wait here," Jere told them when they reached the Blasted Company House. Diar and Jenne waited in the street while he and Firhelm knocked on the door, exchanged a few words with the man who met them, and went inside.

Jenne looked at Diar, but his attention was glued to the door. She pulled her hood up against the rain, though it was more of a light sprinkle and the hood was hardly necessary. She shifted as the silence stretched.

"Do you want to circle around and see if we can watch through a window?" she asked, hoping the suggestion would earn her a few points.

"Drei Jere said to wait here," Diar returned flatly.

She sighed.

Suddenly the door burst open. A heavyset man with the black rose tattoo ran past them into the street, Firhelm on his heels. Diar joined the chase, and together they caught the mercenary and forced him up against the wall of the neighboring building.

"All right, all right, you caught me!" the man said, lifting his arms as Jere came outside. "But I've got nothing to say."

"Nothing to say?" snapped Firhelm, still up in the mercenary's face. "You fled from a watchman. I can have you arrested for noncompliance. You better find something to say."

"A couple nights in jail isn't no bother," the man spat.

"He is afraid," said Jere, studying him. "But not of us."

"Just got nothing to say, that's all," the man insisted, scowling at Jere.

"Perhaps we are using the wrong approach here," said Jere, putting a hand on Firhelm's shoulder. Firhelm released the mercenary, and Diar followed suit. "What is your name?" Jere asked.

The mercenary flicked his gaze from one to another. "Ballas," he said.

"Ballas, a pleasure to meet you." Jere extended a hand. When Ballas made no move to take it, Jere gestured to himself instead. "I am Drei Jere, and this is Watchman Firhelm. We are servants of the city, and as such, we pose little threat to you, it is true. But we may prove useful allies to a man guilty of attempting to murder an Alterran lord. We know you were one of them."

Ballas snorted in derision, and Jenne wondered how Firhelm and Jere had determined he was the man they wanted so quickly. He did not seem to have admitted anything.

It's a good thing we have an Intuiter, she supposed.

"We will be asking you some questions," said Jere, more firmly. "We have the authority to jail you and speak to you there – the threat we pose extends as far as that. Personally, I prefer to discuss my cases in a more relaxed manner, perhaps over a mug of ale at that tavern across the street. But the choice is yours."

The mercenary's movements were slow and suspicious as they crossed the street. Diar walked next to him, keeping his eyes on Ballas and away from Jenne, who walked on his other side. *He's just staying ready in case of another escape attempt*, Jenne told herself, but it felt personal. She had never spent so much time with Diar and held so little of his attention.

Once at the tavern, Jere had Ballas sit and then left to order a drink.

Firhelm sat down across from him, and Diar and Jenne stood behind them while Ballas wiped his face with his sleeve to clear it of rainwater.

"What are you afraid of?" asked Firhelm. "Perhaps your employer?"

"Please," Diar interjected, taking a seat at the table next to Firhelm. "We don't need much from you. Just a confirmation of who your target was. Right now, they think my friend fought you alone, and he's going to be in a world of trouble for it. You don't need that to happen, and it would be so easy for you to prevent."

Firhelm stared at Diar until Diar noticed his attention. "Why don't you let me handle the questions, Initiate."

"Sorry," said Diar, standing and backing up with Jenne, ducking his head.

Why does everyone care so much about saving Jadon? Jenne wondered. It irked her. *It's not like he's even in any real danger. So what if he gets expelled from Eshtem? He's still filthy rich, and one day he'll be a high prince whether he joins the Edrei or not.*

She took a breath to calm down, and then reminded herself that she was going to help them. *Diar cares about this.*

"I don't know what you're talking about," said Ballas.

"One boy. A student. Killed your associates and made you run." Firhelm leaned closer to Ballas as Jere returned and set down a mug of ale. "That's what the official story says. How's that going to affect your reputation?"

Ballas picked up the mug and took a drink, saying nothing. Jere, watching him, shook his head. "You don't care about your reputation, do you? At least, not anymore. Too afraid, I think."

Ballas set down the mug, and Jenne noticed a tremor in his hand. Jere was right about the fear. Jenne furrowed her brow, thinking back to what she had heard about the assault.

"Ask about the Projector," she suggested in an undertone to Jere, who was still standing close to her. If she were a common mercenary who had somehow wound up working with someone who could use Edrei magic, she would find that unsettling.

Jere raised his eyebrows, as if surprised she would say something, but he turned his gaze to Ballas without comment. "The woman who fought with you," he said. "How did you meet her?"

"I don't know what you're talking about." Ballas stared at his mug but made no further move to drink from it. He was starting to sweat.

"Brown hair, shoulder length. Not so tall. Proficient with a pair of daggers. You remember," Firhelm prompted. "Not many women work in your trade. She must have left an impression."

"Yes," said Jere, watching the mercenary. "He fears her. Greatly."

"Was she the one who employed you?" Firhelm asked. "You ran from the contract. Will she be hunting you down for reprisal?"

"She's dead," said Ballas, the outburst born of equal parts fear and anger. He sank lower in his chair, focusing on his ale. "I mean, I don't know what you're talking about."

"The woman I'm talking about isn't dead," said Firhelm. "At least, not as far as we know."

It was a bold gambit, pretending the woman was still alive. But Jenne understood why Firhelm was doing it. They had no other leverage.

"Fauxsight." Ballas's eyes darted up to meet Firhelm's.

Firhelm started speaking again, but Jenne stopped paying attention. He knew the woman was dead. They were not going to convince him otherwise. *Unless…*

As inconspicuously as she could, she tapped Jere on the shoulder and jerked her head toward the tavern's door. She led the way outside, and he followed her as Firhelm continued the interrogation.

"This isn't working," Jenne said.

"A little soon to tell."

"The woman. Not so tall. Did you see the body? Was she about my height?"

"What are you thinking?"

"Could I pass for her? If I had shoulder-length brown hair? And the right clothes? And daggers?"

Jere studied her, considering. "Your build is not dissimilar, though you have a different face." He smiled as a thought occurred to him. "Although, according to Jadon, the woman was wearing a Projection even before the fighting began. It's possible that Ballas saw her true form only as she was dying. He must have seen her wound, though, to be so sure she died."

"Tell me about the wound," Jenne said. "If we can make it look convincing, that should be enough, right? If I'm dressed like her?"

"Maybe." Jere frowned. "But you are not a Projector. And if he never got a good look at her, it might take a Projection to convince him you're the same woman."

"But you're Edrei. Edrei have magic. He'd probably believe you could cancel her powers, don't you think?"

"Maybe." Jere tilted his head, considering. "If there were a Projector in the city we could ask to assist us, that would be better."

"Don't you have any at headquarters?"

Jere shook his head, but he was suddenly smiling. "There might be something else we could try, however."

After two counts of watching a fruitless back-and-forth between Firhelm and the mercenary, Diar was exhausted, frustrated, and starting to grow anxious about making it back to Eshtem before curfew. Ballas was utterly unyielding, though Firhelm had threatened him with everything from the High Prince Hatreth to the dead Projector, who he continued to insist was alive.

Ballas had not said anything at all for the last half count or so, and Diar, sitting at a nearby table as he watched Firhelm continue to talk at the mercenary, was almost ready to give up hope. Diar had sworn to do everything in his power to aid Jadon, but he could think of nothing to suggest to Firhelm that the watchman had not already tried.

Where is Drei Jere? Diar wondered, not for the first time. The Edrei and Jenne had disappeared some time before. Jenne's abandoning the mission did not surprise Diar; she had not even wanted Jadon to escape expulsion anyway. Jere, though, should have been with them. His Intuition might have made a difference.

The door to the tavern slammed open, revealing a brown-haired woman in black leathers with a pair of daggers sheathed at her waist. Diar's attention caught on the wound lacerating her neck. It was a dark red – almost black – partly formed scab the size of a fist, and it leaked trails of blood across her throat.

Ballas went white as a sheet. It was only as she began moving across the room that Diar recognized her. *Jenne?*

"You look like you've seen a ghost," said Firhelm as Jenne settled herself at the bar. Her back was to them, but her position allowed her to view the tavern's exit. Ballas would have to cross her line of sight if he were to flee. "One who looks remarkably similar to a woman I've heard described. You quite sure she has better things to do than come after little old you?"

The door to the tavern opened again, and Jere slipped into the room.

Ballas turned his head away from Jenne. "I've got nothing to say." His voice was an angry half-whisper.

"If you change your mind, I'm sure my associate from the Order will keep her from harming you," said Firhelm, nodding toward Jere. "But if you're determined not to talk, I suppose I'll have a word with her instead." He got up and strode toward Jenne. "Excuse me, madam," he said. "I am Watchman Firhelm, and I have a few questions for you."

Jenne slowly turned to face Firhelm, but her gaze fixed on Ballas. "You," she hissed, her voice an eerie rasp. She had to hiss or Ballas would recognize her voice was wrong, Diar realized, but when coupled with the wound on her neck, it suggested her voice had been destroyed.

How did she do that? Diar wondered, shocked.

Ballas got up and backed into the corner, drawing his sword in panic as Jenne slowly rose to her feet. Firhelm moved a hand to his own weapon, but Diar was too surprised to move. Most of the other patrons were, too, though those closest to Ballas cleared out of his way.

"Madam," Firhelm repeated, but Jenne ignored him.

"What do you want?" Ballas half-yelled at Jenne as he backed farther away, his posture defensive. "I haven't said anything!"

Jere put a hand on Diar's shoulder and leaned closer to whisper. "I need you to do something for me, Initiate. You see Jenne?"

"Yes."

"You see the exit? I want you to focus on that spot right in front of the door. Now, while you're looking at that spot, picture Jenne."

In front of them, Jenne took a step forward. "You ran," she rasped.

"What?" Diar asked. *I'm not a Projector. This isn't going to work.* "I can't–"

"You're going to," Jere said in Diar's ear. "Do exactly as I say. Focus on the spot. Remember Jenne as you just saw her. Imagine her standing in that spot. Get the details right."

"All right," said Diar, focusing. This moment was important for Jadon and for Tamar. If there was even a chance he could do this, he could not afford to fail.

"Now *put* her there," Jere said.

Ballas broke and ran for the door.

Diar, afterward, had no idea how he did it, but for one glorious moment, his focus sharpened to the edge of a knife, and an image of Jenne flickered into existence in front of

Ballas, dropping him in his tracks. The mercenary hit the floor and clambered backward on hands and feet. "I'll do it! I'll say anything!" he yelled, his gaze fixing on Jere.

"Stop!" Jere yelled, surging to his feet, and Diar's focus – and the image of Jenne in the door – evaporated. Jere was holding out a hand in Jenne's direction, and her eyes widened. "This man is under our protection."

Jenne ran out the door. Jere ran after her, and Firhelm crossed the room to the cowering mercenary.

"She's gone now," he said, offering a hand to help him rise. "The Order will see that she stays that way if you explain to them why she should."

The mercenary nodded, still white and trembling.

Diar took a deep breath, trying to grasp what had just happened. They had convinced the mercenary to testify on Jadon's behalf.

In the process, he – Diar Jax, a first-year Eshtem initiate – had Projected.

CHAPTER 20

The Ruling of the Board

Your Majesty,

It is with profound regret that I write to inform you that our fears have been confirmed. Vilinora is dead. The men who took her were led by an Imager, a woman able to change her appearance. She is dead now, slain by my hand, but she answered to someone else. I was unable to learn his identity before I was discovered and attacked. I escaped with the aid of a passing lord and deemed it best to flee the city before my identity became known.

There is more to the story than I dare trust to the post, but I return to you now and will make a full report in person. Be vigilant. I fear war may soon be upon us.

– Your servant, Luc Amand,
First Justicer of Alterra

The six watches after the assault in the streets of Lystra were some of the longest Jadon had ever endured. First there had been the Edrei who found him standing, dazed, over three dead bodies. Jadon, still reeling from the shock and the alcohol, had tried to convince the man he had not killed the woman on the ground between them, despite the fact that her blood was quite literally on his hands. The Edrei had said little and believed less.

Then the man had taken him to Edrei headquarters, where Jadon spoke to the commanding officer and then found himself across from the resident Intuiter, Drei Jere. Jadon tried to explain about the Alterran and the dozen disappearing thugs. None of it made sense, and as he listened to himself talk, Jadon became more and more convinced that he must be describing the events of a dream or a strange waking hallucination.

But the blood on his hands was real, and so was his interrogation with an Edrei Intuiter. Something had happened, and three people had died.

They took him to the city watch after that, where he gave a brief statement. He no longer remembered what he had said. It had not seemed to matter, anyway. The watch had not been planning to charge him. That had been a huge relief at the time, though after his head cleared, Jadon realized it meant nothing. He was a Hatreth prince, and two of the dead had been known criminals. It looked like an assault gone wrong, and that was what they were calling it.

They neither knew nor cared exactly how Jadon had come to be standing over the body of a woman nobody recognized, or to what extent he bore responsibility for her death.

Then the Edrei had taken him back to Eshtem, where administrative aides ushered him into a waiting room in the east tower while Headmaster Regild, Master Miraj, and Master Tamar were summoned. They were disheveled, having been roused from their beds to deal with him in the last watch of the night before dawn. They listened with varying degrees of disbelief while he tried to explain what had happened. When Jadon got to the part of the story where he remembered seeing an apparition of Miraj just before the Edrei found him, it all felt so unbelievably incredible that he omitted that detail. He could tell they suspected him of insanity already; there was no need to confirm it.

As it turned out, there was no need to conceal it, either. Miraj laughed as if Jadon had spoken the memory aloud, and when the masters retired into the hallway, Jadon could hear them arguing, though he could not tell what they were saying. Then Tamar came back and made him repeat his story. He could guess nothing of her thoughts as she asked question after question, pressing him for what seemed like the most irrelevant details. Was he sure the accent of the man in gray had been Alterran? Did he remember what each of the attackers had looked like before the extra men appeared? Had they changed at all with the appearance of the extra men? When exactly had the extra men disappeared? When had he noticed the woman?

She made him describe the black crystal he had found on the street at least a dozen times, but he seemed unable to provide whatever answer she was looking for. It had hardly seemed relevant at the time. The truth was, Jadon had no idea what had happened or what any of it meant, and being pushed to the utter limit of exhaustion was not helping.

When Tamar left, the waiting began. Despite being left to himself in a well-furnished waiting room after a sleepless night, Jadon could rest only fitfully. Whenever he started drifting off, he saw the cold, dead eyes of the woman staring up at him. Over the course of his many interrogations, he had begun to realize that her death, whatever level of responsibility he bore, would mean the end of his tenure at Eshtem and his future as an Edrei.

He had never considered a future in which he did not become Edrei. It had been a sure thing, something he had been told he would do from as far back as he could remember. It had never been his hope or his dream, as it was for so many who crossed the Dragon Arch. He had never even bothered to ask himself if he wanted it. He would become Edrei, just as surely as he would one day become high prince. Wanting or not wanting it was beside the question.

Only now that he was in danger of losing his chance did he realize how much he wanted to stay at Eshtem. The alternative was going home to Hatre steeped in disgrace. His father would fight the expulsion for a time, directing his rage at the Senate and the Drei Masters, but he would have nothing to fight with. Jadon had been in Lystra after curfew, out of uniform, and he had been caught. Eventually, Lord Juaqen would realize that not all his connections and influence could get Jadon out of the trouble he had brought on himself, and then the high prince would come to despise him. Never again would he allow Jadon the opportunity to disappoint him or to become anything other than what Lord Juaqen required of him. If the Order cast him out, Jadon realized, he stood to lose a great deal.

But the Order will cast me out. It was a daunting realization, and Jadon felt sick as he came to it. It no longer mattered what he wanted. The time when he could have done anything to protect his tenure was over. His future was in the hands of others, and only a fool could hope they would take his appeal to the Redemption Clause seriously. His story was too far-fetched.

Why did the man in gray leave? Jadon wondered, suddenly angry. The man in gray knew what had happened. The masters would have believed him. *If he was even real.*

The cut that killed her wasn't mine. Jadon's sword had been bloodless and his dagger still sheathed after the fight. He had at least that much to cling to. *I can't have been the one who killed her.*

Jadon eventually drifted into troubled slumber. A knock at the door jolted him awake. He sat up and rubbed his face as the door opened, wincing as his hand met his bruised left eye. He brought his hand away slowly, thinking.

"That's quite the black eye you have there."

"Master Miraj," said Jadon, blinking. The Drei Master had come in alone.

"Master Tamar asked me to see if I could glean anything further from you before your hearing. We haven't long before I must return to interrogations, but we have a few minutes. Why don't you go over the events again?"

"I don't have a headache," Jadon said.

"Neither do I," said Miraj, taking a seat on the plush velvet chair closest to the divan Jadon had slept on. Resting an elbow on the chair's arm, he leaned his head against his fist as he considered Jadon. "And so?"

"I wasn't drunk last night. Nowhere near drunk enough to hallucinate. I must have really seen four people turn into twelve..." Jadon frowned, finally putting it together. "Magic. It must have been magic. Strong magic." Jadon had always thought of Edrei magic as a subtle thing, easy to miss. The display at the tourney had not been subtle, of course, but that had required the power of two dragons – and even then, the Projections had been obvious fakes, lacking defined features, easy to see through, and sometimes lagging behind their real-world counterparts.

He had never imagined magic could be used to create such a complex and convincing illusion as the extra men he had fought in Lystra. But what else could explain it?

"A powerful Projection. The woman – did she go to Eshtem?"

"No." Miraj gazed at him, his brown eyes unblinking. "Your confusion seems genuine."

"She must have learned some other way."

"A High Wizard's Knight, perhaps?"

Jadon frowned. *He's making fun of me.* According to legend, each High Wizard had kept six human Knights: impossibly strong Imagers who had traded their souls and their service to the wizards in return for immortality. As far as Jadon knew, even people who believed the legends about elves and High Wizards considered the Knights an embellishment.

"Not every Imager goes through Eshtem," he said. "Some must develop their skills on their own. It's possible, right?"

"To learn to Project eight combatants in the level of detail you described, simultaneously? While maintaining alterations to one's own appearance? You are a first-year, and so your understanding of Projection comes from myths and rumors. Trust me when I say that to accomplish anything like what you described would require power and finesse of legendary proportions. Vorsand might be comparably strong in Dreaming. Before him, Merabe One-Strike, the Reader. Sundamar the elf. You may have heard of these people?"

Jadon nodded. They were legends.

"According to Order records, the Dophkan oracle famous for foreseeing the Gysalt Conflict, Trissadari, was a Prophet who never received Eshtem training. Of all the rogue Imagers sought and identified in the many hundreds of years since Eshtem's founding, she was unquestionably the greatest. Her power was perhaps a tenth of what you've described."

Jadon rubbed his forehead. This time he was careful to avoid his injured eye. "The Order must miss some. Perhaps many, over the years."

"The Order makes a point of looking, everywhere it reaches. Those who are missed, are missed because their powers are easily overlooked. We do not miss legends."

"Well, it has to be possible." Jadon leaned forward, elbows on his knees and chin in his hands. "I saw it, and I wasn't drunk."

"Maybe." Miraj twirled his thick, wavy hair with one of his fingers as he continued to lean against his hand, watching Jadon.

After a moment Jadon turned to face him, his eyes narrowed in question. "Were you there? I saw you. That can't have been a hallucination either, but why would she Project you? If she wasn't dead already, she was only moments from it."

Miraj shifted, catching Jadon's chin in his hand. Turning Jadon's head, he peered into first one eye and then the other. "That blow came from a fist, if I'm not mistaken. And yet the thugs you described were all armed. Interesting." He let go of Jadon's face and leaned back. "A detail I missed before, but no mind. You were saying?"

Jadon frowned, trying to think. "I don't remember."

"Can't have been too important, then. Why don't you describe the events of last night for me one more time?"

Jadon took a deep breath and repeated his story. The man in gray, the thugs, the confrontation. The twelve men, the fight. The dagger. The crystal. The dead woman. The Edrei. He had been over it so many times, he could have recited it in his sleep.

"You don't believe me, do you?" he asked after he'd finished, his expression grim.

"I believe that *you* believe you," said Miraj, crossing his arms. "But your story is incredible."

"What did Master Tamar think?"

Miraj shook his head, and then he stood. "You may find out tonight at your hearing. In the meantime, I need to pick up my lunch and return to interrogations. Someone will be by with yours shortly." Miraj walked to the door, pausing when he reached it. "Was there anything else you saw last night that was strange, Jadon? Anything else you wanted to talk about?"

Jadon shook his head. "I think the dead Knight about covers it."

Miraj smiled, bowing his head. "Very well, then. I will see you again at your hearing."

Dark had fallen by the time an aide came to fetch Jadon.

"The Drei Masters are ready for you," the man told him, his voice somber and disapproving. Jadon nodded and rose to follow.

The curfew bell had already sounded, and the other initiates were all shut away in their dorms. The earthy scent of petrichor lay heavy on the air. As Jadon followed the aide down the footpath, the soft patter of their footsteps was all he could hear. The university, like him, seemed to be waiting.

A sudden wind assaulted them as they rounded the library, and a deeper darkness overtook them. Jadon craned his neck to see a large shadow passing above, blotting out the moon and stars.

A dragon. Jadon caught his breath as it passed, stopping to watch. This was the only time he had seen one outside the tourney. Its silhouette was enormous.

"Come along," said the aide, impatient.

"I'm coming." Jadon continued staring as the dragon disappeared, lowering in the sky to the east. He wondered who was riding it, and where they were coming from.

It occurred to him that this might be the last glimpse of a dragon he ever caught.

He resumed walking.

"Still haven't learned respect, I see," the aide muttered.

Jadon frowned as he followed the man down the footpath, mystified by the comment. *What does this aide know about how respectful I have or haven't been? I paused for only a second*, Jadon grumbled to himself as he followed the aide up the steps toward the large double doors of the west tower.

The doors opened into a margarette foyer with winding staircases leading up on either side. The floor was dominated by a deep violet rug. Masks hung on the far wall. One black door stood in the center.

"Wait here," the aide told him, slipping inside. Jadon caught the sound of raised voices before the door fell closed.

He shifted his weight, finding the silence of the foyer oppressive. The suspense was more difficult for him than he would have cared to admit. It felt like forever before the door opened and the aide motioned him inside.

The room was tighter than Jadon expected, and the floor was overlaid with cedar. Twelve magnificent armchairs of varied color and style were arranged in a semicircle across the room from where Jadon entered, backlit by the fireplace on the other side of the room. The room was round, and two more doors were placed at even intervals around the circle. Ensconced torches provided additional light, but the room was laced with shadows.

He could only just make out the features of the twelve Drei Masters staring at him as he stepped inside. The aide closed the door and seated himself on a stool by the door. The other doors, Jadon noted, also had stools standing next to them, but he understood that he was expected to remain standing.

"Initiate Jadon." Headmaster Regild broke the silence. He sat at the end of the semicircle to Jadon's left. The masters, Jadon noted, retained the order in which they had sat during interrogations, with Miraj next to the headmaster and Garadil on the far right.

"Last night, you were caught out after curfew in the city of Lystra, the penalty for which is expulsion. It is the understanding of this board that you have appealed to exemption from this penalty under Section Twenty-Two, Provision Sixteen of the Edrei Charter. Do you still so appeal?"

Jadon closed his eyes and ran through his memories of the night before. Now that he understood he had not been drunk, he had to assume they were reliable. *I saved that man's life.*

"Yes."

"You understand, you can recant now and spare us all the trouble of this hearing." Derrak, Jadon remembered, had tossed him an opportunity to regain the stage during final interrogations, but the master did not appear friendly now. His tone was incredulous and his gaze impatient.

"Yes, I so appeal," Jadon repeated.

The headmaster exchanged a look with Derrak before returning his gaze to Jadon. "Very well, then. This being the case, the purpose of this board is to hear your appeal and render a decision. You may now present your argument."

Jadon cleared his throat. Somehow, he had not expected his hearing to be so formal.

It made no difference. His memories were what they were, and the masters would be no more likely to believe them if he were sitting in a circle with them drinking tea than they were under the present conditions.

"Last night, I was at an inn in Lystra with a few fellow initiates when we received word that a party of Edrei was headed toward us. We took cover as the Edrei entered, split up, and ran.

"I had successfully eluded pursuit when I paused to determine my bearings. I was in the lower city, near the flood wall, when I noticed a man in gray clothes take cover behind one of the buildings across from me. At that time, five figures started coming down the street toward me, all armed and apparently searching for this man. I hailed them but they did not speak to me. The man in gray surprised one, killing him, and ran, only to find the street dead-ended against the flood wall behind me.

"I drew and demanded to know what was going on. The four remaining assailants drew nearer, trapping us against the flood wall. One spoke, inviting me to leave. I saw mercenary tattoos on two of the assailants, and I determined their intentions were to kill the man behind me.

"Since I was not in Eshtem uniform, I claimed custody of the man in gray in my capacity as a Hatreth lord. The assailants attacked us, and then, instead of four of them, there were twelve. The man in gray bid me focus on two of the originals, and I did this. The others landed blows but did me no injury. After a few seconds, the man in gray threw a dagger into the neck of one of the men I was fighting, and then there were only four again. Two were dead, and the other two ran.

"Then I saw that the man I had been fighting, the one with the dagger in his neck, was a woman. The man in gray left, and I was discovered by an Edrei."

Jadon paused, took a breath, and continued. "At the time the assailants invited me to leave, no more than a quarter count had elapsed since the Edrei surprised us at the inn. An additional count and a half would have been ample time for me to make my way back to my dorm on campus, had I taken the assailants up on their offer. Two counts is, I figure, less time than elapsed between the Edrei's discovery of initiates at the inn and the official count that was taken at Eshtem. I could easily have made it back to campus, and my violation of curfew would have gone undiscovered, had I chosen to leave the man in gray to his fate.

"But I stayed, and my intervention saved his life. I thusly appeal to Section Twenty-Two, Provision Sixteen, which clearly states, if an affiliate of the Order is found to have committed an infraction meriting penalty under the Charter because the affiliate has undertaken a good action of praiseworthy intent and positive result, the penalty may be waived under certain conditions. I contend that my case satisfies the necessary conditions. I saved a life, an act unquestionably greater in significance than a curfew violation. I was only able to do so because I was out after curfew, and it is only because I saved this life that my curfew violation was discovered."

Jadon fell silent, and for a moment no one spoke. He studied the floor, finding it a more comfortable fixation point for his gaze than the faces of the gathered masters. There was an argument to be made on his behalf, he knew, and he had made it as well as he could. He just did not see how anyone could believe him.

Verizah, a small second- and third-year instructor with sharp, pale features, was the first to speak. "There is another condition outlined by the provision."

Jadon nodded, meeting her gaze. "I trust the discretion of the board to arrange preventive measures against future curfew violations for me."

"It is worth noting," Verizah continued, now addressing her colleagues, "that even if we decide that the first two conditions are satisfied, we must still face the question of how and whether we should arrange to keep him from continuing to disregard this university's code of conduct. It may prove necessary to expel him because we cannot afford to waste the time and resources to ensure a single student's compliance with curfew."

Jadon resumed his study of the floor.

Estilend spoke next. "Master Verizah makes an excellent point. Moreover, given the history of this particular student, I'd say that curfew violations are far from the only thing we would need to guard against. This incident of being out after curfew – in Lystra, out of uniform – is but the tip of the iceberg. It speaks of a pattern of disregard for this university's expectations, and if we speak of measures that can be taken to rectify the behavior, we must speak of measures that would address the entire pattern, not merely that which we saw last night."

"I don't understand why we're here," said Halce. "This student has earned enough demerits to be expelled three times over, and that *without* the incident last night. When a student shows that much contempt for the rules, we do not ask ourselves how to rehabilitate him. We cut him. Enough is enough."

It was not surprising to hear Halce so set against him. The weaponry instructor had never liked Jadon, but it came as a blow all the same.

"His demerits were offset by the requisite number of merits, as is custom." Porrian came to Jadon's defense. "If he is to be expelled, let it be on account of his actions last night. Previously canceled demerits are not a factor here."

"Well, maybe they should be," Halce insisted. "And I question why we are sitting here talking preventive measures when the student has admitted himself guilty of an expellable–"

"Master Halce, your objections are noted," Regild interrupted. "But I must ask the board to keep in mind that it is not the system of canceling demerits that is on trial here, nor the merits of the Redemption Clause. We are merely here to determine whether it can be applied to Jadon's case, and I ask everyone to keep in mind that the Senator-Liaison will demand a full account of our proceedings as soon as he hears of this. We must each be prepared to defend the logic of our votes in full accordance with the Edrei Charter as it is currently written."

The headmaster stared at Halce until the latter looked away, and then he made eye contact with each of the others, ensuring that they understood the gravity of the situation.

His father's name was no longer a guarantee of his protection, Jadon understood. But it would be a factor.

Somehow that only made him feel worse.

"Now," the headmaster continued, "we have Jadon here to explain himself and to answer our questions. Please save your commentary until we dismiss him."

"I, for one," said Regosh, regarding Jadon with a dubious air, "am still trying to work out the details of your account. Was it four assailants who attacked you and your man in gray, or was it twelve?"

"Four," Jadon answered. "Although, during the attack, eight phantom opponents appeared. I believe the woman who died must have Projected them."

"You do? My, how the plot thickens." Shiell stroked his chin, a sparkle of fascination in his eyes. "I thought the story was he was out-of-his-mind drunk and imagined the entire episode."

"Jadon, were you drinking at the inn before you ran from the Edrei?" Regild asked, to bring the board up to speed on what he and the Intuiters already knew.

"Yes," Jadon admitted, "but I was not drunk, and certainly not drunk enough to hallucinate, although I assumed I must have been when last we spoke. But, upon further reflection, my memories are too clear and complete to be false, and I was not hungover this morning. Nor did I drink enough last night to become intoxicated."

"Is he telling the truth?" asked Verizah, looking from Tamar to Miraj.

"Yes," said Tamar. "He speaks with confidence."

"A confidence that has only recently materialized," Shiell noted.

"Which of you, after stumbling upon a powerful Projection cast by a thug in the streets of Lystra, would not first doubt your senses before figuring out what must be happening?" Tamar challenged. "Add to that that this is a first-year who has experienced nothing of Imaging in his life, outside our brief display at the Eshtem Tourney. One who has not had time to unlearn the Ellyrian norm of never speaking or thinking about magic, a norm we all took years to shed after joining the Order. Add to that a few drinks, and his confusion should come as no surprise. If anything, it lends extra credence to his tale."

"*Extra* credence? To a tale of tangling with a powerful rogue Projector to rescue some mysterious man in gray?" Derrak sighed. "You'll forgive me if his growing confidence has not yet sold me on his story's veracity."

"Master Miraj, what is your assessment?" asked the headmaster.

Miraj studied Jadon. "Are you quite certain that you were not drunk, Initiate?"

Jadon returned his gaze without blinking. "Yes."

Miraj shook his head, turning to the headmaster. "He seems to believe it. But my gift is not equal to Master Tamar's, nor is my read of him as strong. Whether his belief is tainted by his need for it to be true, I cannot say."

"I can." Tamar's mouth was tight and her tone hard, betraying anger. "Though I do not expect this board to take my word for it. I have sent word to the city watch requesting further investigation into this matter, and I move once again that our deliberations be postponed until tomorrow to give them time to produce a witness who can corroborate these claims."

"Again, I deny the motion." Regild looked at her sharply. "In all likelihood, news of this hearing has reached Lord Juaqen in Shenn already, and he could be here in person tomorrow. I do not want him pressuring this decision. We will have done with it tonight."

My father went to visit Shenn. Jadon was unsurprised. The high prince had not been pleased when Jadon reported to him. Jadon had insisted that his solution would create lasting peace in the city, but it seemed Lord Juaqen had decided to monitor the situation himself. Perhaps he had already undone everything Jadon had accomplished.

He found it strange that Tamar had become his strongest

advocate among the assembled masters. She had assigned him more demerits than any other master and had candidly expressed a desire to expel him little more than a month before.

She believed him. That was clear enough. But why she was fighting so hard to make everyone else believe him, Jadon could not guess. In her position, he would have been content to sit back and let the unruly initiate be expelled.

"Well, if we cannot afford to wait for the watch," said Porrian, breaking the silence, "I find myself inclined to give Master Tamar the benefit of the doubt. She *is* our Master Intuiter, and not without reason."

Jadon smiled tightly. He would have thought Porrian would speak for him with more conviction. It seemed, though, that even the masters who would have preferred to keep him around were hard-pressed to justify doing so.

"*Now* you believe her?" Halce objected. "Now that your pet princeling depends on her gift, you put stock in it. Fascinating."

"Master Halce–" the headmaster began, a warning in his tone.

"I will not pretend I fail to see the expedience of giving this young man every benefit of the doubt," Porrian said. "True, I like him, but personal feelings aside, we should all remember the friendship Lord Juaqen has extended to this Order in the very concrete matters of funding and policy, and how quickly that might dry up if this decision goes the wrong way."

Jadon was ashamed to hear the fact so nakedly acknowledged. This board was not meeting to determine whether he deserved to stay. There was no mention of his accomplishments, his victory in the tourney, his success in final interrogations. It did not matter that he was smart, or that he had probably earned more merits during his tenure than any two other initiates combined. They were all agreed that he deserved expulsion.

They were meeting to determine only whether he had provided them with ample grounds to justify it to his father.

"And the point stands," Felade agreed drily. "Master Tamar is not Master of Intuition for no reason."

"Oh, please," Estilend scoffed. "You too, now?"

"Master Estilend–"

"I am not the one on trial here." Tamar interrupted the headmaster, shifting in her seat. "Can we at least agree that if Jadon's story is true, then the provision applies?"

"Without question," Porrian agreed. "I think no one here would deny the good action and positive result of saving a life, or the relative triviality of a curfew violation."

"A curfew violation in Lystra, out of uniform, is not a thing to be set aside lightly," Halce argued.

"Halce, you are not really going to pretend the significance of Jadon's offense ranks even in magnitude with saving a life, are you?" Derrak rested his chin in his hand. "It's not as though he murdered somebody."

"Actually, somebody did wind up dead," Shiell pointed out. "Three somebodies, in fact. And the available evidence suggests Jadon may have been responsible."

"I will pretend you did not just imply the Master Intuiter's appraisal of Jadon's testimony doesn't count as evidence," Tamar said coolly.

"Master Tamar!" The headmaster raised his voice, clearly impatient, and the other masters fell silent. "Does anyone have any further questions for Jadon, or are we ready to dismiss him so that the lot of you may continue your bickering *in private*?"

In the stillness that followed, Jadon wondered why the masters put so little stock in Tamar's ability to read him.

"I have a question." Garadil eventually spoke. "About intent. Jadon, why did you stay to fight alongside the man in gray?"

Jadon took a moment to consider, conscious of everyone's attention.

He understood the question. If the masters could establish that his intent had not been praiseworthy, the provision would not apply, the positive result notwithstanding.

"It would have been cowardly to leave," said Jadon, returning Garadil's earthy brown gaze without emotion. It was not a purely altruistic motive, but eschewing cowardice was praiseworthy enough, and it was something the board would buy from him.

Garadil looked to Tamar, who gave a slight shake of her head.

"Try again, Jadon," she said.

Jadon narrowed his eyes. "It was my duty as a lord."

Tamar shook her head slowly. "Dig deeper."

Now Jadon was annoyed. *What does she want from me? Chroming Intuiters.* He looked away, searching for answers, and licked his lips. Then he returned her gaze. "He was one, and they were four. I couldn't just leave him there to die."

Tamar nodded, then looked to her colleagues. "The other answers were not lies, but this was the truest."

"Some might wonder whether you just took an opportunity to coach him into a better answer," said Derrak, sending a questioning look to Miraj.

"Please, this had *nothing* to do with Imaging, and I trust you are not impugning the veracity with which I represent my Intuition to the board." Tamar was seething.

"I see no reason to doubt Master Tamar," Miraj volunteered.

"Masters!" The headmaster spread his glare across the three of them. "Any further questions *for Jadon*?"

"What makes us so sure we wouldn't have caught him breaking curfew if he hadn't gotten involved in this brawl?" Halce wanted to know. "It would have been a lot of ground to cover with Edrei combing the city. I'm not convinced he could have done it."

"I would be happy to participate in a simulation for you, Drei Master," Jadon returned, though the question had not been addressed to him. His response seemed as relevant as any. "I'm confident I could have made it back to campus within two counts." He took no pride in the assertion, nor did he expect it to aid his case. It was just a fact.

"Surely this case won't come to rest on such an absurd detail," Tamar objected. "The whole purpose of the provision is to encourage affiliates involved in unsanctioned activity to seize every opportunity to do good, even if doing so increases the risk that their activity will come to light. The only questions we should be asking are: did Jadon save a life, and was that deed worthy enough of our gratitude and praise that we are willing to overlook the fact that he was out after curfew when he did it?"

"I am inclined to disagree," Garadil mused. "Even if Jadon saved a life, we should weigh this against not only his being out after curfew last night, but against the whole pattern of his misdemeanors."

"I agree," said Verizah. "And I would furthermore–"

The headmaster held up a hand. "Jadon, why don't you step into the foyer."

The aide opened the door for him, and Jadon left the room. He heard the masters arguing as the door fell shut behind him.

The silence in the foyer stretched. The masks on the walls stared down at him, and he shifted from foot to foot.

Then the double doors to the outside opened, admitting a gust of air and three people.

"Jadon, good. Are we in time for the hearing?"

Jadon recognized Drei Jere. With him came a man in the uniform of the city watch and a nervous, heavyset man with a tattoo Jadon recognized.

"It's happening now," said Jadon, wary of the man with the tattoo. Jere approached the door and knocked softly. The aide opened it and the two of them conferred briefly.

"I am glad that we are in time for you," the watchman said to Jadon. "Though it is only so because of the assistance of your two friends."

Jadon looked at the watchman, confused. "My two friends?"

"Diar and Jenne," Jere specified, his conference with the aide finished.

The watchman nodded. "Jenne bid me inform you that the two of you are now square. I, however, shall remain forever in your debt."

"Do I know you, Watchman?" Jadon asked, frowning. His square face looked familiar, though Jadon could not place him.

"Watchman Firhelm, sir. Formerly of Hatreth."

"From Shenn," Jadon said, all of it coming back to him. The last time he had seen Firhelm, the man had been lying next to a whipping post, covered in blood. "You don't owe me anything," he said. He wished he could forget everything about Shenn.

He glanced from Firhelm to Jere, returning his attention to what they had said earlier. "Jenne and Diar helped you?"

The door to the inner chamber opened. "The Drei Masters will hear from the three of you now," the aide told them. Jere and the others went inside, Firhelm nodding to Jadon on the way. The door closed behind them, leaving Jadon alone again.

The fact that Firhelm seemed to think he was helping Jadon suggested the mercenary was there to corroborate Jadon's account of the man in gray. *But why? How did Firhelm convince him to do that?*

And how were Diar and Jenne involved? Jadon rubbed his head, finding this piece of the puzzle equally perplexing. It would not have been the first time Diar had gone miles out of his way on Jadon's behalf, but this favor struck him as even more curious than the rest. *Why does he keep helping me? What's in it for him?*

He had given Diar an answer during final interrogations. But that had been incidental; they had happened to be standing next to each other, and Diar had deserved a second shot. It had cost Jadon nothing. *He doesn't think he owes me for that, does he?* Diar could not be counting on those kinds of favors to continue. Jadon had barely noticed his roommate all year, despite Diar's reliable assistance in waking him whenever he slept through the morning bell.

Jenne's involvement made more sense to him. A favor repaid made sense, though he would not have thought her the sort to seek an opportunity.

But how did they know to help me in the first place?

Jadon did not understand what was going on, and he did not care for the feeling. He was accustomed to understanding, to controlling, to knowing just how much pressure he could exert where to result in the outcome he desired. Just how far he could rebel without paying a price. He had to jump off the plateau, but he did not have to fall into the river. A man had to die in Shenn, but it did not have to be Drestil Bow. He could celebrate with the Initiative after curfew in Lystra, but if the Edrei showed up to surprise them, he could not get caught.

But he had been caught. He had been caught because he had not foreseen stumbling across the man in gray. There had been no room in his calculations for error, for adjusting to the unexpected. He had used all the slack he knew he could count on the masters to give him. He had used it on purpose, because he knew it was there. He had not imagined he might need to have some left for when he ran out of time to save a stranger without getting caught.

If the masters voted to keep him, it would be because a footnote in the Charter could be bent far enough to apply to Jadon's case – a footnote that had been the farthest thing from his mind when he had decided to fight alongside the man in gray. It would be because the masters were willing to compromise their values out of fear of Jadon's father even further than Jadon had assumed they would have to. It would be because Tamar had inexplicably fought for him, and because Firhelm, Jenne, and Diar had accomplished the impossible task of producing someone to corroborate his story.

It would not be because of anything Jadon had done. If his tenure survived the night, he would be indebted to many people whose aid he had neither sought nor predicted.

Jadon cared for that idea almost as little as he cared for the prospect of being expelled. *Which still very well may happen*, he reminded himself.

After a while, the door to the chamber opened again, and Firhelm came out with the mercenary.

"Don't I get to hear what they're going to do?" the mercenary was saying.

"It is their job to control Imagers," the watchman replied. "You need not fear her any longer."

"Watchman Firhelm," Jadon said, and the man paused. "Thank you."

"You don't ever need to thank me, Your Grace." The watchman gave Jadon a deep nod.

The doors fell shut behind them. Soon the aide returned from the inner room.

"The Drei Masters have called a recess to give them time to process the new information," he told Jadon. "I am to escort you back to the east tower."

Jadon took a deep breath. It would not be a quick vote, either way.

Diar and Jenne parted ways with Drei Jere, Watchman Firhelm, and the mercenary a few miles from Eshtem to take the Initiative shortcut. Jere thought his company would spare them the penalty for being out after curfew, but they agreed it was safest to avoid being seen.

"All that work and we don't even get to see how it turns out," Jenne complained as they crossed the log that spanned the canyon.

Diar said nothing. The strain between them had eased briefly in Lystra, when Jenne had shared his excitement over learning he was a Projector. On the way back, though, he remembered his affection for her, and that she had stipulated they must be friends or nothing. He no longer knew what to say or how to behave around her, so he mostly remained silent.

She glanced at him as they gained the trees.

"I'm sure we'll find out soon enough," Diar finally forced himself to say. It was a useless comment, but he could think of nothing else to speak into the silence between them.

Jenne held up a hand, stopping them both in the darkness.

"Somebody's coming," she said. The trees were starting to thin, and they could see the east complex up ahead. She led him to the west side of the tree beside them and crouched there, looking east.

Diar copied her. Soon two figures came into view. One wore Edrei green; the other was dressed in the black robes of a Drei Master.

"He didn't say, but you're missing the point." Diar recognized Tamar's voice before he could make out her face in the darkness. "He confirmed the scope of her powers as a Projector."

"That doesn't prove she was a Knight," the man beside her replied. Diar and Jenne scooted around the tree toward the north as the two walked past. "How could she have been?"

"You, of all people, should believe in Knights, Vorsand!" Tamar took the man's arm, stopping him. "You spoke to a wizard."

Jenne and Diar shot stunned looks at each other. Vorsand was the Lead Master Imager, which meant he had probably been on campus off and on all year, but this was the first time Diar had ever seen him.

There was a moment of silence as the Edrei gazed at each other, and then Tamar added, "And what of Psedal's Prophecy? Do you think I imagined it? I know we both trusted the panel, but they were wrong about me. Somehow, they were wrong. All the other evidence agrees. I know I'm right, and I need you to speak on Jadon's behalf. Even if you don't see it, do it for me as your friend."

"Even if I wanted to, they wouldn't listen to me." The man – Vorsand – turned away from Tamar as he spoke, aggrieved. "He's a War House prince, Tamar. And after everything I've heard about his conduct here, you can understand why I don't want to speak for him."

"Some would listen," Tamar insisted. "Enough to make a majority. And some things are more important than personal preferences. He's a War House prince, yes. Arrogant, entitled – sure. But he's young, and you know about his rulings in Shenn. He's a better man than Rindarin, at least. We *need* him."

Vorsand's movement had turned him toward Diar and Jenne, and he was scanning the trees in the dark as he considered Tamar's words.

And he was a Dreamer.

"Come out of there," he said, his voice suddenly louder. "We have a pair of eavesdroppers," he told Tamar.

"Come here at once," Tamar ordered. Diar stared at Vorsand while they obeyed, despite his better intentions. It was hard not to stare at a legend. "Diar and Jenne," Tamar noted, her tone softening ever so slightly. "You're late coming back."

"I'm so sorry, Drei Master," said Diar, anxious. "We weren't too late for the hearing, were we?"

"No," said Tamar. "But you're late for curfew. I'll overlook it because you were doing me a favor, but you must get back to your dorms before anyone else sees you."

"We were just on our way, Drei Master," Jenne said, turning to go.

Diar nodded to Vorsand. It did not seem right to leave without even acknowledging the hero's presence. "It's an honor to have met you, Lead Master Imager."

"Drei Master is fine." Vorsand smiled. "First-years?" They nodded. "Perhaps we shall become better acquainted next year. Run along for now."

"Drei Master?" Diar hesitated. "I hope you do speak for Jadon. He's a good friend."

He nodded to the masters and hurried after Jenne.

"Now he's a good friend, is he?" Jenne muttered.

"I better leave you here," Diar said, angling toward the west complex.

"Diar," said Jenne, laying a hand on his arm. He looked at it, resenting the touch and wishing it were more at the same time.

Jenne withdrew her hand. "Are we friends again?"

"I don't know, Jenne," Diar said as he jogged away.

That was a problem for another day.

A half-count later, Jadon returned to the inner chamber in the west tower. The board had summoned him to answer any final questions before deliberations and voting. A brown-haired man in Edrei green was in the room this time along with the assembled masters. Who he was and why he was there, Jadon could not guess, but he sat on one of the stools in the back and said nothing, just like the aide by the door.

A few of the masters wanted to know more about the Projector and the extent of her powers, but Jadon had little to add. His audience was tired, and most of them were ready to be done. The masters had put in a long day, first with second-year interrogations and then reviewing and finalizing results for the first-years. The headmaster and the two Intuiters had worked even longer, having had to deal with Jadon's return in the middle of the previous night.

The headmaster leaned back in his armchair, head drooping against his fist, and then he cut off questions about the Projector and asked if anyone had questions relevant to the case at hand before the meeting was closed for deliberations.

"I do not have any questions," the Edrei in the back of the room spoke up. "But I would like to address the board before deliberations begin, if I may?"

"Certainly, Vorsand," the headmaster agreed. "We would all welcome your perspective."

Vorsand stood and walked to the front of the room. Jadon moved closer to the shadows by the door, watching him with curiosity. Drei Captain Vorsand was a tall man with piercing green eyes, and he moved with a confidence that made the assembly of masters seem somehow smaller by comparison.

"Thank you, Regild," said Vorsand, moving into Jadon's place to address the semicircle of masters. "Masters, as you know, I have only just returned from my latest mission, and I have not yet had the pleasure – or displeasure, as the case may be," he corrected with a twinkle in his eye and a nod to Halce, "of this particular initiate's acquaintance." Here he nodded to Jadon: a brief gesture that was both respectful and cautionary. A nod from a master to a pupil who may or may not turn out to have merit. "Nor was I present for the earlier portion of his hearing, but I have since been made privy to the facts of the case, and I shall offer you my opinion."

There was something about the way Vorsand presented himself, Jadon observed, that made him agreeable to listen to. Whether it was the cadence of his voice or the easy connections he established with his listeners was hard to tell, but Jadon suspected it was more than that. The man was likeable and self-assured, a dynamic combination. And then there were the legends that surrounded him: legends that added an extra inch to his height, the quality of timber to his voice, and a healthy dose of awe to his reception.

Jadon understood why some would choose to hate him.

"It is my understanding that you have before you a student with a habit of running up his demerit count, a student who comes to class late and pays little attention, disrespects his fellow initiates, and has in all likelihood violated curfew and been to Lystra out of uniform on many more occasions than the one where he was caught. Some of you would have liked to see him expelled long ago, for all or any of these offenses, but he remains because his father is Senator-Liaison. Based on this description alone, I would not be inclined to extend this student any leniency. Finally, he has been caught in an expellable misdemeanor, and the Senator-Liaison's arm is not so long nor so powerful as to force you to retain his son in the face of facts such as these."

Jadon studied the ground. There was nothing for him to say in objection to all this, nor would he have been permitted to speak if there were.

"However, these are not the only facts that this hearing demands you consider."

Jadon glanced up to find Vorsand studying him, and for the first time since his hearing began, he felt a glimmer of hope that it might not conclude with his expulsion.

"He is also the tourney champion. First-year final interrogations runner-up. Smart and capable." Vorsand turned his attention to the board. "What does this matter, you may be inclined to wonder, if a student has no character? An Edrei cannot merely be smart and skilled. He must be selfless. Brave. Willing to serve.

"But if this is so, I ask you to consider the events of last night. There can no longer be any doubt of what happened.

Witnesses and Intuiters have confirmed that this student stumbled across a stranger in the dark who was about to be attacked by four armed assailants. The assault had nothing to do with him; the stranger was no one to him. He had every opportunity to turn a blind eye. Instead, he stayed. He took up the cause of a stranger and fought, in the face of unfavorable odds. Then the four assailants became twelve, the odds even worse against him, but he did not flee then, either. In complete disregard for his own safety and self-interest, he risked his life on behalf of a perfect stranger. Selfless. Brave. Willing to serve.

"If this is not the caliber of Edrei we are looking to train here, I do not know what is. Disrespect and dissolution are not things to be overlooked, but they are offenses common in the young – common, dare I say, at this university. They are offenses that one can grow out of, that one can be trained out of. Altruism and courage, on the other hand, are rare, and they are things that cannot be instilled through mere discipline.

"The Redemption Clause exists to empower the executors of the Charter to use discretion in enforcing the Charter's decrees, to remind us that not every offense is alike, that the manner in which an offense is discovered sometimes should make a difference in the way it is treated, that sometimes good deeds outweigh misbehavior, that sometimes, there is room for mercy.

"And so, Drei Masters, you have my opinion: a way should be found to show mercy to this young man."

Jadon, stunned to hear his own character appraised in such generous terms, hardly knew what to feel or think in response. He watched mutely as Vorsand's gaze swept the gathered masters.

Surely now they would rule in his favor.

Vorsand nodded to the headmaster, who returned the gesture.

"Thank you, Vorsand," he said. "I must now ask that the chamber be closed for deliberations."

Vorsand swept out of the room, and Jadon, at a gesture from the aide, followed him into the foyer. The aide came out, too, and shut the door.

Vorsand continued toward the outer doors without a backward glance.

"Sir," said Jadon. Vorsand turned to regard him, and Jadon gave him a deep nod. "Master Vorsand. Thank you for speaking for me." Jadon found himself moved more than he would have guessed that this man from legend would step in out of nowhere and take his side.

"Don't thank me." Vorsand gave him a hard look, shaking his head. "I don't know you, but none of my friends here seem to like you, and I'm inclined to trust their judgment." He looked past Jadon to meet the eyes of the aide behind him, nodding slightly. "What I said in there, I didn't say for you. I'm not even sure I believe it, and if you think it will bring me any personal satisfaction if my influence with the board sways them toward showing mercy to a princeling like you, who has already been given every other advantage, when I am utterly powerless to effect a much smaller measure of leniency for my own family, you are quite mistaken." Vorsand turned and walked outside, a gust of wind slapping Jadon in the face as soundly as the man's contempt.

The wait in the foyer was colder after that.

Why did he speak for me, then? Jadon leaned against the wall, feeling angry for reasons he could not explain. *I didn't ask him to. And what does that Six-forsaken aide think he knows about me, anyway?*

He glanced at the man. "Do I know you?" he demanded.

"We met when you missed the orientation ceremony," the aide informed him. "Your first night here."

Jadon averted his gaze, annoyed. He remembered the aide, now. He had been just as disapproving the first time, and for as little reason.

If Jadon's disappointment in losing Vorsand's approval stemmed from anything other than the man's ability to influence the board, he was only dimly aware of it. But he felt the bitter taste of regret as he continued waiting, remembering the man's curt dismissal.

It was a long time before the door to the inner chamber opened, and then it was only so that one of the masters could hold a whispered conference with the aide, after which the aide left the foyer.

It was an even longer time before the door opened again.

This time the aide opened it, having re-entered the room by another door. Jadon took a few steps inside, feeling no small measure of trepidation.

The masters were standing.

"Initiate Jadon," Regild addressed him formally. "The board has ruled, in accordance with Section Twenty-Two, Provision Sixteen of the Edrei Charter, that the penalty of expulsion will be waived for your infraction if – and only if – one of the twelve leading students in your class who have accumulated no more than five demerits in total throughout the year is willing to take it upon themselves to be held accountable for your future compliance with this university's code of conduct."

Jadon furrowed his brow, realizing that only eleven masters stood before him. Derrak was missing. Curious, but it hardly mattered. "Who are the eligible students?"

"Initiate Vannes," began Garadil, reading from a slate. *They must have sent the aide for that,* Jadon deduced, avoiding the more relevant observation that Vannes would never volunteer to do him any favors. There would be eleven more names on the list. "Initiate Sayler. Initiate Christina. Initiate Nefry. Initiate Saleah. Initiate Ramich. Initiate Idarri. Initiate Lelise. Initiate Jonn. Initiate Claire. Initiate Perleyon. Initiate Matt. These initiates will be sent for and assembled by the last count of Porphyr, at which time they will be made to understand the facts of your case. If any of them volunteers to stand for you, you will be permitted to return to your room in the west complex."

Jadon stopped listening after he counted the twelfth name. Improbably, he knew all twelve of them, by name and face. Impossibly, he had managed to antagonize each one over the course of their first year at the university.

Oh, Perleyon. Why did I open my mouth? If all this had happened two days before, he could have counted on Perleyon to stand for him. Neither of them much cared for the other, but Initiative solidarity would have extended at least that far.

Perleyon would not stand for him now – not after Jadon had pushed him to the brink of throwing a glove down the night before. Idarri, likewise, might have supported him before; she would not now. Not if she wanted to make a match with Perleyon, which by all accounts she did.

The masters may have intended their ruling to be merciful, but the other ten names on the list offered no more hope than Perleyon or Idarri. Jadon could not imagine a world in which any of them would stand for him.

CHAPTER 21

Christina's Code

When the General and the Fanatic first crossed paths, it was at school. He was a War House prince, she a Blood House princess. They bore the expectations of opposing cultures upon their shoulders, and it seemed at the time that he would grow into his mantle and she into hers, with or without the incorporation of Edrei green into their shapes and colors.

No one could have predicted that the two of them would soon break the continent.

> – Anais Fleureve, writing for the *Histories of the Lussonne* some years after the Second Binding

Christina woke to a knock at her door and found an administrative aide waiting to usher her to an important meeting. They stopped to collect Lelise and Idarri on their way outside.

"I wonder what this is about?" Lelise whispered to Christina.

The two of them were friends again, through no fault or effort of Christina's own. Final interrogations had restored her indelibly to the other girl's good graces, as Lelise was only too happy to celebrate Christina's victory as though it belonged partly to her.

"I suppose we'll find out when we get there," Christina

473

returned. As long as Lelise restrained herself from trying to separate Christina from Nefry and his commonborn friends, Christina was willing to return the friendship – though she still found Lelise a far cry from a kindred spirit.

Outside, they were met by another aide leading Claire and Saleah. As they circled the north tower, they crossed paths with a few initiates on their way to the dining hall. If the kitchen was open, it must have been morning; though, judging by the total darkness, there was at least a count left before dawn.

The aides led them along the walkway as far as the west tower, where they caught up to two more aides leading seven boys.

"Good morning, Christina!" Nefry said in an enthusiastic whisper as he fell into step beside her. Lelise eyed him but made way, falling behind with Saleah and Vannes. "Isn't this exciting?"

"Hard to say," Christina answered, watching the aides. Their body language gave nothing away as they opened the doors, led them across the foyer, and ushered them into an inner chamber. They passed another initiate on the way – Jadon, who, along with another aide, was waiting in the foyer. He did not join them inside.

Headmaster Regild and Master Tamar were in the room, speaking quietly as they stood by the fire in the back, behind twelve empty armchairs.

"Initiates, please, be seated." The headmaster gestured. The twelve of them sat while the masters moved to the front of the room.

Christina could not have guessed what they might say, though she found her company encouraging. They were model students, all.

"You have been gathered here because of the entire first-year class, you are the twelve to score highest in the Lists of Achievement while accumulating no more than five demerits. This makes you our most capable and trustworthy dozen."

He gave them a moment to consider that. Smiles broke out as they realized the significance of their achievement.

"The Board of Masters convened last night to decide the case of an initiate caught after curfew in Lystra, who appealed to the Redemption Clause in challenge of what otherwise would have been a quick expulsion."

Lelise shifted forward in her seat, blinking rapidly as she stared at the headmaster to indicate she desired to speak.

"Yes, Lelise?"

"Would this be Initiate Jadon?"

"Yes."

Lelise settled primly in her chair, looking pleased with herself for the obvious deduction.

"It was the board's ruling," Regild continued, "that the clause may apply. However, as you may know, one of the conditions for waiving the penalty of expulsion is that measures can be taken to keep the affiliate from repeating any infractions similar to those of which he was found guilty. The board has decided it is beyond our scope to arrange any such measures through inconvenience to the Drei Masters or the rest of the staff.

"However, as members of Jadon's class, the twelve of you share much the same schedule and activities with him already. It was the board's decision that if one of you, our most trusted twelve, would agree to become responsible for him, we will waive the penalty of expulsion for his offense, as allowed by the Redemption Clause.

"But understand this: by choosing to take on such a responsibility, you would be tying yourself to Jadon's fate. His failures would become your failures; his demerits, your demerits. If he should again be found guilty of an expellable offense, you would both be expelled. This arrangement would continue throughout your training, both here and at Renasche, until either you both make full Edrei, or you both fail.

"The means by which you would ensure his good behavior would be left entirely to your discretion and devices, beyond a pair of locator bracelets that we would provide, and your decision to undertake the task would be irreversible. If it should prove a more difficult task than you expected, or if you should come to regret your decision, there will be neither recourse nor escape. You would swear today an oath of accountability, an oath from which only graduation or expulsion could release you.

"We of the board neither require nor expect any of you to take this on. Volunteering will confer no benefits to you, even should you prove successful. However, we do offer it as an opportunity."

This time Matt leaned forward, his blue-gray eyes catching light from the lanterns that circled the room.

"Please, speak freely," the headmaster invited them.

"An opportunity for what, exactly?" asked Matt.

It was Tamar who answered. "An opportunity to spare your classmate expulsion."

"And why would we want to do that?" Ramich ran a hand through his dirty blond hair as he leaned back in his armchair, scornful. "Pardon me, Masters, but I genuinely do not understand."

"It was the ruling of the board that the Redemption Clause may be applied to Jadon's case," explained Tamar. "He was out after curfew in Lystra when he saw a stranger threatened by a group of attackers. Heedless of both his personal safety and his ability to elude Edrei pursuit, he joined with this stranger to fight the attackers, saving the man's life. The board ruled that the penalty for breaking curfew may be waived in recognition and recompense for the good deed. But our resources are such that in order to reward Jadon's courage in this matter, we would need assistance from one of you."

Christina glanced at the other students, wondering who might volunteer. It was a lot to take on, tying oneself to Jadon's fate, though the masters could hardly have asked any less. They had to ensure whoever became responsible for Jadon took the obligation seriously, or the arrangement would be no more than a charade.

"If any of you would like to question Jadon regarding the incident or the behavior you can expect from him moving forward, he can now be made available to you," the headmaster told them. "However, bargaining with him will not be permitted. If you agree to undertake this task, you must do so voluntarily, with the expectation of nothing in return."

There was a moment of silence, and then Vannes smiled. "I, for one, should like to question him very much."

Jadon watched as the twelve first-years who hated him the most filed into the inner chamber to decide his fate, wishing he could have stayed in the east complex. He did not see why he needed to remain on hand, but the aide had brought him here and told him to wait.

Ramich, Perleyon, Idarri, Matt, Sayler, Claire, Christina, Nefry, Vannes, Jonn, Saleah, Lelise. He ran over their names again, trying to see if there was even the remotest chance that any would speak for him. Perleyon was out. Idarri, too.

The names became only less promising from there. Sayler despised him. Why, Jadon was not sure, but it was clear in every word they exchanged. Claire hated him, too, though at least that one made sense. He had made her cry, and her eyes had flashed with anger every time she saw him after that, including just now, as she passed him on her way through the foyer.

He had humiliated Vannes the day he invited Diar to the practice tourney, and he had taken more than one opportunity to embarrass Lelise in weapons class. This was all nothing beside the national humiliation he had brought upon Ramich in the tourney final. Jadon had humbled his entire class that day by demonstrating how far superior he was to the next best, and Ramich was himself a bully who deserved to be put in his place every now and then – but the fact remained that Jadon had humiliated him, and he could hardly think the Gold House boy might speak for him now.

He had contradicted and belittled Saleah and Jonn all year in politics class, and Master Porrian's praise for Jadon could only have stoked their resentment. Moreover, they were close personal friends with Vannes and Lelise. Christina was another one of their lot, and even closer with Claire, and though he had never antagonized her personally as far as he could remember, their few interactions had trended toward the negative side of neutral, and he could hardly expect her to overlook the injuries he had heaped upon all her friends. He did not know Matt well, but he remembered calling him stupid the day he had considered apologizing to Claire, and of everyone who had been in the room, Matt had seemed the angriest.

That left Nefry, and Nefry did not care for Jadon either. Jadon had laughed at his contributions in class all year, including during the semifinal of final interrogations. Nefry was well learned and Jadon had nothing against him, but some of his notions were so divorced from reality that Jadon could not help but find him comical. It was a reaction unlikely to have endeared him to the little genius.

No, none of them will speak for me. Not a chance.

Female laughter interrupted his thoughts. It was joined by the low tones of a male, drawing closer as two initiates came down the stairs.

Rindarin and Trista. Rindarin leaned closer to Trista and whispered something in her ear. She laughed again.

Somehow, it seemed fitting that Rindarin would appear.

"Jadon. Fancy meeting you here," Rindarin greeted him, the smug ghost of a smile playing at his lips.

"A little early to be up and about," Jadon said.

"Thought I'd show Trista the Imaging room. Take her mind off the Lists." Rindarin tucked a piece of stray hair behind Trista's ear, and she blushed. He settled an arm around her shoulders protectively. "Yourself?"

Jadon returned Rindarin's look flatly as he and Trista came closer.

"Oh, right," Rindarin clicked his tongue. "The twelve most trusted students of your class are deciding your fate right now. I heard about the Drei Masters' decision. Did they ask you to wait out here for that? Seems unnecessary."

He must have bribed an aide. There was no other way he could know, though Jadon could not guess why he would bother. "What do you want, Rindarin?"

"Just checking on you." Rindarin smiled. "We are friends, after all."

Jadon touched his swollen left eye. "My friends were all with me when the Edrei surprised us last night. Maybe you heard?"

Rindarin shook his head sadly. "An unfortunate incident. One of my lookouts told me while I was leaving. I came back to warn the rest of you. Too late for some."

"Really?" Jadon gave a small laugh. Then another thought struck him, and he narrowed his good eye. "All the nights we spent out in Lystra, and the one time you leave early, the Edrei show up. As if someone told them we were there."

Rindarin tilted his head, reclaiming his arm from around Trista. "I returned in time to aid half the stragglers. Led them around the Edrei."

Jadon smiled. "You do love to be seen, don't you?"

"What exactly are you implying, Hatreth?" Rindarin's voice was soft.

"Alaxis and Dreck put in truly miserable performances in their respective tourneys, didn't they?" said Jadon. "We were lamenting it when the Edrei showed up, you know. Analyzing it."

Rindarin studied him. Then he stepped back, shaking his head. "If someone in there should choose to speak for you, I do hope you learn to be more careful with that tongue. It has a nasty habit of getting you into trouble. Come on, Trista, let's get out of here." He offered her his arm. "I doubt they will, though," he said as they walked away, raising his voice. "Trista tells me that none of them likes you very much."

He let the doors fall shut behind them.

Jadon could not imagine what agenda had inspired the second-year to cheating and treachery, but whatever his plans were, they would likely succeed in Jadon's absence.

Somehow, Rindarin, Jadon promised. *Someday. I will figure out what you're up to.*

The doors to the outside opened again. Trista was back, this time alone.

"Claire's in there, isn't she?" she murmured, her body language full of regret.

Jadon nodded, wondering why she had returned.

"I finished one place behind her in final interrogations, you know. One place, and I beat her in the tourney. And I've never had a demerit."

"Guess you just missed out on my execution," Jadon said. He felt very tired.

Trista shook her head. "I am sorry. I do not know what may be between you and Rindarin, but if I were in Claire's place, I would speak for you."

"You would, would you?" Jadon glanced at her. She seemed to mean it, useless as the words were now. "I don't think Rindarin would have cared for that."

"He doesn't truly wish to see you expelled," Trista returned, confident. "He likes you."

"If you say so."

There was a moment of silence. "Well, I should rejoin him," Trista said, glancing toward the doors. "I just wanted you to know. Not everyone hates you. And I regret that I am not in there instead of Claire."

"Thanks." Jadon shrugged, forcing a smile. "Maybe next time."

She let out a breath of air that was almost a laugh, dropping her eyes. When she raised them to meet his, they were utterly sincere.

"I wish you luck."

She nodded, and Jadon nodded back before she left.

He could see what had inspired Dreck's fascination for the Gold House girl. She was well formed, but many girls were beautiful in figure. Her beauty was more than that. There was a grace to the way she moved, an intelligence in her big brown eyes, and an air of total innocence about her. It did not seem right that a snake like Rindarin should hold such a prize.

The door to the inner chamber opened. "They want to question you," the aide said, motioning Jadon inside.

"Question me?" he repeated, incredulous. He entered slowly, and the aide shut the door behind him. Tamar and Regild stood behind him, in the shadows to the right. In front of him, twelve unfriendly initiates occupied tall, elaborate armchairs meant for Drei Masters.

They don't want to question me, Jadon knew. Their faces were closed off and oppositional, with expressions that ranged from dislike to scorn to satisfaction. *They want to get even.*

Jadon liked to think that if he were in their shoes, he would not stoop so low as to kick a man while he was already down. There was no glory to be gained from such a feat, no honor in it. But there could be no escaping it now.

Jadon lifted his chin and prepared to endure a unique sort of humiliation.

"Jadon, as I consider your case and whether I might be willing to speak for you, I find I have a couple questions. First: why were you out after curfew in Lystra to begin with?"

Vannes feigned thoughtfulness, and Christina suppressed a sigh. Everyone knew Jadon had been out celebrating with the War House Initiative. It was an unnecessary question, meant to rub Jadon's face in the extent of his own irresponsibility.

"I was having drinks at an inn," he answered, his voice even and face emotionless.

"You were drinking with friends, I assume?" asked Lelise, all innocence and curiosity. "Which ones?" Perleyon glanced over at her, frowning, and she shrugged. "If I'm to become responsible for him, I should like to know whom I should encourage him to avoid."

"I don't recall," Jadon returned, giving her a flat stare.

"Was this an isolated incident, or have you left campus to drink with friends after curfew before?" Vannes asked, folding his hands.

Jadon turned his stare on Vannes, waited a moment, then said, "Once or twice."

Vannes *tsk*ed in disapproval. "Once or twice?" he challenged.

"Perhaps more." Jadon turned his gaze forward.

"Jadon, I understand you got into a fight with some thugs in an effort to save some unlucky stranger," Perleyon cut in. "Is that how you got your…" He gestured to Jadon's left eye. "…bruise there?" His mouth quirked in a half-smile, and Christina realized the wiry War House boy was enjoying himself as much as Vannes and Lelise, though how or when he had come to despise Jadon, Christina had no idea.

"No."

"Well, how did you get it?" Perleyon insisted. "Not quarreling with friends, I hope?"

Jadon flicked his gaze to Perleyon. "Sounds like you have an idea of what happened already. Perhaps you'd care to explain?"

Perleyon scowled, and the moment passed. *He must have been with Jadon in Lystra*, Christina deduced. Jadon may have been disinclined to sell out his rule-breaking compatriots, but if Perleyon crossed him too far, he had no reason not to.

"After you saved this stranger's life, did he swear an oath to you?" Sayler asked, sounding curious.

Jadon sighed. "No."

"Seems awfully ungrateful," Ramich sneered. "Did you manage to make a bad impression during the fight?"

"I don't know, Ramich. It sounded like he was in a hurry to get a black crystal out of the city. Maybe that's why he didn't stay."

"A black crystal?" Christina asked, her interest piqued. "What do you mean?"

"He dropped a black crystal-like item after the fight, and when I handed it to him, he said, 'This cannot stay in the city.'"

"Please keep your questions relevant to Jadon's behavior," the headmaster interjected, sharing a glance with Tamar.

The poem Nefry had found had described the shards of the White's scepter as "shards of finest crystal." It had also called them white and transparent, but it had warned against their growing "dark with death." It was hardly a direct connection to Jadon's black crystal – and less between that and the high general's shard, which might have become Hezred's magical weapon – but it was enough to make Christina curious.

"Leaving campus after curfew, quarreling, drinking to excess, sneaking around Lystra out of uniform..." Claire spoke next, listing Jadon's offenses blandly. "Sounds like you have quite the list of misdemeanors. What assurances can you offer us that you would behave differently moving forward, should one of us agree to speak for you?"

"If one of you should speak for me, I would like to see said person graduate, since I would like to graduate myself."

"Presumably, you were interested in graduating before," Saleah noted. "And yet you still misbehaved. Could we expect that to change?"

"Would any promise I made inspire you to speak for me, Saleah?"

She shrugged. "I could hardly know before I heard them."

"I, for one, should like you to swear to honor curfew before I could consider becoming responsible for you," Vannes suggested.

"And no more quarreling," Jonn added.

"Or showing up late to class," Nefry supplied.

"I would want you to stop getting demerits altogether if I were to tie my fate to yours," Lelise agreed.

"And would all of that be sufficient, Lelise?" Jadon challenged. "I won't beg. I promise nothing." Then he turned to the masters behind him. "Can't we speed this up?"

"They hold your fate in their hands, Jadon," Regild reminded him. "You should let them take their time with the decision."

Tamar, though, scanned the students suspiciously, and the disapproval in her gaze was not directed at Jadon.

"If any of you have already made up your minds not to speak for Jadon, there is no reason to question him further. You may excuse yourself at any time. But remember that if none of you is willing, we will be unable to apply the Redemption Clause to his case, though we have ruled that his actions warrant it."

Sayler was the first to stand and walk out. He nodded to Jadon and the masters on his way. Matt followed him, and then Perleyon and Idarri. Saleah went next, and then Lelise, who gave a small sigh and tossed Jadon an unsympathetic smile.

Claire made to rise, glancing at Christina to see if she would come. Christina was studying Jadon.

"You can't honestly be thinking of speaking for him," Claire whispered tersely. "After everything he's done?"

Christina, though, found that she *was* thinking about it. Perhaps the others were right to wash their hands of him, to call it good riddance. Jadon was arrogant, disrespectful, and unkind, and she had no wish to see him walk the halls of Eshtem any longer, let alone to become responsible for him.

And yet, if he was expelled today, it would not be for staying out past curfew, for drinking to excess, for being disrespectful or late to class. It would be because he had been caught, and he had been caught because he had stopped to help a stranger.

Perhaps he did deserve expulsion. But Tamar was right. He did not deserve expulsion for what had happened two nights before.

Claire stood and left with a hiss of displeasure. She glared at Jadon as she passed. Jonn and Vannes left next.

Jadon reminded Christina of someone else, as he stood there watching his hopes of a second chance file out the door. He had no friends among them, and he knew it. His posture was defeated as he stood there, hopeless, needing someone to reach out and help him but knowing that no one would.

He was not looking at Christina, not asking her for help. No one expected her to offer it to him, as no one had expected her to aid that other man, kneeling defeated on the road to Lystra. No person, and no code, had asked it of her, would impugn her for inaction. Not *The Ellyrian Code*, not the Edrei Charter. They had not in that other case, and they certainly would not in Jadon's.

Nefry stood to go. "He's no Hezred," he whispered to Christina as he passed, perspicacious as ever. He nodded to Jadon on his way out.

Nefry was right. Jadon was nothing like Hezred. Hezred had been noble, merciful, and kind. All the reports about Hazzar had said as much, and he had been so in his interactions with Christina – even despite his collusion with the outlaws, as far as he could be. With the Order of the Edrei and the whole nation of Ellyrian set against him, he deserved mercy for that compromise. Hezred had been innocent of the charges against him and trying to prove it, trying to expose the true guilty party. He had stood for something greater than himself, had been fighting for something greater than himself, though Christina could guess only the barest edges of what that might have been. Hezred had been worthy.

And Hezred is dead.

Ramich stood and walked out, with a final sneer in Jadon's direction.

Christina was the only one left.

"I have nothing further to add." Jadon's voice was heavy with some emotion she could not place. Regret, maybe, or resignation. "I won't beg."

Hezred had not begged either, Christina remembered. He had not begged Zanner. *Don't watch*, was all he had said to Christina. She had been too late to realize she could have saved him.

Jadon's not going to die here, she reminded herself. *It's not the same at all. Not even similar.*

Christina rose to her feet. She took a few steps toward Jadon and the door.

Hezred was dead now, forever beyond her aid. She knew she had made a mistake with him, a serious moral failure – no

matter what was written in the code or the charter, no matter
what Hezred had thought at the time or how anyone else might
judge her. Her mistake was in the past, though. The truth about
Hezred was buried and erased. She would probably never find
out the whole of it, let alone be able to take up whatever cause
had died with him at the foot of the Brennels.

She had made a mistake, and it was both irreversible and
irredeemable. She could hardly hope to compensate for
it by taking responsibility for some errant princeling. Not
remotely, not even in part.

She looked at the masters.

"I'll do it," she said. "I'll speak for him."

Christina could never make right what had happened
to Hezred – what had happened because she had failed to
speak for him. But this, a student expelled for the wrong
reasons – this was one tiny thing wrong with the Order that
was in her power to fix.

Perhaps it was the only thing wrong with the Order that
would ever be in her power to fix.

Jadon stared at the Blood House girl in front of him. "What?"
he asked stupidly.

"I said I'll speak for him," she repeated, louder, still
addressing the masters. "What do I swear?"

"There is a formal oath," said Regild, glancing at Tamar. He
had not anticipated this, but whether he was disappointed
or relieved, Jadon could not guess.

Perhaps the headmaster did not know himself.

"We'll take you to the graduation chamber. You can swear
there, and we will fit you with the bracelets. Rastilap, would
you fetch them?"

The aide left to obey, and the masters led Jadon and Christina out after him.

"I am deeply indebted to you," Jadon said as they walked. It was overwhelming, and sobering, and he hardly knew what to say. She had given him a second chance at becoming Edrei, at becoming someone he might be proud of, though he still did not know if that was possible. If it was possible anywhere, though, it was more likely in the Order than at Hatre. "If you want gold, land, a favor from the Senate, anything Hatreth can offer, name it. It's yours."

"The black crystal your stranger had," Christina said, lowering her voice. "Can you tell me anything else about it?"

"Not much," Jadon said, lowering his volume to match hers. He wasn't sure if she didn't want the masters to hear, and he had no idea why she cared about the crystal in the first place – but if this was what she wanted from him, he would help as much as he could. "It was about this big." He cupped his hands together, showing a size small enough to rest comfortably in one hand. "Smooth, but multifaceted. Black. Deep black. Master Tamar grilled me about it, too, but I have no idea what it was or why the Alterran thought it should leave the city."

"The man who carried it was Alterran?" Christina asked.

"I think so, based on his accent."

"Do you have any reason to think he might have been a Projector?"

Jadon blinked. This interrogation was even stranger than Tamar's. "No. But... one of the attackers was. She used her magic during the fight."

"Hmm." Christina said nothing else, but Jadon figured his answers must have been less than satisfactory.

"Look, I don't know what your interest in the crystal might be, but I don't know anything else. If you were hoping otherwise, I'm sorry to disappoint."

Christina shrugged and gave a slight shake of her head, dismissing the matter. "I was just curious."

"My other offer still stands."

"I don't want your money, Hatreth, or any favors from your House," Christina returned, as if the idea offended her. "They would have expelled you for all the wrong reasons. The Order should be better, and this is what I can do to make it better. You may thank me by mending your behavior so that I do not wind up expelled on your account."

Jadon took a few more steps in silence, trying to make sense of the speech – to make sense of *her*.

It seemed nobody made sense anymore.

"Thank you," he eventually said. He would rather have given her his princedom than promise to change himself, but what she asked was more than fair. "I have no intention of seeing you expelled."

EPILOGUE

There were some six hundred students waiting when the librarians appeared in the northwest wing of the library with copies of the first-year Lists. There was not enough room for them all in the hallway, so initiates spilled into the central chamber of the library and out into the warm morning air. The sun was just peeking over the horizon, casting the sky into brilliant shades of pink and orange.

Diar was among those outside, shoulder to shoulder with Telius and Liana. Jenne was already inside, having risen at who knew what White-forsaken count to stake out a more favorable spot. Most of the first-year class was somewhere in the library, though some were waiting for the crowd to disperse before trying to view the Lists.

Some already know whether they'll be sent home, Diar thought as he shifted from one foot to the other. He had been eliminated one round after Liana, which put them just above the middle of their class. Some years, the cut fell below that; other years, above.

It would be a near thing. Diar felt he might lose his sanity if he had to wait much longer.

Exclamations broke out as those inside caught sight of the first pages. The librarians would put up the Final Interrogations List first, then the List of Achievement that factored final interrogations together with the Eshtem Tourney. The Final Interrogations List was the list that mattered, though the first pages should hardly come as a surprise. Christina had won, and the order in which the rest of them had finished was already known. The question was where the line would be drawn. Only names above the line would be permitted to continue at Eshtem.

Please, please, please. Diar wished he could press closer, but there was no room, and the last thing the initiates needed was to slow down the librarians by pressing too close.

A few students left after finding their own names, thinning the crowd ever so slightly. Most of them would wait to see the line.

The minutes felt like counts before it came. A collective release of air from the students inside announced its arrival: some sighs of relief, some gasps of horror, even a few outright wails. Then the students started leaving faster, and Diar, Liana, and Telius were able to press inside.

Then Diar saw it: the page with the long black line.

He stepped closer, his eyes devouring names. He started at the top of the page and barely noticed Jenne's name when he crossed it, his heart rising in his throat as he scanned through more and more names after hers that were not his, drawing ever closer to the line.

There. Diar's mouth fell open when he found it.

It was the very last name above the line.

And there, four names below – *under* the line – was Liana's.

Seven sights of the White's beloved. Diar's mind reeled from how nearly he had escaped expulsion.

"So close," Liana whispered, eyes glued to the page with her name in the wrong place. Her eyes were brimming with tears.

"I'm so sorry," said Diar, struck by a wash of guilt. Their performance had been nearly equivalent. *Why should I get to stay, and she has to leave?*

"You will be missed," Telius murmured.

She turned to Diar and managed a small smile. "Congratulations," she told him. "I'm happy for you. For you both," she added to Telius. She turned and squeezed her way out of the library.

"Maybe next time try not to cut it *quite* so close?" Telius suggested when she was gone.

"I'll need to study harder," Diar agreed, still staring up at the list. *One place. One place ahead of the cut. One place removed from losing my chance forever.* "I'll need to study *much* harder," he repeated more softly, this time to himself.

Telius left, but Diar stayed, transfixed, as the crowd continued thinning and more pages were posted. Eventually the librarians finished the Final Interrogations List and began with the List of Achievement, all while Diar continued to stare at his name, sitting right there on the line.

"It's no coincidence, you know."

Diar started, not having noticed when Jenne joined him. "What do you mean?"

"Your name, being the last one above the cut." She nodded to the page. "Drei Jere will have told them that you Projected."

"You mean...?" Diar frowned, not understanding. "What do you mean?"

"The Order doesn't let go of Imagers. Not unless it absolutely must."

"I'm hardly..." Diar considered. Being a Projector was a new identity, one he was unaccustomed to bearing. *But I did Project in that inn. I have Projection magic.* "You think the line would have fallen farther up? They moved it to keep me because of that one instance?"

"I knew you would be safe after that," said Jenne, nodding. "They can afford to keep a few extra initiates if it means they get to hold on to a first-year who can Project. Who knows how many of us owe the rest of our tenure to you?"

"You knew?" Diar turned and frowned at her. "Thanks for sharing."

Jenne shrugged, coquettish. "There was still just a teeny-tiny chance I could have been wrong. Besides… some speculations are only for friends." The words held both a challenge and a question, and her expression carried the same.

"We're friends, Jenne," Diar said as he returned his attention to the List of Achievement. His name would not be last on this list. He had done reasonably well in the tourney, considering his lack of prior training.

It was true, he decided as he stood next to Jenne, aware when she accepted the answer and turned her gaze, too, back to the Lists. They were friends. There could be no more flirting – certainly no more kissing. They came from two different worlds, two different worldviews, and he was not for her any more than she was for him. The reality was painful, but now that he had accepted it, he could move on. Being around her did not change anything or make the pain any more or less.

In short, there was no reason he could not still talk to her. She was still his favorite person at Eshtem, someone he admired and whose company he enjoyed. He did not have to lose her entirely just because they could be no more than friends.

"Good." Jenne's tone was nonchalant, but Diar could tell she was pleased. "Well then, next time I have an important speculation of some kind, maybe I'll tell you."

"I'd appreciate that," said Diar. After a moment, he added, "Have you heard anything about Jadon?"

"His name's at the top of the list," Jenne said. "So, they decided not to cut him. There's a rumor that they put Christina in charge of him to guard against future misdemeanors."

"Good." Diar smiled. "She'll be a good influence."

Jenne shook her head, but she smiled back. "I'm glad for your sake that we helped. Though if somebody's going to teach him to act less entitled, it sure as spitfire won't be the Noraani princess."

Diar sighed. "Will you get angry at me if I ever talk to them?"

"No," Jenne said. "Maybe *you* would be a good influence on them. And they may very well need it," she added, her voice growing somber.

"What do you mean?"

She turned to face him. "Remember in the woods last night? How we heard Master Tamar say that Vorsand spoke to a wizard?"

Diar nodded. At the time, he had been so focused on Jadon and meeting Vorsand that he had barely noticed. But the memory was troubling. "What do you think that meant?"

"One of two things. I did some digging deep in the library this morning, and I found that a panel of Intuiters convened a while back to determine whether the White Plague damaged Master Tamar's Intuition. They think she still has delusions, about the High Wizards. She thinks they're moving again."

"Oh. She said the panel was wrong." Diar remembered that brief conversation with Vorsand. He had not understood it at the time. "Do you think they could have been wrong? What's the other possibility?"

"If Master Tamar is right, then it means the world is in a whole heap of trouble. The Order isn't prepared to fight wizards again. Not by a long shot."

"The woman who died – she was a powerful Projector. A Knight?" Diar turned the possibility over in his mind. It was a lot to believe.

"Vorsand didn't seem to think so," Jenne noted. "The panel could have been right."

"I guess we should hope so." As much as Diar did not like the idea of Tamar's being delusional, it was far more palatable than wizards on the move.

They had nearly destroyed the world the last time, and now there were no elves left to stop them. The Order would have to do it alone, and as Jenne said, the Order was not prepared. Diar did not know if the bulk of the Order even believed that High Wizards existed.

"Why do you think she wanted to save Jadon so badly?" Diar asked after a moment. "She thinks he's important? They need him? The Order needs him?"

"She thinks so," Jenne said. "Why the Order might *need* another spoiled War House prince, I have no idea, but if she's right, it could be good for him to have you as a friend." There was a pause, and then she added, "If the wizards are moving, somebody's going to have to stop them. You and I will have to train harder, at least until we find out whether Master Tamar is wrong."

The resolution in Jenne's voice surprised Diar.

"You think *we* could stop them? A couple first-years who barely made the cut?"

"You keep forgetting you're a Projector, Diar. In a few years, you'll be powerful. Those who manifest early always are."

Diar cleared his throat, realizing it was not just an honor. It was a responsibility.

"With any luck, I'll be a dragon handler before the wizards come for us in earnest," Jenne said. "Then I'll be in a good position to help you."

"Let's hope the wizards hold off a few more years, then."

"Let us hope so, indeed."

It occurred to Diar, as the final page of the Lists went up, that the names he was looking at did not merely represent peers, friends, and competitors.

If the wizards were moving again, the Order was all that could hope to stand against them, and the names on display were the future of the Order.

Somehow, they would all need to be ready.

ELLYRIAN HOUSE & CHARACTER LIST

BLOOD HOUSES

Royal Houses

JINN:

Lady Lelise Jinn
Lord Vannes to'Jinn

NORAAN:

Lord Aander tul'Noraan
Lady Christina tu'Noraan
Lord Illipen tul'Noraan
Lady Rydara il'Noraan

RYDER:

Lady Claire il'Ryder

Noble Houses

FERLORE

Common Houses

CARRIL:

Nefry Carril

ENTEAR

JAX:

Diar Jax

KRENT:

Friada Krent

RIMGARD:

Hazzar ti'Rimgard

WENTRIDGE:

Lozuri Wentridge

Characters from Unnamed Blood Houses
- Adelay
- Lord Jonn
- Kiprim
- Matt
- Riara
- Lady Saleah
- Sayler

WAR HOUSES

Royal Houses

ENTAREN:

Lord Alaxis Entaren
Lord Chase Entaren
Lord Lathew Entaren

HATRETH:

Lady Anna tu'Hatreth
Lord Augame tul'Hatreth
Lord Heraldus "the Great" tul'Hatreth

Lord Jadon tu'Hatreth
Lord Juaqen tul'Hatreth

RITHADUR:

Lord Harral tul'Rithadur
Lord Rindarin tu'Rithadur

Noble Houses

SENDELL:

Lord Dreck to'Sendell
Lord Perleyon tu'Sendell

Common Houses

BOW:

Drestil Bow

ENGUS:

Vasil Engus

HALOWAY:

Elrec Haloway
Morgaine Haloway

KISH

MERETRIL

TARROW:

Keistad Tarrow

WRENK:

Basicus Wrenk

Characters from Unnamed War Houses

Annvar
Enlightened Argest
Lord Arzit
Lord Brell
Chadrie
Cyla
Lady Enna
Lord Fendi
Lieutenant Firhelm (later, Watchman Firhelm)
Private Fren
Captain Gregol
Lord Haf
Sergeant Halomish
Lord Hectibald
Lady Idarri
Kerci
Private Kyl
Lord Regix
Remni
Enlightened Rilad
Tagreff
Mayor Wayse
Weza
Lord Wrayland
Zar

GOLD HOUSES

Royal Houses

RINTON:

Lady Trista to'Rinton

SHALE:

Lord Gossem to'Shale

TARIX:

Lord Ramich ti'Tarix

Noble Houses

ILSAD:

Drei Consul Ocifem
Lady Psedal Ilsad

Common Houses

ADAGAL:

Liana tu'Adagal
Drei Captain Vorsand

KERIM:

Marcellus Kerim

KIRI:

Jenne Kiri

MADRIGE:

Salo Madrige

Characters from Unnamed Gold Houses
Brinnette
Cardos
Elophine
Eridike
Landers
Telius

Characters from Unspecified House Divisions

Adara

Akarlis

Drei General Anandolf

Ballas

Drei Master Derrak

Elad

Drei Master Estilend

Drei Master Felade

Drei Master Garadil

Drei Master Halce

Hezred

Drei Istanosh

Drei Jere

Drei Master Kestigon

Drei Master Legreve

Drei Marsil

Drei Merabe "One-Strike"

Drei Master Porrian

Rastilap

Drei Master Regild

Drei Master Regosh

Drei High General Serend

Drei Master Shiell

Drei Master Tamar

Drei Master Verizah

Drei Zanner

ACKNOWLEDGMENTS

I have been dreaming up the world of *The Ellyrian Code* since I was in middle school, and my heart is impossibly full at the prospect of finally seeing it in print. I have so many people to thank.

First and foremost, thanks (which seems an extremely paltry and inadequate word to express the depths of my gratitude) to Eleanor Teasdale, who read my manuscript and loved it and believed in it and believed in me and convinced the Angry Robot team to take us on. Who knows how long *The Ellyrian Code* might have sat collecting dust on my backburner, or if it ever would have amounted to anything at all, without you and your willingness to champion us. You're my hero.

An incredibly close second and no less important or meaningful thanks to Vicky Hartley, who discovered me in the slush pile at Collective Ink and thought my work was good enough to pass along to Eleanor for her consideration. Over the course of five years and two manuscripts, I sent 97 queries and pitches to literary agents before giving up and submitting to small presses directly, and you saw something in my writing that none of them ever did – and you did more for me and my work than I could have hoped any of them might have. You are also my hero.

Huge thanks also to my editor, Desola Coker, who really "got" my characters and helped me see how to take my story to the next level. I'm so grateful for your insight and advice as well as for your light hand and openness to persuasion on those few points where I wanted to do something different. You've been a delight to work with, and I'm sure everyone who reads the book will join me in thanking you and Eleanor for pushing for more dragons.

Thanks also to the publicity team, the cover designer, copy editor, and proofreader – to the whole team at Angry Robot. Thank you all for making my dreams come true by bringing my baby to market.

Then there is everyone who supported me through the many, many years I spent working on *The Ellyrian Code* before I'd ever heard of Angry Robot. First, my sister Christina Sekutowski, to whom the book is dedicated. I'll never forget how you challenged me to commit to finishing the whole book after reading the first draft of chapter three the summer after I finished high school. It would be another eight years before I finally wrote the end, but who knows if I ever would have made it as far as that without encouragement and support from you and from our other sister, Anne Angel, to whom the greatest of thanks are also due. The two of you read each chapter together with me as soon as I finished them, and these sister "book conferences" were always a great joy and motivation for me to keep producing new material. I don't think I could have done it without you.

Next, to my Inklings writers' group: Abby Morrison, Sarah Binger, Jaime McCall, Pat Daily, and Kimmy Schwarzenbart. Your feedback has been instrumental in shaping the story, the world, and the characters, and I'm so grateful to have had such fruitful exchange and accountability with other writers over the course of so many years.

Huge thanks also to Sarah White, Nathan Cahill, Patrick Fessenbecker, and David McHugh – early readers who offered extensive feedback and great enthusiasm. I hope you can all see how you helped shape and improve the final product. Thanks also to my other early readers – in fact, I inflicted very rough drafts of this project on a large number of people and am so thankful to all who read it and expressed positivity and support and/or offered constructive criticism: Erin Viale, Josh Angel (your tips for the War House Initiative and their vaults and fights were instrumental), Matt Flaherty, John Flaherty, Matt Bork, Ezra LC, Jaemyn Martens, Kimberly Belmarez, Elizabeth Albers, Enye McHugh, John Sekutowski, Megan Horsager, Cody Maynus, Abby Longmore, Abigail Lexen, Devin White, Ben Longmore, Solomon Horn... the list goes on. Thanks to everybody who joined my mailing list before I even knew whether there would ever be good news to report. I heart you all.

I also want to thank my parents, who let me live at home for longer than we might have planned while I wrote, revised, and struggled with my health after college; Brian Wheeler, who hired me at Peet's Coffee and let me work extremely part-time in only the afternoons; Chris Lanser and Joyce Guimond, who hired me at Campus for Kids after Peet's closed and provided a much-needed transition in my life; and Stephanie Jones, who gave me a job in the field that I studied (psychology – what are the odds?), accommodated a work-from-home lifestyle, and sent me a beautiful bouquet of flowers when I signed the publication contract with Angry Robot. I am so blessed to have you as my boss.

A special thanks to my husband, Junior Peterson. Thank

you for being my friend and for marrying me, for making me laugh and for holding me through all the rejections and seeming failure. You're the love of my life, and the book wouldn't be what it became without your influence.

And my final thanks go to you, dear readers. Thank you for letting me share this story with you. I may have mentioned this a couple times already, but it bears repeating: it's a dream come true for me. I hope this installment leaves you eager for the sequel.